D0915947

A Fur Coat for Mama

By Hoyt Walker

ISBN Number 978-0-9768142-6-9

LCCN- Library of Congress control number 2008907245
Published by J. Hoyt Walker Publishing
1841 Lupine Drive Willits, CA 95490

Contents

In Memory of
Hoyt Wayne Walker
The Finest Son
a Father Could Ever Hope For

Acknowledgments

I would like to sincerely thank the following people for their input into this book.

Without their expert help and advice—*A Fur Coat for Mama*—would have suffered greatly.

My wife Stephanie—for her expert listening ear and vital input.

My good friend and fellow writer—JoAnn Smith Ainsworth—for all her technical assistance and good wishes. JoAnn is a great romance novelist. Her latest is *Out of the Dark*. Watch for her books.

My stepdaughter—Jayne Benninger—for her fine photographic work.

To my four excellent editors: Frank and Carolyn Deuel, Gene Stewart, and Charlie Bird.

To Juan Gomez (John)—for his history of the Spaniards of Louisiana (The Canary Islanders) of which he is a direct descendant.

And last but not least—Isidro Juarez (Sid)—for his Spanish Language input.

Thank you one and all.

Foreword

A Fur Coat for Mama is a family oriented story that projects moral values and a fierce determination for survival in a tough time—the 1940s. It's a fictionalized story of the Walker Family of Sugar Grove—my family. It's the story of a boy and his dog, and what a dog he was. His name was Old Trailer, and he had a one in a million nose. He was an actual phenomenon in real life and he was my soul mate. Lots of the story is actual fact—I know because I was there; I was the little boy in the story, and Old Trailer was my dog.

CHAPTER ONE—Tough Times and My Soul Mate

The time was in the early forties, and even though things weren't quite as bad as they had been, the lasting effects of the Great Depression were still hanging around, and the Walker family of Sugar Grove, Arkansas was continuing to struggle for existence. There were three of us kids still left in the nest—Dorothy, 12 years old—Nellie 10, and me—Hoyt, 9. My older brother George and sisters La Vada and Audrey had already married and moved out to begin families of their own, and Dad and Mom were in their middle forties. Mom and Dad also had another baby boy, two years before Dorothy that they named JD, after Dad's initials, (James David), but Mother's milk dried up suddenly because of an undiagnosed fever and the baby started to lose ground immediately; he never was able to digest cows milk properly. Dad and Mom tried everything they knew to keep the little boy alive, but JD's struggle came to an end on the morning of his first birthday and he was buried in the Sugar Grove Cemetery.

After the beginning of World War II, the cotton market, which was what our family was always involved in, started making a comeback and Dad and Mom once again became involved in the meager existence called sharecropping. Sharecropping was an agreement between a landowner and a tenant farmer where the tenant and his family would plant, raise and harvest a crop and receive a portion of the profits. The whole family was involved; it took a tremendous amount of labor before a bale of cotton was ready to be sold.

Times were still terribly hard, and there was never anything left over from one year to the next. Dad would have to go back to the bank in Booneville every spring and borrow money against the next year's crop to feed the family and buy seed to plant again. As tough as times were for the Walkers they were among the stronger of the people in the area and were constantly being asked to reach out and help friends who were not so fortunate. We finally found out the hard way that being too caring and compassionate had a very serious down side when we were suddenly stuck with two bank notes that Dad had cosigned. Dad and Mom were especially vulnerable when there were children involved, such as when a family's cow would die and leave the children without milk. Luckily for us, the president of the Citizens Bank in Booneville, CX Williams, was also a compassionate man. The old banker, who would loan Dad money on a simple handshake, finally called him in and gave him some very plain and to the point advice. "Dave, you've got to stop what you're doing! You're just too danged generous for your own good, and people are starting to take advantage of you. To protect you and your family I'm going to halt this process right here and now. I will not approve loans to anyone else who has your name on their note, so you can just tell them that right up front. It's going to be mighty hard for you and your family to repay what you've already absorbed without adding any more to it. Your word is as good as gold to me, Dave, and you know you can count on me when the chips are down, but trying to save the whole damned world is not something one man can do!"

"Yeah, I should know that by now," Dad replied soberly, "but it just seems like each case is more desperate than the last. I just can't seem to say no after I hear their sad story."

"Dave, these are terribly hard times. I know it's hard to look the other way when you see people in distress, but you've got to start doing it! You're putting your own family at risk trying to save everybody else! Now, I apologize for being blunt like this, but sometimes that's the only thing that works!"

"You've been a true friend and helper to me and my family, CX, and I certainly appreciate what you're doing right now. We'll get this debt paid off, but it's going to take a while. Thanks for everything, old friend," Dad said, clasping the old banker's hand.

After Dad got home and explained what had happened at the bank to Mother they both breathed a sigh of relief. "I'm not sorry we did it," Mama responded. "What we did was right, but there comes a time when you just can't reach out any farther; I'm glad it's over."

"$250.00 is a lot of money to come up with when things are this tight," Dad acknowledged, "but if the Lord is willing and the creek don't rise, I guess we'll get it paid off someday."

* * *

The newest Walker kids were total opposites from the first three. We all had sandy-blond hair like Daddy, while the first three had dark hair like Mama. Dorothy, the older of the second batch, took being the big sister very seriously. She was cautious of everything and insisted that Nellie and I, the two free spirits of the group, follow Mother's orders to the letter whenever we were away from home. I personally, grew up under something of a handicap because I was Mama's last baby and she knew it. Even though Mama probably didn't recognize it, she cut me a lot of slack, and a lot of times my sisters weren't too happy about that. There's one thing Mama didn't cut me any slack on though; when I got to running contrary to her wishes, the peach tree tea (thrashing with a peach tree limb) would be just around the corner, and she always gave me enough to get my head pointed in the right direction.

The fourth and last new member of the Walker family was called Old Trailer. He was a pup out of Old Blue, Dad's long time hunting buddy, and a female dog that my Uncle John owned; he called her a feist. Whatever a feist was she sure gave Trailer some intense fire. He was about 35 pounds of pure vengeance when it came to things he didn't like, such as poisonous snakes or other critters that might harm his family. It took him mere seconds to literally destroy the largest timber rattlers, copperheads, or cottonmouth water moccasins, and he was a virtual fighting machine when other dogs got too close to his family or their livestock. Trailer was born with an unbelievable canine gift that began to blossom as he and I started growing up together—a gift that drew the attention of some very unsavory individuals, but it was also the key to getting—a fur a coat for Mama.

Old Blue, the patriarch canine of the Walker clan and father of Old Trailer had died at a ripe old age a few months back, and Daddy buried him near his favorite sleeping spot in the back yard. It was a very sad day for the Walkers because Old Blue was a legend in his own time, but Trailer was destined to become even greater than his dad. He came into our family on a cold winter morning when I was five years old. For as long as I could remember Old Blue had always been our family dog, and even though I liked him, he didn't pay much attention to me—a 5-year-old kid. He was Dad's dog and that's just how it was. What I didn't know was that he had sired a litter of puppies just down the lane and one of them was destined to change my life. One morning Daddy was just returning from a visit to Uncle John and Aunt Lilly's, and I could tell that he was hiding something under his coat. I immediately decided I had to know what it was because it was doing a whole lot of wiggling and grunting—like a puppy with a very full tummy. Suddenly Daddy opened his coat and there he was—a carbon copy of Old Blue—only he was little like me! Oh my goodness! When Dad handed me that wiggly black and white pup, my heart fell on the floor—it was love at first sight. I finally had me a dog of my own.

Daddy knew that Old Blue was getting up in age and would soon have to be replaced with a younger dog, but at that moment Daddy's thoughts for the future meant nothing to me; this was my pup, and I wasn't going to let anyone forget it. I named him, "Old Trailer," on the spot. From that day on, Old Trailer became the encompassing factor of my life. He was my pal, my confidant, my getting into trouble specialist. He was a hunter from the beginning, and wherever he went to do his hunting that's where I went. It was obvious from the beginning that he had an outstanding nose. Even as a small pup he would find things that would totally delight his little master—like a baby cottontail rabbit hiding in the grass, or a nest of newborn mice out in the hay barn. Old Trailer was the last thing I thought of before going to sleep and the first thought I had on awakening. As soon as my feet hit the floor we were up and at it again.

Unfortunately puppies grow up much faster than little boys, and by the time Trailer was six months old, he was already an accomplished hunter, spending most of his days away from home with Dad. I had a little problem with having to wait in line to hunt with my own dog, but as soon as he was off duty, he and I would be heading down to the little branch creek near the house to harass the critters that lived down there. I finally had me a real pal, someone I could relate to. I'd found me a soul mate! I loved my sisters very much, but I was a boy, and I needed to do boy things.

That winter started out really scary for our family, not only did Mother and Dad have the usual lack-of-money-in-the-wintertime-blues, they also had to come up with money to pay on the bank note. Things were really starting to go downhill fast when a sudden stroke of good luck happened to come our way that started changing everything for the better. Here's the story.

CHAPTER TWO—The Little Gold Mine

"Hey, look Mama, it's starting to snow outside," said Nellie, running to the front window, followed by Dorothy and me.

"Yeah, I figured it was going to start anytime," Mother said. "It's really gotten cold in the last few hours."

"We've been pretty lucky up until now, though," Dad said, walking over with the family. "Usually by the middle of November we've already had a lot of snow. I sure hope it doesn't get too deep. Come on Hoyt; let's go finish stacking the back porch full of wood. There's no telling how much it'll drop tonight."

"I want it to snow enough to make snow ice cream, at least, " I said wishfully, as I followed Dad out the back door with Old Trailer hot on my heels.

"Oh, me too!" Dorothy said, excitedly. "Nellie, let's go see how many flavorings we can find in the cupboards. I know we've got vanilla and lemon."

"I think we have coconut and pineapple in there too," Nellie added, following Dorothy into the kitchen. "Let's get all the flavorings and the sugar out and set everything on the counter, and tomorrow morning when we wake up maybe we'll get to eat all the snow ice cream we want."

"Not until after breakfast," Mother interjected, as she walked into the kitchen. "When the cows have been milked and breakfast is done then you can make all the ice cream you want."

"Oh goodie, I can hardly wait," said Dorothy, with a little squeal of delight. "Since tomorrow is Saturday and we don't have to go to school we'll have two whole days to play in the snow, and make different flavors of ice cream."

"Son, how about you run on out to the shop and grab the wheelbarrow for us," Dad suggested, as we walked outside. "We want to make short work of this job; it's really starting to come down."

"Okay Daddy," I replied, heading towards the shop on a full run with my arms spread wide, my head thrown back and my tongue stuck out as far as I could get it, trying to intercept the large soft snowflakes.

It only took about 30 minutes to stack the back porch full of wood, for both the heating stove and the cook stove and to bring in enough kindling to last for a week or so, and by the time we had finished, the snowstorm was in full force.

"I think we've got it, Son! Let's get in out of this slush," Dad said, heading to the back door, stomping his feet. "If it keeps this up, we'll probably have a foot or more by morning. Hey, catch him and get all the snow and junk out from between his toes," Dad said, as Trailer came running up behind us. "We don't want to get yelled at!"

"Yeah, that's for sure!" I added, taking care of Trailer's feet with an old towel from the soiled clothes basket. "Man, I sure hope the robins come in this winter like they did last year," I said. "I've got me an old wash pan clear full of nice round creek gravel to shoot in my bean flip."

"That's good, Son—next to quails, robins are about the best eating birds out there; they have a nice meaty breast."

"Yeah," I agreed enthusiastically. "Hey, Daddy, why doesn't black rubber work as good for slingshots as red; it doesn't stretch the same."

"Yeah, I know, Son. But the difference in the rubber is a much bigger problem than a young man wanting to make a bean flip can understand."

"What do you mean, Daddy?" I asked, uncertain of his meaning.

"Well, I'll try to explain it to you the best I can. You notice me listening to the war news on the radio all the time—right?"

"Yeah, but I don't know what it's all about."

"Well, Son, the whole thing in a nutshell is that there are some real nasty people overseas who are trying to take over the whole world and make all the rest of us their slaves."

"And that's why you listen, to see who's winning?" I asked.

"That's right, but to answer your question about the rubber—it's been about a year now since the rubber plantations where most of our good live rubber—the red kind—has fallen to the enemy. The black stuff that doesn't stretch well is called synthetic rubber. The government had it created to take the place of the regular kind so our Jeeps and army trucks can operate. It seems to work just fine for tires and inner tubes—anyhow, there's still about half of that tube of live rubber out in the shop; that'll last you a long time."

"Why do the bad people want to take over the world, Daddy?"

"It's because they're too dadburned lazy to work and feed themselves, Son. They want someone else to do all the work while they sit on their behinds. Your Uncle Elmo is over there, right now, trying to help stop the bums. He drives a landing craft for the Navy."

"Daddy, what if the bad people come over here?" I asked, with a worried tone in my voice.

"Don't you fret about that, little man," Dad said, ruffling my short hair with his big rough hand. "If they come over here, your pa will get his double barreled shotgun out and chase them all right back where they came from."

Suddenly I felt an overwhelming rush of pride and love for my daddy. Nobody could hurt us, Daddy wouldn't let them!

"Let's take our coats off out here on the back porch and shake as much of this snow off as we can, Son."

"Hey, Hoytie, come into the kitchen and see all the ice cream stuff Dorothy and I have found!" Nellie called out, as we came in the back door. "All we have to do tomorrow is get the eggs and the cream."

"And the snow too—silly!" Dorothy added, with an impish grin. (Snow ice cream was made with the same ingredients as regular ice cream except it was poured directly onto a pile of fresh soft snow in a large bowl and stirred up thoroughly.)

"The way you kids are carrying on, you'd think it was Christmas," Mother declared. "You're probably going to be seeing a lot more of this stuff than you want to before spring gets here."

"Hey, how about pouring me a cup of that coffee, Hon," Dad suggested, as he and I passed through the kitchen. "The boy and I are heading straight for the heating stove to thaw out—right, Man?"

"You betcha," I replied, holding my hands up just as close to the stove as I could, like Daddy. "My fingers are frozen!"

The large freestanding heater was used for heating the house in general, and it did a very good job of that, but it was a dangerous thing to be close to, so we did most of our after supper family get togethers in front of the big stone fireplace where everyone could get comfortable. A few years back I received a very harsh lesson about making contact with that old stove. Mama had bought me a pair of one piece pajamas and for some reason the little back potty door would never stay buttoned. Early one morning while the house was still cold, Dorothy and Nellie each had themselves a kitchen chair right up close to the stove and were cutting pictures of dressed up ladies out of a Montgomery Ward's catalog; they called them paper dolls. Nellie had just finished cutting out another paper doll, and she dropped it and it went fluttering towards the floor. Well, being the helpful little brother I was, I quickly stooped over to get it. Wow-eee! My soft exposed little hiney made full contact with that red hot metal. Holy mackerel!—around that room I flew like all the demons of hell were chasing me, screaming my brains out with the girls trying to capture me to see how bad I was burned. Needless to say, I carried that quarter sized blister on my rear for quite a while as an extreme reminder—you'd better keep your mind on what you're doing when you're close to the stove!

* * *

"Hey, we've got company," Dad announced, walking over to the front window. "Someone is pulling up in a taxi cab."

"Who do you think it is, Dave? It's almost dark out there." Mother said, from the kitchen.

"It looks like Steve Walker, but what would he be doing here this time of year? He always comes in the spring or summer."

"Yeah, that is strange," Mother agreed, as Steve began to disembark and set all his stuff out on the ground.

Steve was Dad's first cousin, and he was a very unusual type of fellow. Whenever he came, he always worked just as hard as everyone else at whatever the rest of the family was engaged in, but he wore a white shirt, necktie and dress pants no matter if he was slopping hogs, picking cotton or whatever, and he just never seemed to get dirty like everyone else. Steve was a first class gentleman. He was a barber by trade, and I know he worked in Albuquerque, New Mexico, other than that he was a bit of a mystery to me. He had to be a man of means because when he came, he often stayed a month or more. I liked Steve very much; he called me Hootie.

"Come on kids—let's go help him," Dad said. "He's got lots of stuff to bring in."

"Get your jackets on," Mother commanded, as we all ran in from the kitchen. "Gosh—looks like he's moving in!" Mother said, observing all the gear Steve had brought.

"Hey, Hootie! How's my favorite young man?" Steve called out, as the girls and I came rushing out.

"I'm just fine, Steve," I replied, grabbing him by the hand.

"And who are these two beautiful young ladies? This can't possibly be Dorothy and Nellie!"

"Oh, Steve, you know it's us!" Dorothy said, putting her hand up to her face with a shy smile.

"We haven't grown that much," Nellie said. "You're just joking with us, Steve!"

"Well, there's one thing I'm not joking about girls; you ladies are getting prettier every time I see you."

"Cousin, what could bring you to this neck of the woods in this nasty weather?" Dad asked, grasping Steve's hand for a vigorous handshake.

"Well, Dave, I've learned something I think you ought to know about. Let me pay this gentleman his fee, and get him headed back to town, and I'll come in and tell you all about it."

"Come on gang; let's hustle this stuff in before it gets wet," Dad said, grabbing two large suitcases and heading up the walk.

"I've got the spare bedroom ready," Mother informed, pointing through the open door. "Take everything right on in. Steve, how are you?" Mama asked, as Steve came in carrying the last of his stuff.

"I'm just fine, Dell, and I'm seriously looking forward to putting my feet under your table again. Whatever that is you've got cooking in there,"—Steve indicated, pointing towards the kitchen with a big smile—"has already got my attention."

"It's just a pot of pinto beans with corn bread and fried salt pork on the side, but we've got plenty of it. As you already know our house is your house," Mama said, extending her hand. "We're a little tight nowadays, but you're more than welcome to share what we've got."

"That's exactly why I'm here, Dell. You and Dave have always shared your home and your life with me—always made me feel comfortable and welcome, and I think it's high time I return the favor. I have gained some information that I believe will help you folks out. You could very well be sitting on top of a little gold mine down here and not knowing it."

"My lands, Steve, what can you possibly be talking about—a gold mine!" Mother repeated, with a quizzical look on her face. "I'll certainly want to hear more about that," she said, pointing her index finger at Steve, "but right now, you go on into the kitchen and pour yourself a hot cup of coffee and get warmed up. The girls and I will finish getting you settled in."

"Hey! Cousin, I want to hear more on that subject you just mentioned there. What is it you're talking about anyway?" Dad questioned, as he began pouring both himself and Steve a large mug of steaming coffee. "Right now, we're scratching the financial bottom of the barrel."

"Yeah, that's what my son Jess told me," Steve said, as he walked into the living room. "He heard through the family grapevine that you folks were really hitting it tough, and I felt I might have knowledge that could give you a wintertime job."

"Well, that certainly is a welcome thought!" Dad replied, enthusiastically. "Tell me about it."

"Last summer, I took me a little tour up into the north country. In fact, I went just about as far north as any man in his right mind would ever want to go. I ended up in Yellowknife, a small town in the Northwest Territories of Canada. Now, to make a long story short, I met an old trapper up there that taught me the art of mink and ermine trapping. I realize you folks don't have ermine down this far south, but I would almost guarantee that there are mink on these creeks, and if there is, Dave, I can teach you how to catch them."

"Why do we want to catch them, Steve? Are they really good eating?" I asked, trying to figure out the reason for the excitement.

"Well, Hootie, they might be edible, but the real reason people want to catch them is they fetch a pretty penny on the open fur market. Their skins are used to make fur coats for fancy ladies that live in the big cities. A small female mink will bring 12 to 15 dollars and a large male can bring up to 35."

"Oh my goodness!" Mother exclaimed, walking over next to Dad with hope gleaming in her eyes. "Dave, maybe this is the Good Lord's way of helping us out of this bind we've gotten ourselves into."

"Well, Hon, at this point in time, I'm ready to accept help from about any direction, as long as it's honest. Whether it was Steve's or the Good Lord's idea or both, I want to hear more about it," he said, putting his arm around Mother affectionately.

"There is a slight possibility that I'm barking up the wrong tree here, Dave. There may not be any mink this far south. We do know there's an active fur market though because you sell other hides like possum and coon, don't you?

"That's a fact; I do."

"And fox and bobcat too," I added, exuberantly.

"But you've never seen any mink sold?" Steve reaffirmed.

"No, I don't believe I ever have," Dad replied, shaking his head.

"Well, no matter! They can still be here and people just don't know it. They are the smartest animal out there. A man can trap a whole lifetime and never catch one if he doesn't know how."

"Is that a fact?" Dad replied, in amazement, with his eyes firmly glued to Steve's face. "Let's pull us up a chair here by the fireplace and you can tell me all about it."

CHAPTER THREE—Yellowknife Jack

"Yellowknife Jack is the nickname of the old trapper that taught me the art," Steve said, as he pulled up a chair across the fireplace from Dad and sat down.

Quickly I slid in between them on the floor where I could see and hear good. I was determined not to miss a thing.

"He says that generation after generation of mink can live out their lives on small creeks and even canals and people never know they're there. They're absolute creatures of the night. In the area where Jack lives, he dominates the mink and ermine trade, but his success comes at a price. Nobody around there will associate with him because he won't tell them how to catch mink and ermine. They all want to cash in on something it took Jack half a lifetime to figure out and he just won't give it up. The jealousy is unbelievable."

"How in tarnation did you get him to teach it to you?" Dad questioned.

"Well, he's a very lonely old guy, and I suppose I was just in the right place at the right time," Steve replied. "I'd been slowly working my way up through Canada for about six weeks, stopping a few days here and there, and I was approaching the end of my northern adventure—a community called Yellowknife. I knew I was pushing my luck being that far north, but I really wanted to know what was up there. I've always been interested in the types of wild life that inhabit different areas. I thought it over, and decided I had a couple of days before I actually had to start back, so I parked myself at the local hotel and ventured on down to one of the nearby creeks to see what all I could learn. Well, I'd been down there for about an hour, and I'd already spotted a moose and a couple of young grizzly bears prowling around the edge of the woods across the creek from me when suddenly a large arctic wolf—as white as snow, came charging out of the thicket, stopped dead still and glued his beady eyes firmly on my person. Man, what an awesome creature! The only part of the picture that I didn't like was, he was on the same side of the creek as I was and only fifty feet away! Knowing that wolves usually run in packs, I thought to myself, "my Lord, what am I going to do if others come out?" I knew that I couldn't outrun a pack of wolves, so I figured to stand very still and if extreme measures were needed, to jump into the current of the fast moving stream next to me. As we stood there in a virtual face-off with the deep green eyes of that huge wolf glaring down his long snout at me and the short hairs on the back of my neck starting to stand up, something very unusual began to happen. He started to wag his trail and walk directly at me, but he still had those beady green eyes locked on me. Now let me tell you, there was a whole range of thoughts running through my head about then and every one of them was something along the line of—let's get the heck out of here, but I knew I'd best not move a muscle. When he got within about twenty feet of me, with me standing there as rigid as a fence post in sheer panic, suddenly something equally strange began to unfold. A soft grumbly voice from out in the edge of the woods said, 'Well, if Sam likes you I guess I like you too,' and out hobbled a grizzled old fellow with a big black beard, walking with a gorgeous hand carved cane that would sell for about a hundred dollars in the city.

"'I'm sorry if Sam scared you,' he mumbled, from under his massive beard. 'The locals and I don't get along too good, so I always let Sam be my introduction committee. If he likes a person then I'll usually like them too!'

"'Well, that's very comforting to know!' I confessed, shaking my head, 'but I can tell you one thing, mister—Old Sam just about made me soil my pants. My knees are still trying to buckle.'

"'Sorry about that!' he mumbled, again shaking his head, with a slight grin wrinkling his upper lip. 'They call me Yellowknife Jack, but my real name is Jack Hopkins. Where you from, anyway?' he asked, extending his hand.

"'My name is Steve Walker, and I'm from Albuquerque, New Mexico; I'm a barber down there. I'm just up here looking around for the summer.'

"'Yeah, I came here about twenty years back just looking around,' Jack chuckled. 'I used to live in Los Angeles, California, but there are just too dang many people down there to suit me. Hey, my cabin is back there about a quarter of a mile. What do you say we go on back and make us a cup of something hot and talk awhile? Sam and I don't get much company. Like I said, me and the locals haven't hit it off too well.'

"'Something hot sounds just fine to me,' I agreed, as Sam began rubbing up against my leg like he wanted me to pet him."

"Did you pet him, Steve?" I quickly asked, with my attention firmly fixed on Steve's face.

"Yeah, I did, Hootie."

"How did it feel to pet a real live wolf? I bet that was really something!"

"Don't interrupt Steve, Son!" Dad commanded. "You can ask him questions later; right now I want to hear about that little gold mine!"

"It's all right, Dave; we've got plenty of time; let him talk if he wants to. It's just like petting a regular dog, Hootie, except a wolf's hair is very coarse on the outside, but right next to the skin it's totally different," Steve said, looking me directly in the eyes.

"How's it different, Steve? What's it feel like?"

"It feels just about like goose down," he replied. "Sam was just starting to put on his winter coat. In the summertime the old hair sheds off and they get a thinner coat for warmer weather. Nature has prepared the wolf well to survive in the Arctic. Their outside coat is long and coarse so it sheds water, but next to the skin is soft and fine to hold in the heat."

"Okay, Son, now let Steve finish. This is very important."

"Well, it took us about 30 minutes to get to Jack's cabin because he had to stop a few times to rest his leg. He told me he had hurt it a few days earlier when Sam and a big black bear were having a territorial dispute out on the front porch. It seems he ran out the back door with his rifle, intending on having bear steak for supper, but instead he slipped on the frozen porch and almost broke his ankle. Anyway, we finally got to the cabin, and Jack made us a cup of hot tea—said he never did learn to like coffee. Well, I never was much of a tea man either, but after I'd gagged down a few cups and with the exceptional conversation, I decided it wasn't all that bad. Jack had a good tight cabin supplied with everything he needed to live the solitary life. While we were sitting there talking, he said that spraining his ankle had certainly put him in a bind. Well, being the inquisitive type, I asked him what the trouble was. He said the trouble was that trapping season was going to start in two days, and that's how he made his living, and he couldn't possibly do it because of his injury."

"So that's what you meant by being at the right place at the right time," Dad spoke up.

"Yep, there's no other way to put it. Well, the knowledge that he was all alone and crippled to boot, really made an impact on me, and I decided I was going to help the old fellow out if it was in my power. I looked his ankle over and decided it would probably be a couple of weeks before he would be using it to any degree, but in reality it was closer to a month. I was just lucky as heck to still be able to get out of there before the winter set in for good. Old Jack is a virtual genius at trapping. He has learned every quirk and nuance that the weasel family has. Mink and ermine are both branches of the weasel family. He has mastered the art to an unbelievable degree, and I am his only student."

"Man, I sure hope there's mink here," Dad said, shaking his head. "This could be just the break I need to get my family back to solid ground."

"If they're here, Old Trailer and I will catch them," I exclaimed excitedly, running my hand over Trailer's head and ears. "Won't we boy?"

"Well, if he does, Hootie, he'll probably be the first dog in history to do so," Steve said, grinning at me. "They're some wary critters."

"Old Trailer's got the best nose there is—huh Dad! If they're there he'll find them—won't he?"

"He has a terrific nose, Son, but whether he can use it to get mink is yet to be seen."

"Old Jack uses number two Blake and Lamb steel traps, and he is highly successful." Steve proclaimed. "I suppose there might be other ways."

"Well, we definitely want to go with the proven method," Dad said, "and it sounds like old Jack has it down to a science."

"There's no doubt about that," Steve agreed, nodding his head, "and even though I was there only twenty-five days, those days wore on into the night. Jack was a college mathematics professor in his former life and perfection is all that he will accept. He had a real need to talk, and details are his strong point. I learned his trapping skill both verbally and hands on."

"Kids, it's time for bed," Mother interrupted. "Tomorrow is another day."

"Aw, Mama, please let me stay up just a little longer," I whined. "I want to hear what else Steve's got to say."

"You go on to bed, like your Mama told you," Dad insisted. "We'll be going to bed soon."

CHAPTER FOUR—Blake and Lamb
Steel Traps

I was the first one up the next morning, and the first thing I did was run and look out the front window to see how much snow there was. Old Trailer saw me come hurrying by, and jumped out of his sleeping box over behind the stove and quickly followed me to the window doing his usual good morning hand licking and tail wagging routine. I wasn't able to see clearly through the icy window so I jerked the front door open and we ran out onto the porch. The whole world was covered in about a foot of brand-new powder snow, and it was still snowing lightly. Trailer was just as delighted as I was because he bolted off the porch and went blasting around the front yard dashing and darting here and there—breaking up the smooth new surface. Suddenly I heard a familiar shrill bird call, and I quickly glanced up to the top of the big willow tree in the front yard, and there sat three of the biggest robin red-breasts meant? I had ever seen. Suddenly my mind was filled with superheated excitement and I went running around the house to the back porch to get my slingshot and a pocket full of creek rocks. My prayers had been answered; there were robins flying in every direction.

"Good morning, Hootie," Steve exclaimed from the front porch, as I came running past. "I see you're all ready for action!"

"Yeah," I said, taking aim at one of the birds in the willow tree. "There are robins everywhere!"

The gravel left my slingshot heading straight for the closest robin, but much to my dismay it traveled on a slight curve and missed by a mere inch, sending all three birds off in a flurry of feathers.

"Dadburn it, that rock had a flat spot on it and it curved." I said, with disgust in my voice.

"Yeah, that was always my problem with bean flips," Steve said, with a big grin. "I never could find good rocks."

"I'll get the next one," I insisted, pulling a handful of rocks out of my pocket to choose from.

"I think I'd better get on back in the house," Steve said, running his hands over his bare arms. "It's too cold out here for me. Your dad's just about got the heating stove fired up."

* * *

In a couple of hours the snowstorm suddenly changed to brilliant sunlight as the clouds gave way to the morning and Old Trailer, my constant companion, and I went chasing after the elusive robin flock that had moved into the area to feed on the last of the wild persimmons.

"Hey, Hoytie, have you killed any robins yet?" Nellie yelled, as she and Dorothy headed to the barn with their milk pails.

"Not yet," I hollered back, "but I almost had one on the first shot," I replied excitedly.

"As soon as we get the milking done and have our breakfast we're going to make snow ice cream," said Dorothy. "We'll call you when we're ready."

"Okay," I replied, following Old Trailer down toward the creek.

Well, the whole hunt seemed to be full of almosts. Several times I got feathers but no meat to take home, and after about two hours of near-miss frustration the hunger pains in my stomach started turning my head back toward the house.

After I'd had my breakfast I found myself facing a really tough situation. There were two special events going on in the house at the same time that I really wanted to be a part of, and I was terribly torn between them. Steve was discussing trapping with Yellowknife Jack and his big white wolf in the front room, and the girls were in the kitchen making all kinds of snow goodies; it was a terrible dilemma. It took me a whole two seconds to figure out how to handle the situation. I got me a big bowl full of coconut flavored snow ice cream and went in by the stove to eat it where I could hear everything Dad and Steve had to say. Ha—I had the best of both worlds!

"If it doesn't snow anymore tonight we'll be able to check for mink sign tomorrow," Steve exclaimed. "If we find any, we're going to have to buy you some traps. It takes about two weeks to get them when you order from the catalog, but since the season doesn't open until the first of the month there's a good possibility we can get it done."

"About how much does each trap cost, and how many are we going to need?" Dad asked. "As you already know I'm pretty well strapped for cash."

"Dave, I came prepared to set you up in business—that is, if there's any business to be set up. To answer your question though, number two Blake and Lambs cost about $2.50 each and you will need about two dozen. That's $60 worth of traps. "

"Do you think that'll be enough?" Dad asked.

"Well, it's plenty to start with," Steve replied, "but you're going to need replacements now and then because inevitably a person will misplace or forget where he set one. You'll need to keep your stock up so you can take maximum advantage of the time you have. The season is only three months long."

"Your $60 will be the first thing that gets paid back, if there's never another nickel made," Dad declared.

"You don't worry about that, Dave. You and Dell have spent your lives reaching out to help others. Now it's your turn. I just hope there's mink down here."

"Yeah, it does sound a bit like a pipe dream, I'll have to admit, but you've always been a man with a sharp mind, Steve, and if you say it's a possibility that's good enough for me."

"Old Jack makes around 3 to 4 thousand dollars every season, but that's both mink and ermine."

"Man, if I could only make enough to pay off that danged banknote and a little extra to buy the kids some Christmas, I'd be delirious."

"If there's mink here, that banknote will fall fast. It's the first thing that gets paid off," Steve answered.

"After your $60," Dad reminded, pointing his finger at Steve.

* * *

Unfortunately, the girls and I had to go to school on Monday, the very day that Steve and Dad had chosen to go to the local creeks to check for mink sign. Even though I did my very best to concentrate on my lessons, over and over I would catch myself down on the creek with Dad, Steve, and Old Trailer. There was a fierce burning delight going on in my mind at what they were going to find. Somehow I just knew they were going to find mink and that our lives would be changed for the better. When school was over I ran the whole half-mile home leaving the girls far behind. When I got there, Dad, Mom and Steve had the Sears and Roebuck catalog laid out on the kitchen table and were in the process of ordering two dozen, number two, Blake and Lamb steel traps.

"Hot dang," I yelled. "There's mink—isn't there?"

"There absolutely is, Hootie; there are lots of mink here," Steve said, scuffling my hair and giving me an affirmative wink.

"Oh man!" I exclaimed. "Maybe we'll even make enough money to buy Mama one of those gasoline powered washing machines we saw in Fort Smith the other day, Daddy."

"Cash money buys anything you want," Dad assured me. "The only problem is figuring out how to get it."

"Since these mink here have never been trapped before," Steve said, with an affirmative wink in Dad's direction, "we'll have enough of them caught and sold to put you folks well into the black, before the rest of them even figure out there's a problem."

"What does in the black mean, Steve?" I quickly replied.

"To be in the black, Hootie, is to be financially secure—to have money in your pocket to jingle—to be debt free."

"Oh my Lord," Mother said, shaking her head and putting her hands prayerfully up to her face. "If this family could only be so blessed!"

"It's going to happen, Mama," Dad said softly, encircling her in his arms. "The mink are here, and Steve is going to teach me how to catch them! Things are going to be getting better, starting right away."

"I'll also need to teach you to pelt them out and prepare the skins for market, Dave," Steve added. "Furs sell for a much better price when they've been taken care of properly."

"I want to learn everything too, Steve, just like you teach Daddy!" I exclaimed. "We're going to make so much money; we might even be able to buy a car!"

"A car!" Dorothy questioned, as she and Nellie came in the front door. "Who's going to buy a car?"

"Maybe we are!" I replied, with a persnickety tone in my voice. "There are all kinds of mink down on the creeks!"

"Now hold on here kids; let's not get carried away," Dad cautioned. "There are a whole lot of very important things that have to be taken care of before we could ever think of buying a car."

"I'll certainly agree with that!" Mother said, shaking her head. "We are going to be heavily in the black, as Steve puts it, before something like that will ever happen, so let's, not count our chickens before they hatch. Dreams have a curious way of vanishing right in front of your eyes. I've been there and seen it lots of times."

"Dell, I know what you're saying," Dad agreed, running his hand through his thinning hair, and looking Mother square in the face. "I know how many disappointments we've gone through, just as well as you do, but at least now we've got some forward motion. Now our family has a dream to pursue!"

"I probably want to believe it even more than the rest of you, Dave," Mother said, shaking her head and wiping a tear from her eye. "I know we haven't got much right now, but we've still got each other, so I'm just going to hold on to that and keep trusting in the Lord, and if it's meant to happen, it will."

BLAKE AND LAMB STEEL TRAPS

"That's great, Hon," Dad replied, holding Mama close and comforting her. "All Steve and I need is a little time. Steve's done this before. He's seen it happen, so just relax and keep an open mind—that's all we ask."

"That's the truth, Dell; within the next month you'll see honest cash money start coming into this house again to take care of the needs. If I don't miss my guess, in two or three months, your household will be debt free."

"Steve, I certainly don't want to seem negative or unappreciative of what you're doing. I know you've come a long ways and put out a lot of effort to give us this chance, but there's been so many dreams that have come and gone in the last few years. It's just hard for me to put much faith in anything any more."

"I thoroughly understand where you're coming from, Dell, but let me tell you this. There are lots of mink here! I saw their tracks, and I know without a doubt they are mink. Just bear with us for a few more weeks, and I'll prove it to you in cold cash. You wouldn't argue with cold cash, would you?" Steve said, with a sly grin.

"Absolutely not," Mama said, putting her arms around Steve, with tears flowing profusely down her cheeks. "I'm so sorry, Steve, for being such a doubting Thomas. I guess I've just become hard and closed minded since the times have gotten so tough. Please forgive me, dear friend. Maybe I can at least make it up to you a little bit," she said, stepping back and taking Steve by the hand. "Come on into the kitchen and let's sample those beans and salt pork to see if they're up to snuff."

"Dadburn, that's what I've been waiting to hear," Steve acknowledged. "I'm hungrier than a three toothed hound dog."

A FUR COAT FOR MAMA

CHAPTER FIVE—The Fur Coat
and Attention Problems

After supper was over, the grown-ups talked for about another hour then went to bed, but there was an air of excitement in the house that was different from anything we kids had ever experienced. There was something about the possibility of having money that made us want to think about what all a person with money could buy. I was lying in my bed with my eyes wide open thinking about all the mink we were going to catch when I started hearing giggling noises coming from the girls room. I quietly crept across the hall and opened the door just enough to stick my head in. The girls had the catalog up in bed with them and they were laughing at something they had seen. "Hey, Hoytie, come on in!" Nellie whispered, gesturing with her hand.

"We can't sleep," Dorothy whispered with her hands framing her mouth, "so we're looking at things we would like to buy."

"That's a great idea," I replied, as I quietly closed the door behind me. "I can't sleep either; I'm just too excited." Suddenly we began hearing a familiar scratching noise at the door—evidently, Trailer couldn't sleep either.

"Hurry and let him in," Nellie said. "We don't want to wake up Mama and Daddy."

As soon as I got Trailer inside and settled down, we all converged on the catalog. Trailer was being a pain wanting to get petted, so the only way I could get to look at the catalogue was to put his front feet up on the bed and get on my knees beside him on the floor. The girls, of course, wanted to look at frilly girl things, and I wanted to look at bicycles and

Red Ryder BB guns but as we were turning the pages suddenly we came across beautiful ladies wearing all kinds of fancy fur coats.

"Hey, look at that!" I exclaimed, pointing to the pictures excitedly. "That's the kinds of coats Steve's been talking about!"

"Oh my gosh, Dorothy, look at this beautiful white one!" said Nellie. "It's made from 100 percent, prime Alaskan ermine fur, and the brown one, is—"

"Prime Canadian mink," I blurted out, looking around Nellie's arm at the catalogue.

"Hey—look, over here on the next page!" Dorothy exclaimed. "There's even one made from raccoon and one from bobcat."

"Holy mackerel, girls, we're going to be rich!" I proclaimed, with a wide eyed grin.

"Let's see how much each one costs," Dorothy suggested, looking down at the bottom of the page "Oh, my Lord!" she exclaimed, pointing to the white one, and looking at Nellie and me with actual shock on her face. "It's over a thousand dollars!"

"It can't be that much!" Nellie objected, looking down at the price list. "You've got to be reading it wrong."

"No I'm not," Dorothy insisted, with irritation in her voice. "I know what a thousand dollars is. Hey, look at this brown one!"

"That's the mink one," I interrupted. "That's the kind of furs we're going to get!"

"Well, it's not that much cheaper," Dorothy said. "It's eight hundred and ninety-nine dollars."

"Oh my goodness!" Nellie exclaimed, when she finally got to where she could read the prices. "You're right, Dot. That is unbelievable."

"When I get big, I'm going to catch lots of mink and sell them and buy Mama a fur coat just like this one right here," I said, pointing to the one made from mink.

"Fat chance," Dorothy replied, with a sarcastic tone in her voice, "but even if you could, to spend that much money for a coat would be stupid. That's probably almost enough to buy a car."

"That is unreal," Nellie said, looking closely at the lady wearing the mink coat; "she looks almost just like Mama!"

"Wowee! She really does," Dorothy acknowledged, looking closely at the lady's face, "and she's even got long black hair that she wears up in a bun like Mama. I'm starting to see what you mean, little brother. Mama would really look great in one of these."

"Look, Trailer," I said drawing the catalogue over in front of me and pointing to the mink coat. "This is Mink; this is what we're going to catch, boy; smell it!"

"You silly thing," Dorothy grinned. "He doesn't know what you're talking about; he's just a dog."

"He is not just a dog, Dorothy!" I blurted out, defiantly. "He's super smart, and he's got a one in a million gift; Daddy said so. He doesn't even need to put his nose to the ground to trail an animal down. He just smells the air and goes straight to where they are."

"Well, if your dog is so all-fired intelligent, why don't you and him catch us a whole bunch of mink, and Nellie and I will sew Mama a fur coat. We do know how to sew," she said, with that uppity big sister look.

"Fine! That's just what we'll do," I snapped. "We'll show them, won't we boy?" I said, pulling Trailer over close to me; "we'll show everybody."

"I wonder what kind of lining a fur coat like that would have," Nellie contemplated. "It would have to be something really nice—probably silk or something like that."

"You won't ever have to worry about that, Nell!" Dorothy said, with a grin and a snicker, as Trailer and I started beating a hasty retreat back to my room.

"You might be counting your chickens before they hatch, big sister," Nellie cautioned. "Little brother has a very strong will about him, and I did hear Daddy say that Trailer is an exceptional dog—anyhow it would be fun to think about sewing a thousand dollar coat."

* * *

THE FUR COAT AND ATTENTION PROBLEMS

The last two weeks before trapping season seemed like an eternity to me. With all the talk of trapping going on and the new adventure we were just about to have, I was really having problems concentrating when I was at school. Mr. Roberts, our teacher, was a kindly old gentleman that had dealt with farm children all his life and he knew that something had my attention other than my studies. One afternoon when he was letting school out he held me back for about ten minutes to talk to me. "Hoyt, you're a fine young lad, and you've always worked well for me," he said, looking me straight in the eyes, "but it's obvious you've got something else on your mind nowadays other than your studies, and it's going to reflect on your report card unless you straighten it up. I'm talking to you man-to-man now, to see if we can get this problem under control, otherwise, I'll have to talk with your Mom and Dad."

Boy, that really shook me up because I knew there would be big trouble heading my way if he did; I might even get my butt paddled. As soon as I got home I got my homework schedule out and got down to the business of catching myself up.

* * *

Two days before the trapping season was going to begin the mailman pulled up down at the front gate and began blowing his horn. I went running out of the yard and down the lane. He was laboriously dragging a medium-size cardboard box out the door of the mail truck.

"Man, I don't know what's in this thing," he exclaimed; "whatever it is, it's heavy."

"It's mink traps," I volunteered enthusiastically. "There are two dozen of them."

"Mink traps? Never heard of anyone trapping for mink in this neck of the woods."

"Well, we're going to, and we're going to catch a whole pile of them!" I exclaimed. "Steve learned how to do it from Yellowknife Jack, and he's the best there is!"

"Yellowknife Jack, huh?" the old mailman grinned. "Is this Steve coming with the wheelbarrow?" he asked, pointing up the lane.

"No, that's my Daddy. He's the one the traps are for."

"Lots of luck, son; I'd say you're going to need it."

When we got the box loaded I grabbed the handles of the wheelbarrow and headed up the lane wobbling back and forth like a drunk sailor with Dad following along behind me.

"Let's open her up and have a look," Steve commented, as Dad and I came through the gate and approached the front porch. "We want to make sure we've got what we need. Day after tomorrow we're going to be putting them to work."

As Dad and Steve started tearing into that big cardboard box, I was so excited I felt like I was going to explode. This was man stuff, and I was right on top of it.

"Yep, I'd say we got what we paid for," Steve stated, as he picked up a shiny new steel trap in each hand and began looking them over. "Old Jack says a number one's too small and a number three's too big." 'You want to be able to hold them, but not damage the fur.' "Dave, I am fully confident that these traps are going to be the catalyst that will start your family back to financial stability."

"Steve, my friend, for the first time in an awfully long while, I'm starting to feel some hope and a little confidence coming back, and man, does it ever feel good!" Dad said, reaching out to vigorously shake Steve's hand.

* * *

That night after supper, Steve began to expound the complicated animal science behind Yellowknife Jack's trapping success. 'You can make an animal do anything you want him to if you understand how he thinks,' Jack would say. 'Learning how to think like he does and figuring out what makes him tick is the difference between success and failure. Mink and ermine are much craftier than most other animals; they follow an entirely different set of rules. Catching possum, coon, fox, and the like is on the scale of grade C mathematics, but if you want to catch mink and ermine you need to be functional in advanced algebra.' "Old Jack has two log books: The first one is full of notes and sketches of different types of sets, and different types of tests that he has run, and the second is the final results. You've heard the old saying of having a mind like a steel trap—when you're around Jack for awhile you'll realize, he's the prototype—the one they named the saying after," Steve said, with a chuckle. "He's one sharp cookie. One of his favorite tricks is to lure two or three mature male mink into the same area and cause them to lose control." 'When you get them out of their own area and mess with their heads a little they're a lot easier to catch.' he would say with a big smile.

"Well, how does he do that—get them out of their area—I mean?" Dad asked, hesitantly.

"He is very observant of the female mink he catches. When he catches one that shows signs of being in, or just coming into season, he will meticulously remove the urine bladder and save every drop. 'It's priceless,' he says. 'You can draw males from as far as a 100 yards in all directions by using a drop here and a drop there, and before long you've got two or three big male furs to add to the female you caught from the area.' In cash money, Dave, you're talking about a hundred dollars or more," Steve said, looking straight at Dad.

"Man, that is some unreal knowledge, Steve!" Dad agreed, grinning and shaking his head. "With a few tricks like that up your sleeve a guy could get into the black pretty quick."

"That's what I'm telling you," Steve replied, nodding his head. "It's like money in the bank, and that's only one trick. When I get through tuning you up, you'll be just about as unpopular as old Jack is up north. It burns people bad when they see someone making good money and they can't figure out how to get in on the deal."

"Boy, that's for certain. I've been there and done that plenty of times, and it doesn't feel good! Well, I'm not going to be nasty, but from this day forth, my family is going to receive the benefit of all my efforts; other people will just have to look out for themselves. I'm going to be tight lipped just like old Jack, and take maximum advantage of the situation. Hey, how does he handle the urine once he collects it?" Dad asked.

"He's got a Vicks nose drop bottle with a rubber bulb and glass tube dispenser that he uses when he really wants to load a place up, but most of the time he uses short broom straws about three inches long. He just dips the straw in—flicks it lightly with his finger then drops it, and mind you, he is always wearing rubber gloves. The quickest way to scuttle your program is to touch anything in the mink's area with unprotected hands. Washing your boots and gloves after every use, and wearing a new set of clean clothes after every trapping foray is an absolute necessity. You've got to be squeaky clean to make this business work. That's why the average trapper will never catch a mink. If the mink knows you're there, you're out of business before you start. Your washing has to be done with soap that has no scent whatsoever. Plain old homemade lye soap is the very best."

"Boy, we've got that one covered!" Dad said, looking over at Mom with a comical grin.

"Yeah, it just so happens that's the only kind we ever have!" Mama added, looking at Dad sarcastically.

CHAPTER SIX—Revenge Is a Stinky Business

"Okay, kids, it's time for bed," Mother announced. "Tomorrow is another day."

"Aw please, Mom," I begged. "I really want to hear what Steve's talking about!"

"This is mighty interesting stuff to your boys, Mom," Dad ventured. "Let's allow him to stay up a little while longer."

"Alright but just another hour. He's still got to go school you know."

"Thanks Mom!" I said, excitedly. "I want to be a trapper just like Steve."

"Before you learn how to trap, little man, you're going to learn to read, write and do your multiplication tables properly," Mother said defiantly, "so get that into your hard little head! This family is not going to grow up without schooling, like their mother and dad."

After Mama and the girls left the room, Steve began to really get down on the art of mink trapping. He was absolutely loaded with unbelievable tricks of the trade, and each one he talked about was like fire running across my brain. Before he stopped I was so pumped up I was like an over-charged battery, about to explode! All that night I dreamed about catching mink and making loads of money, and life was such a joyous thing. Unfortunately, with the coming of the dawn I was quickly reminded that I was still a little kid that had to be getting ready for school.

Steve and Dad were already putting on their hip boots and loading their packs full of steel traps, rubber gloves and all the other stuff they would need for the day. Oh God, how I wanted to go with them! I didn't want to be a kid anymore. Mama's insistence on me growing up with an education was really starting to get in my way. Unfortunately, she was a lot bigger than me, and very determined, so I reluctantly began getting ready to go to school—"Rats! I never get to do anything that's fun," I mumbled to myself.

Getting through the next few days at school was about the hardest thing I've ever done. Knowing that Mr. Roberts was watching every move I made and trying my very best to concentrate over the knowledge that Dad, Steve, and my dog were off on the creek doing exactly what I wanted to be doing was horrible. Each evening though after I had muddled through my homework I would get my batteries recharged by learning all the new stuff that was going on, as Steve and Dad relived the events of the day. What really made those rerun hunts so satisfying for me was the fact that I could be petting my super dog—Old Trailer—as the stories of the day were unfolding, and a lot of the talk was about him too and what a fantastic sense of smell he had. While Dad and Steve were setting traps down along the creek, Trailer would be out in the woods nearby working his magic on the denizens of the forest. At the end of the day they would usually bring home two or three squirrels or a rabbit or two to be added to Mama's dinner table.

It had been a full week since the first traps had been set and still no mink had been caught. I could tell that Daddy was really starting to get worried, but Steve showed absolutely no concern.

After supper that evening, Mother and the girls decided to do some work on Mama's Singer sewing machine, and Dad and Steve grabbed themselves another cup of coffee and retired to the fireplace with Old Trailer and me hot on their heels.

"Dave, I can tell you're starting to get a little antsy because we aren't catching any mink yet," Steve remarked, pulling up a chair by the fireplace. "There's no need to worry though; we're going to get them. If we can't catch them one way, we'll try something else. There's lots of mink here, and we'll get just as tough as it takes to get the job done. Hey, Dave—I know this may be a bit of a tall order," Steve said, "seeing as how it's right in the middle of winter, but I need a fresh fish to build us an attractant lure. Is there anyway to catch fish this time of year?"

"Daddy, I could catch some perch down on—"

"Son, your Ma would skin both of us alive if I let you out of school to go fishing, and you know it," Dad interrupted. "Steve and I will have to handle this by ourselves," he said, as I scowled in protest. "We could probably set out a few bank lines and come up with a catfish or two. Would catfish work?"

"Catfish will do just fine," Steve acknowledged.

"How do we use fish?" Dad inquired.

"You ferment it in a capped fruit jar by the fireplace for about a week, and then you drain off all the liquid and use the nose dropper and straw method. We'll just have to experiment a little until we find out what makes these critters respond. Fermented fish is a very strong attractant to a mink, and if I don't miss my guess this little, come on, will turn the tide in our favor. When we figure out their weakness, we'll start cashing in."

"Man, Steve, I am so thankful you're here," Dad said, shaking his head. "I could never have learned something as complicated as this all on my own."

"Having the right information is the key to success in any situation, Dave. This secret is well guarded because there's top money in it. Once you learn it, you should have it all to yourself down here."

"Boy, now I see why old Jack guards this thing so closely, Steve. You're right—he had to be a genius to figure this all out. Man, I sure hope I can absorb enough to get me by."

"You will, Dave, and the fun is just about to begin," Steve said, with a chuckle. "All we need is that catfish and a few days for fermentation, and we'll be in business, but you'd better remember one thing—hold your breath when you're using it," he said, with a grin. "It smells bad enough to gag a maggot."

"I can imagine!" Dad replied, with a sour look on his face. On that note the lesson came to an end, as Steve let out a big yawn and stood up.

"Gentlemen, I think I've had enough for today."

"Good night, Steve," Dad said; "Son, it's time for bed. You've got school tomorrow."

"Whoopee, I can hardly wait," I thought begrudgingly to myself.

The next day after school, I was delighted to see Old Trailer come running down the lane to meet us as we approached the house. Dad and Steve had apparently gotten home earlier than usual. Trailer seemed overly excited as if he was trying to communicate something of his day's adventure to me. "Hey boy—how's my best buddy?" I said, dropping to my knees and throwing my arms around him for a big hug. "Man—what's that stinky stuff you've got all over you," I yelled, shoving him away!

"I don't know what it is," Dorothy replied, with her nose wrinkled up, "but it smells terrible."

"Yeah, Hoytie, keep him away from us, he'll get our school dresses all smelly," Nellie added, backing up a few steps.

"Okay, Sis," I said, running on ahead with Old Trailer out in front. As I started opening the yard gate, Daddy and Steve were just coming out of the house to sit on the porch. "Hey, Dad, what's that weird smell on Old Trailer?"

"That's the sweet smell of success, Hootie," Steve volunteered, with a satisfied grin.

"It sure doesn't smell all that sweet to me, Steve," I replied. "What is it?"

"It's mink musk, Son," Dad answered. "We caught our first one today and he was a dandy! That knot-headed dog of yours dug up the carcass after I had it buried and rolled on it. I guess he wanted to get better acquainted with mink."

"Well, at least, now he knows what they smell like if he does decide to become a mink dog," Steve said, with a big grin.

"He will, Steve; I know he will!" I yelled. "We're going to catch a whole pile of them aren't we boy!"

"More power to you, Son; I sure hope you do," Dad replied.

REVENGE IS A STINKY BUSINESS

"Hoyt, come on in the house and get some other clothes on," Mother called out to me. "You're going to have to give that dog a bath or he's not coming in this house tonight."

"All right, Mama," I replied, following behind her as she walked to my bedroom.

"Here," she said, opening the bottom drawer of my dresser and taking out some of my older clothes, "put these on. They're a little ragged but they'll do for dog bath."

"Boy, mink sure don't smell very good do they, Mama?"

"That's a fact, Son, but I guess we'd better get used to it. Steve said the one they brought in today, will bring around $25. For that kind of money I guess we can learn to tolerate it, can't we?" Mama stated, with a big grin.

"Yeah, Mama, we sure can," I agreed, grabbing her around the waist to give her a big hug. "I want to see the skin; where is it?"

"It's hanging out on the back porch. After you have yourself a quick look, fetch the wash tub, and draw us some water. We'll have to heat it up a little on the cook stove though, so we don't freeze your dog to death."

"I'll do it right away, Mama," I exclaimed, running down the outside hallway.

The mink skin was turned inside out and every last bit of fat and tissue had been removed. It was stretched over a thin board about a half inch thick which had been rounded at the front end so it would slide in smoothly and just wide enough to keep it good and tight. Looking at that mink fur and fantasizing about going to the fur market with Steve and Dad, really started a fire inside of me. "Someday I'm going to be just as good a mink trapper as Yellowknife Jack," I declared to myself as I turned to go get the tub.

After supper and the rerun trapping events were over and with my eyelids just about to close and Mother ushering us kids off to bed, I suddenly became aware of a new addition to the fireplace hearth—a half gallon fruit jar stuffed full of fresh catfish. Steve was about to get down and dirty on the local mink population, but at that particular moment I was just too pooped and sleepy to get excited.

* * *

All week long I kept rushing home from school hoping that Dad and Steve would have more mink skins stretched and hanging out on the back porch, but somehow things just weren't working out. The mink were really being stubborn and Dorothy could see that I was getting stressed out over it. On Friday as we were walking home from school, she suddenly decided she was going to needle me about it. "So, Hoyt, how long do you think it's going to be before Nellie and I will need to get the lining and the buttons for Mama's fur coat? How many mink have you caught so far? I've forgotten. Was it 12 or 15?" She asked, with a snicker. "Oh, you haven't caught an-ny! Well gee, I thought that super snifter of yours would have caught at least one by now," she said, with a big grin.

"Dorothy you shouldn't tease Hoytie like that," Nellie protested. "You're his big sister, and treating him like that just isn't right."

"Oh, I'm just kidding. He thinks he's such a big shot," she added, as I took off for home on a run.

"You just wait, Dorothy," I yelled, back. "You just wait; I'll show you!"

"You're pushing him too hard, Dot, and if I know Hoyt he will find a way to get you back. You just remember who started it all when the payback comes."

"Oh what could he possibly do—just get mad—anyhow, I was only kidding."

When I got home there wasn't anyone in the house, and I headed straight for my room to change out of my school clothes. I figured Mama was probably around the back of the house somewhere, hanging out clothes or something, and I was heading around there when I spotted the catfish jar setting on the hearth. "Hmmm—I just wonder what kind of smell it is that mink are attracted to," I thought. "Since I'm going to be a trapper, maybe I ought to find out." I picked up the jar and gently began unscrewing the lid. I had only gotten my nose about halfway to the mouth of the jar when the most ghastly odor I had ever smelled in my entire life ran up my nose, down my throat and felt like it went out my ears—I started gagging instantly! I barely got the lid back on and set it back down before my stomach began retching—trying to empty itself. Jimminy whillikers—I didn't think I was going to make it outside in time! I had never smelled anything close to that bad in my entire life. It took about five minutes before my stomach started settling down. "Wow! It's no wonder mink smell bad if they eat stuff like that," I thought as a visible shudder shook my whole body. I had barely got straightened up when Dorothy and Nellie started coming up the lane. Instantly a scheme started forming in my mind on how to get Dorothy to smell the fish jar. I truly felt that payback was in order because of her rudeness to me, and making her stomach turn upside down would suit me just fine, but how could I coax her to smell it? All afternoon I tried to think of ways to get Dorothy to smell the catfish jar, but nowhere in my devious little brain could I come up with the solution. I was just about to give the whole thing up when it all suddenly started falling into place. Dorothy had a small jar of cold cream that she was purely in love with (cold cream was as close to makeup as Mother would allow her to have), and she guarded it like a hawk. Every night she went through a ritual of applying her beauty cream—as she called it and prissing around the room playing grown-up, looking at herself in the mirror. She wouldn't even allow Nellie to touch it, because she said that Nellie was just too young, which, of course, really frustrated Nell. Suddenly my whole concentration went from mink trapping to getting even with Dorothy. Somehow I had to get myself a small supply of that "gag a maggot juice." I knew that Mother and Dad used quite a bit of Vicks nose drops so I went out on the back porch and went through the garbage can, and just like I had hoped, there it was, Yellowknife Jack's favorite applicator system. Now all I had to do was get it all cleaned up and remove all traces of the Vicks smell, and I was in business. I could kill two birds with one stone—be practicing the application of mink lure and getting even with Dorothy at the same time; what could be better?

* * *

The next week turned out to be a little piece of heaven for me. By mid-week I had Dorothy about to freak out, and Steve and Dad were bringing in two or three mink a day by using the new fish lure. I found out the broom straw method was the best for my purposes because I could leave just a slight trace of the yuk smell in exactly the places I wanted, without over-doing it. First I started by putting three teeny droplets into her cold cream jar and stirring it in thoroughly, then I added just a trace to the collar of her school blouse and a larger droplet about midway of her skirt in the back. Each day she was changing clothes because she knew there was something wrong; she just couldn't figure out why she couldn't get rid of that phantom odor. She was constantly checking the bottoms of her shoes and smelling her hands. I could hardly contain my glee. As soon as she would hang her clothes out for the next day I would be biding my time to sneak in and doctor them up. I felt so smug and successful I couldn't believe it was that easy. I had brought her to the point of absolute panic in only three days; payback really felt good, but just when I was getting into the swing of the whole thing, something unexpected started blowing my plan. I started feeling sorry for her because people were moving away and didn't want to sit next to her at school. As mad as I was I still loved her, and I didn't want to see her being treated that way. Getting even was one thing, but degrading her to others wasn't right, and I knew it! That evening she broke down and started crying on the way home from school. Man that really threw a monkey wrench into my process. I took off running and left her and Nellie far behind. I wasn't ashamed of what I had done, but on the other hand, I didn't feel like torturing her anymore either. I hid my yuk bottle in my room for safekeeping and started concentrating on trapping again.

* * *

That week Steve and Dad caught six mink, two boars and four sows, as Dad and Steve called them—two males and four females—and I watched them remove the urine bladder from one of the females and put the liquid into the same type of bottle I had. Steve had brought several in his suitcase. That was a total of 7 mink that had been caught, and I was getting some really good lessons in pelting and making stretcher boards. This was my kind of life.

"Dave, if I don't miss my guess, there's a hundred dollars or more hanging on that wall right now," Steve projected, as he and Dad added the newest skins to the collection. "Now you see how fast it can add up."

"Steve, I am flabbergasted at this whole thing. This is by far the fastest and easiest money this dirt farmer has ever seen made," Dad said, smiling and shaking his head.

"It's like I said before, you've just got to give the process time to work. In another two weeks that banknote of yours will be history."

"Steve, Dell and I have talked this over more than once, and we want you to take your trap money, right off the top and then at least half of everything else that's made is yours. The bank won't push me for the money; they know they'll get paid."

"No, Dave, this is my gift to you and your family. I have sufficient income to do this without hurting myself. The payoff for me will be when we can walk into your bank and see them tear up that note and to know that you and Dell will have a chance for a better life. I've set my feet under your table an awful lot of times without you ever flinching or asking me for a penny. Now it's your turn to be humble and accept what I'm offering, and I don't want to hear anymore about it from either of you—okay?" Suddenly Mother walked out of the kitchen onto the back porch, and one could tell that she was very touched. She had overheard the conversation between Dad and Steve.

"Steve, our home is your home, for now and always," she said, wiping tears on a handkerchief she took from her apron pocket. "Why don't you guys come on into the kitchen and let's get all this family together. Supper is on the table."

A FUR COAT FOR MAMA

"Now that's an offer I won't turn down," Steve replied, with a big smile. "Dell, there's the first hundred dollars against that banknote," Steve said, pointing to the furs hanging on the wall. "Like I just told Dave—in another two weeks that note will be history."

"There's no way this family can ever repay this act of kindness, Steve, but since friendship is always an ongoing process, I'm going to start by feeding you a good hearty supper. You boys get washed up and come on in here."

* * *

Right after supper, Old Trailer and I were in my room when Nellie, Dorothy and Mama came in.

"Hoytie, Dorothy has something she wants to say to you," Nellie said, as Mama gave Dorothy a little push forward.

"Little brother, I'm sorry for how I treated you," Dorothy said, with tears starting to well up in her eyes. "This week has been horrible for me, and I've seen just how much I need my family. Please forgive me; I won't ever do you that way again," she said, giving me a hug.

"Now Hoyt, Dorothy has apologized to you and asked for your forgiveness," Mother said, "so I'm counting on you to be a big man about this and forgive her too. I want you kids to be good to each other. Nellie told me what has been going on, and I have given Dorothy a sound talking to, so this is over right now—okay!"

"Okay, Mama," I replied, as I reached under the bed and pulled out the mink lure bottle.

"What's this?" she asked, rolling the bottle around in her hands.

"That's some of the stinky catfish juice that Steve and Dad are using for trapping," I said. "I was really mad at Dorothy for being mean to me, so I was putting it on her clothes to make her stink." Suddenly Dorothy's face flushed bright red, and her eyes looked like they could shoot fire.

"Why you little bum! How could you do something like that to me? You—you!"

"Now just a minute, Dorothy," Nellie said, stepping in front of her. "Do you remember what I said about payback, and you asked what he could possibly do? Well, that horrible time you suffered is what he did. You did deliberately start this whole thing, you know!"

Suddenly Dorothy's face dropped as she realized the small bit of cruelty she had initiated had come back to haunt her. "Oh my gosh, Hoytie, I am so sorry," she said, dropping to her knees and throwing her arms around me.

"Please forgive me! I will never treat you bad like that again; I promise!"

"And you won't talk bad about Old Trailer either!" I added.

"I certainly won't; I promise. You can count on your big sis from now on," she said, with tears still running down her face. "You're just too dadburned smart and ornery to be treated little any more," she said, with the best attempt she could make at smiling.

"Okay then, Big Sis, I accept," I said, throwing my arms around her.

"Now that's the way I want my children to act," Mama said, pulling Nellie over into a group hug with Dorothy and me. "We're a family that loves and takes care of each other, and that's just how it's going to stay. Kids, it's bedtime—tomorrow is another day."

CHAPTER SEVEN—The Fur Market and Big Trouble!

Dad and Steve trapped until the middle of January before they decided they had enough cured mink furs to take to market. They had 17 market ready and five more that needed a little more time. Luckily for me the market was only open on Saturdays, so for once I got to do the man stuff without being shuffled off to school. I was higher than a kite! We removed the boards from all the cured furs then tied them all into a single bundle and slipped it inside a clean burlap bag. "It's going to be a chilly ride in the old wagon getting to Booneville," Dad had just said, when suddenly Mama spoke up from the living room. "I think that's Maxy pulling up in front of the house, Dave."

"Alright, Mom," Dad replied. "Son, run out and tell him to come on in. Steve and I still have a little more work to do here."

"Hey, there, young Mr. Walker," Maxy shouted, as I came running out of the house. "Would your daddy happen to be at home?"

"He sure would, Maxy," I replied excitedly. "We're just getting ready to go to town to sell a bunch of mink hides. Do you want to come with us?"

"Mink hides," Maxy repeated, with an almost startled look on his face. "Where'd you guys get mink hides?"

"Daddy and Steve—they caught them down on the creek!"

"Hey, come on in here pal," Dad said, swinging the front door open. "I've got someone here I'd like you to meet. Steve, this is my good buddy Johnny Maxwell, alias Maxy. Maxy, this is my first cousin, Steve Walker."

"I'm mighty proud to meet you, Steve," Maxy said, extending his hand.

"Likewise, sir. Dave has told me a lot about you."

"Well, I hope at least some of it was good," Maxy said, with a crooked grin. "Hey, I hear you boys have been doing some trapping—and you've caught some mink; is that right?"

"We've got seventeen!" I quickly interjected, "and there's five more out on the back porch we're not even taking."

"22 mink," Maxy stammered—"Man that's hard to believe! I've never heard of mink being caught around here before."

"Yeah, neither did I," Dad admitted—"it's all Steve's doing!"

"Let's have a look at them. If they're good enough, I just might be able to set you fellows up with a better than average deal."

"How's that, Maxy?" Dad inquired, as they headed for the back porch.

"Dave, there's a mutual friend of ours that has a real need of good mink pelts. Mel Flood has gone into the fur buying business, and he's having to import most all his mink fur from Canada."

"Man—when did that happen? I thought he was still in the beverage business," Dad exclaimed.

"No, he's been out of that for about a year now—said the heat was just getting too close. Have you fellows heard about that new coat factory that went in last year in Fort Smith—Magnus and Son's? Well, Mel is their main furrier, and he certainly would like to have a source of good fur closer to home. He buys the run of the mill stuff—possum, coon and the like in Booneville at the Market where you boys are heading, but the mink and ermine are most all coming out of Canada and Alaska."

"I don't believe you're going to find any ermine this far south," Steve replied, "but these mink pelts are very near as prime as the Canadian ones I trapped in Yellowknife—North West Territory."

"No kidding! Well, if that's the case, you boys are in the money! Mel says Canadian fur is just about the best there is. This new factory uses several different types of fur, but I'm sure you already know the real money is in mink and ermine. I didn't have a clue there was mink in this neck of the woods."

"Here, have a look for yourself," Dad said, sliding the bundle out and taking off the binding.

"Man, I am amazed these mink came from around here. I don't know a whole lot about fur quality," Maxy admitted, looking very closely at the individual skins, "but from what I can see—these look great. Are there lots of them, or are they pretty scarce?"

"No, there seems to be plenty of them," Dad acknowledged, "but it takes a real master of the art to get them. Without Steve's Canadian trapping experience, I would never have stood a chance, and neither will anyone else who doesn't know the game."

"Well, I'll say one thing; you fellows are off to a roaring start!"

"Not exactly," Steve added, shaking his head. "It took me a lot longer to figure them out than it should have. We're actually a little behind schedule. We've got them nailed down now though—right Dave?"

"I sure hope so," Dad said, with a bit of uncertainty in his voice.

"Ooh yeah—I'll guarantee you, by this time next month we'll have two or three times this many ready to go."

"Well, I'll guarantee you, our fur buying buddy is going to love that!" Maxy replied, looking at Dad with a big grin. "Hey, let's throw these in the rumble seat of my Model A, and I'll take you boys right on up there."

"That's a mighty generous offer," Dad said. "We were already starting to dread the trip in the open wagon."

"Hey, I'm glad to be of help," Maxy said, "Besides, I told Mel I would keep an eye open for any good fur in this area, so this could be good for both of us. He might even make me a subcontractor, and I could earn a nickel or two myself."

"Well, there's one thing I know for sure," Steve replied. "You've already earned yourself a tank full of gasoline just as soon as we get to town!"

"That's a fact," Dad agreed, "and a bowl of chili at the Train Car Diner. They make the best dadburned chili I've ever had!"

* * *

Within minutes we were all loaded into Maxy's Model A and headed towards town. Oh man—I was finally living the dream—my first trip to the fur market!

The market was located inside a very large warehouse building in the far edge of the wagon yard, and the Train Car Diner (a compact little eating place inside a rail car) was sitting right out in the center. We had to walk right by it, and one could already smell the wonderful aromas from within as the cook got his specialties ready for the day.

"Man, if that stuff is half as good as it smells," Maxy said, raising his graying eyebrows over an aggressive Arkansas smile, "we just might want to have us a couple of bowls. My belly is suddenly feeling the need."

"Yeah, mine too," Dad added, rubbing his tummy through his coat. "Fellows, this chili is a true bargain at a quarter a bowl, and since soda pop is just a nickel, and since I now have a renewable source of income I can count on, we're just going to belly up to the bar and eat all we want—I'm buying!"

"Man, that's the best news I've heard all day," Steve acknowledged. "My mouth is already watering."

"I know what you mean," Dad replied. "With a Grapette or an orange soda pop on the side, this chili is a meal fit for a king, and another thing I really like about this little joint—not only is their food top rate, but they always give you plenty of crackers to eat it with."

"Boy, that's one of my pet peeves," Maxy declared, "when they skimp you on the crackers."

"I really like Orange Crush a lot," I interjected, taking decidedly longer steps to try to stay up with the men, "but I think I like Grapette just a little bit better," I proposed, using my prior knowledge of the diner to hold a position in the conversation. "I just wish they made those bottles bigger."

A FUR COAT FOR MAMA

"I'll certainly agree with that, Hoyt," Maxy added. "That's another one of my gripes. Six ounces is way too small for something that tastes that good. Maybe we ought to consider having us a double there too," he grinned, pointing at me with his index finger. "After all, Dave did say we could have all we wanted, didn't he?"

"He sure did," I agreed, with a satisfied grin. "I might just have a Grapette and an orange too!"

"Now you're talking—that wasn't so hard to work out, was it?" Maxy grinned, looking across at Dad.

"You boys are liable to bankrupt this endeavor before it gets off the ground," Dad said, looking at Maxy and me with a sour grin.

* * *

We were one of only two or three automobiles which had parked in the wagon yard. Most all the cars which came to town, parked out on the main street where the storefronts were more accessible. The wagon yard was for the use of people who still used animals to travel with, which in our area was probably about three out of four families. There were about 10 or 12 wagons and teams sitting around at the different tie up spots with their horses and mules still attached. It was pretty much a standard practice to place feeding bags on your animals and give them enough grain to keep them occupied while you were doing your business.

"Here, Son, make yourself useful," Dad said, handing the bag of furs to me. "Since you want to be a trapper, you might as well learn the business from the ground up."

"I've got it, Daddy!" I replied, grabbing the bag and rolling it up onto my shoulder.

"Now Son, you want to let Steve and me do the talking. You might accidentally say something that would give our secret away. We're going to give them the old Yellowknife Jack treatment," Dad said, with a wink.

"Yeah—tight lipped!" I whispered, excitedly.

"You've got it! This is our thing and we've got to protect it."

At that moment I felt like I was nine feet tall and six feet wide; I was finally involved in the action.

As we entered the back of the big warehouse through a heavy wooden door, I was suddenly exposed to a part of the fur business that I had only heard and dreamed about. There were four merchants plying their trades at four separate buying stations about twenty feet apart with several people standing around the front of each waiting to sell. It was comfortably warm inside the big building and the air was pungent with the smells of the different kinds of furs that were being traded—a little fox, a little skunk, a little raccoon—you name it—it was there. The stove-pipe on the big barrel heater sitting some twenty feet back behind the stands was glowing cherry red, and there were several old guys sitting around the stove soaking up the free coffee offered by the buyers—all four had a big pot on.

"That's Mel's station up at the front there," Maxy pointed, as we made our way through the crowd.

"Well, what do you know? It's the boys from Sugar Grove!" Mel hollered, as we walked up. "Gentlemen, it is truly a pleasure to see you. It'll be just another minute, and then we can talk," he interjected as he counted out five one dollar bills and a small amount of change to his last customer. "Thanks Frank—see you next week."

"Yeah, I sure hope it's better than this one," the man grumbled, shoving the money deep into his overalls pocket.

"Dave, how the heck are you!" Mel exclaimed, extending his hand across the counter.

"I'm doing just fine, my friend," Dad replied, shaking Mel's hand affectionately. "Hey, I've got someone special here I would like you to meet. This is my cousin Steve Walker from Albuquerque, New Mexico," Dad gestured, as Steve stepped forward to greet Mel.

"I'm always glad to meet another Walker boy," Mel said. "Steve, it's a pleasure."

"Likewise, sir," Steve acknowledged, nodding his head.

"And who is this young man carrying this big load of furs? I'll bet these are all mink hides, right?" he said jokingly.

"That's just what they are alright," I replied, rolling the bag off onto the counter.

"This is Hoyt, my youngest son, Mel," Dad announced.

"Well, Hoyt, it's a fine pleasure to meet you too. Me and your pa go way back. Now, let's see what kind of furs you brought me today," he stated, reaching inside the bag.

"They're all mink hides just like he said!" Maxy declared, shaking his head with a wide grin.

"Well, I'll be danged. You weren't kidding me, Hoyt! Where in the cat hair did you boys come up with these beauties? This is prime mink fur, gentlemen!"

"Dad and Steve caught them down on—" immediately, Dad silenced my enthusiasm with a quick nudge of his elbow as two other guys came walking up behind us.

"I'm sorry, Daddy," I whispered. "I forgot."

"It's alright, little man," Dad said, with a smile.

"How many of these do you boys have?" Mel asked, clipping the binding cord with his pocket knife.

"I believe there are 17 there," Dad answered.

"17 mink?" one of the guys in back of us whispered, pushing in closer trying to get a better look. "That's a pile of money," he mumbled under his breath.

"Man—fellows, this is the kind of stuff I've been looking for!" Mel exclaimed, holding the individual furs out for close inspection. "These skins have been properly taken care of too," he said, turning one inside out to check the actual fur. "You boys have done well."

"Steve has trapped the Canadian northwest," Maxy quickly volunteered.

"Well, you're a craftsman, Steve; there's no doubt about that. I'm sure you already know this knowledge is like money in the bank to whoever possesses it."

"Dave and his family are very special people to me," Steve replied. "He's the only person I'm ever going to teach it to. Whatever he does is his own affair. As soon as he feels comfortable to be on his own, I'll be heading back to my barbering practice in Albuquerque."

"Dadburn it, Steve!" Mel exclaimed, shaking his head. "Are you sure you've got to do that? I was already having visions of you boys setting up a little fur empire down there at Sugar Grove and me being your number one pal and fur handler," Mel said, laughing as he spoke. "This is brand new country, boys! These are the first local mink I've seen or heard of, and if there were others being sold I would certainly know about it," Mel said, looking first at Steve then at Dad. "That puts you guys right on top of the heap!"

"Well, like I told you, whatever Dave wants to do is up to him, but I have another life that I'm very attached to, and I need to be getting back to it."

"Dave—just to entice you to expand into this new business venture, I'm going to extend you the best price possible. I'm going to pay you $15 for each of your female skins and $30 for each of the males. That's pretty much scraping the upside of the market. The way I figure it, you've got nine females at $15. That's $135, and you've got 8 males at $30; that's $240. 240 plus 135 is $375. How does that sound to you?"

"That's more money than I've seen in a coon's age, partner," Dad replied, reaching over to shake Mel's hand, "and I have a powerful need of it."

"Gentlemen, how many furs like this do you think you're going to be able to generate in a 30 day period?" Mel questioned.

"I'm going to let Steve answer that," Dad replied. "He's the expert."

"If we have good luck and the weather doesn't get too severe—being on the conservative side—I'd say we're going to have at least 50."

"Good grief! That's a ton of money," one of the men standing behind us blurted out as they both turned and started quickly walking away.

Mel reached under his stand and pulled out a metal cash box and began to count out the money that Dad and Steve had coming. Just as he had finished counting out the full $375 into a stack on the table top, suddenly instead of two guys looking on there were five.

"Dave, that's your money; pick it up, and let's get on out of here and go have that bowl of chili," said Steve, looking back nervously at the inquisitive onlookers. "After we do that we've got a date with the Citizens Bank," he reminded, as Dad began picking up the large stack of cash.

"Hey, Walker, where'd you boys get them mink at anyway?" a tall husky onlooker asked, as Dad stuffed the large roll of bills into his overalls pocket.

"We had them imported from Canada," Dad quipped, as he turned and started walking away with a crooked grin on his face.

"Good answer, Dave!" Steve smiled, as we all headed for the back door.

"See you boys next week," Mel called out after us.

* * *

"Well, Dave, you've already started raising eyebrows," Steve declared. "Those fellows are definitely interested in what you've got going."

"Yeah—just my luck, too!" Daddy mumbled, in a very negative tone. "It just had to be those knot headed Sloyd brothers. They only live about a mile from where we've been trapping. I sure hope they don't cause us problems."

"Dave, those boys will be a problem to anyone and everyone that makes contact with them, and you guys are no exception," Maxy stated, shaking his head. "It's damned unfortunate they had to see that money. I'd highly recommend we get right on over to the car as quickly as we can. That bunch is unpredictable."

"Hey, aren't we going to get that bowl of chili?" Dad questioned. "I sure was looking forward to that."

"Yeah, we'll have our chili," Maxy replied, "but let's give it a few minutes. Unless I'm badly mistaken we're going to have to deal with that bunch of creek bottom slime before we're through. I saw some real aggression pop into old Dud's eyes when he spotted that pile of cash."

"Dud, that's the name of the leader—the big husky one?" Dad questioned, looking backwards toward the door of the fur market.

"Yeah, and he's a real, dyed in the wool nut case too!" Maxy replied. "They figure just because they were raised down on that creek, it belongs to them—and that means the mink and whatever else is down there."

"You're kidding!" Dad replied, in disbelief. "I knew those boys were a bit dense, but I didn't know they were that bad."

"Oh yeah, they've turned into a bunch of real-life thugs in the last few years, and they'll do whatever they can get away with. Since their mama passed away a couple of years back they've totally gone wild. Now instead of farming, they just live off of whatever they can steal and catch hunting and fishing. That old place where they were raised down there is falling down around their ears and they're too lazy and stupid to fix it back up. The old lady was the brains for the whole bunch; unfortunately she took it all with her when she left."

"How long has their daddy been gone?" Dad questioned.

"He died about ten years back. I guess he was just about as worthless as the boys, from what I hear."

"How'd you learn so much about them anyway?" Dad asked. "I had no idea you even knew the bums."

"My sister and her husband bought 50 acres of bottom land right down there close to them, and they've had nothing but trouble from that bunch. Boys, I've got a couple of 18 inch crowbars I use for tire irons under the back seat," Maxy said, as we approached the Model A. "If we have to we'll knock some knots on their thick skulls. There's no use trying to run from them; sooner or later, they'll have to be dealt with."

"Yeah, I'd say you're right there," Dad agreed, with a bit of uncertainty in his voice, "but maybe we're just overreacting here, Maxy."

No sooner had Dad gotten the words out of his mouth than the harsh reality of what Maxy had predicted began taking place. The back door of the fur market flew open and out they came—all five of them, heading in our direction, almost on a run.

"Hey, Walker," the big chubby one yelled. "Are you guys going to tell us where you got them mink, or do we have to rip your kid's ears off?"

"That's just what I figured!" Maxy chuckled, shaking his head and reaching under the back seat. "Here Dave," he said, handing Dad a hefty crowbar. "Hang this on the back of your pants so they can't see it and I'll do the same. If they give us trouble, lay into the side of their heads with it."

"I'll do exactly that if it becomes necessary," Dad agreed, slipping the bar onto his belt. "Ain't nobody going to rip my boy's ears off while I'm around."

"Steve, I've only got two crowbars. You and Hoyt get in the car—lock the doors and roll up the windows. I think Dave and I can handle these ruffians, but if they should get the best of us—the keys are in the ignition; run over the bastards if you have to, but don't let them leave here with Dave's money."

"Gotcha," Steve, agreed, sliding over under the wheel. "Anyone who gets that money away from Dave is going to have a set of tire tracks right up his backside, before he knows it. Hey, Hootie, didn't I see the stock of your bean flip sticking out of your pocket awhile ago?"

"You sure did, Steve; I take it everywhere I go."

"Have you got anything in your pocket to shoot in it?"

"No, I always get my rocks wherever I'm at," I replied. "All I've got in my pocket right now are three real good marbles and a steely ball."

"Little buddy," Steve said, looking at me with the seriousness of the situation reflected in his face, "when we get out of this mess we're in, I'll buy you a whole danged hat full of brand-new marbles—whatever kind you want, but right now, I think you ought to load up that steel ball and get ready for action. I think your pa and Maxy are going to need some help before this thing is over, and you and your bean flip just might be what makes the difference. Your target needs to be that big one out in front there with the rock in his hand. You need to shoot him just as hard as you can. Try to drive that steelie ball right through his ornery hide."

"I'm ready to go," I whispered, adjusting the steel ball in the leather of my slingshot.

"Where'd you boys get them mink hides anyway?" the big aggressive fellow challenged, as the group came to a halt about ten feet out in front of Dad and Maxy. "You got them down there on our creek didn't cha!" he accused.

"We saw you guys down there!" one of the younger boys sneered, in a high pitched voice.

"That money is ourn and we intend to get it," the tall skinny one professed, moving in close enough that I could see his yellow rotten teeth.

"What you're going to get, is something you're not looking for!" Dad replied, with a little chuckle and a threatening bit of cynicism.

"There's not a thimble full of brains among the whole damned lot of you fools, is there?" Maxy grumbled, looking at the group with a scowl. "Nobody owns Sugar Creek, especially not you bunch of clods, and you're danged sure not going to get your hands on the money these boys earn trapping down there. Now why don't you go on home before the whole lot of you get your heads bashed in."

"You don't really think you two pencil neck farmers are gonna whip all five of us—do you!" the big one scowled. "Now give us that danged money Walker or we're gonna take it."

"Okay, Hootie—get ready," Steve whispered, as he leaned across me and slowly began rolling down the window. "Do you think you can shoot between your Dad and Maxy and nail that big guy?"

"You bet I can, Steve; that'll be easy. Where do you want me to shoot him?"

"See how his coat opens up when he moves his arm backwards. Shoot him square in the bellybutton if you can."

Gently, Steve reached out the window nudging Dad on the thigh with his hand. As Dad's eyes quickly glanced downward, Steve whispered, "Dave, step aside just a little more; we need some shooting room here." At that very instant the big man began raising the rock over his head, threateningly.

"Gimme that money or I'm gonna bust your damned skull!"

"Get him, Hootie!" Steve yelled. Suddenly the live red rubbers on my slingshot were at maximum pull and Dud's bellybutton was shining like a new moon. Whack—the steel ball slammed right into his tender protruding navel. The two pound rock he was holding was suddenly loose in the air as he let out a blood curdling yell and grabbed his belly.

"Ai-ee—Jesus!—I've been shot"—he squalled, running backward a few steps clutching his big belly. The large rock tumbled from about eight feet in the air and the skinny one looked up to see what had happened to it just in time to have it smack him right on top of the left foot.

"Oooh—God damn you—Dud, you broke my lousy foot!" he whined hopping backwards a little ways dragging his left leg.

"You sawed off little runt, I'm going to get you for that if it's the last thing I ever do," Dud yelled, glaring at me through the car window—"you can count on it! Man, am I going to get you good," he threatened, looking down at an egg sized blue knot that had suddenly appeared where his belly button used to be. "I'm going to take pleasure in twisting both those big ears right off your skull!"

"Boy, you laid it on him good, Hootie!" Steve said, laughing and putting his arm around me protectively. "You're going to really need to be careful from now on though—never let these guys catch you off away from home."

"Yeah," I agreed, looking out the window at Dud's menacing stare and sliding my hand subconsciously up over my ear.

"Hey Dave, what's going on over there?" a familiar voice rang out loudly from across the wagon yard.

"Daddy, it's Uncle Ike and Cowboy," I yelled, as the Sloyds started regrouping to begin another push on Dad and Maxy.

Ike and Cowboy were both on horseback, and within seconds they were skidding to a running dismount in back of the attackers. "Now those bums will get it," I cried, jumping out on the opposite side of the vehicle.

"Dave, what's happening here?" Ike yelled, over the noise of the impending encounter.

"A strong armed robbery is what's trying to happen!" Dad yelled, backing up against the car again with his tire iron slashing out in front of him. "These guys are trying to take the money Steve and I made trapping down on Sugar Creek."

"That money came from our creek, Ike, and it's rightfully ourn!" one of the younger boys yelled.

"Dud! You boys are pushing on the wrong man this time," Cowboy asserted, stepping right up into the face of the belligerent leader. "I know Dave Walker well enough to know that whatever he's got belongs to him, and he came by it honest! You boys may think you've got something going here, but it's not going to fly. You bunch of jerks have got ten seconds to turn around and start heading out of here, or we're going to stomp the living hell out of the lot of you." Cowboy threatened, as he and Ike began pulling off their jackets. "Dave, give me that crowbar—I'm going to bash me some skull!"

"That's our money, Cowboy!" Dud insisted defiantly, shaking his oversized fist and glaring at Dad. "These guys came down to our creek and stole it right away from us."

"It takes brains and effort to catch mink, Sloyd," Maxy declared, "and you lazy bums don't have neither. You've lived on that creek all your stupid lives and didn't even know there was mink there, so go on home and shut up!"

"Walker, this ain't over!" Dud yelled, as the group started reluctantly backing away. "One way or t'other, we'll have what's ourn."

"I don't want anything that belongs to you, Sloyd," Dad replied, "but there's one thing you boys better keep in mind—you come around me or my family again with this pushy attitude, and I'll put a bullet through you, before you can blink your eyes! You better remember that!"

"That's our creek, Walker," said the tall skinny one, "and what's down there is ourn. You guys had better stay away from there."

"Sugar Creek is a public stream, Wag," Ike stated. "If you push on Dave like this anymore, you'll be dealing with me and Cowboy, and we'll make no qualms about busting your thick heads!"

"Dave, I am truly sorry about this," Steve said, stepping out of the car. "I figured you could handle not being real popular if the money was good enough, but I surely didn't expect anything like this."

"This doesn't change a thing partner," Dad insisted, with defiance in his voice. "Those mink belong to whoever can catch them, and I intend to keep right on with the process you've taught me. My family's future is at stake, and besides, now I've got backup," he added, looking down at me with a wink and a grin.

"I put him up to that, Dave," Steve admitted. "I hope it was all right."

"All right—it was more than all right!" Dad said, with an ear to ear grin—"it was a stroke of genius! Did you see that goose egg that popped up on old Dud's belly? They'd better think twice about messing with the Walker boys again—right Son?"

"You said it, Daddy! Next time I'll put knots on all the bums!" I said. "I'm going to save up all the steely balls I can find."

"Hey Steve, it's been awhile since I've seen you," said Ike, reaching out to shake Steve's hand. "How long have you been down here?"

"About six weeks now, Ike. I thought I was doing Dave a big favor by teaching him how to catch mink, but, suddenly I'm not so sure. Cowboy, how are you doing nowadays?" Steve asked, reaching out to grasp Cowboys hand.

"Not too bad, Steve, although I sure could use a job right now. Ike and I have been working at a sawmill outside of town here until the snow shut us down."

"If I had any work, I would certainly be glad to use you at my mill," said Maxy, shaking hands with Ike and Cowboy, "I had to give it up too about a month back."

"Cowboy, I can tell you one thing you've got going for you," Steve said. "Even though this old horse has aged a bit since I saw him last, he's still the best looking piece of horse flesh I've ever laid eyes on. Did you ever get him trained to ride properly?"

"Yeah, after about two years of fighting with him, I finally started using my head. I take him out to the racetrack about two or three times a month and run the tar out of him. The rest of the time I can handle him pretty well. He holds the three quarter mile track record here at the Booneville horse track."

"Well, you and he sure make a handsome pair," Steve answered. "Man, that set of Mexican spurs you're sporting is really something. I don't believe I've ever seen a pair quite like those."

"Yeah, these spurs are very special to me. I've had them about 15 years now."

"Very special is not quite the word," Ike replied, with a sarcastic chuckle. "I'm not sure but I think he even sleeps with them on."

CHAPTER EIGHT—Maynard's Diner and a New $5 Bill

"Ike, since you and Cowboy are always hungry, and always broke, and since I owe you a big favor for saving our bacon just now, why don't you tie those nags to the car bumper, and come on with us over to the diner and talk a spell," Dad suggested. "I'll buy you boys all the chili you can eat."

"Hot damn! I'm sure not about to turn that offer down," Cowboy replied, with his usual enthusiasm—"I'm starved!"

"Ditto," Ike affirmed with a big grin—"lead the way brother; we're right behind you!"

"Boys, I'm having me a big bowl of chili and an Orange Crush," Dad announced as we all started filing into the little diner. "You boys can order whatever you want; it's on me."

"I'm having what you're having," Cowboy said, following Dad in the door.

"Yeah, me too," Ike agreed. "If there's one thing I've learned in life, it's—don't ever look a gift horse in the mouth."

"Okay, that's three chili's with Orange Crush," Dad said. "Steve—Maxy, what are you boys having?"

"I'm going to stick with Hoyt," Maxy replied. "He's the hero of the day, and besides we've got a possible double-header going. What are we having partner?"

"Let's start out with Grapette, chili, and lots of crackers."

"Yeah, that sounds good to me too," Maxy replied. "We'll just let our appetite dictate what happens next."

"I'm going to go with you boys," Steve said. "I think you're getting the best of this deal."

"We need six bowls of chili, three bottles of Orange Crush, and three Grapettes," Dad informed the cook, as we all started lining up on the tall bar stools along the counter.

"You've got it!" The cook smiled, adjusting his chef hat, and turning to the big wood heated range adorned with several large bubbling pots.

"Hey, Maynard, is that you?" Cowboy asked, standing up and looking inquisitively at the cook—"Hell, yes it is you!"

"Well, what do you know; it's my Cowboy cousin!" the cook responded, turning from the stove and excitedly reaching across the bar to Cowboy. "Long time no see, cuz."

"Yeah it's probably been about two years now; wouldn't you say? Hey, what the heck are you doing in here anyway?"

"Man, I own this place. Well, me and the Citizen's Bank owns it. I invested in it about four months back."

"Maynard, I can tell you one thing," Dad quickly asserted, "this little joint has a track record of always putting out the best danged chili in this whole area. I'd say you've got yourself a real winner here."

"Yeah, I think so too," the cook replied. "That was why I invested in it. I really loved the food, and the old couple who owned it wanted to unload it so they could retire; I got a real fine deal on the place. I had it right in the contract that they had to train me for two full months before they could leave. Man, I've learned more about chili in the last few months than you can shake a stick at. I know I've got it right because I'm a confirmed chili addict, and I've gained 20 pounds since I bought the place."

"Hey cousin, I'd like to introduce you to my friends here. Fellows, this is my Uncle Jim's boy, Maynard James. Maynard, this is my good buddy, Ike Walker—that's his brother Dave over there, and the short guy sitting right next to Dave is his boy, Hoyt. He's a mean man with a bean flip. On the other side is Steve Walker, Dave's cousin, and last but not least is Maxy; he owns a sawmill over near the foot of Flood Mountain."

"Gentlemen, it's a real pleasure to know all of you," Maynard replied, "but instead of making your grumbling stomachs wait while we go about shaking hands, I'm going to give you what you came in here for—chili!"

"Yeah, with lots of crackers!" I interjected loudly.

"You can't eat chili without crackers," Maxy drawled, shaking his head and smiling at me.

"Hey, what was all that ruckus out in the wagon yard awhile ago?" Maynard inquired, as he began ladling out steaming bowls of aromatic chili to all of us. "Was that you guys?"

"It danged sure was!" Cowboy replied. "Those stupid Sloyd brothers were in the process of robbing Dave here, when Ike and I came along. He sold a bunch of mink hides at the fur market and they thought the money should belong to them because Dave and Steve caught the mink down on Sugar Creek close to where they live. Can you believe that! They think Sugar Creek is theirs!"

"Man, those guys are out of control," Maynard said, as he finished the chili orders and started setting out the soda pop. "Now who wants orange and who wants grape?"

"Ike, Cowboy, and I want orange," Dad replied.

"And the rest get grape—and oh yes, lots of crackers," said Maynard, setting our soda pop and a large basket of crackers on the counter. "Well, I'll tell you one thing; those hillbillies had better steer clear of my place from now on; they came in here last week and ate their bellies full and refused to pay me. If old man Swint and those two big boys of his hadn't showed up just when they did, I fully believe the bums would have robbed me too. They were already starting to come behind the counter."

"No kidding!" said Cowboy, shaking his head. "Man, you've got to have some kind of protection in here, Maynard. You can't let those guys get away with that. If they think they can push you around, you're in big trouble."

"That's the way I figured it too," the cook replied. "I've got a little surprise waiting for them if they show up again. There's a sawed off twelve gauge, laying under the counter now."

"Letting the bums know you're not going to take their crap is probably about all you'll need to do," said Cowboy. "Bullies are all cowards at heart. Hoyt over there, did a pretty good number on them with just a bean flip, awhile ago. He shot the holy hell out of old Dud, so if they find out you've got a shotgun under there, they'll definitely leave you alone."

"He shot Dud with a bean flip?" the cook questioned, loudly, looking over at me and then at Cowboy.

"Man, did he ever!" Ike interjected, slapping his leg and laughing as he spoke. "Old Dud's belly button looked like a big blue Easter egg. Man, that had to hurt like the dickens," he groaned, shaking his head. "Hoyt you did everybody in this whole area a major favor by whacking that bugger! That was the best use of a bean flip I've ever witnessed!"

"I shot him with a steely ball," I exclaimed proudly—"It was my best marble shooter."

"Well, partner, you sacrificed it for a fine cause," said Maxy, with a wide grin. "You're the only one that got a lick in on those scum bums. They will certainly remember you."

"Yeah, that's what I'm afraid of," I mumbled under my breath.

"I promised him a hat full of brand new marbles, if he used that steel ball," Steve said, opening up his wallet and taking out a new five dollar bill. "Here boys, slide this down the counter to the bean flip man."

"Thanks, Steve," I said quietly, picking up the crisp five and holding it out for inspection. "This is the most money I've had in my whole life," I said, tucking it away in my front pocket.

"Hoyt, my man, you are definitely my kind of guy," the cook said, walking over directly in front of me in his chili stained white apron and tall chef hat. "I'd have easily given ten bucks to see you lay the steel to that bum," he grinned, pointing his index finger at me. "Somehow I feel better now—a little bit vindicated, you know Just for that, everything you eat and drink today is on the house," he said, shoving the cracker basket over closer and setting me up another soda pop.

"I want an orange this time," I insisted, draining the last drop from my Grapette bottle, and setting it noisily on the counter.

"You've got it partner," Maynard replied, reaching down through the crushed ice into his pop box and fishing out a heavy brown glass bottle. "Orange Crush—there you go, Little Buddy—drink up!"

The feasting went on for about another 15 minutes as everyone continued enjoying the specialty of the house and good conversation. Suddenly Steve broke the silence, "Dave, we need to be getting over to the bank. There's a chore we need to take care of over there before closing time."

"Yes sir, there definitely is," Dad agreed, sliding a five dollar bill across the counter to Maynard. "I think that should cover it."

"That will more than cover it, Dave," the cook said, heading for the cash register.

"Keep the change, Maynard, and keep the chili coming," Dad insisted, as we all started filing out.

"Thanks fellows, I sure appreciate the business," Maynard yelled, as the door slammed behind us.

CHAPTER NINE—Sugar Grove Boys Enterprise and the Sloyd Brothers' Larceny

"Hey Dave, just how hard are mink to catch?" Ike questioned, as we headed back to the wagon yard. "Cowboy and I can't find a thing to do that pays anything."

"Yeah, we've tried all over the whole area, and there's just nothing available," Cowboy proclaimed.

"Well, it is a complicated process, fellows, but it's nothing that good old boys can't learn. I'm living proof of that. I actually wanted to talk to you boys about possibly throwing in with me. Steve is just about to head back home, and I don't relish being down on that creek bank all by myself, now that I know how irrational those ignorant people are."

"I think that would be a very wise idea, Dave," Steve agreed. "From what I witnessed a little while ago, I wouldn't trust those ingrates in any way shape or form. There's no telling what they would be capable of if they caught you off by yourself."

"I can tell you one thing, Dave, if you'll take the time to teach Cowboy and me to trap, we'll make sure those lunkheads don't cause you any problems."

"Yeah, we'll put the hurt on them fast if they start messing around," said Cowboy. "We really need a job, Buddy."

"Alright then fellows, how about we meet at my house Monday morning, and I'll take you boys out and start your training. You're both going to need a pair of hip boots, and somehow we'll have to wrangle some traps for you."

"Dave, I'll leave you my boots and the rest of my gear," Steve offered, "that might help a little."

"Thanks, Cousin," Dad replied. "It definitely will. Maxy, how about you, would you be interested in learning to trap mink?"

"I certainly would, Dave. I would consider it an honor to be one of your students. This kind of opportunity doesn't come along every day."

"Then it's settled. We have just formed us a mink trapper's co-op. All we need now is a little time, and those mink will be in trouble."

"Gentlemen, since Mel is our contact with the money, and since he is highly interested in quality mink fur," said Maxy, "why don't I put the bite on him for a loan to get us started properly. If we promise him an exclusive on all our pelts he might even furnish the stuff we need free. In fact—I could head over there right now and put it to him."

"Now, by jove, that's what we needed," Dad replied enthusiastically—"a manager! Go to it pal; see what you can turn up."

"Hot damn!" Cowboy exclaimed excitedly, slapping Ike on the back—"the old gang's together again!"

"Yeah, now all we need is old Doc, said Ike, with an approving grin. "I'm starting to feel better all ready."

"Dave, let's get on over to the bank," Steve insisted, adamantly. "I want to get that note taken care of. Tomorrow morning I need to be heading home. I would like to stay longer, but I have other duties that need attending to."

"I understand, good buddy," Dad replied. "What you've done here will never be forgotten."

"I wish you boys all the luck in the world with this project, but I certainly don't envy the situation you're looking at," Steve admitted. "I want you to promise me you'll be very careful. I'd hate to be the catalyst that gets all of you killed."

"Don't worry cousin. We'll take care not to let those ruffians get the upper hand on us."

* * *

Monday morning was a very hectic experience for the Walker house. Steve was in the process of packing to leave, Mother was trying to get us kids fed and off to school, Ike and Cowboy were already there ready to get started on their trapping lesson, and on top of it all Maxy came pulling up in front of the house blowing his horn.

"Hey, Ike, how about one of you boys run out and tell him to come on in," Dad suggested.

"We'll take care of it, Dave," Cowboy agreed, as he and Ike quickly headed for the front door with their coffee mugs in hand.

Our whole family was really sad to see Steve leaving; he was like a godfather to us. The evening before at the dinner table he had presented Mother with the $250 banknote paid off in full. It was a very touching moment for Mother and Dad. They knew for certain that without Steve's assistance that note would have been around for an awful long time throwing a dark shadow over their family, but out of the resourcefulness of his mind and the goodness of his heart Steve had single handedly built a financial bridge to rescue us.

"Dave, I just wonder if I could pay Maxy to haul me to town," Steve questioned. "I know you boys are in a fizz to get out on the creek bank, and you having to haul me to town in the wagon is going to eat up most of your day."

"We'll find out just as soon as he gets in here," Dad replied, "but we'll get you there one way or another partner. You can count on it."

"Hey Daddy, what's that Uncle Ike and Cowboy are carrying?" I asked, looking through the front window. "It's a big cardboard box."

"You've got me there, son," Dad replied. "Why don't you go check it out?"

"Hey Uncle Ike, what is that?" I asked, as they slid the heavy box up onto the front porch.

"That's number two Blake and Lamb steel traps, young Mr. Walker," Maxy volunteered, as he came up the walk carrying two brand-new pairs of hip boots. "There's another box just like that one still in the back of the car. We're going to catch us some mink, Little Buddy," he exclaimed, looking at me with a big excited grin.

"Hey Maxy, what does S- G- B- Enterprise mean?" I asked, reading the big lettering on top of the box.

"Sugar Grove Boys," Maxy exclaimed loudly, as Dad and Steve came out the door. "Is that handle all right with you guys?"

"I suppose that about sums it up," Dad replied, grinning and nodding his head.

"Mel has agreed to front our little adventure if we'll give him first bid on all our furs," said Maxy.

"Well, we were going to sell to him anyhow," Dad proclaimed, "but there's no doubt, this will get him and us where we want to go faster."

"That's the way I figure too, Dave. I got us six dozen new traps and three sets of hip boots. By the way, Mel's got a store room there at the market that's chock full of everything a person would ever need in the line of trapping. He's not only a buyer he's a product supplier."

"Is that right?" Dad replied. "That boy is a real go getter. That will certainly be a convenience to us. Ordering through the mail takes entirely too long. Hey Maxy, Steve would like to know if you could possibly run him to Booneville to the bus station; he needs to catch a bus back to Albuquerque, and then maybe we can get in a short day of trapping."

"You bet I can; Steve, it would be my pleasure. I'm really sorry to see you leave, but I'm certainly glad about all the knowledge you've leaving behind. I know Dave will do it justice, but learning from the hand of the master would have been a real treat."

"Well, there's a very good chance I'll be coming back this way next winter to see what all you boys have gotten into. It's been a real pleasure meeting you Maxy, and it sure was nice seeing you and Cowboy again, Ike."

"Okay, boys," Dad prompted. "How about giving us a hand with Steve's gear?"

* * *

The weeks following Steve's departure showed a dramatic change in the lives of the Walker family. With the absence of the big note hanging over their heads and a new source of income, Mother and Dad were like birds out of a cage. They laughed and were more relaxed than I had ever seen them. Dad had Maxy and the boys lined out on Sugar Creek and its neighboring branches and the back porch was loaded with mink skins which was a delight to me because I got to watch all the pelting of the mink and making of the stretcher boards. What I liked the most though was going to the fur market and the ritual stop at Maynard's. At the close of each trapping day the talk would go on into the night, and Mother always had to drag me reluctantly out of the middle of it all to put me to bed. Mel was delighted with S. G. B. Enterprise and was constantly asking if the guys needed more traps or anything else. Everything was going forward in leaps and bounds. The guys took to mink trapping like ducks to water, but suddenly without warning, everything started going down hill. First it was Ike who came home saying that one of his traps was gone. "Well, a person is going to lose a trap now and then," Dad had told him, and the incident was dropped, but the following week both Dad and Maxy had traps come up missing. Dad kept a small notebook of exactly where his traps were set, so he knew he hadn't forgotten their location. Someone was stealing their traps, and it was obvious they were traps with mink in them or they couldn't have been found in the first place.

Well, if that wasn't bad enough, Old Trailer was really starting to act strangely. Dad and the guys would come home telling about him running through the woods looking up, as if he was trailing something running in the treetops, but the winter woods were absolutely barren of leaves and they all swore there just couldn't be anything up there or they could see it. What was even more perplexing was after his running spree he would tree in the muddy creek bank in a hole the size a crawfish would make. Man, having my hero dog go off the deep end was just about more than I could bear, but little did I know, the real shocker was just around the corner. One evening after Trailer had done the running thing, three times in one day, I overheard Dad telling

Mama that Trailer might be getting "the running blues." I cried myself to sleep that night holding on to him because "the running blues" was a death sentence to any dog that got it, and I just couldn't bear the thought of my soul mate being taken out into the woods and shot in the head (the only known cure for the disease). The condition would usually start with the dog's eyes dilating larger than normal, and it was very noticeable. It would even happen in bright sunlight. If the condition lasted more than a minute or two the dog would usually lose control and start running and howling like they were scared absolutely to death. Sometimes they would start jumping and snapping like they were trying to catch butterflies or something out of the air. It was an unpredictable situation. Ultimately, if let go, they would end up biting some of the family, usually the children. They could never be trusted again even though they would sometimes return to normal for a short time. I personally saw two neighbor dogs destroyed because of it. One of them had bitten the family's little girl through the hand. The other dog was killed before it hurt anyone because he was showing the same symptoms. I was constantly watching Old Trailer's eyes for any changes, horrified of losing my best friend. Dad and Mom never knew I had overheard their conversation. It was a terrible secret for a kid to hold inside; I didn't even tell my sisters. I just wasn't going to admit it was even a possibility.

* * *

As the season continued, the Sugar Grove boys were starting to lose more and more traps, and their patience was starting to wear very thin. It was obvious that the Sloyd brothers had to be the culprits because the trap robbing had to be done very early in the morning, before Dad and the boys got there, and the Sloyds were the only ones close enough to be doing it. The absolute clincher came when Mel told the crew that one of his competitors had been getting mink hides from the Sloyd boys. Man, that lit an immediate fire under S. G. B. Enterprise. Ike and Cowboy were ready to go down and thump the dickens out of the whole bunch immediately, and Maxy was feeling pretty much along the same lines, but as usual the voice of reason and common sense intervened.

"Fellows, I am just as upset about this as you are," Dad exclaimed, with the stress of the matter showing in his face, "but we just can't afford to lose our train of thought right now, or we'll really be in trouble. We only have six weeks left in the season, and you fellows are just starting to be productive. We really need to hit it hard from now until closing day, and we can still come out on top. Getting into a big hassle will thoroughly disrupt what we've got going. The money is here right now—it won't be, later!"

"I understand what you're saying Dave," Ike replied, "but we can't afford to let those bums keep on stealing from us like this. They're not ever going to quit unless we force them to. That's got to be 2 or 3 hundred dollars they've pilfered from us already. I say we go down and pay them a quick unannounced visit and put a stop to it once and for all. Bust a couple of heads—break an arm or two—put a little fear into their lives—that'll back them off. If you and Maxy don't want to come, Bud and I will take care of it."

"You bet we will!" Cowboy replied. "There's nothing I'd like better."

"Fellows, I definitely understand both your points, of view," Maxy quickly interjected, "but I sincerely believe we need to stop right here and discuss both sides of this matter before we make any decision. I'll go either way; whatever decision we make, I'll agree to, but I want to talk about it first."

"Yeah, I think you're right on that point," Cowboy agreed; "this needs to be thoroughly hashed out. Ike, I feel just like you do. I'm madder than hell and I'd like to bash the tar out of those knot heads right now, but Dave has a point. He's always been the man with the plan, and I'd like to hear what all he has to say, before we do anything rash—okay?"

"All right, brother, you've got the floor," said Ike, looking over at Dad. "Let's hear what your solution is, but I still say we ought to put the fear of God into those culls."

"There'll be time for that later if it's necessary, Ike, but right now is our time, and we need to use it wisely. Getting all flustered and letting it dominate our thoughts won't make us a nickel."

"Like I said brother, you've got the floor. Let's hear what your solution is."

"I'm sure you boys have noticed the only mink we're losing are the ones caught in dry sets. That's because they're out in the open where they can be seen. Every water set we've scored in has retained its catch because the mink was instantly drowned and concealed by the water. It's a mink's nature to jump into the creek when he's in trouble. Fellows, it's well within our power to deny these thieves any more of our hard earned money. All we need is to restructure our program a little bit, and we can still end this season with a good lump of cash in our pockets. If we can out think some of the trickiest creatures on God's green earth, we can certainly handle a bunch of creek bottom clods who can barely tie their own shoes."

"I hear what you're saying, Dave," Maxy acknowledged, "but isn't that going to drastically cut down on the number of sets we're able to make? Only about half of what we're doing now is in the water."

"Yeah, Dave, isn't that going to mean catching fewer mink?" Cowboy asked.

"It might at first, fellows, but we all know that a mink is a water oriented creature. No matter how far he strays he will always return to the creek, and from now on that's where we need to be targeting him. His den is in the creek bank—he'll always come back there. Dry sets just don't get it when you've got a bunch of thieves following you around, plus a water set is much more humane; the animal doesn't suffer for hours. That's the one thing I hate about this whole danged business, and this change will stop all that. This way when he hits the trap he'll go into the water and drown instantly, leaving a minimum of disturbance to the ground in the area and no indication that there's a mink to be had when the thieves come by. It will be imperative though that we know the exact location of every trap, so we'll all need to carry a short pencil and a note pad.

We'll use a rusty bailing wire 6 or 8 feet long on each trap. It's the exact color of the leaves and dirt; we'll bury it an inch or so deep where it's thoroughly hidden then tie it under the water to a tree root, or we might need to carry some short stakes to drive into the creek bank below the water line. We can pick us up a crooked stick on the creek bank to fish out the wire when we see the trap is gone."

"Man, I see your reason for carrying a note pad now," Maxy replied. "It's really going to be a tricky business trying to keep up with all our locations."

"Changing plans in the middle of the game is always tough," Dad admitted, "but just think how much more frustrating it's going to be for the Sloyd boys when they see us still selling mink hides and they're still spending all those cold mornings out there searching their brains out and never finding a thing."

"All right, Dave, you've convinced me. I'll try about anything that will frustrate that bunch of thieves," Ike replied. "I'm ready to do it if these other boys are."

"You can count me in," said Maxy. "Let's give it our best shot."

"Yeah, I think we're doing the right thing here, Ike," said Cowboy, slapping him on the shoulder. "After trapping season is over though those boys had better keep a low profile. I think I'm going to want a little payback."

"Yeah we'll go get our steel traps back and a few hundred dollars worth of skin off their damned heads," said Ike, with a sadistic grin. "Nobody is going to steal from us and walk away unscathed—right Bud?"

"My thoughts exactly!" Cowboy agreed.

CHAPTER TEN—Old Trailer's Dilemma

Just before school time Wednesday morning, Dad said, "Hoyt, I'm going to lock Trailer in the smokehouse for a few days, and I want you to leave him in there. I'm afraid he's going to get caught in one of our steel traps."

"But why can't he stay in the house with Mama, Daddy? It's cold out there!"

"Your mother is going to do a lot of house cleaning and if he gets out, he'll follow me and the guys off to the creek, so you leave him in there, do you hear me? I made him a real good bed and your Mom will water and feed him good. Now you go on to school."

"Yes Daddy, but it's so cold out there!"

"Come on, Hoytie, or we'll be late for school," Nellie urged.

"Get your lunch off the table, Hoyt," Mama prompted.

"I just wonder why Daddy is really locking Trailer up," Dorothy pondered, as we walked out onto the front porch. "It sounds like he thinks he's got something really bad like—rabies—or maybe—the running blues."

"He doesn't either, Dorothy—don't say that. He doesn't have nothing wrong with him," I said, with my lip puckered out and tears starting to come to my eyes. "Daddy just doesn't want him to get hurt that's all."

As we left the front gate and started down the lane, Dorothy put her arm around me, and looking me straight in the eyes, she said, "Hoyt, do you know something about Trailer that we don't?"

It was easy to see that Dorothy and Nellie weren't buying the whole thing, either.

"Hoytie, you know something you're not telling us!" Nellie interjected, getting on the other side of me and putting her arm around me too. "I want you to tell us everything you know; why is Daddy really locking Trailer up?"

"Oh God, Sissy! I heard him tell Mama that Trailer may have the running blues," I blurted out in a storm of pent-up tears and emotions.

"Oh my lord, honey!" Dorothy said, in a half whisper, putting her hand up to her face. "It just can't be true! No wonder you're so upset," she said hugging me closer.

"Yeah, Hoytie, I'm really sorry, but maybe it's just a mistake," Nellie said hopefully, stopping and hugging me. As we all three stood there in the middle of the lane holding onto each other, Dorothy said, "There's one way we'll know for sure what Daddy is thinking, and we'll know tonight," she exclaimed, as we all started walking again.

"How Dorothy? How can we know?" I whined.

"If Daddy lets Trailer come in the house tonight, then he's just protecting him from getting caught in a steel trap," Dorothy speculated, "but if he doesn't, then he really does think there's something bad wrong."

"I know he does, Dorothy," I replied, with anguish in my voice. "I can tell the way he acts, and he told Mama that Trailer might have the blues. He didn't know I could hear them talking. He said Trailer did that running thing three times yesterday. I know that's why he's locking him up. He's afraid he's going to go out of his head and bite somebody. "

"Well, what do you think, Hoytie?" Nellie questioned. "Do you think Trailer is really seeing something up in the trees?"

"He certainly is, Nellie. I know Trailer, and there's nothing wrong with him. I've been watching him really close and he doesn't have that strange look in the eyes like a dog with the blues. Their eyes look really weird. The little black things are almost as big as their whole eyeball."

"Maybe Daddy and the guys just can't see that well," Dorothy questioned. "It's pretty dark down there in the forest."

"Yeah, especially in the winter time," Nellie added. "Maybe their eyes are just not good enough to make out what Trailer is seeing."

"But what if Daddy shoots him and he doesn't even have the blues? What are we going to do?" I cried; "I think I'll just die if Daddy kills my dog."

"Oh, honey don't say that," Dorothy begged. "We'll think of something."

"If I was there I know I could see what it is he's after," I said. "I know I could! It's got to be something really small like a young weasel or something like that. They're so little and skinny you can hardly see them, and they can run like the dickens."

"Somehow we've got to find out what it is he's after," Dorothy proposed, as we approached the schoolhouse.

"Hey, maybe we could sneak him out on the weekend and take him down to our creek and see if he does that running thing down there," Nellie suggested.

"Yeah, next Sunday; we'll do it, okay!" I replied enthusiastically. "Daddy says after he does the running thing he trees in a really small hole, almost like a crawdad would make. Trailer is really smart and I know that whatever he's chasing through the trees is what he's treeing. We've just got to find out what it is."

"We'll take us a shovel and dig it out, and then we'll know," Dorothy stated with a determined look on her face.

"Well, it's not going to be a crawdad, I'll guarantee you that," I replied adamantly. "Crawdads can't run in the tree tops."

"Come on, let's get on into the school house before the bell rings," Nellie urged as we headed up the steps.

"Hoyt, Honey, I want you to just forget about all this for now," Dorothy pleaded. "You need to keep your mind clear and do just as good as you can today. Trailer's a really good dog, and Daddy knows it, so you just give it a rest; everything's going to be alright—okay?"

"Okay Sis, I'll try," I replied as we entered the cloak room to hang up our coats and leave our lunch bags.

"Let's get on over to the stove and warm up before class," Nellie suggested. "My hands are frozen."

* * *

"Hey, Hoyt! I've got a new sack of marbles we can play with at recess," Jimmy Killian, called to me as we approached the big cast iron heater with most of the students huddled around it.

There were only twelve of us in the whole school, and Jimmy and I were the only second graders. We were great marble shooting buddies. A couple of the older boys were up on the stage with Mister Roberts helping him get things set up to start the school day. One was filling the big crock water jar so we could all have a drink during the day, and the other one was pulling the rolling world map out from behind the curtain to get it ready for use.

"Let me see your marbles," I said enthusiastically, as Jimmy approached holding out a small green mesh bag.

"They're cat eyes!" he declared. "There are twenty five of them in there."

"Man, those are beauties," I replied, quietly rolling the sack around in my hands for a better look. "How much did they cost?" I inquired. "I've got five dollars to spend!"

"Five dollars!" Jimmy exclaimed. "Man, Hoyt, you can buy 500 marbles. This bag cost a quarter, and there's 25 marbles in there, so that's a penny a piece."

"Students, those of you who wish to warm up, need to do it now," Mr. Roberts announced, as the girls and I pushed in closer to the stove. "Class will begin in five minutes, and I want you all to get comfortable before we start. As usual we're going to start the day off with a song."

Mr. Roberts always liked to get us thoroughly woke up and alert before he started the day's lessons, so he would usually lead us in a couple of rousing songs that we all knew by heart. "Amazing Grace," and "Love Lifted Me," were two of his favorites. We also sung several others such as, "You Are My Sunshine," and "My Bonnie Lies Over The Ocean." He would reach into his big desk drawer and pull out his little short director's stick and with a couple of sharp raps on the corner of his desk to get everyone's attention his arms would begin to wave and the quiet chilly school room would be filled with music. Sometimes we would sing only one song and then he would tell us a story. It would usually be a true historical event that happened in the immediate area. He considered local history to be a vital part of our education. I really liked his stories, because they were always fun and exciting.

"Good morning students; I am truly delighted to see all your shining faces. Let's all take our seats now, and we're going to get the day started. I've decided to change things around a little and tell you a story first, and then we'll sing. This story is about the first train to come to Boonville, as it was told to my father by his father—my grandpa," he added.

"Oh, man, this sounds like a good one, Jimmy!" I whispered, as we sat down next to each other in the front row seats.

"Now, as you can imagine," he declared, pointing his index finger at the class, "the first train coming to town was really a big thing, and everybody and their dogs knew about it. In those days there was about a mile of open space on the south side of the railroad tracks in the middle of town, and there were hundreds of families present with their wagons all lined up waiting to get their first glimpse of an iron horse, or a locomotive, as they were commonly called, and it was well over due. It was supposed to have been there at 12 noon, but it was already getting on towards 1 o'clock, and the hot afternoon sun was really starting to take its toll. Everyone was getting bored and some folks were starting to fall asleep sitting in their wagons, but all of a sudden the noise factor at the other end of town began to rise and everyone started to perk up and take notice. Moment by moment it continued—getting louder and louder, until it sounded like a huge tornado was heading straight in their direction. The tension level really started to mount as billows of black smoke began appearing above the treetops and the ground started shaking all around them. Suddenly around the corner a half mile away, came a giant black machine belching fire, smoke, and steam, and making a God awful racket. When the hundreds of horses and mules spotted it roaring up the tracks toward them pandemonium broke out. Everyone was fighting like crazy to keep his position along the tracks while his animals were trying desperately to vacate the scene. Well, at first they were doing a pretty good job of holding things together as the train approached closer and closer, but it just wasn't to be because the train crew and engineer were a mischievous lot. They really liked a good practical joke, and this long line of wagons was made to order. As soon as the train got up even with the excited mob, one of the crewmen ran out onto the front of the train and started yelling and waving his arms. 'Get those wagons out of the way,' he squalled. 'We're going to turn her around.' Well, seeing as how the train reached clear back to the end of town, the whole crowd suddenly lost its bravado, and common sense went out the window as they all flew into a panic, trying desperately to turn their rigs around and get the heck out of there. What a mess," Mr. Roberts groaned shaking his head. "It took them about half an hour sitting out on the outskirts of town thinking on the situation to finally figure out they had all been the brunt of a ornery practical joke. 'That thing can't leave the tracks,' one old guy grumbled with a crooked grin. 'They were only joshing us.' Most everyone came back, but they all left their rigs a good distance away, and came cautiously walking forward with their whole family in tow, to check out the first locomotive to come to Booneville. After they had thought it over and shook hands with the boys on the train, most of them had a good laugh about the whole thing and thought it was a grand affair, but as usual, there were a few soreheads that just wouldn't give it up; it just wasn't funny at all to them. 'Those guys should all be fired,' they complained!"

Mister Roberts gave us a few minutes to talk and get the giggles all settled down after he finished his story then he said, "Okay students, let's see your hands; who wants to choose the first song of the day." Immediately almost everyone's hand shot up, including mine and Jimmie's.

"I recognize Mister Hoyt Walker in the front row," he said. "What's your choice young man?"

"I'd like to sing 'Love Lifted Me,'" I replied, full knowing that was one of his favorites.

The story, the songs, and the camaraderie made the day move forward smoothly and before long we were all engulfed in the learning process and Mister Roberts was in complete control of our minds. "Learning one's multiplication tables properly," he told Jimmy and me, "is the first step into the world of business, and whether you're going to be a farmer or a banker you've still got to know them. I want you boys to copy your sixes over twice and study them between yourselves. I'll be around in a few minutes and check to see what you've learned."

At first recess, Jimmy and I battled it out in a mean game of marbles, and we speculated on how big a can I was going to need to hold a cache of 500. At lunch break which was a whole hour, the entire school had fun playing ball, with Mr. Roberts pitching to everyone. All we had to play with was a rubber ball and a bat made from a rough hewn cedar plank. Our bat looked an awful lot like a canoe paddle, but all in all, we had a glorious time. That afternoon the girls and I left the school and our friends with a bit of an after glow, but as we started getting closer to home the harsh realities of life started coming home to rest.

* * *

At the dinner table that evening, the girls and I could already tell that Old Trailer wasn't going to be coming in the house. The atmosphere was very tight, and Daddy was entirely too quiet. Right at the end of the meal he broke the silence. "Kids, your mama and I have to tell you something that's not easy for us to do. We love Old Trailer just as much as you do and we don't want anything bad to happen to him, but we love you even more, and we have to do what we think is best to keep you safe. I'm not absolutely sure, but Trailer may be coming down with the blues. Now Son, I can already tell you're starting to think the very worst, or all those big tears wouldn't be building up in your eyes, but it's not necessarily a fact yet—we just don't know. What your mom and I are doing is for everybody's good. We're going to take good care of your dog but he's going to stay in the smokehouse until I'm certain about his condition. Son, you've been around dogs long enough to know that the running blues is a very serious thing, and rather than have him hurt some of us we're just going to stay on the safe side."

"But Daddy, he doesn't have the blues," I insisted, between sobs and bouts of tear wiping on my shirt sleeve. "There is really something up in the trees that he's chasing."

"I suppose there's always a chance I'm wrong, but I've been around a lot of dogs in my day, and I've never seen anything like this in my life. He's just not acting right!"

"Daddy, his eyes are perfect. He doesn't have that weird look like a dog with the blues."

"Well, little man, you're just going to have to trust me and see how things work out. Sometimes life is very unfair. Old Trailer's a fine dog. He's got the best nose I've ever seen, and you can bet your bottom dollar I'm going to give him every chance, but if worse comes to worse—there's nothing I can do."

"Oh God, Daddy, I just can't think of you shooting him in the head like those other dogs I saw," I said between uncontrollable sobs. "Trailer's not just a dog; he's my very best friend. I've had him since he was a baby pup. You gave him to me!" I said, in an outburst of discouragement and tears. Suddenly I found myself leaping to my feet and flying down the hallway to my room. I just couldn't stay there any longer. I had never done anything disrespectful and contrary like that in my whole life, and I had no idea of how Dad was going to react, but I was devastated beyond hope. Deep down inside of me though I knew he had to do what any father would do to protect his family, and I was really sorry for him, but I was even more sorry for myself and especially Old Trailer, an innocent victim that didn't even know what was happening to him.

About 30 minutes after Mother and Dad went to bed I heard a gentle creaking of boards in the hallway and I stuck my head out from under the covers to see the girls quietly opening my door. They had their lamp with them and they both got inside the room before they spoke.

"Hey Hoytie, are you still awake?" Nellie whispered.

"Yeah, I can't even think of sleeping!" I answered, sitting up in bed.

"We know what you mean," Dorothy agreed. "This is so horrible. Old Trailer has slept in the house since he was a puppy. It's got to be so awful for him wondering why he's been abandoned by his family."

"Yeah, especially when there's really nothing wrong with him," I replied. "I don't know why Daddy can't see he's not sick," I said, with a discouraged tone in my voice. "He's just as frisky and alive as always."

"He sure is," Nellie agreed. "We went with Daddy to feed him awhile ago. Daddy let us pet him, with him standing close by. I'm like you Hoytie, there just don't seem to be anything wrong with Trailer. Daddy must be basing his fears on something other than the way he acts."

"We petted him real good, little brother," Dorothy said. "We hugged him and told him we loved him, and that you love him too."

"I just don't know what to do," I said in desperation. "I'm not going to let him get killed! If I have to I'll go get him and run away from home."

"Oh no, don't you even think of such a thing!" Dorothy pleaded. "It's so cold out there you'd both freeze to death in a matter of hours, and besides, Daddy's got him locked in. He probably figured we would try to take him out while he was away from home."

"Oh no, now we can't even get him out to go down to the creek on Sunday like we planned!" I lamented. "Why is Daddy being so mean?"

"He thinks he's doing what's right, little brother, and he may be," Nellie reasoned. "He's just trying to protect us. It's what any good father would be doing. I just hope and pray that Trailer is really all right and we can all get back to normal soon. It would be an awful thing for our whole family if he really does have the blues."

"Oh gosh, sissy, don't even talk like that!" I begged, cringing from the thought. "If Trailer was sick, he would act like it; wouldn't he?"

"We've got to get back to bed, Little Brother. We all have to go to school tomorrow," Dorothy said, as they both put their arms around me. "When we say our prayers tonight let's all ask the Good Lord to make this nightmare go away, and maybe when we wake up everything will be all right."

"Yeah, we'll all ask him to let Old Trailer not be sick, okay?" I mumbled, clinging on to the girls for one last hug.

"We certainly will, Hoytie," Nellie assured me. "Now, just try to put this out of your mind, and go to sleep; everything's going to be fine."

* * *

It was a long terrible night. I don't know if I could actually hear Old Trailer whining or if it was just my imagination, but when morning came I felt like I hadn't slept a wink, and the girls really had to work to get me out of bed. I was so exhausted and distracted the next day at school that I couldn't concentrate at all, and Mister Roberts really got frustrated with me. At the end of the day on Friday he scolded me really bad, and I almost broke down, but I held it back long enough to get outside the school house. He sent a note home with the girls saying that he wanted to speak to Dad and Mom Monday morning before school time. "Oh my goodness, Hoytie, I just don't know what to do," Nellie said, as we started walking home. "I know how awful you feel already, and this note is going to make things even worse."

"I think we need to give the note to Mama," Dorothy suggested, in a speculative tone. "She can tell Daddy at the right time. Don't you think that would be best, Little Brother?"

"I guess so," I replied sullenly. "I can't help how things are, and neither can Old Trailer; I don't know what to do! I just wish Daddy would shoot me too and get me out of my misery."

"Oh please honey, don't talk like that," Dorothy pleaded, putting her arm around me, as we walked. "Surely the Good Lord won't let anything so cruel happen to a beautiful creature like Old Trailer."

"I don't know, Dorothy. I just don't know. How do we know he even hears us?"

"God hears everything, Hoytie," Nellie reassured me, with a pat on the back, "and besides we're going to keep right on praying until he does. Please don't give up hope. Old Trailer needs all of us."

"Yeah, I know, Sissy," I responded, as we walked up onto the porch. "I need to go straight to my room and lay down. Maybe I'll fall asleep," I said, with a big yawn. "I'm so tired. When you give Mama the note, tell her I'm really sorry—okay?"

"We will, honey. You don't worry about anything," said Dorothy "It's going to be okay. Tomorrow's Saturday so you can sleep as long as you want."

Evidently I conked out immediately and slept really hard for three or four hours because when I heard someone tapping lightly on my door I thought it was already morning. "Come in," I said groggily, sitting up in bed as Mama entered the room carrying a small tray of food.

"How's my favorite Little Man?" she asked, as she set the tray on the stand by the bed, and sat down next to me.

"I think I feel better now, Mama," I smiled, as she ran her hand through my hair and caressed my face. "I was so tired today. I didn't sleep at all last night. I'm really sorry about not doing well at school."

"That's okay, Son; I know you had good reason," she said, leaning over to give me a warm motherly hug. "Sometimes, no matter how hard we try we just can't make things happen the way we want them, but we have to keep on trying anyhow—hoping things will be better tomorrow."

"Thank you, Mama," I said, hugging her back with tears starting to flow again. "Mama, I am so afraid for Old Trailer. I think I'll die too if Daddy kills him," I said bursting into tears. "He's just like my brother!"

"This is a terrible thing, Son, but I suppose we'll live through it. When I lost your little brother I thought I would die of grief for certain, but I didn't—people are tough. We'll just have to put our faith in God and whatever happens—happens. Hey! I brought your favorite supper—a big glass of cold sweet milk and a nice piece of warm cornbread to put in it," she said, with her comforting mama smile.

"Thanks, Mama; I'm really hungry," I said, sitting up straighter in bed and reaching for the tray.

"You'll feel better when you get something in your tummy. You eat now then go right back to sleep, okay? We'll worry about tomorrow when it gets here. Good night, my Little Man," she said as she turned to leave.

"Good night, Mama—I love you!"

"I love you too, Son. Now finish your supper and get some rest."

* * *

At first I thought I was only dreaming or wishful thinking because I knew it had to be very early in the morning, and in my heavy sleep state I wasn't able to think too clearly. Suddenly as the noise at the door continued I jerked myself partially awake, sitting straight up in bed. "There it is again—but it can't be!" I said to myself as I jumped out of bed and quickly made my way to the door in the darkness. As I gently opened the door a crack, suddenly out of the darkness of the hallway a crazed animal was all over me. I fell backwards on the floor as the door shoved open against me. It was Old Trailer my hero dog, my buddy, my pal. Somehow he had gotten out of the smokehouse and I was holding on to him with him licking my face and hands, whining and quivering all over. "Oh my goodness boy, how did you get out?" I pondered, petting, hugging, and holding on for dear life. Suddenly nothing in the whole world meant a darned thing except what was happening right there in my bedroom. Me and my dog were back together again! It took a few seconds to get the kerosene lamp lit with him trying to be petted, but I finally got it done. He was so attention starved I could hardly hold on to him to check him over. He seemed to be just fine, but I could tell he was really scared of being locked up again because he kept looking backwards at the door. Quickly, I lifted him over onto the other side of the bed, covered him up and blew out the lamp. I knew I wasn't supposed to have him in bed with me, but since Mama had said we would worry about tomorrow when it gets here, I figured I had a little leeway. Trailer hadn't been in bed with me since he was a tiny puppy, but he hardly moved a muscle all night long. He definitely knew we were breaking the rules and needed to be quiet. It took awhile for us to settle down and go to sleep since we were both so wound up. I was insanely happy to have my pal back, even for a little while, and he was certainly glad to be out of the cold smokehouse.

I woke up to hear mother stirring around in the kitchen making coffee. In another few minutes Ike and Cowboy knocked on the front door and came in for their morning mug, followed by Maxy arriving in his model A, and within the hour Mother had them all coffied up, fed, and off to the creek bank. Old Trailer and I kept a low profile while all that was going on. After the guys left I heard Mama come to the girls' room and ask them if they wanted to go down to La Vada's, our older sister's house, for awhile. It was only about a mile down the road. Suddenly I was hoping against hope they were going to say no because if they did we could take Old Trailer to the creek. My heart jumped when I heard them both tell Mama that she could go ahead that they needed to stay home and do some homework for school, and they might come down a little later. It seemed like forever until I heard her shut the door behind her and leave. I waited for a few minutes extra to make sure she was really gone then I jumped out of bed, followed by Old Trailer and went racing to the girls' room.

* * *

"Oh my God, Hoyt, how did you get him out?" Dorothy gasped. "What if Daddy sees him!"

"Daddy's already gone, Dorothy, and he's going to be gone all day," I replied.

"Hoytie, why is Trailer out of the smokehouse?" Nellie demanded. "Daddy is really going to be mad at you!"

"He got out all by himself, Nellie. He came to my room early this morning. I don't know how he got out, but I'm glad he did," I said, passionately, running my hands all over his blue ticked coat.

"Well, I can say one thing," Nellie ventured, dropping to her knees to pet Old Trailer, "there just can't be anything wrong with this dog; he looks just as normal ever."

"I know that, and you know that, Sissy. What we have to do is prove it to Daddy, and now is our chance. We've got to go down on the creek and dig out one of those things Trailer is treeing and see what it is."

"I think you're right, Little Brother!" Dorothy agreed. "That's the only way we're going to save Old Trailer and stop this nightmare we're in. Let's get into some of our old clothes and go do it."

"I'll bring my bean flip and some good rocks to shoot in it too," I replied, heading into my room.

In about 15 minutes we were out in back of the house ready to go. "Oh good, you've got the shovel," Dorothy remarked to me as we started past the smokehouse.

"Hey look!" Nellie pointed. "There's how he got out; he dug under the wall."

"Oh man, I wonder if we should cover it back up," I replied, looking at the hole apprehensively.

"No sir-ee! We're going to leave it just like it is," Dorothy answered. "If Daddy gets home before we get back that hole is our alibi. We didn't take Trailer out—he dug out."

"Before we come back home," I declared, looking the girls straight in the eyes, "we're going to know what it is Trailer is after; we just have to."

"Well, there's only one way to make it happen and that's to quit talking and get to it," Nellie stated. With those words ringing in our ears we headed off towards the creek with Trailer out in the lead.

We hadn't been at the creek more than five minutes when Nellie yelled. "Hey look—I think Trailer is already after something!"

"Yeah, but it's not what we want him to be after," I replied, as Trailer rushed up to a large pile of driftwood on the creek bank and started running around it. "He probably saw a water moccasin go under there."

"Well, at least it shows he's his normal self; he still hates snakes," Dorothy insisted.

"We need to get across the creek somewhere," I said wishfully, as I ran and pole vaulted across a small stream on the handle of the shovel. "All the best woods are on the other side about a mile farther down."

"Let's go on up to that big sandbar where we usually cross," Nellie suggested. "It's only about another hundred yards and we can scoot across on that big log and not get our feet wet. I hate cold feet and squishy shoes."

"Yeah, it's too cold out here to wade across," I agreed. "Come on boy!" I yelled, trying to get Trailer to leave the woodpile and follow us.

It took us about 10 minutes to walk to the sandbar and scoot across single file on the frosty log.

"I wish I could do it as easy as he does," Dorothy sighed, as Trailer came running across the log after us without so much as a care.

"Alright, buddy, let's go hunting!" I yelled, taking off after Trailer on a trot. "We need to get on downstream where the timber is heavier," I suggested, looking back at the girls. "If those things are in these woods that's probably where they're going to be."

"Yeah, and we really need to hurry," Dorothy reminded. "Mom is probably only going to stay down at La Vada's for two or three hours, and we need to be back before she gets home."

After a faster than usual trip through the timber along the creek, we were finally entering the dense woodland where I wanted to hunt. It seemed like only seconds before Trailer struck a hot trail and started running and barking occasionally with us following as close behind as we could. "He's got something up this tree right here," I yelled as we all three ran up to where he had stopped. "Darn, it's just a fat old gray squirrel," I said, as I ran around to the other side of the tree, catching the squirrel off guard. "I sure wish we had a gun. We would take him home for dinner."

"Shoot him with your bean flip, Hoytie," Nellie suggested.

"It would take too long to get him, Sis. They just keep going around and around the tree where you can't get a good shot at them; besides we've got something more important to do."

* * *

It took me a few minutes of coaxing to get Old Trailer to leave the squirrel tree. He just couldn't understand why we didn't shoot that squirrel and take him home. After leaving the squirrel tree, we pushed steadily forward into the dense woodland where the big timber was with high hopes of learning the identity of Trailer's mystery creature. Within the next couple of hours he treed two more squirrels and chased two cottontail rabbits into logs, but he did absolutely no running looking up into the trees like Daddy had described. "Dang it; what are we going to do?" I asked the girls. "I just can't stand the thought of taking Trailer back only to have him locked up again."

"Maybe we need to be closer to the creek, since he always trees those things in the creek bank," Nellie suggested.

"Yeah, let's get closer in," I agreed. "We're probably just too far away."

"Hey, look at that!" Dorothy pointed. "He's sneaking up on something." Trailer was sneaking through the forest like he was trying to surprise an animal on the ground, then he raced forward a few yards and started looking up as if something had been on the ground but had suddenly taken to the trees.

"What was it, Dorothy? Did you see it?" I asked, impetuously.

"No I didn't, but Old Trailer sure did, or he wouldn't be acting this way! There's darn sure something up there, but what?"

"This is exactly what Daddy said he does!" I reminded the girls excitedly, as we all took off running as fast as we could. Trailer wasn't moving all that fast because he was concentrating on the tree tops as if he was clearly visualizing something running up there.

"Can you see anything, Hoytie?" Nellie questioned, as we ran along looking up in the trees.

"No, I sure can't," I replied, with total frustration in my voice. "Do you see it, Dorothy?"

"It seems like I should be able to, but I don't," she confessed, shaking her head. "I can't understand this. Now I know what Daddy was talking about. Whatever it is though seems to be heading towards the creek."

"Let's run on ahead and see if we can spot it as it comes down out of the timber," I suggested.

"That's a great idea," Nellie agreed. "Come on, Dorothy—let's hurry."

Slowly but surely Trailer kept coming straight toward the creek where we were standing, but when he got within about twenty yards he started veering away, as if the elusive creature had spotted us and changed course. "Look at that!" I yelled. "Whatever it is saw us; it's turning downstream."

"That is unreal," Dorothy exclaimed, shaking her head. "It can see us, but we can't see it!"

Suddenly Trailer started running super fast into the thick bushes as if he were trying to intercept his quarry coming to the ground. We couldn't see him anymore because he was a ways downstream in the huckleberry bushes.

"What do you think happened, Hoytie?" Nellie yelled. "Do you think he caught it?"

"I couldn't tell," I yelled back. "Let's try to get through this brush where we can see."

It took us a few minutes to make our way downstream to where Trailer was, and when we found him he was standing in a small open spot resting, with his tongue hanging almost to the ground and his sides heaving. "What was it boy? Did you catch it?" I asked as I dropped to my knees beside Trailer and began looking intensely around him on the ground.

"There's nothing here!" Dorothy exclaimed, in a disappointed tone. "Now I'm beginning to see what Daddy meant. It looks just like he's chasing something up there. This is awful!"

"Yeah, Hoytie, I don't know what to say," Nellie replied sadly. "I would have bet anything he was after something. This is heart breaking!"

"Oh no," I said, in despair. "I just can't believe it. I won't believe it!" I said, shaking my head defiantly. "I know he was chasing something. He just didn't catch it!"

"We need be getting back home and put him back in the smoke-house before Daddy gets back," Dorothy acknowledged, sadly.

"Yeah we've got to fill in that—hey look at this!" I said, suddenly taking hope. "He's got blood on his mouth. He caught something and it bit him through the lip."

"Little Brother, he probably did that on a thorn bush," Dorothy replied despondently. "Come on; let's get on home."

* * *

"Come on boy," I said, half heartedly, starting to follow the girls. We had only gotten a few yards through the bushes when I looked back to call Old Trailer one more time and saw he was going back into the brushes. I stopped for a second to see what he was doing only to see him coming back out. "Oh goodness girls, look at that!" I yelled at the top of my lungs.

"What is it?" Nellie questioned, as they both came running back through the brush.

"Oh my Lord! What's that he's got in his mouth?" Dorothy yelled excitedly.

"That's a female mink, girls," I said proudly, as I went running back and picked up the limp carcass lying on the ground in front of Old Trailer. "Oh man, you're alright, Buddy!" I said, falling on my knees and throwing my arms around my dog. Suddenly a torrent of delightful tears was wetting the blue ticked fur beneath my face.

"Wait until Daddy sees this," I sobbed, hugging and holding on to Old Trailer. "I knew there wasn't anything wrong with you, fella. This is a $15 mink," I said, looking it over closely. "Look, he snapped it right through the head; it didn't damage the fur at all. Oh my gosh, boy! Oh, I am so happy," I cried out, hugging and rubbing Trailer all over. "Let's hurry and show it to Mama," I suggested, picking the mink up by the hind legs, and heading back through the bushes.

We had barely gotten out of the huckleberries and started forward again when Trailer started running and looking up into the trees again. "Oh no," Dorothy said, almost despondently. "He's doing it again!"

A FUR COAT FOR MAMA

"Oh well, Sis, we do want to make Mama a fur coat, remember."

Since we were already near the creek when we started, it didn't take long for the critter to abandon the tree tops, and Trailer had it treed very quickly. He was already about a foot back in the clay bank when we found him; he was digging furiously.

"That hole isn't very big," Dorothy observed. "I just wonder if it's a mink this time."

"I sure hope so," I answered, with a big smile. "Wouldn't it be something if we got another one?"

"Well, mink aren't all the same size," Nellie stated; "maybe this is just a smaller one."

"Here, hold Trailer back," I said, taking him by the collar and pulling him out of the hole. "Let me get in there with the shovel for awhile." I dug until I was about 3 feet back into the bank and needing rest, then I backed out and Nellie let Old Trailer back in. It had only been about five minutes since Trailer had started digging when suddenly he really started getting intense and one could tell that something new was happening. He started whining and moving his head around like he was in very close proximity to another animal that might be a danger. "Everyone get back," I yelled, just as the action started happening. Suddenly a flash of very dark brown appeared in the hole and Trailer came backing out of the hole slinging something like a rag doll. He had a mink right by the head, and it had hold of the side of his jaw. For a second there we couldn't tell who had who, but in a second more, Trailer dropped the lifeless critter in front of us and looked up for our approval. It was another sow mink just about the same size as the one before.

"Oh my gosh, now we've got two of them," Dorothy yelled ecstatically.

"How much money is that one worth, Little Brother?" Nellie wanted to know.

"Well, it's just about the same size as the other one. That's about 25 or 30 dollars we've made already. Hey, look at Trailer," I said. Trailer had run back into the hole and was acting like there was something still in there. In another instant a brown flash came shooting out on both sides of Trailer's head as two mink made a last-ditch attempt at freedom. For a second it looked like they had both gotten away clean. One dove into the creek and disappeared, and the other one ran into a little rotten tree stump on the very edge of the creek.

"Man, that's a big old Male in that stump," I hollered, as Trailer began to claw and bite off chunks of rotten wood from the mink's hiding place.

"Hey Hoytie, get on the other side of the stump with that shovel," Dorothy suggested. "You might be able to pry it right out. It doesn't look very strong."

"That's a great idea, Sis," I said, running around to the other side, but suddenly Old Trailer ran backwards with the mink in his mouth slinging it furiously. The whole front of the little stump had caved in under his onslaught. "Good Lord!" I yelled. "We've got us a big male now!"

"Oh my goodness, he's got to be worth a lot more than the others. He's more than twice as big," Dorothy yelled.

"I'll say he is," I hollered. "He's worth at least 25 to 35 dollars. That's about as big as mink get," I proclaimed, using knowledge gleaned from Steve and Dad.

"Holy cow," Nellie shrieked. "I really like mink hunting! We've made a whole pile of money already."

"Hey, we better hurry home," Dorothy reminded. "Mom is probably already back, and she'll be worried to death about us. If she sees Trailer has dug out, she really will be. She still thinks Trailer is sick, you know."

"Sick, my eye," I replied, as I continued petting him. "He's just the super dog I always knew he was. He's the best mink dog in the whole danged world," I said putting my arms tightly around him. Suddenly from deep within Trailer's chest I felt the vibration of a serious growl starting. I quickly jerked back uncertain of what was happening.

* * *

"Why's he growling?" Nellie, asked, noting the shocked look on my face.

"I don't know, Sis," I said, quickly moving back a little.

"He's not growling at you, Hoytie," Dorothy whispered. "It's something down there," she said, pointing down the creek. Trailer had his attention fixed on the huckleberry bushes downstream where we had caught the first mink.

"There's got to be somebody down there," I whispered, apprehensively. "I just wonder why they're not coming on up here." Suddenly Dud Sloyd's threat to twist my ears off if he ever caught me away from home came back with startling clarity. "Girls, I think we had better take our mink and get on out of here fast. I don't know who that is but it could be those darned Sloyds, and as you know, they're a bunch of jerks." I quickly took off my belt and ran it through Trailer's collar, and with each of us carrying a mink and me leading Old Trailer, we beat a hasty retreat out of the deep woods towards home. Even as we were nearing the crossing place, Old Trailer was still looking backwards and straining on the leash, and I had the distinct feeling that the Sloyd brothers were following us just out of sight.

"I wonder why they would do that?" Dorothy questioned, looking backwards.

"Because they're a bunch of ignorant knot heads," I answered. "They're not like real people, Sis. Daddy says they're meaner than a cottonmouth water moccasin, and twice as dumb." I had never told the girls about the wagon yard encounter because Daddy didn't want to scare everyone.

It was a little harder scooting back across the big log over the creek carrying a shovel and a mink too, but in about five minutes we were safely on the other side and headed up the hill with our catch. There couldn't have been three happier kids in the whole world. We were ecstatic about our hunting trip to the deep forest and thrilled out of our minds to know that our dog wasn't sick, but the real icing on the cake was to find out that he was a mink catching whiz. Mama's fur coat wasn't just a pipe dream anymore, it was reality.

"I just wonder how many mink it's going to take to make a coat," Nellie pondered, as we topped the hill and headed into the backyard.

"I don't have any idea," I replied, "but I can probably find out from Mel, when we go to the fur market the next time."

"It would definitely go by the size of the mink," Dorothy reasoned. "If they were all as big as that last one, it wouldn't take very many, but the smaller they are, the more we're going to need."

* * *

"Where have you kids been?" Mama questioned irritably, as she opened the back door and started coming down the back steps. "I've been looking all over for you! What's—what's that you've got there, and what's that dog doing out?" she demanded, trying to take in the whole scene all at once.

"They're mink, Mama!" I yelled. "This is what Trailer's been chasing in the treetops. There's nothing wrong with him at all."

"Well, my lands!" she said, putting her hands up to her face, "but how did you kids get them?"

"We dug them out of the creek bank where Trailer treed them," Nellie quickly responded, holding out the shovel.

"Yeah, and Trailer killed them," Dorothy added gleefully. "It was really fun, Mama!"

"Well I'll swear, and your Daddy thought that dog was going out of his mind," she said, shaking her head. "But, how did you get him out of the smokehouse with the door still locked?" she asked, with a puzzled look on his face.

"He dug under the wall, Mama," Nellie explained, pointing to the side of the house. "See this big hole."

"Well, I guess it's a good thing he did! He might have saved his own life. Wait until your Daddy sees these," Mama said, looking at the mink and shaking her head. "Man that one is a big thing," she said, with a smile—"he's going to fetch a pretty penny!"

"Come on girls! I hear Maxy's Model A out front," I said excitedly. "Let's go show Daddy."

"Hey, what do we have here?" Uncle Ike asked, as we came running up with the whole crew starting to unload.

"Hey, Dave, look what these kids have!" Cowboy called out, looking back at Dad coming around the car.

"Son, what's that dog doing out?" Daddy demanded before he even saw the mink.

"He dug out, Daddy," I quickly replied.

"My God, where did these come from?" he exclaimed, as he spotted the mink lying on the ground in front of us.

"This dog and your kids got these all by themselves down on the creek, Dave," Mother defended, as she approached the group. "Trailer dug his way out of the smokehouse, and the kids took him hunting and this is what they came back with."

"He's chasing mink in the treetops, Daddy. That's why he's running looking up," I explained.

"Yeah, and then he trees them in the creek bank," Nellie added gleefully. "There's not a thing wrong with Old Trailer, Daddy, except he's too smart for his own good!"

"Well, it sounds like you've probably got it right, Sis," Dad confessed, shaking his head. "It would seem that I've made a terrible blunder."

"They thought they had gotten clean away, when they ran into their holes," Dorothy said, jumping into the conversation excitedly, "but we brought a shovel with us and we dug them all out. It was really fun—I can't wait to do it again!"

CHAPTER ELEVEN—Daddy Eats Crow
and Doctor Cedric Comes to Visit

"Boy, I can say one thing," Dad said, looking at the other guys with a crooked grin, "I've got me a whole lot of crow to eat here, but I'll admit I deserve every bit of it. I'm really happy your dog's not sick, Pal," he said, squatting down in front of me. "It would seem that your wind hunter here has taken hunting to an even higher level. There's virtually nothing known about what he's doing, Son. They say only one dog in a million is capable of it, but this critter of yours has raised the bar even higher. Good Lord, he must think I'm stupid," he said, shaking his head and looking over at Trailer. "I hate to think of the money I've lost calling him off. I'm really sorry I didn't think this thing out more thoroughly. I know you were telling me he didn't have the symptoms of the blues, but I was so caught up in trapping and trying to make what money I could that I just wasn't hearing you. You have my sincere apology, Son. Next time, we'll sit down and talk it over man-to-man."

"That's okay, Daddy," I said, grabbing him around the waist with a bear hug.

"Now comes the hard one," he said, dropping to one knee and calling Old Trailer over to him. "Old buddy, you have turned out to be one heck of a canine. You figured out right away what I wanted to catch, and you were doing your level best to help me; I just wasn't savvy to how intelligent you actually are, but now that we're on the same wave length, I'm seriously looking forward to having you do that little trick that started all this ruckus. I'm going to carry that little short handled shovel on my pack from now on, and I'll dig in every hole you point me to. I'm sorry for the way I've treated you," he said, pulling Old Trailer over to him. "You now have my full attention."

Just as if on cue, Old Trailer raised his head and started licking Dad on the face. "Well, I hope that means I'm forgiven," he said, smiling and rubbing Old Trailer's ears. "I also want to apologize to the rest of my family that has gone through this bit of trauma on my account. From now on I'm going to listen to what all of you have to say. We're going to make it a family affair." At that moment all of us including Mama gathered around Dad for a family hug.

"We're one happy family," Mama said, "and that's the way it's going to stay."

"I remember that line," Dad replied, with a smile, hugging Mama closely.

"Your family is used to you being a good level headed person, Dave Walker, and we're glad to hear you're not going to close us out anymore—right kids?"

"Right!" everyone echoed, as I pulled Old Trailer up by the front feet into the family hug.

"Dave, why don't you go on into the house with the family—get cleaned up and relax," Maxy insisted. "You folks need some time together."

"Yeah, we can handle this, Dave," Ike agreed. "We've got plenty of boards already, so all we'll have to do is skin them and slip them on a board. In the morning we can rework them if we need to."

"Do you want to keep those separate?" Cowboy asked, pointing to the three mink on the ground.

"That's up to the kids," Dad answered.

Quickly Dorothy, Nellie and I began whispering among ourselves and we all agreed that to try and keep the mink for our project would give away the secret—"go ahead and sell them, Daddy," I blurted out. "We're just happy Old Trailer is alright."

"Okay boys, I'm going to go get me a hot bath," Dad announced.

"We'll come in a little later after we're finished," Maxy said, as they headed around the house carrying the mink.

"I'll put a full pot of coffee on," Mama added, as we all went up onto the front porch.

* * *

"Dave, before we start settling down there's something you need to know about," Mama mentioned, with a bit of a somber tone in her voice. "Come on into the kitchen and let's all sit at the table. Mr. Roberts sent a note home and he wants to see us about Hoyt," Mother said, pitching the note over in front of Dad.

"I'm really sorry, Daddy! I couldn't think about anything but Old Trailer," I confessed.

"Well, I can certainly understand how that might happen, Son. I think you did just fine handling it as well as you did. I'd say the problem is solved now though, wouldn't you?"

"It sure is, Daddy! As long as Old Trailer's alright, I'm alright."

"Okay Pal, I'll take your word for it. Monday morning I'll go to school with you kids and we'll get it all straightened out; meantime, Mama, how about a cup of that good smelling coffee then I want you to get me some bath water on. I've got mink up to my eyebrows."

"This is the last of this pot," Mama said, as she poured Dad his coffee. "I'll get a new one on for the other guys."

"Ike and Cowboy will probably stay for supper too," Dad speculated, "but I sincerely doubt if Maxy will. His missus will likely have supper waiting at home."

"There's food enough to feed whoever wants to eat. I'll get you some bath water started right now."

"How about making enough so the guys can wash up too?" Dad said. "They're definitely going to need it."

"Yeah, I already had that planned," Mama said. "I don't like stinky smelling people at my supper table. Kids, you can eat right now and go on into the living room out of the way. Get around the table, and I'll fix you up."

After we kids had eaten, Mother had me fetch the wash tub out of the storage shed, and she went about setting Daddy up in their bedroom and pouring him a nice hot bath from her three large water kettles.

"Man, we've got to go to market!" Cowboy yelled, from the back porch. "This place is just about maxed out."

"Yeah, I'll second that motion; we need some of our boards freed up," Maxy agreed. "Dave's new system is really starting to kick in."

"That's an understatement," Ike declared. "We're getting more mink now than we were before."

"I got one yesterday that was caught by one toe," Cowboy chuckled. "If that had been a dry set that mink would have been long gone. Hey, we're going to have to take some of these down before we'll have a place to hang these five new ones."

"Boys, here's you some nice warm water, a bar of my new lye soap, and a clean towel," Mother offered, coming onto the porch with the wash pan and kettle.

"I think she's trying to tell us something, fellows," Maxy chuckled.

"You're definitely right about that," Ike affirmed with a sly grin. "You'd better scrub up good if you want to put your feet under Dell's table."

"Well, if that's all it takes, I'm certainly willing to oblige you, Dell," said Cowboy, starting to roll his shirt sleeves back. "I don't know anywhere I'd rather eat, than at your house."

"Well, thank you, Cowboy. You know you're always welcome. It's a real pleasure to have you boys. Dave will be out in just a few minutes; he's just finishing up his bath. Fellows, it looks to me like you need to take some of these furs to town," Mother observed, looking around at the crowded situation.

"Yeah, I think next Saturday we should take the day off and do just that," Maxy agreed. "We'll see how Dave feels about it."

"This just goes to show how many furs we were losing," Cowboy reminded. "When you bring them all home they add up fast."

"We probably lost about 20 mink to those rotten bums," Ike projected.

"Yeah, and that means they've got 20 of our steel traps," said Cowboy. "When the season is over we'll find out from Mel how many new traps we've had to buy then we'll know how bad to skin their heads up."

"Supper's ready whenever you are," Mama announced, turning towards the kitchen.

"I'm right behind you, Dell. I don't really care if these guys get to eat or not," Cowboy answered, leaving the porch, with a sarcastic grin on his face.

"I'm coming! I'm coming!" Ike yelled, moving hurriedly towards the wash basin. "The smell of that food is driving me crazy. I'm so hungry my stomach thinks my throat's been cut."

"Mrs. Walker, I'll take a cup of coffee if you don't mind, but June will be waiting dinner on me, so I'll need to be leaving pretty soon."

"That'll be fine, Maxy. I'll get your coffee right away, but it's really too bad you can't stay and eat with the boys."

"There'll be other times," Maxy replied.

"Now, old man, you look and smell a whole lot better," Mama remarked, with an approving smile, as Dad entered the kitchen.

"I feel a whole lot better, too, old woman. What is that awesome smell you've got going in here?—suddenly I'm starved."

"Well, I'm just waiting for everyone to get around the table. I've got a big old pork roast that's just falling off the bone, with potatoes, parsnips, and rutabagas on the side. I've got hot biscuits and cornbread, and you can have your choice of sweet milk, coffee or water."

"My goodness, Mrs. Walker, you're sure making it tough on this hungry old boy," Maxy grinned. "Suddenly, coffee just doesn't seem to cut it," he said, observing the spread Mother had on the table.

"Well, why don't I make you a small plate, Maxy, and you can still eat when you get home."

"I guess I might get away with that," said Maxy, with a bit of uncertainty. "Walking away from your table with an empty stomach is just about more than my feet can do."

"There you go; that should keep the hunger pains down until you get home," Mama said.

"Good grief, Della Walker, that's enough food for two people!" Maxy complained, looking up at Mama. "I can't eat all of that. If I did I certainly couldn't eat anything when I get home!"

"Just eat what you want, Maxy. Old Trailer always gets the leftovers anyway, and he deserves a special meal tonight too. By the way, boys, you've got apple pie for dessert, so pace yourself," Mother cautioned.

"I'm a dead man!" Maxy mumbled, as he tasted a small bite of the tender meat dipped in brown gravy. "Dell, this is absolutely fantastic," he groaned, shaking his head. "Trailer, I've only got one thing to say to you pal—it's every dog for himself tonight, and I got here first."

"See, you just didn't know how hungry you really were," Mama taunted with a devious smile.

"Hey, Dave, that back porch is really loaded with fur," Ike mumbled, around a jaw full of food. "We've got to do something pretty quick."

"Yeah, I noticed that," Dad replied. "I was thinking that maybe next Saturday Maxy and I should go on in to the fur market while you and Cowboy hold down the fort. You know, just go on down on the creek and check things out."

Suddenly everything got really quiet, and Dad looked over at Maxy with a wink.

"It doesn't sound like that idea went over too big, Dave," Maxy mumbled, grinning from ear to ear.

Suddenly Ike stopped eating and pointed his fork at Dad. "You knot heads had better be kidding. Going to the market is the only part of this darn job that's any fun."

"Don't worry, Ike," Cowboy threatened, giving Dad and Maxy the evil eye. "I'll have Maynard poison them if they come in the diner without us."

"Okay, boys, I give up," Dad chuckled. "Next Saturday it is. We all need a day off, and this is something that can't wait."

"Oh goodie," I yelled running in from the living room. "I want to go too, Daddy."

"Yeah, I didn't figure on leaving my backup man behind. Boys, before Saturday, we need to see how many furs we have that are fully cured and make sure they're market ready."

"We want to go too, Daddy," Dorothy insisted, as she and Nellie came running into the kitchen.

"Yeah, Daddy, we caught mink," Nellie said; "we want to go with you to sell them!"

"Now girls, this is a man thing," Mother interrupted. "That fur market is not a place for little girls. We'll get the sewing machine out and do some fun things of our own. Now go on back in the front room until supper is over."

"Aw, why can't we go, Mama?" Dorothy whined, as she and Nellie reluctantly headed back to the living room.

* * *

"Hey, Mama—Daddy! Dr. Cedric's here. He's coming up the walkway right now," Nellie announced, in her shrill voice.

"Well, it's about time that old scamp paid us a visit," Mother commented.

"Yeah, it's been a long while since we've seen him," Dad said. "I just wonder what he's been into that's kept him so long."

"You guys just eat your supper," Mama said. "I'll bring him on in. He'll probably be hungry too."

"Hey, Dave, have you ever heard what was in that big old safe we found in the Flood Mountain caverns that time?" Cowboy questioned.

"You mean Dave's Caves," Maxy quickly corrected. "Since the county has recently designated them a historical site and Dave's the one that discovered them they've recently been named them after him."

"I still can't believe that," Dad said, grinning and shaking his head. "Finding a safe place to hide from the revenuers was all I was trying to do."

"Weren't we all," said Ike. "I guess about that time everybody was running from the law around these parts—even old Doc got roped into the situation. Man, that was one hell of an adventure."

"No, to answer your question Ike, I haven't heard a thing on it," Dad replied. "Maybe Doc will know something about it by now."

"Well he certainly should since the county made him the head man up there," said Maxy. "Doc is a very educated man in several fields, and archeology is just one of them."

"Come on in here, Doctor Cedric," Mama said, swinging the door wide open. "What's that you've got in those big bags?"

"Well, I didn't get a chance to see you folks at Christmas time, so I brought it with me. Here Kids, hold these while I give your mama a belated Christmas hug then I want one from each of you. There's a present in this sack for all of you, and the other one is for your mom and dad."

"Oh my gosh, Doc Ced—a store bought slingshot!" I yelled excitedly, "and a sack of steely balls. Oh thank you so much. This is the best bean flip I've ever had."

"Thank you, Dr. Cedric," Dorothy said, as we gathered around the doctor to give him his hug. "Sewing stuff is just what we wanted, right Nell?"

"Yeah, I've never seen this many colors of thread in my whole life!" Nellie replied gleefully, "and there's lots of different sizes of needles too. Wow, Dorothy, we've got more sewing stuff now than Mama. Thank you so much Doctor Cedric."

"You're very welcome kids. Dell, it's such a fine pleasure to see you again. I've really missed all of you," the doctor said, engulfing Mama in his big arms. "How is my favorite family doing?"

"We're just fine Doc, but I was starting to think you didn't love us anymore."

"That'll never happen, woman. I've been wanting to set my over-sized feet under your table for months now, but it seems like something always comes up at the last minute to prevent it."

"Well, you're here now," Mama said, "Come on in here; I've got a whole room full of people wanting to see you."

"Holy Toledo! The Old Gang is here!" the doctor yelled, excitedly. "This is like old home week, boys."

Instantly everyone pushed himself away from the table and stood up to properly greet the doctor.

"Doc, how the heck are you?" Dad asked, grasping the doctor firmly by the hand.

"I'm just fine, Dave," the doctor grumbled, "but I'm so danged busy I just can't seem to get any one thing actually completed before something else is pulling me in another direction. The historical society is always yelling at me to spend more time up at the caverns, and I really want to but the people of Reveille have got me running around like a chicken with its head cut off. One would think that as old and ugly as I am they'd get themselves a good looking young doctor and let me off the hook."

"You wouldn't have it any other way, you old scamp, and you know it," Mother said, patting the doctor on the shoulder affectionately. "Boys, you're going to have to shove around here a little bit. We've got to get the doctor a chair in here somewhere."

"Let me shake hands with everybody before I sit down, Dell. I'm as hungry as a bear, but I'm even hungrier to see everyone. Ike, Cowboy—how've you boys been? Dang, it's good to see you fellows again. Remember that great time we had exploring the caverns when we first found them?"

"Yeah, I remember, Doc, but I also remember we weren't just there because we wanted to be—the revenuers were hot on our trail trying to throw our butts in prison. To tell you the truth I didn't think we were going to get out of that scrape alive," Ike said, grasping the doctor's hand with both of his in a double handed shake.

"Doc, it's really great seeing you," Cowboy said, reaching for his hand. "There's just one thing I'm proud to say that's missing from this festive occasion though!"

"What's that, my friend?"

"Pinto beans," Cowboy replied, shaking his head. "Remember all those danged beans we ate while we hiding from the law? I don't think I'll ever willingly eat beans again. You were the only one of us guys that didn't suffer in that ordeal!"

"Man, I do like beans," the doctor grumbled, shaking his head.

"I distinctly remember," Cowboy exclaimed looking around at the other guys with a sour grin. "Well Doc, out of all this wonderful food Dell's got laid out here I'm proud to say there's not one damned pinto bean present."

"Man, what a downer!" the doctor exclaimed quickly scanning the supper table. "Dell, how could you do that to me? You know I'm a confirmed bean addict! Well, since you didn't know I was coming I guess I'll let it slide this time," the doctor replied with a big grin. "Maxy, how's everything with you and June? Are you still sawing a little lumber?"

"No Doc, I had to give it up for the winter. I'm into a brand new adventure. What you see right here at this table, is the entire crew of the Sugar Grove Boys Enterprise. We're heavy into mink trapping."

"Yeah, Mel Flood was telling me about that, but I didn't know you were involved. Mel says you boys are doing quite well too. I stopped by to see him this morning when I was in Fort Smith. He sent you boys a little message which I'll tell you about a little later on."

"Come over here and have a look on the back porch before you sit down, Doc," Mama said, swinging the back door open, "then I'll make you up a plate of food and get you seated,"

"Good Lord, there's wall-to-wall mink out here! Old Mel is going to be happy to see you boys coming."

"Well, this Saturday we're going to do it," Dad replied. "We've got a real good catch."

"Man, I'll say you have," said the doctor, heading back towards the dinner table. "I had no idea there was that many mink in the whole of Arkansas. How did you fellows get into this business anyway? There's got to be a lot more behind this thing than meets the eye or there would be all kinds of other people doing it."

"Yeah, it's a complicated affair, Doc. My first cousin Steve Walker learned it up in the Canadian northwest. He was here for the first of the season."

"Sit down right here next to Dave, and I'll get you a plate, doctor."

"Thanks, Dell, you're a woman after my own heart. Boys, according to Mel Flood, those furs you've got out there are worth a sizeable amount of money. I would be very careful about who knows you've got them. There are people around here who are desperate enough to hurt you over that kind of money."

"Yeah, we've already run into a few of those. The Sloyd brothers for starters," Dad replied.

"Dave, that's the same name that Mel sent you the message about. He said to watch out for the Sloyd brothers. They're planning something against you. It seems that one of his fur buying friends was getting mink skins from them and somehow you interfered with the process."

"They were stealing half of our mink!" Maxy exclaimed loudly, shaking his head. "Dave figured out a way to hide our traps to throw them off. That's what interfered with their mink selling."

"Well, in any event, one of Mel's competitors gave him the warning for you boys. It seems that the Sloyds—Hmm—Sloyd—that's a very unusual name, and I've heard it before somewhere—well anyhow, they were boasting that not only were they going to get even with you but by next season they would be able to catch every mink on Sugar Creek."

"Man, that's a mighty tall order for a crew like that, but we'll keep our eyes open anyway," Dad replied, as Mama slid a heaping plate of food in front of the doctor.

"Man, does this look good! Della, I've been daydreaming of this moment for months now."

"Hey, Doc, what ever happened to that big old safe we found in those caverns on Flood Mountain?"

"Yeah, did that thing ever get opened up?" Ike questioned. "It's been an awfully long time now, and Bud and I have often wondered what was in there."

"You're certainly right about it taking a long time," the doctor replied. "I know it's hard to believe, but that safe has been sitting in a vault in Fort Smith all this time. The Mel Flood estate and the Logan County Historical Society finally got to open it about two weeks ago. As you know that safe was the property of the Confederacy, and a part of those caverns were used to hide and maintain a contingent of the Confederate army in the region. Just recently it was designated a historical monument. Mel Flood's grandfather General G.P. Flood was in charge of the whole area surrounding those caverns."

"Why did it take so long?" Ike asked, looking quizzically at Doc Cedric.

"Well, as usual, Ike, politics reared its ugly head right at the wrong time. The state of Arkansas got wind of the safe right after the caverns were opened up and they sent the sheriff up there with an impoundment crew to confiscate it. It took a solid week for that bunch of goof balls to get that thing out of that cavern and down off the mountain. Man, what a riot! Before they were through, they wished they had never heard of that danged safe, but their problems were just beginning. Mel Flood is not a man to be trifled with. He quickly filed a lawsuit in the names of the last 50 men that served in General Flood's outfit and also those who were found to have died in the line of duty. We found evidence in the general's files that determined the last payroll and a goodly amount of reserve was still present in that safe. Mel intends to give every dollar to its rightful owners. The process is going on right now trying to locate them or their heirs."

"Did you get to look at the stuff that was in there, Doc?" Cowboy asked.

"Yes, Cowboy, I sure did. We ended up having to cut the back out of that old safe with an acetylene torch. The door was rusted shut. We figured there would probably be some fire damage to the contents, but we had already tried everything else we knew."

"Well, what was in there, Doc?" Ike asked impatiently. "Was there any gold?"

"You bet they're was, Ike! There were six dried up old leather saddle bags that contained a total of $62,000 in beautiful $50 Confederate gold pieces. Boys, that was a sight for sore eyes! Boys, as we were pouring all that gold out into a large wash basin to count it," said the doctor with a noticeable melancholy tone to his voice, "I ran my hands through it several times for you boys and remembered how it was—all of us there in the cavern house for all those months together. I miss it like hell! (Pardon my French)" he said, with a slight crack in his voice. "That was the most gratifying time of my whole danged life. Hey, I guess I'm getting a little too emotional here," the doctor said, wiping his eyes with the back of his hand.

"Well, what else was in there, Doc?" Cowboy asked. "There had to be a lot of other stuff!"

"Now, fellows, Doc Ced is hungry, and he needs a chance to eat," Mama said. "You guys just hold up a little while until he gets the edge knocked off his appetite."

"It's all right, Dell; I'm going to get started right now," said the doctor, shoveling a large fork full of food into his mouth. "We're still in the process of going through it all, Cowboy, but there was 55 thousand dollars in confederate notes, which of course, aren't worth the price of the paper their printed on and a couple of other things that caught my interest," the doctor mumbled around a jaw full of food."

"Go on, Doc, tell us everything you saw," Dad urged. "This news has been a long time coming."

"Well, Dave, there was a set of plans that the South had drawn up to build an infernal machine in hopes of saving the Confederacy. It seems that Mel's grandpa was not only a top class general, but he was also a highly respected engineer, and the Southern leaders were asking his advice on their project. There was also an interesting document written in French—a story right out of the pages of history concerning this immediate area of Arkansas. It's called the Legend of Petit Jean. In French it means, The Legend of Little John."

"I've heard of that," Maxy replied, "but what the cat-hair is an infernal machine?"

"I've never heard of none of that stuff, Doc," Cowboy replied, scratching his head, with a confused look.

"I think you've got us on the short end of the education scale here, Doc," Dad said. "How about bringing it all down where a country boy can understand it?"

"Tell us about that infernal machine thing. What was that anyway?" Maxy asked.

"Yeah that sounds like something really bad!" Ike interjected. "How was it supposed to help the South?"

"The term, infernal machine, was the name given to an underwater attack vessel for destroying or sinking surface warships. We call them submarines nowadays, and as you know, they have become an accepted part of warfare, but that wasn't always the case. The South was heavily out gunned and they were faced with certain defeat unless they could come up with a way to turn the odds in their favor. To attack the massive Union flotilla from beneath the waves seemed to be their only hope."

"Why did they call the machine that, Doc—infernal?" Ike asked.

"Well, back in those days, war was fought in a gentlemanly fashion, Ike. Infernal, means diabolical, or evil—of the devil, so to speak. It was considered to be cowardly to attack one's opponent without giving him a fair chance. It was like back stabbing or bush-whacking a person."

"I just wonder if that thing was ever built, Doc," Dad questioned.

"Well, Dave, I guess it doesn't really make a whole lot of difference— they still lost the war. If it was built though, it just might have been the first such craft in the world. There was considerable fire damage to the top of the first page of the plans where the name was. It was pretty well illegible.

The name of it ended in—ley—possibly The Conley, or The Finley—maybe we'll find some more documentation on it later. It seemed to be a six man propeller driven craft with a crank handle running all the way through the center where everyone could turn at the same time."

"That's really interesting, Doc," Dad replied. "It's too bad that knowledge wasn't carried on from way back then. We might have something more capable of handling these Nazi U-boats that are taking such a heavy toll on us right now. You mentioned a legend concerning this area. What was that all about?"

"I've heard that legend mentioned a few times before," Maxy replied, "but I've never gotten the gist of what it's all about."

"It's called The Legend of Petit Jean. It's actually a French love story. It's supposed to be a real account of how Petit Jean River, and Petit Jean Mountain, got their names. It's a pretty lengthy story, but I could do a quick summary if you'd like to hear about it."

"I think we would all love to hear it, Doctor Cedric," Mother piped up. "Anyone who says otherwise won't get any dessert," she said, smiling at the crew around the table.

"You definitely have the floor, doctor!" Ike said with an approving grin.

* * *

"Okay then, here we go. Arkansas is a small part of what is known as the Louisiana Purchase. The United States bought it from the French back in 1803—almost 530 million acres of territory. The Louisiana Purchase comprises all or part of 14 different states in present day America. So that's the reason there are lots of strange sounding names around. They have become such a part of our everyday lives that we use them and never think twice about their origin or what they mean. We usually shorten or Americanize them a little such as us, calling Petit Jean River—Petty Jane River, like we do. Now that you understand where I'm coming from I'll tell you the story. The name, Petit Jean, belonged to a young French cabin boy whose real name was Jean Rowland. Petit Jean, or little John, as he was called aboard ship, was desperately poor; his father was dead, and his mother was very ill. Little John was her only support. When this story began back in 1789 he was probably 12 or 15 years old. Little John considered himself very lucky though because he had a job he was proud of. He was scheduled to sail with the tide on Tuesday, the 14th of July, on the good ship, *Au Monet.* He lived in the seaport town of St. Nazairre, France. On the morning of his departure he was heading up the gang plank carrying his sea chest when he was approached by a beautiful aristocratic young lady with curly red hair.

"'Garcon,' she whispered. 'I would like to speak with you.' Her name was Adrienne Du Mont, and she was destined to become royalty. She was betrothed to Bertie, the fat bumbling nephew of King Louis that her aging father was forcing her to marry, but she literally hated the sight of the man. In the course of a few minutes quiet conversation, Adrienne offered Little John more money than he had ever seen at one time in his entire life—more than two years ship wages, to buy his name, his sea chest, and his position on the ship.

"'Ce'st impossible Ma'm'selle; you are a girl.' he answered. 'Sealife is rough—the sailors—Ma'm'selle!'

"'They will not know I am a girl!' she whispered. 'Come—please say you will help me,' she pleaded. '500 francs is a lot of money!' She wanted desperately to be aboard that ship but she knew her presence there would expose the man she was in love with, Jean Jacques Chavez. He was fleeing for his very life. The nephew of the king had attacked him with drawn sword because Bertie had seen Adrienne smiling at him. Chavez had merely been protecting his life but the clumsy nephew was killed in the incident. Adrienne's true love was secretly leaving for Nouvelle, France—what is now the southern United States. He had promised to send for her as soon as he could, but Adrienne was convinced that if he left without her she might never see him again because of the great distance and the hardship involved.

"'Five hundred francs, Ma'm'selle?' whispered Little John, questioningly.

"'Oui, 500 francs,' Adrienne repeated. 'I have it right here in this bag.'

"'Oui, Ma'm'selle,' said Little John with a huge smile. 'I will do it! My mother will be so happy that I do not have to leave. She is very sick, and there is no one else to take care of her.'

"'What is your name, Garcon?' Adrienne asked.

"'Jean Roland, Ma'm'selle, but they call me Petit Jean aboard ship.'

"'Thank you, so much, Jean Roland. You will be in my heart and in my prayers always.'

"'Quickly returning home with the sea chest, Adrienne Du Mont, the red-headed darling of St. Nazairre, cropped off most of her auburn colored hair and smeared the remainder with black dye, and donned the humble clothing and identity of Petit Jean, the little cabin boy. She boarded the ship, did her chores well, and was accepted completely by the captain and the crew, and after months of hardship at sea, the ship finally arrived in Nouvelle Orleans, what we know as New Orleans, today. A terrible mosquito borne fever was raging in the area, and Jean Jacques Chavez almost immediately fell ill. Adrienne, still in disguise as Little John, nursed him for weeks almost back to total health, before she also fell ill. One night in a feverish stupor she revealed her identity to her true love then immediately fainted and fell to the floor. Chavez quickly rose from his sick bed and took over her care. In the weeks to follow she began to regain a little of her strength, but unfortunately the pressing affairs of trying to make a life in a new land had to be addressed. The captain of the *Au Monet* was sailing on up the Mississippi through the mouth of the Arkansas, and on up to where the confluence of an unnamed river flowed below a huge blue mountain. It was there that he and Jean Jacques Chavez had conspired aboard ship to start a new French settlement. Adrienne's care was turned over to a kind Indian woman named Nonie Perry, and Chavez sailed on up river. From this point on the story becomes clouded and vague, as if it has been fragmented and lost in the pages of time. No one seems to know whether Petit Jean ever made it to her home beneath the big blue Mountain.

Some say she did—others say no, she did not. Anyhow, that's The Legend, and that's why the river that Sugar Creek flows into and which goes on to meet the Arkansas and the mighty Mississippi bears the nickname of a little cabin boy from the distant past. It was brought here to us more than a hundred and fifty years ago, by a red headed beauty, all the way from France."

"My goodness, Doc Ced, that's a wonderful love story," Mama said, with the impact of the story still showing on her face. "Someday when you have plenty of time, I would really like to hear the whole thing."

"We'll make it a point to do that, Della Walker," the doctor replied, reaching out and taking Mama by the hand. "At least maybe there's something I can do to show my vast appreciation for your kindness and generosity."

"Just for those kind words, Doctor Cedric," Mama said, pointing her index finger at him. "You're going to be the first one to get a piece of my deep dish apple pie."

"Hey, that's not fair, Dell," Ike complained loudly. "We were here first."

"Yeah, Dell, Doc came in last," said Cowboy. "You're playing favorites, here!"

"Aw pipe down you knot heads, or I'll only give you half a serving," Mama said, with a sideways glance at the guys. "You're lucky I'm even feeding you at all!"

"Doc, that was really a fascinating story," Dad agreed. "I'm like Dell, though, I'd really like to hear it all from beginning to end as soon as possible. Little John River, that's a whole lot easier on a country boy's tongue."

"Yeah, I've always wondered about that name, Petit Jean. It just didn't seem to fit in this neck of the woods," said Ike.

"Well, now you know the reason," the doctor replied.

"That's definitely an enlightening story, Doctor Cedric," said Maxy. Now when I go past the river or the big blue mountain I'll have a better appreciation of the French and their historical contribution around here."

"I didn't have a clue that the French were ever around here," Cowboy replied.

"Well, they certainly were," Doc Ced answered. "Even the little town called Magazine a few miles from here has a French name. To them it meant a place to store ammunition—or an ammo dump. Sometimes the word is just used to mean a store."

"No kidding!" Maxy replied. "Doc, I had no idea there was such a history in this area. I would really like to pick your brain some more about it one day when we get time."

"I would be more than happy to oblige you, Maxy. As you know I'm a bit of a history buff, and I'm a big mouth to go with it," he said with a grin.

After a lengthy visit with everyone, Doctor Cedric didn't feel like driving home to Reveille at night, so he stayed over with us. Mama made me a pallet on the floor and the good doctor slept in my bed, which he did fairly often. Very early in the morning he arose and headed on home. He had two morning appointments, he said, so he couldn't stay for breakfast.

CHAPTER TWELVE—Old Trailer Super Dog and Our Secret Project

In Mother's Monday morning school ritual, she treated Daddy—to his chagrin, just like he was one of us kids. She got him out a clean but well worn pair of overalls and one of his nicer long sleeve shirts and made sure he was absolutely clean-shaven and his hair was combed just right. It was easy to see that Pappy wasn't all that thrilled about being thrown into her school routine. "We may be poor," Mother mumbled, as she stooped over to pick a small piece of lint off of Dad's overalls, "but we're going to put our best foot forward. There old man, you look pretty good now."

"You'd better be careful, old woman, I might just decide I want you to come along with me," Dad replied, with a bit of exasperation on his face. "This is your son too, you know, and his problems belong to both of us," he grumbled, scuffling my short hair.

"Well, maybe this will prompt you to think things out a little better next time before you make serious decisions—running blues—my word!" Mama said, with an ornery grin. "Now get over here around the table and I'll get you all fed. Nellie, you or Dorothy get you kids some milk. You'll want coffee won't you, Dave?"

"Oh gee, Mama, are you actually going to let me have coffee?" Dad answered, in his falsetto voice. "I figured you were going to make me drink milk with the rest of the kids." That one really caught Mama off guard. One could see she had a big grin on her face as she turned around but she didn't seem to have an appropriate comeback. "Now I see what you kids are going through every day," Dad whispered, looking over at Mama. "I'll have to start treating you better." It really tickled us to see Mama and Daddy verbally jousting with each other.

Within minutes after breakfast, everyone including Dad was lined out on the road making the half mile hike to school with Old Trailer leading the way. Dad had told Maxy and the boys the night before that he would be a little late because he still had some more crow to eat. As we were approaching the school, Mr. Robert's Model A was just pulling into its graveled parking space in the front. "Mr. Walker, and all the little Walkers," he called out cordially as he got out. "How are you folks this fine morning?"

"We're just fine, Mr. Roberts," Daddy replied. "I've come to see you about the boy."

"Well, I'm sure it's something we just need to talk over. All in all, Hoyt is a mighty fine lad, and you've got two fine young ladies coming along there also," he said, smiling at Dorothy and Nellie. "Come on into the school and let's get us a fire going," he said, as we entered through the back door. "This old building is as cold as a rock on mornings like this."

"Yeah this 3 inches of new snow we got last night didn't help things a lot," Dad replied.

"Hoyt, grab us a couple of handfuls of that split pine kindling out in the wood room," Mr. Roberts said. "These pieces of oak wood are just a little too large for this stove and it takes some real effort to get them going."

"Here you are, Mr. Roberts," I said, running in with a small arm load of kindling. "I got the piniest stuff I could find."

"Thank you, young man; that will be just fine. Now, we'll wad us up a few sheets of this old newspaper and put it under the kindling and that should do the trick," he said, removing a kitchen match from his pocket. "Okay, I believe that's got it. Now let's pull us a chair over here by the stove, and we'll have us a little chat before the other students get here. First of all, Mr. Walker, I know Hoyt well enough to understand that he wasn't just being ornery, but you also know that I have to get to the bottom of what the problem was so I can keep his attention focused."

　　　　　　　　　　　　　　A FUR COAT FOR MAMA

"You're right Mister Roberts, and I accept full responsibility for what was happening. Hoyt and that little black and white dog outside are joined at the heartstrings. They've grown up together and they're inseparable. Well, I was under the impression the dog was possibly coming down with the running blues, which as you know, has no cure. It was a terrible shock to the whole family and especially Hoyt, when I decided to lock the dog in the smokehouse until I could be sure of his condition."

"Now, I'm beginning to understand," said Mr. Roberts, leaning back in his chair and nodding his head. "When something gets between a country boy and his dog, it will definitely affect his attention span—no doubt about it."

"Well, the problem has been resolved and not only is the dog not sick, we've found out he's a canine genius, to boot. He's taken hunting to a brand new level."

* * *

"Now, Mr. Walker, even though I'm a little pressed for time this morning, you've got my interest peaked white hot on this canine genius stuff so tell me about it. I've never heard of such a thing!"

"I know this is going to sound a bit screwy, but I swear to you it's the God's truth. Throughout my lifetime I've heard old time hunters talking about a thing like this, but I just discounted it as folklore."

"Now, Mr. Walker, I still don't understand; what this thing is you're referring to?"

"The possibility of an especially gifted dog that's capable of a hunting trick akin to magic, Mr. Roberts. It's a thing so rare that few hunters have ever heard of it, much less seen it. It's called wind hunting or winding."

"Now, you've really got me going! Please continue, and hurry before the rest of the students get here; I've got to know about this."

"Okay, I'll try to speed it up a little. As I'm sure you know most dogs put their noses down close to the ground to trail an animal—not a wind hunter. They hunt with their heads up, running and smelling the air as they go. When you put Old Trailer on the scent of an animal, you take him to where you saw the animal or where you know or suspect the animal has been, and that's the only time you will ever see him put his nose down. As soon as he gets the scent he will run straight away, up to 20 or 30 yards in one direction then he'll come straight back past where he started and go 20 or 30 yards in the other direction. After that he'll head off into the woods and within two to five minutes he will usually have the animal treed. Somehow, through using that process, he is able to go almost directly to wherever the animal is out in the woods. What would usually take other dogs half an hour to accomplish; he can do in just minutes."

"That's unbelievable!" Mr. Roberts said, shaking his head. "He's triangulating the animal's position, plus he's running in different directions to see where the scent is the strongest then he's follows the scent upwind, to where the animal is. I've never heard of such a thing. You said he was a genius; well if he's doing that he certainly is."

"That's not all, Mr. Roberts. We knew he was a wind hunter before, but what really started this whole matter and caused such a problem was something altogether different but just as unreal."

"Man, what could he possibly do to top the fact that he's using doggy trigonometry to locate his prey?" Mr. Roberts said, smiling and shaking his head.

"I know how strange this sounds, but this is what he was doing that got him into trouble. When me and the boys were down on the creek trapping we started noticing that Old Trailer was really acting weird. He would run through the winter woods, looking up into the leafless treetops as if he were chasing something on the timber. Well, it seemed obvious to me and my trapping partners that if there was actually something up there we could see it too. We were dead wrong! There was something up there—little female mink that were all but invisible to the naked eye. Anyway, that's what led me to believe he might be getting the blues. The boys and I tried desperately to spot anything that might be causing him to do that, but after weeks of not seeing anything we finally just gave up on it."

"I can certainly understand why it caused such a commotion," said Mr. Roberts. "When a group of people who have been raised hunting can't see it, that's a pretty good indication there's nothing there."

"Well that's the conclusion we came to, but we were wrong."

"We couldn't see them either, Daddy, and we really tried hard," Dorothy interjected, enthusiastically.

"Yeah, but they were really there and Old Trailer knew it!" Nellie blurted out. "He treed three of them in little holes in the creek bank, Mr. Roberts, and we dug them out; we took a shovel with us."

"He treed three mink and you kids dug them out?" Mr. Roberts repeated, questioning Nellie's statement.

"They certainly did, they probably saved the dog's life!" Dad replied, nodding his head affirmatively. "That's where I made my mistake. I didn't dig in the holes. I was convinced that nothing of any value could be in a hole that small. Man, was I mistaken. Those little buggers are worth 12 to 15 dollars each. Trailer had learned that I wanted to catch mink, and he was using his special gift to help me, and I was too dumb to understand."

"That is amazing, Mr. Walker. That dog could be worth a little fortune to you and your family. Hoyt, I certainly understand why you were so distracted now. This Trailer dog of yours is no ordinary pooch. He's that one in a million the old-timers were talking about. Sometime when it becomes handy, I would really like to go hunting with you and see him in action, but right now, kids, we've got to get ready to start the day; your classmates are beginning to arrive. Thank you so much for coming in, Mr. Walker. This has been a very enlightening experience. Kids, what I would suggest is that you get your heads together and make up a good show and tell program for your classmates for next week. You can bring in that super dog of yours, Hoyt, and maybe you girls could bring in those mink skins you caught and tell everyone how you dug them out of the bank and how much they're worth. I'm going to refill this stove then we're going to get school started."

The day at school started off as usual with an inspiring old hymn called Love Lifted Me. Mr. Roberts was very high on morality and kindness and he took great care in pointing his students in the direction of a courteous dignified life. It was easy to see that Mister Roberts was not a rich man, but he was always clean and had his thin wispy hair well combed. Sometimes when I was close to him I would get a little whiff of rose scented hair oil.

"Students, today I'm going to start your learning experience with the proper way to treat the elderly," he said, walking back and forth on the stage. "If sometime in your future you should happen to be in a large city, such as Fort Smith and you should observe an elderly person that seems to be unsure about crossing a busy street, there is a proper and dignified manner in which to give them aid. Many elderly people, who have worked hard all their lives and have been outstanding citizens, can one day find themselves in situations where they can no longer see well enough or they just may not have the mental ability to handle situations that require making quick decisions. First of all you need to gain their confidence by approaching them properly so they won't be afraid of you. By using an endearing tone of voice as you approach, you can make them feel at ease. "May I be of assistance to you, Auntie? This is a very busy street, or may I help you cross the street, Uncle? In some cases they may refuse your help, but that's okay, you offered. A great deal of the time though you will find they are very grateful for your assistance. Life is very harsh in a lot of ways kids, but by making the part of it you are concerned with better, others may want to follow your lead, and in some small way the world will be a better place because of you. People want to follow someone with a strong position on life, and it's the duty of everyone who leads, whether he is a teacher, a minister or a political figure to lead in a manner that justifies his position. A teacher who won't teach or a preacher who won't preach is as useless as mammary glands on a side of bacon," he said dramatically. "That's all on this subject. Take a five minute break while I chunk up the fire up a little." As Mister Roberts closed the senior ethics class with a bang and hopped down off the stage, he left the entire student body of the Lick Creek Valley School with a huge grin gracing their face. The stern old ethics professor had a fine sense of humor.

* * *

The school day went along just about as usual with all the students involved in their studies and Mister Roberts expounding his individualistic viewpoint of reading, writing and arithmetic, then just before school was about to let out for the day, he called me aside and said, "Hoyt, I have a little present for you; see me after school is over." Well, as one can imagine, I was in stitches waiting to see what his present was going to be. I had already snitched to Nellie and Dorothy that Mister Roberts was going to give me a present, so they were waiting with me as all the other students filed out. "Come on up here to my desk," said Mr. Roberts, walking past us up onto the stage. "These little books belonged to my granddaughter, Nancy; they're called comic books, or funny books," he said, reaching under the top of his desk, and pitching the curious little books out on top. "They were printed by a man out in California, called Walt Disney. One of them is called Donald Duck and the other one is called Mickey Mouse. Mr. Disney has even made a cartoon type moving picture featuring the characters in these books. If you kids would like to have them, you're more than welcome."

"Oh yes, Mister Roberts, we would love to have them," I replied. "Please tell your granddaughter thanks for us."

"I'll certainly do that. Mister Disney is trying to start a business with these little cartoon characters; I don't know if it will ever catch on or not, but Nancy seems to like them."

"Please tell Nancy hello for us," Nellie said, "and that we would really like to meet her sometime."

"I'll do that. I'm sure you girls would have much in common. I know you girls like to sew and so does Nancy; she and Kathryn, (my daughter) make most of her school clothes."

"Oh, we do too," said Dorothy excitedly. "We've got all kinds of sewing stuff."

"Then it's settled. I'll bring Nancy to school one day and introduce you."

"Oh goodie I can hardly wait," said Nellie. "That will be so much fun."

"Hey, I was really impressed with you kids digging those mink out of that creek bank. That takes some real spunk, and I want all of you to know that I highly respect people, especially children, who have a spirit of individualism such as you do. They go on to make good strong citizens."

"We've got a secret project Mister Roberts," I said, looking sheepishly at Nellie and Dorothy. "Can you keep a secret?"

"I certainly can, but is it going to be all right with your folks if I know?"

"Well it's actually them we don't want to know about it," I replied, as Mr. Roberts began raising his eyebrows in a doubtful manner.

"Oh, it's not anything bad," Nellie quickly interjected.

"Yeah, it's actually something really good," said Dorothy, "but it's also something that's a really hard job, and we don't know just how to get started at it."

"Well, what is it you kids are scheming to do anyway? If it's technical help you need, I would be glad to advise you."

"Oh, would you please?" Dorothy pleaded, putting her hands together. "We need the advice of an adult really bad, but we can't let Mother or Daddy either one know about this."

"Yeah, it's really a secret. We want to make Mama a mink coat," Nellie said, as Mr. Robert's eyes widened in amazement.

"Old Trailer is a mink catching machine, like we told you this morning, Mr. Roberts," I reminded, "but we don't know how to put the skins together to make a coat."

"I can say one thing; you kids don't lack anything on motivation. That is a very ambitious project you've undertaken."

"The way we figure it, Mister Roberts, since Daddy has to sell all of the mink he catches, so fancy ladies in the big cities can wear fur coats, we're going to use our mink to make Mama one. She's just as fancy as anyone else's mama. If anyone deserves a nice coat, she does," I said defiantly.

"I am pleasantly stunned by what you kids are planning," said Mr. Roberts, shaking his head, "and what is even more stunning is the excitement I'm feeling. I don't have the slightest doubt that you are going to complete this project. Somewhere in the near future you are going to present that special little mama of yours with a beautiful new fur coat, and I'm telling you right now, I think it's just wonderful. If you kids need any help I will be very glad to assist you, and I'm almost positive you can count my wife in too. She's a fine seamstress and she has a heavy duty sewing machine that would be just great for sewing a mink coat."

"Oh my gosh, girls, it's actually going to happen!" I yelled, grabbing Dorothy and Nellie and hugging them both together.

"Hey, don't leave me out; we're partners now!" said Mr. Roberts, surrounding us all three with his big arms. "I'll talk to my wife Katie tonight, and I just know she'll be delighted to be a part of our team. She is really good at planning and executing large sewing projects. This is a very exciting thing we're doing, kids!"

"Oh, Mr. Roberts, you don't know how much this means to us," said Nellie, wiping a tear with her hand that suddenly ran down her cheek. "Mama has worked so hard all her life and never had anything really nice. I just wish there was someway we could pay you for helping us!"

"Sis, there is!" I quickly replied. "We'll just catch a few extra mink. We're going to need stuff for the coat anyway—pretty buttons and silk for the lining and stuff. Mr. Roberts could sell the extras and keep part of the money!"

"Ohoo—yes, Hoytie! I had forgotten all about that!" Nellie exclaimed happily. "We will pay you, Mr. Roberts! Oh, this is going to be wonderful!"

"Kids, I will definitely sell your mink for you to get whatever you need for the coat, but you're not going to pay Katie or me anything," he said, looking at all of us with a gentle smile and pride in his eyes. "This will be a labor of love—a time to practice that which I have always preached—good people helping each other. The only thing needed to get this project going is for you to get the mink and tan the hides. Your mother is going to be so proud—not just of her new coat," he said, looking at us admiringly, "but that she has three gutsy children with the gumption to attack such an audacious project. This will be a moment in time we can look back on with pride—the time we got our heads together to make a fur coat for your Mama. Let's shake on it partners." Instantly we all grabbed his hand in a four way handshake. "There now, that clinches the deal. You kids get on home; your folks will be wondering what has happened to you."

"Thank you again, Mister Roberts. We'll see you tomorrow," I yelled back, as we all three went running to the front door of the school house.

"Oh my goodness, I can't believe it!" said Nellie, with absolute glee in her voice.

"Me neither!" Dorothy yelled back with a little squeal of delight. "Let's hurry home and get out our new catalogue. Maybe there are some new styles of fur coats in it."

"Yeah, now all we need is to catch us a bunch of mink and tan their hides," I said, confidently. "Come on girls, let's run. Maybe we can go down on the creek for a little while, if Daddy is home with Old Trailer."

CHAPTER THIRTEEN—The Mink Season Closes and the Walker Kids Learn a Good Lesson

The last two weeks of February were very intense for our whole family. The end of the mink trapping season was coming up on the last of the month, and Daddy and the boys were trying hard to set every trap they possibly could, to eke out every hard-earned nickel before the season closure. Our show and tell program at school was a raging success, with Old Trailer getting petted by the entire student body, and every kid there wanting to have a dog just like him. He really enjoyed being the center of attention, and the girls and I felt like really big stuff getting to answer all kinds of questions about mink hunting.

Even though Old Trailer hunted with Dad and the guys five days a week and treed mink almost every day, for some reason he seemed to like to hunt with me and the girls best. I guess it was because we gave him special attention. Daddy sometimes had to call him two or three times in the mornings because he wanted to stay at home with us. "I can't figure what's happened to that dadburned dog," Dad said, one icy morning as he looked at Trailer still asleep in his box. "Seems like he'd rather stay home by the fire, than go hunting."

"Well, Dave, you did say he must really think you're stupid," said Cowboy, with a big grin. "You know as intelligent as he is it probably didn't take him long to put us all in the same boat."

"Yeah, he's probably got us all figured out by now," said Ike. "He just doesn't want to hunt with a bunch of clods like us." Whatever the reason, he became obsessed with going down on our creek, and he pestered us night and day. We wanted to catch those mink just as much as he did—probably worse—but sometimes the weather was just too bad or it was dark outside; it didn't seem to matter to him. Knowing we had the support of Mr. and Mrs. Roberts really added a new dimension to our coat building plans, and every possible chance we had of getting down to the creek, we did. We set us up a mink station out in the hayloft of the barn, to take care of our catch, but by the end of the trapping season we only had six mink—two males and four females. After we would skin them and put them on stretcher boards we would hide them in a little cavern we had made in the haystack to finish curing. We used an old tablecloth that Mama had thrown into the garbage to do all our skinning on, so there would be no evidence left to give our secret away. We always washed it and dried it thoroughly then rolled it up and stuck it under the hay with the skins.

* * *

The season closing was a real letdown for us kids. Old Trailer was still treeing mink and we had all the help we needed to make Mama a beautiful fur coat just like the pictures in the catalogue, but suddenly we weren't allowed to get the skins anymore—dagnabbit, it was so frustrating! Then one evening a day or two later our problem seemed to be solved. We were having a coat powwow in the girls room, discussing our problem when Nellie said, "well, we're not going to sell the skins, and I think that's all the season is for—people who are catching them to make money. They probably wouldn't even care if you're just going to catch a few to make a coat out of."

"Yeah, that's got to be right," I agreed, exuberantly. "Mel has already stopped buying, so nobody's probably going to give a hoot if we just catch a few more to finish Mama's coat."

"Let's do it." Dorothy quickly agreed. "It shouldn't take but two or three weeks and we'll be finished anyhow."

In the next few days everything really started looking up, and we added 6 more mink to our hiding spot for a grand total of 12. The problem came when Mr. Roberts found out.

"Well, how many mink did we end up with, partners?" he asked a few days after the season had closed.

"We've got twelve now," I quickly replied, as we all three ran up onto the stage after school had let out. "In another two or three weeks we'll probably have enough."

"Now, wait just a minute, young Mr. Walker. Did I hear you right? You're not still hunting after the season has closed, are you?"

Suddenly the girls and I looked at each other with an oops—maybe we shouldn't have told him expression.

"I take it by the looks on your faces you have been catching mink since the season has closed."

"Well, Old Trailer just keeps on treeing them!" I said, in a bit of a blame shifting tactic.

"Kids, that is no excuse. Old Trailer is an animal, and he doesn't know about seasons, but you do. I understand that you couldn't ask your folks about this, but you've got to stop immediately. There's a very big fine to be caught with illegal mink skins."

"We just thought that since we weren't selling them for money no one would care," Nellie stated.

"Yeah, we thought we could finish it real quick," Dorothy replied.

"I understand how badly you want to continue with this project, but there's always next year. At the speed that mink machine of yours works," he said with a smile, "it won't take more than a month or two into next season and we can start putting that coat together."

"Oh, that's going to be so much fun!" Nellie giggled.

"Now, there's a lot of figuring to be done in the process of making a fur coat, kids, so what I'm going to do is make you out an arithmetic assignment that will allow you to continue working on the project, but before I do that I want to tell you why you should always respect the game laws. Laws are made as guidelines for the general public to follow, and the reason there has to be laws is because there are lots of folks who would keep right on hunting and trapping until there wasn't any wildlife left. Now you wouldn't want that to happen would you—where there weren't any more mink left down on your creek!"

"Oh no, Mr. Roberts; we sure wouldn't!" I replied, as the girls and I shook our heads.

"Yeah, we would never want something like that to happen," Nellie agreed.

"Okay then, but before I assign you your math lesson, I want to tell you a couple of good reasons why the mink season closes when it does. As spring comes and the weather starts warming up, mink begin losing their heavy winter fur—the kind that's good for making coats. Their spring and summer fur isn't worth anything. If you kids will remember, I know you've all heard your Dad talk about prime fur."

"Yeah, I remember," I quickly acknowledged. "Prime means really good."

"That's right, Hoyt. Now you kids wouldn't want part of your mama's coat to be pretty and the rest of it ugly and shedding hair, would you?"

"Oh no, we sure wouldn't," Dorothy replied, shaking her head. "That would be awful!"

"All right then, that's the first good reason to obey the seasons, but there's an even better one. Mink and all other wild creatures have to have time to reproduce and raise their young. Our forests and streams have good hunting and fishing because the game laws are there to protect them. If you keep catching wild things out of season, sooner or later they will start having babies to care for, and if you catch the mother the young ones will all starve to death."

"Oh that is so horrible," Nellie said solemnly, as Dorothy and I shook our heads in unison.

"We won't ever do that again, Mr. Roberts. We're really sorry. We just didn't understand what we were doing," Dorothy replied.

"Yeah, I'll make Old Trailer stop treeing them, right now," I acknowledged. "We're sorry, Mr. Roberts."

"Well, that's good. You kids are fine young people, and it's a real pleasure for me to be your friend as well as your instructor. What you need to do now is let the pelts you've got finish curing then I'll store them in my freezer for you until next year."

"Thank you very much," I replied, "but what if those new ones we caught aren't any good?" I questioned. "We don't want to ruin Mama's coat."

"These you've got are still alright, Hoyt, but when the weather really starts warming up that's when the problem begins. Now, your math lesson is to take a ruler and measure an average sized male mink skin and then a female and see about how many square inches each one is going to produce. In the following classes, we will also need to know your mother's height and how long her coat needs to be. In essence you will be figuring out how many mink you're going to need to catch next year. Dorothy, your math lessons have taken you into figuring the area of squares and rectangles, so I want you to be the teacher and explain everything to Nellie and Hoyt. Now, remember young mister Walker, as intelligent as that pooch of yours is, he still doesn't understand about seasons, so it's up to you to tell him when."

"I'll make him stop, Mr. Roberts—I promise."

"Okay then, get along home with you. I'll see you tomorrow morning."

As soon as we got home we got right on our math assignment. We got a ruler, pencil and paper and went out to our mink stash in the barn loft. We got out a male and a female skin, and Dorothy proceeded to teach Nell and me how to figure the area of a square. Later on after Mother and Dad were in bed we got one of Mama's coats and took it over to the girls room and went to work. In about an hour of intense measuring and re-measuring we came to the conclusion that we were going to need from 36 to 40 mink skins.

Two weeks later Mama's coat project ended for the season when we placed all the cured mink skins into a big paper sack and snuck them off to school with us. We were a little stressed out to know it would be a whole nine months before we would see them again, but we were exhilarated to know they would be in safe keeping and that Mr. and Mrs. Roberts would give us the assistance we needed to complete our project.

CHAPTER FOURTEEN—Spring Finally Comes and Mama Picks Dangerous Greens

After a long winter of eating mostly canned stuff out of the garden, the first greens of spring were a special delight for Mother and Dad, and they anxiously awaited their arrival. As the weather warmed up and the snow pack commenced to melt an amazing thing began happening down on the local creek banks. Wild onions and *poke salat* (German word for salad) began shoving their way through the loose soil to the sunlight. The pungent little onions were mostly all top with a small white bulb on the bottom. They were at their best at about 6 to 8 inches tall. After several months of winter time survival food they were a very welcome addition to our diet. The only thing I never learned to like about wild onions was the cows enjoyed them just as much as we did, so for a couple of months in the spring we always had onion flavored milk—Yuk. The only remedy for the problem was to take a big bite of onion first then the milk would taste perfectly normal. Poke salat, or poke weed, is a thing Southern folks grow up with, and the recipes on how to prepare it are passed down from generation to generation. The plant, which grows to 5 or 6 feet tall in its adult form, is very toxic, but in its young stage, (usually at about 12 or 14 inches tall) the large leaves can become wonderful early greens if prepared properly. One must know precisely how to do it and be very selective of the leaves which are chosen, using only vibrant green ones with no yellow. The stalk part is never eaten; it has way too much acidity to deal with, but the leaves can be boiled and leached out to become very edible. Old timers swear that poke salat is chock full of vital nutrients. Lots of people only boiled it once and poured off the water before using it in their favorite recipes, but Mama was very cautious with the food she was feeding her family, so she always boiled the greens twice making absolutely certain there was no toxicity left.

* * *

For about a week after the poke salat started to appear, Mother had been going to the creek below our house to gather it. She was canning up a supply for next winter. One Friday afternoon, we kids were just coming home from school when Mother ran out onto the porch and began hollering for us to quickly come inside.

"What's the matter, Mama?" I asked, as she hustled us all into the kitchen and began looking out the back window.

"Girls, I want both of you to get over here and watch the top of that hill where it comes up from the creek, and see if anybody comes over it. Hoyt, how do you load this thing?" she asked, picking up Daddy's .22 rifle which she had laying on the table.

"I'll do it Mama," I said, jacking the bolt back to expose the firing chamber.

"Here," she said, sliding a box of shells over in front of me. "Put one of these in there quick."

"Mama, what's wrong?" Dorothy begged, almost in tears.

It was not like our Mama to dramatize anything, and we knew that something very traumatic had happened. Her dress was torn, her long black hair was hanging full-length down her back and there were two large bloody scratches on the side of her neck.

"Oh, Mama—please—you've got to tell us what's wrong!" Nellie pleaded, turning her eyes quickly away from the window.

"I was attacked by a bunch of men down on the creek while I was picking greens. If it hadn't been for Old Trailer, I don't know what I would have done," she replied, wiping tears with the corner of her apron. "He was still chasing after them when I left. One of them ran up and grabbed me, but with Trailer biting him, I was able to get away."

"Where's Old Trailer at now, Mama?" I asked nervously.

"I really don't know, sweetheart. As soon as I got loose I took off up the hill. It looked like they were trying to catch him. One of them had a blanket he was trying to throw over him."

"Oh, Mama, I sure hope they don't hurt my dog!" I whined.

"Me too, Son, but right now we've got to concentrate on what we're doing here. Put these shells in your pocket and get out on the porch. If you see any of those bastards start shooting at them."

"I will, Mama. If they hurt my dog, I'll kill them," I said in a vengeful tone.

Mama had to be really distraught for her to use such a smutty word in front of her children. Bad language was just not something she condoned.

"I haven't seen anybody yet, Mama!" Nellie nervously reported, as she continued to observe the hill.

"Okay, baby, just keep watching. Oh, I sure wish your daddy would come home."

"I'm going out on the porch now, Mama" I said, opening the back door a crack and sliding through.

"Shoot at their legs, Son. We don't want to kill anybody if we don't have to."

"Mama, I see Old Trailer coming up over the hill!" Nellie yelled. "So far there's no one following him."

"Oh thank God. Son, get him in the house just as quick as you can, and keep your eyes on that hill."

"I've got him, Mama!" I yelled, shoving the door open and grabbing him by the collar.

"Oh, my goodness, kids, I think your daddy's here," Mother sighed, running to the front of the house, then out onto the porch.

It was easy for the crew to see there was something strange going on, as Mother started motioning them all to hurry into the house.

"Something's wrong here boys," Dad said, seeing the way Mama was acting.

"Yeah, I've never seen Dell like that before!" Cowboy exclaimed, as they all began to unload.

"Me neither," Ike agreed. "I sure hope she's alright."

Within minutes of their arrival, Mother had the whole S. G. B Enterprise crew in the house. They had been off on Petit Jean River, scouting for new trapping territory for next year.

"Dell, what's the matter?" Dad asked—"who did this to you?"

"I was attacked by some men while I was picking greens, Dave! I was just lucky Old Trailer was there biting the heck out of them or I don't know what I would have done!"

"The Sloyd boys," Ike said, with a scowl—"that lousy bunch of crud. We'll make them pay for this, Dell—don't you worry!" he said, taking Mama by the hand to comfort her.

"Yeah, we'll bash their damned brains out," Cowboy agreed, coming around to the other side of Mama. "Nobody's going to mess with you while we're around—right guys?"

"Right," the crew said in unison!

"Was it the Sloyd brothers, Dell—were there five of them?"

"I only saw three and they all had rags tied over their faces. There could have been more in the woods, but three is all I saw. One of them grabbed me around the neck and by the hair, but with Old Trailer running around biting him, I was able to jerk free. I left about half the hair in his hand," Mama said, feeling the back of her head, with a grimace on her face.

"Those bastards! They've crossed the line this time, fellows," Dad growled with fury seething in his voice. "There've laid their scummy hands on my family—nobody does that and walks away from it," he exclaimed, comforting Mother by putting his arm around her.

"What do you want to do, Dave?" Cowboy questioned. "You call it; I'm ready which ever way you want to go."

"Yeah, Brother, we can't let this go un-answered," Ike declared. "If we do, it's just going to invite a whole lot more of the same. Those boys have got to be taught a lesson. It's likely to be one of your kids here they're messing with next."

"Yeah, I'd say you're correct on that point," Dad replied. "They've already threatened to rip off my boy's ears. I guess it's time to heap that fire on their heads you were talking about, Ike. I had hoped to avoid direct contact with that bunch of culls, but this leaves me no choice."

"Dave, I understand what a hard spot you're in here," Maxy said, "but this is not a time for you to lose your self control. Whether you know it or not, Buddy, you've been my mentor for a lot of years now. I've been taking lessons on your cool under fire tactics. In my opinion, what you are considering is not in your best interest, and it's just as likely to hurt your family as it to help it."

"Maxy, I've always known you to be a man with a good level head," Dad answered back. "Tell us what you've got on your mind. I'm highly open for suggestion, right now."

"It appears to me there are only two things we can do. The first one is what you guys are considering—go down and rough them up and take the chance of killing some of them, and possibly going to prison ourselves, or get our heads together and out-think the bums. We know they have definitely singled you out, and it's evident that we have to respond, but the way you side-stepped them and saved our trapping season was such a piece of genius—well, somehow I just believe if we get our heads together—remember what you said—if we can out think a mink—!"

"We can surely out think a bunch of country bumpkins!" Cowboy finished the phrase.

"Exactly!" Maxy replied.

"Yeah I remember," Dad acknowledged, shaking his head, "but that was before they attacked my wife. I'll agree that violence should never be a man's first choice, but I get a little out of hand when people start messing with my family."

"I can definitely relate to that, Dave, but your common sense has always been the outstanding factor of who you are, and people know you for it. If you will just back off and give yourself some time to think, I believe you'll realize this is not the time for swift reprisal, but the time for some very heavy thinking. As much as we would like to obliterate that bunch of scum, the laws of the land frown heavily on that type of action, so whether we like it or not we need to get the authorities abreast of what's going on here. Ike, I do believe you're right; I think this is just the beginning of what the boys are planning to do, and there's no telling where it's going to lead."

"Okay, guys, let's sit down over here at the table and get comfortable. Mama, would you put us on a pot of coffee please? We've got some hard thinking to do."

"Maxy, the law isn't going to help us down here in the backwoods!" Ike said, shaking his head. "They'll just come down and nose around a little and say they don't think there's been any crime committed, and they'll be right! We can't prove anything has happened, so that will be the end of it, and we'll still be stuck with the problem."

"That could be true, Ike, but at least we can bring them up to date on what's already happened: the wagon yard incident, the mink stealing and what has just occurred. If the creek bottom boys insist on keeping up the harassment, they could be spending time down on the Tucker Farm where they won't be causing us any more problems, but we'll definitely keep your plan on hold, Ike, as a last resort. We will stop them one way or the other; you can count on that!"

"That sounds like rational thinking to me," Dad agreed. "I'm ashamed of letting myself go like that. That's the second time in the last month I've allowed my emotions to cloud my better judgment. Now I'm the one who's taking the lesson," he said with a smile. "I'm ready to listen to what everybody has to say, now. Let's see if we can come up with a plan."

"You've pretty well heard what I had in mind," Maxy replied. "It's too late to do anything today, but tomorrow we need to get on up to the police station in Booneville and tell them everything that's been going on."

"I think you've got something there," Cowboy agreed, "then if we have to kill some of those hair brains we'll have the law on our side!"

"Yeah, I'll have to agree; that sounds much better," Ike confessed. "Having the law on our side would be a very comforting thing. There's no telling where this Sloyd stupidity is going to lead, and we don't want to end up on the wrong side."

"Fellows get your mugs ready," Mother interrupted, heading for the table with her big glazed coffee pot. "This stuff is strong and hot. If this doesn't stimulate your thinking process, nothing will."

"Thanks Dell, we need all the help we can get," Dad agreed, shoving his mug over towards her.

CHAPTER FIFTEEN—Mama Makes Hominy and Big Dan and the Law Come Calling

After having her poke salat program messed up, Mother was really challenged to find something progressive to do outside the house. Being inside when the sun was shining and the weather was finally decent just didn't get it with her. On a brisk but clear Saturday morning, she said, "Kids, today we're going to make us some hominy. It's sunny out there, but it's still cold, so get dressed for it. We're going to be out there most of the day." After we kids had gotten properly dressed, we headed out through the back porch, which was strangely empty, and followed Mother into the backyard. "Dorothy, you and Nellie take these two buckets and go to the corn crib and fill them with shelled corn. Son, I want you to help me get my big kettle out of the storeroom then we've got to gather us up enough wood to do our job." Instantly, Nelly and Dorothy grabbed the two buckets, which were about 2 ½ gallons each and headed off towards the barn on a run, as Mother and I headed for the storage shed. Homemade hominy was one of the Walker family's staple foods and I liked it very much, especially when it was smashed up and fried in the form of little cakes. Mother made hominy about two or three times a year, and she always made enough each time to can up a few jars for the winter as well as have enough to eat several meals fresh. We made it from dry yellow corn. Although we had white corn, everyone in the family agreed that yellow tasted better; it had more good corny flavor. The process of making hominy was a bit on the dangerous side because a very caustic chemical, (lye) had to be used to remove the hard outer coating of the corn so the inside part could be cooked. Lye came in a little short round can about 3 inches tall and 3 inches across, and in the center of the label it displayed a skull and crossbones with the ominous words—Caution-Poison—prominently displayed above and below the skull. After the outer coating had been removed, the corn could be boiled just like cooking a pot of beans. The longer you cooked it the more the corn broke down, and released its wonderful taste. I liked it best when it had been cooked and re-cooked a few times and the gruel became thick and soupy around the corn. Mother's hominy making process went as follows: first she would get her 15 gallon cast iron kettle, which was always kept spotlessly clean, out of the storeroom and set it up in the backyard then she would fill it about half full of water. Next she would add about 5 gallons of dry yellow corn and build a roaring fire around the kettle which was designed for outside use only. It had four short stout legs which were always set on small flat rocks so they wouldn't sink into the ground and spill the contents. After the water began to boil the lye would be cautiously added—about two or three tablespoons to start. She used a wooden paddle about 3 feet long that Dad had made special to stir the contents of the pot to make sure the lye was evenly dispersed. Mama monitored the process very closely by occasionally checking a single grain of corn picked at random from the pot. Occasionally she might choose to add just a smidgen more lye if she didn't think the job was getting done. It took quite a few minutes for the durable coating to start breaking down, but eventually one could feel a slickness starting to happen and over a period of 10 to 15 more minutes all of the slick would disappear and the process would be complete. At that point Mama would begin her cleansing process to remove all the lye. We would bring her bucket after bucket of water from the well as she washed and rewashed the contents of the pot in small batches until she was perfectly satisfied that not a trace of the chemical remained. When we were finished the big pot would be allowed to cool and was thoroughly washed before being put back in storage. There was also another process which was much the same as making hominy, the making of homemade lye soap. Mother used the same pot with a very hot fire around it, but in the soap process she would be adding the lye to scalding hot oil which had been rendered from pork fat. That event took place in late autumn after hog killing time. Most every family in our area used lye soap made in that fashion. For hand washing and heavy duty scrubbing purposes Mama would always make at least one batch to which she would add a certain amount of sifted wood ash, as fine as face powder, to act as an abrasive. It was always such amazement to me to watch what adding that small amount of lye would do to that pot of scalding oil. Within seconds of adding it, one could see a congealing effect starting to take place, and just a few minutes more as Mama continued to stir the contents it would begin to look like very thick yellow pudding, and the process was finished. She was very careful to add only enough lye to thicken the oil. Adding more than the oil could absorb would leave excess lye in your soap and it caused a stinging sensation on the skin when you used it. In a few hours after the contents was thoroughly hardened Mother would return with a large butcher knife and carve the contents up into usable sized bars.

* * *

For most of the morning, Mother was thoroughly engrossed in her hominy making process, but about lunchtime just as she had finished washing the last batch, preparing it to be taken into the house, Old Trailer ran to the edge of the hill overlooking the creek and started barking. "Kids, let's pour some water on the rest of this fire and get into the house," she said, gazing out towards the edge of the hill with a worried look. "With your daddy gone, I don't want to be taking any chances." Daddy and the rest of the crew had left early to go in to Booneville to the sheriff's office, and it was easy to see that Mama's trauma of the day before was still fresh in her mind. "Hoyt, run out towards the hill a little ways and call your dog. Get him back here as quick as you can. Nellie, you and Dorothy grab a pan of this corn and let's get on into the house." Instantly I left Mama and the girls putting out the fire and went running towards the hillside scanning the horizon for the Sloyds and hollering for Old Trailer at the

A FUR COAT FOR MAMA

same time. It was pretty obvious that he had seen or smelled something down near the creek that he didn't like because his eyes were riveted down there, and he was barking with a very strong intensity.

"Come on boy; we've got to get back to the house," I said, grabbing him by the collar, and forcibly taking him with me. In about five minutes we were back at the house and I was tugging Old Trailer inside.

"Hoyt, lock that back door behind you and get the .22 out," Mama called from the front room. "I'll bring the shells to you. Girls get over there at your post and keep your eyes on that hill. Here's the bullets, son. Load it quickly and get out on the porch. Remember, shoot their legs!"

"I will Mama," I said, as I slid an extra long range shell into the chamber, and headed to the porch. About 30 minutes went by with everyone on high alert—me and Old Trailer keeping watch on the porch with the .22 and the girls still watching the hill from the window. Finally, Mother decided there wasn't likely to be anyone coming and we all began to calm down a little. Mama was the driving force behind all our lives when Daddy was gone, and when she was scared we kids were terrified. There was one thing I knew for sure though as long as I had Daddy's .22 in my hands nobody was going to come up that hill without getting some lead in his hide because I was used to shooting squirrels and rabbits, and people made a lot bigger targets.

"Hoyt, you can come back into the house now, but leave the gun out there. We're going to try and get this family back to normal. I've got to get some supper started and a pot of coffee on; Daddy and the boys should be getting back soon."

"Hey, Mama, there's two cars coming in off the highway, right now!" Nellie yelled, looking out the front window.

"It's Daddy and the guys, Mama, and there's another car following them," Dorothy announced, loudly."

"It's a law car, Mama!" I yelled, crowding in between Nellie and Dorothy to get a better look; "it's got a big star on the side."

"Well, my lands, I didn't expect they'd come all the way out here." Mama said, pushing in closer to the window. "Now don't any of you kids go running out there. This is very serious business, and we need to let your daddy handle it without us getting in the way."

"Mama, they're probably coming to talk to you!" Dorothy exclaimed, looking Mama straight in the face.

"Oh my goodness, I'll bet you're right, honey!" Mama agreed, as they approached the porch with Daddy in the lead. "You kids find your-selves something to do and stay out of the way!" Mama said, straighten-ing her hair up and fixing the front of her dress.

Well, there wasn't much chance of us leaving the scene and Mama knew it. Never in our lives had a law man been to our house before, but we did make ourselves scarce, for the time being.

"Come on in, Sheriff. This is my wife, Dell," Dad said, as he opened the door and walked in.

"It's a pleasure to meet you Ma'am," the burly young officer said politely, as he walked into the living room followed by all the gang.

"This is Sheriff Dan Shipley, Dell. He's come to talk to you about your encounter down on the creek."

"Just call me Dan, Ma'am."

"I'm glad to meet you, Dan, and you can call me Dell. It makes it easier to talk to people when you use their first names."

"I heartily agree."

"Come on into the kitchen, guys. It just so happens I've got a pot of coffee brewing," Mama said, turning back towards the kitchen.

"Dell, is that fresh hominy I smell?" Cowboy asked, as he walked into the kitchen removing his hat and sniffing the air.

"That's definitely hominy," said Ike, doing his own sniff test—"I don't know whether it's fresh or not."

"It's as fresh as it gets," Mother remarked. "The kids and I made it today. Dan, you can have this seat right here at the end of the table," Mother said, pulling out a chair. "Do you drink coffee?"

"I certainly do," the big officer replied with a smile. "I take it black."

"Everyone just sit down here around the table, and I'll get the coffee as soon as it's ready."

"Mrs. Walker, I'm definitely staying for supper tonight," Maxy volunteered with an assuring grin. "I haven't had homemade hominy in a coon's age."

"Maxy, you and I are on a first name basis now, so quit that Mrs. Walker stuff," Mama scolded, looking at him with a smile.

"It's just force of habit, Ma'am," he said shaking his head—"oops, I mean Dell. I guess I'm going to need a little more practice," he admitted, with an embarrassed look.

"Don't worry about it," Mama said. "You'll always be welcome at my table. Okay boys; shove your mugs out here. The coffee is ready."

After everyone had gotten himself a big mug of coffee and downed a couple a hefty swigs, Dad said, "Dan, any time you want to talk to Dell about the incident, just go ahead. It's very unlikely you're going to get her to sit down when supper is this close."

"Yeah, I can certainly understand this is not the best time, but if it's all right with you Dell, I'd just like to ask a couple of things about what happened down on the creek yesterday. Dave has already explained to me that you didn't recognize any of them because they had masks over their faces; is that correct?"

"That's exactly right. For the life of me I can't understand why anyone would do a thing like that. It appeared to me like they were actually trying to catch the dog, and I just was in their way. One of them did grab me by the hair, but Old Trailer bit him two or three times on the legs and I was able to jerk free. They had an old blanket they were trying to throw over the dog, but every time they tried to grab onto him he would really lay into them. I'll guarantee you one thing, whoever it was will have some serious dog bites on their hands and legs."

"That will be proof enough to hold them for trial. I'll know right away when I pick them up if it was them. So, they didn't injure you any other way except jerking some of your hair out?"

"Well, they did scratch me pretty bad on the neck here," Mama said, walking over to Dan and leaning over where he could see the marks.

"That sorry bunch of scum," the Sheriff mumbled. "Your neck is badly bruised, Dell. You're darned lucky your dog was there to give you some support. So what would make them want that dog? Is he a pure-bred, or is he worth money?"

"He's definitely not a purebred," Dad replied, "but there is a quality about him that would certainly make some people want him if they knew about it."

* * *

"Dave, I think I've got it," Maxy interrupted. "Those jug heads had to see us digging mink out of the clay bank where Trailer was treeing them, and since they couldn't learn how to catch mink with traps they've decided your dog is the next best bet."

"That's got to be it, Maxy!" Dad said, shaking his head. "Man, those guys are unbelievable. That dog would never hunt with them if they had him."

"Okay, now this is starting to make some sense," Dan said. "Trailer is a mink dog, and mink are worth a lot of money. They would definitely be interested in a dog like that. What a bunch of lunkheads. I had them all in jail about a week ago for ripping up Maynard's diner."

"Maynard's diner!" Dad exclaimed.

"Yeah, that little train car diner down at the wagon yard."

"Hey, we know that place well; that's our favorite eating spot. Maynard is Cowboy's cousin," Dad replied.

"I was afraid of something like this," said Cowboy, shaking his head and looking apprehensively at Dan. "I sure hope they didn't hurt old Maynard!"

"Naw, they just roughed him up a little and dumped a couple of big pots of his chili on the floor. It's too bad he didn't blast the bums. It would definitely have been self defense. I guess he held them back for quite awhile but somehow they distracted him and got the gun away from him. It's just lucky for Maynard that a passerby saw what was happening and alerted us. Those boys are some sorry people—they've got to be stopped!"

"You sure don't have to convince us of that, sheriff," Maxy acknowledged. "They've been a pain in our rear for months now."

"I'm almost sure they were down on the creek again a couple of hours ago," Mama said. "The dog was barking really hard looking down the hill."

"He was just about to take off when I grabbed him," I proclaimed, as Old Trailer and I followed by the girls made our entrance into the kitchen.

"Dan, this is Hoyt, Nelly and Dorothy," Mama said, pointing to each of us, as Old Trailer began making his rounds among the guys for his usual petting session.

"And I bet that's Old Trailer," Dan said, observing his interaction with the guys.

"Yeah, that's him all right. He's the best mink dog in the whole world!" I announced proudly. "That's why they were trying to steal him."

"Well, they're probably not still down there, but I think I'll go on down and have a look around anyhow. It was nice meeting all you folks. I'll drop back by before I leave."

"Would you like us to go with you, Dan?" Dad asked. "We'll give you all the help you need, but we don't want to get in your way."

"Naw, it's just a routine look-see. I can take care of it. You boys just go ahead and finish your coffee. Does this door lead to the outside?" he asked, pointing to the back porch.

"It sure does," Mama replied. "Just go straight down the hill from the house to the creek, and the area right along this side is where it happened. By the way, you've got about 30 minutes until supper is going to be served, and you're definitely invited. I've got a big pot of chicken and dumplings and fresh hominy."

"Wild horses couldn't keep me away, Dell! I thought you'd never ask," Dan smiled, as he closed the back door behind him.

MAMA MAKES HOMINY AND BIG DAN AND THE LAW COME CALLING 145

"Yep, it does feel better having the law on our side," Ike confessed, with a sigh of satisfaction. "They've already had problems of their own with those dummies so now they know what's up."

"Exactly," Maxy replied, nodding his head in agreement. "Now we're started off on the right foot."

"Dan seems like a fine fellow, doesn't he?" Dad said. "I liked him right from the beginning."

"He does appear to be a conscientious young man," Mother agreed.

"Hey Daddy, maybe I should go with him to show him the exact spot where they attacked Mama!" I suggested hopefully.

"No, Son, if he'd wanted us to be there he would have told us. We'll just let him do his job and when he gets done we'll feed him one of your mama's special suppers. If that doesn't put him soundly in our corner nothing will."

"Man, that's a fact," Maxy agreed. "Dell's cooking could charm a rattle snake out of his buttons."

"Aw, you guys cut it out," Mama said, with an embarrassed grin. "What kind of cobbler do you knot heads think you want for dessert, blackberry, peach or apple? I've got to get it on right now."

"Let's take a vote," Cowboy insisted. "Everyone who wants blackberry raise his hand. Okay, that's four for blackberry. Now how many for apple? Only one, Dell, and he doesn't count anyway," Cowboy said, grinning at Ike.

"It looks like the blackberries have it then," Mama said, heading for the pantry.

The conversation around the table continued on for another 30 or 40 minutes as the aroma of Mother's cobbler became more and more bodacious. Suddenly at the back door came a soft rapping noise with the sounds of someone cleaning their shoes on the back porch rug. "It sounds like our dinner guest has arrived, Mama," Dad said, pushing back from the table. "Come on in here young man," Dad said, as he pushed the back door open.

"Well it was just about like I figured," Dan suggested, following Dad towards the kitchen. "There wasn't really anything conclusive to tie the Sloyds to the incident. It appears you were right about the number of people, Dell. I could only find three other sets of tracks besides yours, but I did find that handful of hair you're missing. I've got it tucked safely away in my pocket, as exhibit number one. When I file my report that will be ample evidence there actually was an attack on your person."

"I sure thank you for coming out here to help us, Dan," Mama said. "People living in the country can't always count on getting police help just when they need it, and we certainly appreciate what you're doing."

"You're very welcome. I just wish we could get more people to cooperate with us the way you folks are. Law enforcement in the outlying areas could become a regular thing if people would let us know what's going on right when it starts happening instead of letting it get out of hand. I realize people have to take care of some of their own problems, but there's also a time to ask for help."

CHAPTER SIXTEEN—Screams in the Night and the Sloyd Brothers Disappear

"Why don't you come over here and sit where you were before, Dan?" Mama suggested, "and we'll get supper under way. What does everyone want to drink? We've got coffee, water, sweet milk and buttermilk."

After everyone had chosen his drink and Mother started bringing the food to the table, Dan posed a question that quickly got everyone's attention. "Since you folks have lived in this area for a long time and have had your problems with the Sloyds, have you ever heard any rumors about there being a woman involved with them, or about there being sounds of screaming and crying coming from around their place late at night?"

"It's funny you should ask that, sheriff," Maxy quickly replied, "because my sister and her family live within hearing distance of them, and they swear they have been hearing that type of noise occasionally for as long as they've lived there. At first they thought it was some kind of animal like a panther or a large bird, and they didn't pay that much attention to it, but they have been there for several years now and it continues to this day. My Sis just mentioned it to me again the day before yesterday. Do you know anything about it?"

"We've had several reports on it, but most of them say just about what you've told me. One old lady even went so far us to say she thought it was the ghost of their dead mother walking through the woods around the house late at night crying."

"Yeah, that's something I forgot to tell you," Maxy added. "It only happens late at night."

"My goodness, we've never heard anything like that before," Mama interjected. "Have we, Dave?"

"No, that's a first for me, but I'll tell you one thing, there's not a whole lot I would put past those old boys. I'd say they're capable of just about anything. Why is it the sheriff's department hasn't gone down there and checked it out?"

"Well it's only been the last few months we've started hearing about it, and it's always just little bits and pieces—nothing substantial. With all this new stuff they're getting into though, I'm guessing we'll be checking it out sooner rather than later."

"You know, even as kids those old boys were mean to the core," said Cowboy. "When I was 10 years old my family moved down to the bottoms fairly close to where they lived, and we went to the same school over at Sugar Grove. For the first two weeks after school started they sent me home with a bloody nose or something, every day. Finally my Dad sat me down, and gave me a stern talking to. 'Son, somehow you've got to convince those boys you're not going to take what they're doing to you. We've got this land rented for a cotton crop, so that means we're going to be here for at least a year. The quicker you take care of this problem the better off everybody's going to be.' Old Dud was just about my age, and all the others were younger, but they sure liked helping Dud beat up on me. On the way home from school the next day after Dad had talked to me I could hear them sneaking up behind me walking faster and faster to catch up, but I didn't even turn around; I just kept right on walking. When Dud finally got close enough to grab me by the back of the coat, I whirled around and smacked him right in the nose with everything I had. Instantly, I knew I had him! His knees almost buckled, and he just stood there like he was dumb struck. I quickly plowed another haymaker, right into his fat lips, and down he went. As I leaped on top of him the rest of gang took off for home like a bunch of scared rabbits. In about half a minute old Dud was blubbering and begging me to stop. I made him say, calf rope, uncle, I give up, and a few other choice words of surrender, before I decided I was through. I told him I would beat him up everyday if he and his pack of rats didn't stay clear away from me. Then I gave him one last hard punch in the side of the head for good measure, and sent him home holding his ear, squalling his brains out."

"So that's the reason they seemed to be afraid of you up at the wagon yard," Dad assessed. "I wondered about that."

"Yeah, they're all cowards; when you get them separated they suddenly lose their bravado."

"Well, it's definitely a good thing to have that bunch afraid of you," said Dan, shaking his head.

"Folks, everybody better be warned; I've got a big pot of chicken and dumplings heading to the table, and it's piping hot," Mama said, holding the handle of the big kettle with a towel in each hand.

"All right—Dell! I can't wait to get my teeth into some of those!" said Ike, concentrating on the big pot as Mama slid it gently onto the table.

"I'll get the biscuits, hominy and the poke salat on the table in just a minute then we can start eating."

"Man, I don't think I've ever seen this much excitement over supper before," said Dan, with a bit of humor in his voice.

"That's because you haven't eaten at Dell's table yet," Maxy said, with a reserved smile. "Supper at this house is an event you don't want to miss."

"I believe it," Dan smiled, as Mama proceeded to slide a large bowl of freshly cooked hominy over to the middle of the table. "Suddenly I'm hungrier than a mother wolf nursing 12 pups!"

* * *

The Walker family saw a lot of Big Dan in the next two weeks. The Sheriff's Department really got on with its investigation of the Sloyd brothers, and Dan would frequently stop in to give Mother and Dad a report on the process. Two times he just happened to drop in right at suppertime and during the meal he would give Mother and Dad a full update. For the first two weeks the department kept a stake out at the

Sloyds house waiting for them to come home, all to no avail. Evidently the boys had been expecting the police to come their way because in the two weeks they were there they never saw hide nor hair of them. Even though the police didn't get their hands on them the constant presence of a police vehicle pulling in and out of the driveway certainly did a lot for the Walker family's nerves, especially Mama's.

As the weather continued to get better Mama became obsessed with getting her garden ready, and getting her a new batch of baby chicks to raise as fryers, and also some to replace her older hens that had just about stopped laying. Early one spring morning Dad and I had been down to the barn hooking up the mules and getting ready to plow up the garden, when he and I made a startling but welcome discovery. "Hey, look over here in the corner, Son! Can you believe that?" Dad said, just above a whisper. "Your mama is sure going to be pleased about this. Let's tie these mules up to the rail here and go have us some breakfast and tell her about it."

"Oh, yeah; let's do, Daddy," I agreed, "and I want to tell Nellie and Dorothy too!"

As we walked into the back porch, Dad announced loudly, "Dell, that old sow we thought was all pigged out had six little ones last night, and she may not be through yet."

"Oh, Mama, they are so cute," I said excitedly, heading towards the girls room on a run.

"Well isn't that a nice little surprise!" Mama replied, as she opened the oven to take out a pan of biscuits. "At least that's a little money we can save. I just thought she had gotten big and fat."

"Yeah, that would be the logical assumption since we don't own a boy pig. Evidently we got a little help from the neighbors," Dad said with a chuckle.

"Well you know what they always say—love will find a way!"

"Well in this case, I'm certainly glad it did," Dad replied, as the girls and I came running out of the hallway heading for the back door.

"Now you kids take a quick look at those pigs and get right on back here," Mother insisted. "I've got breakfast ready, and as soon as we eat we're all going to get outside and go to work."

"Okay, Mama," Nelly yelled, as we headed out the back door.

* * *

The next few months brought a lot of changes around our place. Mama got her new chickens all settled in, our garden was up waist high and doing really well, and the pigs had grown to 50 pounds or more and we were having to build new pens to hold them all. The so called, pigged out old sow ended up having three more for a grand total of nine. Everything seemed to be right with the world, and the Walker family was enjoying life. Even the Sloyd brothers weren't causing any problems in the area. In fact, Maxy's sister attested that the disturbing sounds late at night had even stopped. The whole area was taking a well-deserved sigh of relief—but ominous signs that things weren't quite as well-off as they seemed to be were starting to pop up here and there, like people's chicken houses being raided with all their eggs and part of their chickens gone, or maybe a steer found dead with only its hind legs missing. The first big alarm came when the store at Sugar Grove was burglarized. The thieves took ammunition, flashlights and batteries, and lots of canned goods.

CHAPTER SEVENTEEN—Sugar Grove Under Attack and Man Hunt for the Sloyd Boys

Shortly after the burglary, Maxy's sister reported the disturbing noises had started again, but this time she said it sounded different. The police immediately checked it out but found nothing new. It was as if the Sloyds had vanished from the face of the earth, but left their evil deeds behind them. The clincher that they were still around came when two families near Sugar Grove, who were known to have had problems with the Sloyds, both had their houses burn to the ground the same night.

"It's got to be them, but why hasn't anyone seen the bums?" Ike questioned, as the crew was gathered around the table in an early morning coffee session.

"Oh yeah, it's them all right; there's no doubt it!" Cowboy responded, expressing his usual scowl at the mention of his childhood foes. "They've just found themselves some new little gimmick they're working."

"That's got to be right," Dad agreed. "They're the only people around here who are criminal minded and ignorant enough to be doing something like this, but where can they be hanging out, and why can't the law catch up to them?"

"Somewhere they've got themselves a secret little spot, Dave," Ike drawled, leaning back in his chair and scratching his head. "They're kicking back and enjoying life as usual at everyone else's expense."

"Yeah, and laughing at the rest of us like we're all a bunch of damn fools!" Cowboy added, with a belligerent look in his eyes. "Wait until I get my hands on old Dud again—I'll choke his fat eyeballs right out of his head!"

"I'll tell you one thing, fellows," Dad, stated, "if old Dan and his crew don't get their act together here pretty soon, we're going to be giving them some help. The Jacksons and the Duprees aren't the only ones with houses that can get burned, and as you know, we are very high on the scum bags' list. It's just a matter of time until they show up."

"No doubt about that," Maxy agreed. "It appears this short respite we've been enjoying has actually allowed them to get better organized. They've become more elusive and a whole lot more radical than they've ever been. The thing I'd like to know is where have they been for the last three or four months? We know they're not invisible, so why haven't people spotted them sneaking around? Is it possible they left the area for awhile, and now they've just gotten back? I think if we got our heads together on the subject, fellows, we might be able to come up with some answers, and maybe we can cut them off at the pass; you know—get in front of them instead of behind them."

"Man, I'm certainly for that," Dad replied. "Somehow we've got to get those bums out of circulation. Being around them is like trying to live with a mess of scorpions nesting under your house; you're always up tight whether you're getting stung or not."

"Yeah, it's too bad decent folks have to put up with vermin like that," Cowboy added. "What we need to do, is stomp out their nest with them in it."

"I agree with that," Dad confessed.

"Dave, I think you've just stumbled across the answer," said Maxy, with a touch of excitement in his voice. "The Sloyds not being seen can merely mean they're sleeping all day and staying up all night doing their mischief. You're seldom going to see scorpions out in the daytime. They only come out when predators that prey on them are asleep."

"That's got to be it, partner! There's your new gimmick, Cowboy," Dad said, smiling and shaking his head, "and that's also why the law hasn't been able to lay their hands on the bums. They've found themselves a cozy little hiding place and they're sticking tight in the daytime."

"Yeah, and raising hell all night!" Ike interjected, with a lusty chuckle. "That's exactly their style! By the way, Dave, that's a good name for that bunch of scum, the scorpion brothers."

"Yeah, I like that, Ike! It fits them perfectly," Cowboy agreed. "I hate scorpions almost as bad as I hate the Sloyds!"

"Gentlemen, now we've got our thinking caps on," Maxy said, smiling and nodding his head at the rest of the group. "What we need to do now is figure out where that secret place is and go nail their hides to the wall."

* * *

"Hey guys," Mama said, bringing the coffee pot off the stove to give everyone a warm up. "I've been listening to your conversation from the living room, and I feel you may be overlooking something significant."

"What would that be, Dell?" Maxy questioned, turning to face Mama.

"That noise your sister has been talking about for so long. She said it had remained almost exactly the same every since they've lived there until right now. If that's a naturally occurring sound, why would it change just when all this mean stuff is starting to happen?"

"Yeah, that's a good question, Dell." Maxy agreed, nodding his head at Mama. "But what if it isn't natural and the scorpion boys are responsible for it. Man, the implications of that could be staggering!" Maxy said, shaking his head.

"Man, I see what you mean!" Dad replied, looking around at the gang, wide eyed. "Discovering the answer to that one might be the straw that breaks the camel's back."

"Yeah, or yanks out the scorpion's stinger," said Cowboy. "I tell you right now; there isn't anything I would put past those guys!"

"Fellows, it's practically a certainty they're behind these incidents," Maxy stated. "Assuming it is them—they've got to be hiding somewhere right there close to where they were raised!"

"Maybe it's a boyhood hideout they built when they were kids," Ike said thoughtfully.

"Hey, man, you're not going to believe this," Cowboy quickly responded, "but I actually remember hearing them talk about digging a tunnel once, when we were all going to the Sugar Grove school."

"No kidding!" Ike interjected, sitting up straight in his chair.

"Yeah, they were talking among themselves about wanting to hurry home to work on it."

"Now we're getting somewhere!" said Maxy, energetically. "Did they say where it was located? Was it hooked to a cellar or something?"

"Hey, they'd never have told me anything. I hated their innards, and they knew it," Cowboy replied, with a chuckle. "Man, I wish I'd have listened closer!"

"That was some good thinking, anyway, Bud," said Ike, punching Cowboy on the shoulder. "That's got to be where the bums are. They're still right there on the home place."

"Boys, we're bringing this thing to closure," said Maxy. "I knew we could out think those creeps if we tried hard enough."

"But the law has been crawling all over that joint for months now," said Cowboy. "How are they getting in and out without being seen? They're definitely coming and going to do their dirty work!"

"Yeah, that's a hard one to figure," Dad replied, "but the fact that they're doing it and getting away with it can only mean one thing, they've got it really well camouflaged, and they're able to go in and out right under the nose of the law. It's got to be something pretty clever."

"I think we've got this thing just about thrashed out," Maxy said. "We've established, with very little doubt, they're still right there where they've always been, and they are in a very concealed location that the law's probably walking all over."

"Well, if the law can't find them," Ike said skeptically, "what chance do we have?"

"Hey, the big difference is, we know what to look for and the police don't," Dad replied. "We're going to be looking for a hidden tunnel or a trap door setup leading to an underground bunker."

"How about if I go down to my sister's place for a few nights and check out that mysterious noise? Maybe there is a connection between the noise and where they're hiding. If that proves to be the case it would give us a real leg-up in locating them. At least maybe we'll finally get to the bottom of what the noise actually is."

"That sounds like the right move to me," Dad replied. "While you're looking into that the rest of us will be keeping our eyes peeled for the bums."

CHAPTER EIGHTEEN—Night Watch and Devastation Strikes

Ike and Cowboy stayed at our house for the next three week as a precautionary measure, and between them and Dad, the house, the barn and the livestock were kept under 24-hour surveillance. I had to sleep on a pallet on the floor and let them have my bed, but I didn't mind; they were just like big brothers to me, and it was really exciting to have young men in the house even if they weren't my age. Sometimes when I would wake up in the middle of the night and a new shift was starting to take place, Old Trailer and I would take a turn sneaking around the place in the dark with whoever was coming on duty. It was like playing cops and robbers with my friend Jimmy Killian, except this time it was dead serious. I had to keep Old Trailer on a rope to keep him out of the way because the guys didn't want him running around out in front of them.

Although everything had been normal around the Walker house since the guys had been staying over, there had been three more structure fires in the Sugar Grove area and Big Dan and the police department was running around like chickens with their heads chopped off. They knew exactly who they were looking for, but no matter how hard they tried or how many stakeouts they used they couldn't find hide nor hair of the Sloyds. Dan stopped by three times on different occasions to give Dad and Mom an update on what all was happening. He said the whole Sugar Grove area and surrounding parts was as nervous as a big bowl of Jell-O with everyone wondering who was going to be victimized next.

"If I ever get my hands on those Sons a Bitches again," Dan said, in a fit of rage, "it'll be a long time before they ever see the light of day—I'll grant you that—Oh, I'm so sorry, Mrs. Walker!" he said, when he realized the language he had used. "I sort of let my temper get away from me there! Please excuse me!"

"Your frustration is understandable, Dan," Mother smiled. "You merely put into words what we're all feeling. It's hard to believe those boys have turned into such worthless trash. It seems like only yesterday they were just children tagging along after their mother down in the bottoms."

"Hey Dan, how are you guys going to prove it was them even if you do catch them?" Cowboy asked. "What's to keep some do-gooder judge from turning them loose for lack of evidence?"

"We've got the evidence to nail them right now. We've had their fingerprints on file since they tore up Maynard's diner. We've got them placed at three of the five arson sites. They're stupid enough to just keep on using the same starting method every time—a pop bottle full of gasoline with their finger prints all over it. Two times we weren't able to lift prints because the bottle was partially melted, but we've got all five of their prints off the three bottles. Fingerprints don't do us much good though until we can lay our hands on the bums!"

"Well, the boys and I have been seriously discussing their possible whereabouts," Dad said, "and we've come to the conclusion they're hiding out somewhere right there on the old place."

"Now, that's awfully hard for me to believe, Dave," Dan replied, shaking his head. "The boys and I have gone over that farm with a fine toothed comb. What makes you think they could still be there?"

"The fact that all the skullduggery is happening in walking distance of that old place, is the best reason."

"Yeah, you've got a point there, but where in the dickens can they be?" Dan asked, shrugging his shoulders.

"What we figure is, they've got themselves some kind of an underground bunker system," Dad replied. "Cowboy, tell him about the tunnel you heard them talking about."

"A tunnel!" Dan exclaimed.

"Yeah, when we were just kids, we all went to school over at Sugar Grove elementary—that is—when they showed up. One day I overheard them talking about hurrying home to work, on the tunnel. They didn't say where it was, or anything else."

"Hey, now, that's a new concept!" Dan said, looking at the other guys with excitement showing in his face. "Suddenly the prospects in this case just got a lot better. That's a piece of work, boys! I can see right now, I should have been listening more instead of talking. What else do you guys know that I should be hearing?"

"Well, we're still waiting on another possible piece of the puzzle," Dad said.

"Hey, tell me what you've got going, Dave!" Dan exclaimed, "I want to hear everything."

"Well, a few days back, Maxy spent some time down at his sister's place trying to hear that mystery noise that his sis is always talking about. He didn't have any luck hearing the noise, but he put his sister and her husband on high alert, and they're going to call him the instant they start hearing anything."

"So, you guys feel there might be something real about that noise then?" Dan questioned.

"I'll have to admit we're grabbing at straws," Dad admitted, "but that noise is the only possible lead we could come up with that might take us to where they're hiding out. Of course, there's a very high probability it's just a naturally occurring sound."

"Holy hell, I almost hope it is!" Dan said, shaking his head. "Otherwise this could get mind boggling."

"Yeah, that's the same conclusion we came to," Ike replied. "But even though we think they're still right there, it's probably going to take some kind of real breakthrough to ever locate them, and that noise could possibly be it."

"Boys, it's obvious there's been a lot of work gone into these thoughts and it makes the hair stand up on the back of my neck to think what you may be onto. As soon as I get back to the office in the morning, I'm going to start looking through the missing persons files from this area."

"Well," Ike spoke up, "I can tell you one missing person without you even having to look. Bobbi Jo Wilcox has been gone for two or three years now. She's listed as a runaway by your office, but Bobbi Jo's parents say she was not the runaway type; she would never have left home without telling them."

"Oh my God, I remember that now! Fellows, I hope this is all just far out speculation, but we're going to chase down every possible lead until we get to the bottom of it all. You've gotten a lot deeper than my people have been able to."

"We may be just chasing butterflies," Dad replied, "but somewhere there's an answer to it all."

"That's a definite fact, Dave. I want you guys to keep right on top of it, and keep me posted—especially on what happens between Maxy and his sister. I want to know immediately if those sounds start happening. Please don't try to take any action on your own, though! This thing may be bigger than all of us. I'm going to leave you my card and you can call me night or day," Dan said, sliding a card out of his wallet. "My home phone and my office are both listed there."

"We'll tell Maxy to keep you updated on the whole affair," Dad said. "We decided a long time back we needed the law involved here, so we'll definitely wait for your lead. When your adversary is as irrational as the Sloyd brothers, there's no telling where it's all going to end."

"It's already gotten way too far, Dave," Dan said with a grave look on his face, "and hearing what you boys have just told me makes me shudder to think where it may be going. I figured we were just dealing with a bunch of mischievous farm boys out of control."

"Yeah, that's what we thought in the beginning, but as you see, these are some very dangerous people."

"No doubt about that," Dan replied, as he headed out the door. "I'll be in touch."

* * *

The third night after Big Dan's visit, the very thing that Dad and the guys had been guarding against, started happening. It was about 2:00 in the morning, and Dad had just taken over the watch from Cowboy. Within a minute or two of him leaving the house, suddenly Ike sat straight up in bed and yelled—"Hey, Bud, get up! Hoyt, get the lamp lit just as quickly as you can!"

"What's wrong, Uncle Ike?" I asked, rolling off my pallet, and fumbling in the dark trying to light the lamp.

"Ike, there's something going on out there," Mama hollered, suddenly appearing in the doorway with her lamp.

"Yeah, it's down at the barn, Dell, and Dave hasn't even had time to get down there. The pigs are squealing really bad. Cowboy, get your clothes on; we've got to get out there quick."

Within two or three minutes from the start of the commotion the squealing had all stopped, and everything outside fell dead silent.

"Well, whatever was causing the problem must have left," said Cowboy.

"Let's hope so," Ike replied, as they headed for the back door. "Maybe it was just a stray dog jumped into the pen for a few seconds then took off."

Suddenly a .30-30 began firing a long series of slow deliberate shots.

"That's got to be Dave, but why would he be firing so slow?" Cowboy questioned, turning and looking at Mama.

"Dell, I suggest you and the kids get in your bedroom and lock the door," said Ike, as Dorothy and Nelly's heads appeared in their doorway.

"We'll go out and see what's going on, and let you know just as soon as we can."

"Son, grab the .22 and shells for it and get on in my room just as quick as you can."

"Okay, Mama," I whispered. "I'll be right back!"

"Come on girls; get on in here," Mama said, gesturing with her hand and opening the door wider.

"What's the matter, Mama?" Dorothy asked, with a scared look on her face.

"We don't know right now, Honey, but I'm sure we'll be finding out soon enough. I just hope your daddy's all right."

"Oh Mama, I don't like this!" Nellie said, sitting down right next to Mama on the bed.

"I know, Sweetheart; I don't like it either," Mama agreed, putting her arms around Nellie and Dorothy.

"Okay, I've got it," I said, sliding through the door and locking it behind me.

"Where's Old Trailer at, Hoytie?" Dorothy asked. "I'd feel a whole lot better if he was in here with us."

"Me too Sis, but he's outside with Daddy."

"Kids, let's all kneel down here on the side of the bed, and I'm going to ask the Good Lord to take care of us," Mama said, as we all slid to our knees. "Dear Lord, we have always honored you in this house and tried to keep your commandments as best we could. Now we would like to ask for your guidance and protection. We know the evil that is trying to harm this family has no power against thy greatness. Please take care of us all, in the hour of our need; I ask you in the name of our Lord Jesus, Amen."

It seemed like forever that we huddled there in Mother and Dad's bedroom waiting to hear what was happening outside, but it couldn't have been more than 10 or 15 minutes. Finally at the back door we heard Daddy's voice calling out. "Hey Dell, can you hear me?"

"That's Daddy!" I yelled, ecstatically. Quickly everyone headed for the door with Mother in the lead and me behind her with my .22. As we approached the door we heard Dad calling to us from outside. "Dell, I don't want you and the kids to be scared. I'm not hurt in any way but I'm thoroughly covered with blood. Unlock the door and let me in. I've got to change out of these clothes and get back to the barn."

"Oh my God, Dave, what has happened?" Mother cried out, putting her hands up to her face.

"Quick, let's get in the house," Dad said, looking backwards. "Those creeps may still be out here somewhere. I know this looks bad, but as far as I know I'm not hurt."

"Oh my goodness, Dave, please tell us what's going on!" Mother pleaded, with desperation in her voice.

"Those lousy Sloyds have brutalized our livestock. I had to shoot every last one of our hogs. Some of them were dragging themselves around the pen with their entrails hanging out, and others were just stabbed through the body with some kind of long bladed knife and left to run around the pen squirting blood straight up in the air! I don't know anything about the rest of the animals."

"Oh Lord, Dave; I can't believe this is happening to us!" Mother gasped, with shock starting to show in her face.

"Yeah, it's really got me rattled too. I feel like I'd like to hug all of you close to me right now, but as you can see I'm in no shape to touch anybody."

"Daddy, where's Old Trailer?" I asked quickly. "Is he with Uncle Ike and Cowboy?"

"I think so, Son. I asked Cowboy where he was when I took over, and he said Trailer was with him earlier, but he hadn't seen him in a little while. He's probably down there with the boys by now though. Dell, grab me some old clothes to put on. I've got to get back to the barn."

"I'll just be a second," Mama replied. "Girls, come and give me a hand. Dave, what are we going to do?" Mother asked turning around to face Daddy as she started to leave the room. "We can't let all that meat go to waste. Those hogs were our wintertime survival."

"Yeah, I know what you're saying, Dell, but right now my major concern is keeping the family, the house and my barn safe. We don't know if they've done all they're going to or if they're still out there somewhere waiting to hit us again. When morning gets here and we can see what we're doing there's a good chance we may be able to save some of the meat. It's definitely been bled out good enough. Girls, stay in the other room for a while," Daddy said, to Nelly and Dorothy. "I've got to get out of these clothes."

CHAPTER NINETEEN—Old Trailer Dog-napped and Hoytie Loses Control

"I'll be right back with something you can change into," Mama said, as she and the girls turned to leave.

"Son, I want you to stay here at the house with Mama and the girls and keep your eyes peeled; watch the outside of the house from the porch and the windows as much as you can. The boys and I will have to be down at the barn for a while longer at least, but when we decide to come back we'll holler at you before we get here. If you see anybody else sneaking around, put a bullet hole in them. I'm counting on you to keep the girls and your mother safe."

"Okay Daddy, I sure will!" I said picking up the .22. "Do you want me shoot at their legs?"

"Shoot at whatever you can hit. They'll more than likely be trying to burn the house, so stop them any way you can. Shoot then quickly reload and keep shooting until you nail them or they run off. These people are animals, Son. We've got to get just as tough as it takes. If I hear you firing I'll get right on back here just as quick as I can, but I'll holler to let you know it's me."

"I'll watch everything good Daddy. I'm going to load my gun now and get out on the porch. Daddy, please look for Old Trailer. It's not like him to stay away like this."

"I'll do the best I can, Son. I'll be heading to the barn as soon as I get dressed, but I'll let you know ahead of time."

"Okay, I'll be careful."

"Dave, the girls and I are really scared!" Mama said, coming out of the hallway and handing Dad his clothes. "Somehow we need to let the law know what's happening down here!"

"As soon as I get back to the barn I'll have Cowboy run up to the Youngs' house and use their phone to call the police. By the way, where is that card Dan gave us?"

"It's right here on the table." Mama said, handing Dad the card.

"Hoyt's going to be guarding the house with his .22 so I want you to keep a close eye on him. He's out on the porch right now. I told him to shoot anybody he sees messing around the house. The boys and I will call out before we approach—okay?"

"Alright, but the first thing I would like you to do when you get back down there is send Cowboy to call the police."

"I'll do just that. I'll leave Ike at the barn as soon as we get things squared away, and I'll come on back here with you and the kids."

"If we get out of this mess alive I think it's high time we have a telephone of our own," Mama stated.

Over a period of about 30 minutes and umpteen trips through the inside of the house looking out the windows and the outside porches checking things out, suddenly I heard Dad's voice calling to me from the back of the smokehouse. "Hey, Son, it's me. I'm going to be coming in by way of the back porch, so get your finger off the trigger."

"Okay Daddy, I'll set the gun right here in the corner," I said, as Dad made a run for the back porch.

"Daddy, is Old Trailer at the barn?" I asked, as Dad slipped in the back door and sat his .30-30 in the corner.

"I didn't see him, Son, but he still may be down there, or he may have chased off after the Sloyds. He'll probably be back in a while."

"Daddy, I'm afraid they've already killed him like they did the hogs or maybe they stole him like they were trying to last time!" I said, with a real tightness in my voice. "He'd of been here by now if there wasn't something bad wrong; I just know it."

"Try not to think about it right now, Little Man," Dad said, pulling me over close to comfort me. "This is a very dangerous situation we're dealing with and we need to stay focused. It won't be but a few hours until daylight will be breaking and then we'll be safe. We'll find your dog, don't you worry about that. He's one of the Walker bunch, and anybody that messes with him messes with all of us."

"Dave, is that you?" Mama asked quietly, as she crept through the kitchen towards the back porch.

"Yeah, it's me, Hon," Dad replied, in a subdued voice. "Cowboy just got back. Big Dan and some of his officers are headed this way right now."

"Oh thank goodness. Let's hurry into the bedroom and you can tell the girls; they're scared to death."

"Mama, Old Trailer's gone!" I said, with a quiver in my voice.

"Now Son, that's not necessarily true," Dad said, stopping and turning back towards me. "He could show up at any minute. You just hold a stiff upper lip there, young man. Things will work out—you'll see!"

"Okay, Daddy, I'll try," I said with a big lump starting to form in my throat.

"Come on into the bedroom with us, Little Man," Mama said. "Right now I want all my family together."

* * *

About twenty minutes later three police cars with their red lights flashing came roaring off the main road in a cloud of dust and Daddy went running out with his flashlight to meet them. "Dave, is there a way to get our vehicles back to the barn?" Big Dan asked, as he stood half in and half out of the lead squad car. "We've got enough lighting equipment on our vehicles to light up the crime scene if we can get back there."

"Yes sir, the gate to the pasture road is right on down here another 20 yards," Dad said. "Just follow me and I'll let you in."

Within minutes, the three squad cars were parked at strategic areas and had their spotlights trained on the house and the barn and

A FUR COAT FOR MAMA

there were three officers with flashlights and drawn weapons scouring the area.

"All we have to do now is stay inside and let these boys do their job," Dad said, as he returned from the barn.

For the next two hours Dan and his men aided by Cowboy and Ike went over the whole place with a fine tooth comb, and finally deciding that the Sloyds were actually gone, Dan came to the house to give Dad and Mom a report.

"Well, folks, it seems your hogs bore the brunt of the attack, but we did find a soda pop bottle full of gasoline in the corner of your barn, Dave. Evidently you must have surprised them and they didn't get the wick lit properly."

"That's a good possibility; when I heard the pigs start squealing I headed straight to the barn, and when I was about 30 yards away one of them shined a flashlight directly on me. I hit the dirt and laid there for a couple of minutes covering the area with my Winchester; finally I jumped up and ran to the door and began shining my light around inside, but they were already gone."

"They beat a quick retreat when they saw you had discovered them," Dan said. "It's darn lucky you got there when you did. Dave, what are you going to do with all that meat? Do you have any way to save it?"

"Not much of it, I'm afraid. Pressure cooking it in fruit jars would probably be the only way, and at best we could save maybe a 100 pounds or so."

"Well, I've got a thought that might work out better for you, and you wouldn't be stuck with such a terrible situation."

"Hey, we're all ears," Dad said, looking over at Mama. "Tell us what you've got in mind."

"My brother-in-law, Frank Jones, has a small locker plant in Boonville. Farm butchering is how Frank makes his living, and he's very good at what he does. Now if you boys would remove the entrails and take care of that part of it, I'm almost certain Frank would come out and pick your hogs up and process the whole batch for half the meat."

OLD TRAILER DOG-NAPPED AND HOYTIE LOSES CONTROL   **169**

"Oh my goodness," Mama said. "That would be wonderful!"

"Yeah, that sounds more than fair to me, Dan," Dad added. "Did you say it's a locker plant?"

"Yes sir—and you can rent a locker there to keep your meat in for $2.50 a month or $25 a year."

"Dave, that sounds really good to me," Mother said, with relief showing in her face. "That way we can have fresh meat as well as salted."

"Hey, if you'd like to salt the middling down and keep them in your brine box here at home, I'll bring them down to you as soon Frank has them ready."

"Boy, that sounds like as sweet a deal as I've ever run into!" Dad exclaimed. "Under the circumstances, Dan, I think we'll accept your offer, and we would like to salt the middling. I'm very partial to having fried salt pork with my breakfast now and then."

"Now and then, my foot," Mama replied, with a grin. "He'd eat it three times a day if I'd cook it."

"Yeah, I do like my salt pork," Dad agreed.

"Okay then, I'll get on back and set it up."

"How does he take care of the outside of the hog?" Dad asked. "Does he skin them or does he have facilities to scald and scrape them?"

"Well, he's sort of got his own thing. Over the years he's developed a system that's fast and efficient and all his regular customers prefer it over skinning or scraping. He uses a large acetylene blowtorch and thoroughly singes the hair then he rubs it off with a clean burlap sack. He usually does it two or three times. The skin turns out just as smooth as you could ask for. His customers swears it give the meat a nice smoky flavor."

"Well, if they like it I'm sure we will too," Dad replied. "What do you think, Dell?"

"Oh, yes, that sounds like a wonderful idea—not having to deal with this problem is a godsend."

"Alright then—it's four a.m. right now, so Frank could possibly be getting out here by 5:30 or 6:00."

"That will be just great, Dan. The boys and I will take care of the off-fall so he can just pick the meat up and go."

* * *

"Daddy, aren't you going to tell Dan about Old Trailer?" I asked despondently, as Dan was starting to leave.

Suddenly Dan turned on his heel and said, "What about Old Trailer, Hoyt—I don't remember seeing him out there."

"He's gone, Sheriff Dan!" I said, with my head hung, and tears starting to run down my face. "He would have been here if there wasn't something wrong. I know they've either stolen him or maybe even killed him!"

"Now, Son, you may be overreacting here," Dad said, a bit impatiently. "As soon as it gets daylight, we'll all spread out and make a major search for him. With everything going on like it's been, we just haven't had the time."

"I'll tell you what, Hoyt," Dan asserted, pointing his big finger directly at me, "as soon as I file my report at the station and get Frank headed down this way, my deputies and I will come back, and we'll find your dog or know the reason why!—okay?"

"Okay," I said, with a weak smile and my bottom lip quivering. "He's my very best friend, Dan, and I'm really scared for him."

"Well now, I wouldn't be much of a lawman or a friend if I didn't help you get your pal back, would I? I'll see you in just a little while, partner!" Dan said, with a wink and a smile.

* * *

It seemed like it took forever for daylight to finally arrive and all the activity at the barn to get finished up. Dad and the boys worked their hearts out taking care of the hogs—getting ready for the butcher to come and take them away, but in all that time there wasn't any sign of Old Trailer. Since early daybreak I had been running up and down the top of the hill above the creek yelling for him—that's as far as Daddy would let me go, but Trailer was nowhere to be seen, and the impact of his absence was becoming more and more unbearable. Once I saw a cottontail rabbit come running out of the brush down by the creek, and my heart leaped with joy thinking my black and white pal—my soul mate—had jumped him out of his hiding place, and would soon come streaking out after him, but as the seconds began to pass and the rabbit disappeared into the thicket, my hopes started to fade and the impact of my loss was overpowering. Suddenly I found myself collapsing to the ground in a fit of uncontrollable sobbing. How many minutes I laid there I can't really say, but before long I heard Nellie and Dorothy yelling for me in the distance—somehow I just couldn't respond.

"Oh, Hoytie, don't cry," Dorothy said quietly, as she and Nellie finally spotted me and came running up to where I was.

"Yeah, little brother, let's hurry on back," Nellie encouraged, kneeling down beside me. "Dan is here again with his deputies to hunt for Trailer. "They want you to show them where he would most likely be."

"He would already be here if he could come," I said despondently. "They've either stolen him or they've killed him! Old Trailer's gone, girls," I said looking them both straight in the face. "Now we're never going to be able to finish Mama's coat," I said, venting my anguish in a torrent tears.

"Oh God, honey, please don't cry," Dorothy said, cradling my head in her arms. "Maybe Trailer's just hurt real bad and can't get back. Maybe all he needs is for us to find him and carry him home."

"Yeah, Hoytie, Old Trailer needs all of us. Now come on; let's go find him," Nellie urged, wiping tears off my face with her skirt tail. "We need to hurry; everybody's waiting."

"Come on over here, kids," Mama motioned, calling us aside as we entered the kitchen through the back porch. "Dan wants Hoyt to go with them down on the creek, to hunt for Old Trailer, but I don't want you girls down there, so don't even ask! I don't really want you down there either, Little Man," Mama said, running her fingers through my hair. "Under the circumstances though, there doesn't seem to be any choice."

"I've got to get my dog back, Mama," I said, with a slight break in my voice. "I just have to!"

"I know, Honey," Mama consoled, hugging me close to her, "but there's just some things in life that mamas have a problem with, and seeing their children be put in harms way is one of the worst."

"Mama, why can't we go help hunt for Trailer too?" Nellie pleaded. "He's our friend too."

"Yeah, Mama, we want to go too—please!" Dorothy begged.

"No girls, this is not a time for children to be out in the woods, especially little girls. Those criminals may still be out there, and if they are there's likely to be shooting. I don't want my family hurt. Dan has promised to send Hoyt straight back to the house as soon as he's finished with him. Now I want you girls to either stay here in the kitchen or go to your room for awhile. Come on Son, you'd better get on in there," Mama said, taking me by the shoulders and heading me toward the door.

As I walked into the living room in front of Mama, I was shocked at the scene that greeted my eyes. It was an armed camp ready for war. Uncle Ike, Cowboy, Maxy and Dad all had their Winchesters in hand and their side arms strapped on, and all three of the officers were standing up in front of the group. "Dave, except for being a mink dog, which you've already explained will never hunt for them, why would the Sloyd brothers want Old Trailer?"

"The only possible benefit they could ever hope for would be to raise pups out of him and hope the pups will inherit his sense of smell."

"Hey, that's it Dave!" Maxy quickly interrupted. "Remember the warning—by that time next year they would be able to catch every mink on Sugar Creek and get even with you at the same time. They want to raise a bunch of pups that will hunt mink for them."

"That's got to be it," Dad agreed, shaking his head. "By the time Trailer was six months old he was already a hunting whiz, and those snoops were probably watching out of the cane break seeing everything that went on."

OLD TRAILER DOG-NAPPED AND HOYTIE LOSES CONTROL

"Hoyt, come on up here to the front," Dan urged, pointing in my direction. "Tell us a little bit about Old Trailer."

"What do you want to know, Sheriff Dan?" I asked, making my way through the guys to the front of the room.

"Well, does he ever just go off hunting on his own?" Dan asked, looking me straight in the eyes.

"No sir! He has never done anything like this before," I replied, "and he always comes when I call him. They've either hurt him real bad where he can't get home, or they've stolen him. He would be here right now if there wasn't something wrong!"

"All right then Little Buddy; it appears your dog has been abducted!" Dan asserted, putting his heavy arm around my shoulders. "First I want you to take us to the spots where you and Trailer like to hunt, and we'll have a good look around, but if he's not down there, I'm going to send you straight back home like I promised your Mama, and the rest of us are going to head on down the creek to see if they've left any kind of trail. If it's within our power we'll find your pal today, but if we don't, the boys and I will be back tomorrow morning with our secret weapon," Dan said, looking down at me with a wink and a grin—"Old Waldo—the police department's blood hound."

"What's a blood hound, Sheriff Dan?" I asked quickly. "What does it do?"

"Well, a blood hound has a super sense of smell, Hoyt—just like old Trailer does, but they use it for a totally different purpose. Blood hounds are used a lot in police work. We use Waldo to find things that are lost—like missing people or even dogs or horses. Whatever you want him to track down, you just give him the scent, and if it's anywhere in the area he'll find it."

"But what if there isn't any blood; can they still find it?" I asked, looking up at him with a perplexed look on my face.

"Oh, yeah, there doesn't need to be any blood, Hoyt. That's just the name of the dog. We'll get Old Trailer's blanket out of his sleeping box over there and give Waldo a good sniff, and he'll go right to where your dog is; I guarantee it."

"Oh thank you so much, Sheriff Dan," I said, grabbing his big hand in both my own and shaking it.

"You're very welcome, little buddy," he replied, patting me on the back. "I know how it is to lose your buddy. Men, you are now deputized, and you represent the law of Logan County. I know all of you guys to be men of good character, and I expect you to act according of the rules I've laid down for you. Now let's go take care of this problem," he said firmly. "Remember, we want them alive if it's possible, but if they start firing on us—defend yourselves. These rogues have given the people around here enough trouble, and it's high time they were brought to justice. Everybody be careful and keep your eyes peeled for Hoyt's dog. It's almost a certainty they want him alive, so it's likely he'll be in a cage or some kind of pen."

"Hoyt, now you come straight back home," Mama reminded, as we all started filing out the back door.

"I will Mama," I replied soberly. Mama knew, without a doubt, that I dearly hated the thought of coming back.

Within half an hour the group had cautiously but thoroughly covered all my good hunting spots along the creek without finding hide nor hair of the Sloyds or Old Trailer, and the time I had been dreading was at hand.

"Now Hoyt, you go straight home!" Daddy warned, pointing his index finger up the hill in the direction of the house. "Those thugs are still on the loose, and as you know old Dud has already threatened you!"

"I know, Daddy," I said despondently, "but I want to help find Old Trailer. He's my dog, and I want to go!" I said a bit more determined.

"Now Son—that's not an option! Your mother is waiting on you. Now get going!" he commanded, as the men started regrouping to head down the creek.

Begrudgingly I started hiking back up the hill, hating every step I took. "I'm a boy," I mumbled defiantly, "and I shouldn't have to stay home with the women. I'll be glad when I get grown up!" I complained, kicking at every rock I saw on the trail. "Trailer's my dog. Why can't I hunt for him? I could probably find him quicker than anybody!"

Just as I was coming to the top of the hill I saw Doctor Cedric's Model A pulling off the road into our driveway. "Oh no!" I thought to myself. "I don't feel like visiting!"

Doctor Cedric was one of my most favorite people, and I was always happy to see him, but right now I just wasn't in the mood to visit. I just wanted to get my dog back!

CHAPTER TWENTY—Hoytie's Gone!
and Doctor Cedric's Warning!

"Doctor, it's always great seeing you," Mother said, smiling and showing him in, "but you sure have come at a depressing time. Your favorite family is in real trouble!"

"Oh no, I was afraid of something like that," the doctor replied, engulfing Mother in his big arms in a comforting hug. "I've been hearing about all the trouble going on in this area, so I thought I'd better get over here and see if you folks were alright."

"Hi Doctor Cedric," Dorothy said, as she and Nellie came shyly forward to receive their usual bear hug.

"Hi, Sweethearts," the doctor replied, folding his arms around the girls. "How are my favorite young ladies? Hey, where's the boy?" the doctor questioned, looking around the room.

"He should be getting back any minute, doctor," Mother replied. "In fact he should have already been here. Come on and I'll make you a cup of coffee and tell you about what's happening,"

"Well, what is happening, Della; what's going on?" the doctor asked, taking himself a seat at the kitchen table.

"For quite a few days now, Doc, we've been trying to protect ourselves against the kind of thing that's been happening in the Sugar Grove area—you know—people getting burned out and having their livestock killed."

"Yeah, I've heard a lot about that lately," the doctor acknowledged. "So what have you been doing to protect yourself?"

"We've had Ike and Cowboy staying with us for several days now, helping Dave keep a watch on things even through the night. We knew we were likely to get hit because of all the problems Dave and the Sloyds had over the mink trapping, but we were starting to feel like maybe we were going to get past it all. That was just wishful thinking, Doc!" Mama said shaking her head.

"Now good lady, you need to stop right here and tell me exactly what has happened here," the doctor said, sensing Mother's tension.

"Those dirty Sloyd brothers, Doc—last night they brutalized our poor hogs, and we had to kill them all," Mother replied, with the trauma of the whole thing suddenly spilling over into her voice. "But the worst part is they've either stolen Old Trailer, or maybe even killed him and we don't know what else they've done yet."

"Della, where's Dave at, and where's the boy?" Doctor Cedric questioned, taking Mama by the hands and looking her straight in the eyes.

"Hoyt should have been here already, Doc. I'm really starting to get worried about him too. Girls, go out on the porch and keep an eye open for your brother. If you see him, get him in this house immediately."

"Now, Della, I realize you're under a lot of pressure here, but you need to just answer my question. Where are Dave and Hoyt, and what's going on?"

"Dave and the boys are with three law officers down on the creek trying to track down the Sloyds, and maybe find Old Trailer. Doctor, Hoyt is in total shock over losing his dog, and I don't know what's going to happen if we can't find him."

"Where's Hoyt at now, Della?"

"The guys took him down on the creek to show them where he and Trailer usually hunt. They were hoping that Trailer had just gone off hunting by himself and they might find him down there somewhere! They promised to send Hoyt straight back home, and he's way overdue. He should have been here an hour ago. Doc, that dog means everything to him, and I'm afraid he's gone off on his own trying to find him, or even worse, those damned Sloyds may have taken him," Mama said, in a torrent of tears. "I just don't understand how people can do something like this."

"Della, there have been scum like this as long as there have been people on this earth. People have had to deal with it throughout the ages. Piracy—highway men—bank robbers; then there's your home grown variety of creeps like these. They're all a bunch of lazy thugs that have learned it's easier to prey on their neighbors than live by the sweat of their own brows."

"Doc, I think this ought to be fairly hot," Mama said, sliding a large mug of coffee in front of the doctor, and sitting down across from him.

"Della, is there a rifle I can use?" asked the doctor, taking a hefty sip of his coffee, and lowering his eyebrows in a determined stare.

"There's the .22," Mama said, pointing to the rifle sitting in the corner.

"That's a bit light. I have my .32 revolver in the car; I'll just use that. As soon as I finish my coffee I'm going to take a little trip down around the creek and see if I can pick up Hoyt's trail. With this kind of trauma working on the lad there's no telling what's he's likely to get into if he goes off on his own. It probably would've been better if Dave had just taken him along so he would know exactly what's happening. I know it would have been dangerous, but leaving him alone in a traumatized state was not the right thing to do!"

"It's all my fault, Doc," Mother replied, frowning and wringing her hands, "he was supposed to come straight home. With all this horror that's been going on I was only trying to protect him."

"You're a fine mother to your family, Della, and you made the same decision most every mama would make," the doctor responded, reaching across the table and patting Mother's hand. "Sometimes though, there are complicating circumstances that get in the way, and this is one of those times. Do you know how to shoot that gun over there?" the doctor asked, pointing to the .22.

"Yeah I know how to shoot it, but I probably couldn't hit anything that wasn't right in front of me. Nobody's ever showed me how to aim it. Oh God, Doc," Mama cried with her hands over her face, "I just can't believe this is happening to my family."

"Well, maybe the guys will get lucky and nail that bunch of rabble, and end their terror reign. Right now though, the whereabouts of young Mister Walker is our prime concern."

"He's not out here, Mama," Nellie yelled, sticking her head in the door.

"Okay, Baby, you girls come on back in the house now. Doc we're going to lock the doors and wait for you, so as soon as you learn anything, please hurry back and tell us."

"I'll do exactly that, good lady," said the doctor, emptying the last of his coffee mug and standing up.

"Mama, there's a bunch of people coming up the hill," Dorothy yelled. "I can't tell who it is yet, but it might be Daddy and the guys!"

"Oh my God—I sure hope that's who it is!" Mother replied, hurrying towards the corner to get the .22.

"Mama, it is—it's Daddy," Nellie yelled running into the house. "They're all coming up the hill right now."

"Oh thank God," Mother sighed, laying the rifle on the table. "Can you tell if your brother is with them?" Mother asked, as she and the doctor headed out the back door.

"I can't see him, Mama," Dorothy reported, as the hunting party approached.

"Well, I guess we'll know soon enough, Della," the doctor grumbled. "They'll be here in a couple of minutes."

* * *

"Hoyt's not with them, Mama," Nellie confirmed, as the group entered the back yard.

"Well gentlemen, it would appear your quest was unsuccessful," the doctor said, as the group approached the porch.

"Yeah, we hit a bit of a snag, Doc," Dad replied. "It's certainly comforting to see you here. I hope you brought your doctoring gear."

"I never leave home without it, Dave," the doctor replied. "What's the problem?"

"My deputy here took a bullet in the left arm," the sheriff said, motioning for his deputy to come forward. "It went through clean, but he's bleeding pretty heavy."

"I think we can handle that without any problem," the doctor replied. "Cowboy, how about grabbing my bag out of the back seat of my car?"

"I'll be right back," Cowboy replied, heading around the side of the house in a brisk walk.

"Dave, where is Hoyt?" Mama asked nervously, looking Dad directly in the face. "I haven't seen him since you guys left."

"Dell, I gave that boy strict orders to come right home!" Dad answered, with frustration showing on his face. "Where in tarnation could he have gone anyway? This complicates things even more than they already are."

"Oh God, Dave—if that bunch of trash hurts my boy!"

"Now, Dell, don't go jumping to conclusions here," Dad said, taking Mother in his arms. "We've got enough problems without adding anything to it! The boy has probably just wandered off. We've got enough people here—we'll spread out and find him, but let's wait for Doc to patch this old boy up before we say anything."

"Okay, but as soon as he finishes, I want every grown-up in this house out looking for Hoyt!"

"You can count on it, Mama; I'm certain they'll all want to help," Dad said, taking Mama by the hand and heading toward the kitchen.

"Hey I'd better get busy and get the doctor some water on to heat. Dave, tell him to use our room if he needs to lay his patient down. That bed in there is higher and he won't have to stoop as much."

"I can certainly appreciate that, good lady," said the doctor suddenly appearing in the kitchen doorway with his medical bag. "This old back doesn't stoop nearly as well as it used to."

"I'm putting some water on to heat right now, Doc. Do you think this one pot full will be enough?"

"That should be plenty, Della. I think all I'll need to do is wash the wound up and bandage it. Have you told Dave about the boy yet?" the doctor asked, setting his medical bag on the table.

"Yeah, she just told me, Doc. That knot head—when we find him I'm liable to make him wish he'd have done what I told him."

"Dave, that will definitely be your prerogative, but from a medical viewpoint—I'd like to caution you—don't be too hasty with the chastisement. Sometimes the connection between children and their pets can be unbelievably strong, and a painful separation can do them grave harm. That's when they need full understanding from their loved ones."

"Doc, as you well know, Dave and I are both uneducated and there are a lot of things we don't understand. We need you to tell us a little more about what it is you're cautioning us against. We certainly don't want Hoyt to come to harm out of our own ignorance."

"Yeah, but we don't want him running his own show neither!" Dad replied, with a stern parental look on his face. "Children will take unfair advantage if you allow it."

"I understand your reservations, Dave, and I thoroughly agree. Children must have proper parental guidance, but on the other hand, you certainly don't want Hoyt to fall into the category I'm talking about—watching a child waste away when there's nothing physically wrong with them is one of the most devastating things a parent can endure. There have been cases in history involving children and animals that started out just as innocent as this that turned into problems no doctor could possibly treat."

"Oh my gosh, Doc Cedric—That is scary!" Mama said, with uncertainty showing in her eyes. "We need advice on how to handle this—It's seems awfully complicated."

"It is complicated, Della; that's why I'm warning you folks up front. Children and animals have a special connection that is not well understood. I need to be getting back in there to my patient, but I'll tell you of this one incident that I personally know about; a friend of mine was involved in trying to treat it. A 9 year old girl had a Shetland pony, and when the pony got pneumonia and died the girl went into a state of psychological trauma, and nothing my doctor friend or the girl's parents could say or do could turn her around. All she wanted to do was sleep because she dreamed about her pony. It seemed she just couldn't deal with the harshness of reality. Children can be very resilient in some cases, but when it becomes a thing of the heart and mind—you'd better watch out. If the attachment is strong enough it can overpower the child's will to live. That's what I'm fearful of, Dave; Hoyt and that dog are soul mates. There's an unbelievable bond between them."

"There's no doubt about that," Dad replied, shaking his head. "Now I'm starting to understand where you're coming from, Doc. By the way, what happened to the little girl in the pony case?"

"Well, after about a month of almost constant sleep her internal organs began shutting down and she lapsed into full coma—she only lived about another month. In essence, the shock of losing that little pony caused her to lose her grip on life, and no one knew how to help her—we still don't!"

"Oh my God, doctor, that is so horrible," Mother gasped, putting both hands up to her face.

"Yeah, that throws a whole new light on the subject," Dad conceded, putting his arm around Mama's shoulders.

"What should we do, Doctor?" Mama begged, with tears starting to run between her fingers—"I'm so scared!"

"Well, we've got to find the boy first; then we'll just have to play it by ear—making every effort to get his dog back as quickly as we can is what needs to happen."

"Doc, we're going to let you call all the shots from here on out!" Daddy stated, shaking his head. "We don't want to do anything that's going to jeopardize our boy's life."

"Della, as soon as that water boils a couple of minutes, call me. I'm going to take your advice and put the patient in your bedroom."

"I'll go clear off the night stand so you'll have a place to work from," Mama said.

As Mama passed through the living room among the guys, Sheriff Dan was just standing up to address the posse.

"Boys, up until now, the Sloyds were only wanted for destruction of property and vandalism, but the intense hail of lead we ran into down in the woods there awhile ago has changed things—attempted murder of police officers is now the charge. We were very lucky to get out of that ambush without loss of life. They were trying to kill us, gentlemen, there's no doubt about it. Tomorrow morning we're going to start this hunt all over, and we're going to chase those bums right to where they're holed up."

"But even with the dog, Dan, we're only going to be able to follow one of them at a time, while all the others get away," said Cowboy.

"Well, they can confuse the issue a little by splitting up like they did today," said the Sheriff, "but in the end we're going to hunt them all down; it's just of a matter of time."

"Following one of them is probably as good as following them all," Dad suggested, as he entered the room. "If I don't miss my guess they'll all end up at the same place."

"Yeah, you're right, Dave." Cowboy admitted, with an embarrassed grin. "I guess I'm just in too big a hurry to nail those rats. They're all going to be heading back to their secret hole in the ground wherever that is."

"That's the only place they've got to go boys," said the sheriff. "All we have to do is find that secret spot and the game is over. Nobody in these parts will hide them or give them aid."

"Sheriff, if you don't mind, I've got something very urgent I need to talk to everyone about," Dad said, walking towards the front of the room. "As all of you know, Hoyt was supposed to come straight home from the creek. Well, he didn't, and he's still gone, and Dell is fit to be tied. There's a good probability he's just gone off on his own hunting for his dog, but there's also an outside chance that the Sloyds have had something to do with his disappearance. At any rate as soon as the doc gets our buddy in there patched up I would like to solicit all your help in finding our boy."

"I don't believe there's a man here that doesn't feel this takes top priority, Dell," Dan said, standing up and looking around the room— "right Men?"

Instantly the room was alive with positive reinforcement from everyone.

"I need that water now, Dell," said the doctor making his way through the crowd to the kitchen. "I'll have this job finished in 10 or 15 minutes, and we can hunt up your boy."

"Thank you Doc, and I'd like to thank all you other guys too," Mama said. "Without your help right now our family would be devastated. Facing something like this alone is unthinkable."

"That's what neighbors are for, Dell," Maxy reminded; "it's our duty to help each other."

"Folks, I'm going to go get Waldo while Deputy Anderson is getting patched up," said the sheriff. "Wherever your boy is, Dell, Waldo can find him. Franks—you stay here and keep your eye on things. I'll be back just as soon as I can."

As Big Dan made his exit and Doctor Cedric began treating the wounded officer, Mother turned back into her kitchen and began building up the fire in the cook stove.

"Girls, run to the root cellar and get us a big batch of potatoes, and a half dozen parsnips—oh yes, and a half dozen yams too. We need to get started feeding these people. When Dan gets back they need to be ready to perform. Your brother's life could depend on it. Bring a couple of big onions and a few cloves of garlic too."

* * *

Within the hour, Dan was back, and Mama had only his very large appetite to contend with. Soon the whole gang was standing outside ready to start the hunt.

"Boys, I want you to spread out over this whole area leading down to the creek and look for any type of sign that Hoyt may have been there," Dan instructed. "Be careful and have your weapons ready. We don't know yet just what to make of this whole thing, but we do know there's a plucky little boy lost out here, and it's up to us to find him. Dave, I'd like for you to show me and Waldo exactly where you last saw Hoyt, but before we go I'm going to need something of Hoyt's that has his scent on it."

"How about his pillowcase?" Mother suggested.

"That's an excellent choice, Dell," Dan answered. "That should have only his odor on it."

In seconds, Mother was back with the folded up pillowcase and Dan was tucking it into his back pocket. "Okay, gentlemen, let's get on with the process. If anyone finds anything—call out—otherwise, we'll all meet at the bottom of the hill and put Waldo on the trail."

It didn't take long until the guys had covered their respective areas and were arriving at the creek—all with negative reports. "Well boys, I guess it's up to Waldo now," said the sheriff, taking the pillowcase out of his pocket and holding it out to the bloodhound.

Waldo began shoving his oversized nose into the crumpled up pillowcase almost like it was something alive—shoving against it and drawing in large breaths of air. After he was satisfied with his odor collection, he let out a couple of low soft rumbles from deep in his chest and began to scour the area that Dad had pointed out. In a few seconds he headed up the hill meandering back and forth a few yards this way and that but always returning back to the well used trail in a slow meticulous search.

"It would appear he's heading straight back to the house," Deputy Anderson said, as he trudged along behind the sheriff and Waldo, wearing a brand new pillowcase sling on his arm.

"Yeah, or the barn," the Sheriff replied. "Sometimes finding a kid is really hard because of their hyperactive nature, but Waldo will find him wherever he went. It's just going to take a little while."

"I just wonder if he could be hiding out in the house somewhere," Dad pondered. "He was really frustrated at me for making him stay home!"

A FUR COAT FOR MAMA

"Hey, I bet that's it, Dave," Ike speculated. "He's probably mad at you, and he's off sulking somewhere. He does consider Old Trailer his next of kin—you know."

"Yeah, I should have let him go with us," Dad answered, shaking his head. "That's what complicated this whole affair! He and that dog are inseparable, and I ignorantly separated them."

"Dave, don't be too rough on yourself," said the doctor, struggling along a step or two behind Dad and the others. "Being a parent is a tough business. You and your missus were just trying to protect the lad. Sometimes we just have to take a lesson and start over. We'll probably find him here in a little while and everything will be all right."

"I sure hope so, Doc. What bothers me is—with a little forethought, this could have all been prevented. I never once stopped to consider the boy's feelings. That dog is the center of his world."

"Yeah, hindsight is always 20-20, Dave," Doc Ced agreed. "Unfortunately, being human puts us at a slight disadvantage. We have to wait for the outcome of our actions to see if we did it right or not."

"Gentlemen, we're heading to the barn," said the Sheriff, as Old Waldo began a slow deliberate turn followed by the Sheriff and the rest of the gang. "Fellows, let's spread out a little," said the Sheriff. "If there are any of the bad boys still around here, we don't want to make easy targets for them."

"Doc, let's you and I take the side door over here," Dad suggested.

"That's a good idea Dave," Dan said, in a low voice. "Boys, some of you go around and come in the back way, and be extremely cautious with your weapons," he added as several of the guys began checking the readiness of their side arms. "I don't anticipate any problems here, but it's better to expect trouble and not have any than the other way around."

Dan, his two deputies and Old Waldo went straight through the front entrance way; Maxy, Ike and Cowboy went around and came in through the back; and Dad and the doctor entered through the side door. Soon everyone was standing in the center of the breezeway looking up at the hayloft with Waldo bellowing his low soulful bark.

"I'll check it out," said Cowboy, quickly stepping up onto the ladder leading to the loft. "There's nothing up here," he quickly reported, looking up into the upper level—"just a few tons of hay."

Suddenly, just as if Waldo had heard Cowboy's report, he lowered his head and began pulling the sheriff towards the back end of the barn.

"He was here, boys; that's a certainty," Dan said, as the 120 pound blood hound dragged him forward. "The problem with tracking kids is they leave trails over the top of trails, and it takes a dog time to sort out the new from the old. Waldo thinks he may have left heading in this direction, so let's give him every chance to prove himself. He'll eventually locate him."

"Boys, it would seem to me that all of us don't need to be following this dog," Maxy concluded, with a concerned look on his face. "In another hour it'll be getting dark. If there's any other way for the rest of us to be helping, we need to be doing it."

"I was thinking the same thing," Dad agreed. "Maybe part of us ought to go search the house and the out buildings, while the rest stay with Waldo."

"That would be fitting, gentlemen," the sheriff agreed. "This late in the day, speed is of the essence. Unfortunately, Waldo has only one gear, and that's somewhere around compound low! My deputies and I can handle this end. You boys do whatever you feel is needed. If any of us find anything we'll let everyone else know immediately—okay?—or if the trail starts to leave this area I'll let you know."

"That sounds good, Dan," Dad replied, as he and the crew started leaving the barn. "We'll keep in touch."

In the next hour Old Waldo left the barn three times checking the surrounding area only to return to the barn again, and start barking up the ladder.

"Gentlemen, we have an impasse here," Big Dan admitted, as Dad and the guys returned to the barn through the front breezeway.

"Yeah we've had the same luck," Dad said. "We've searched every nook and cranny of the house and out buildings. This is really starting to get serious."

"Especially with night coming on," the doctor added. "Even if he hasn't met foul play, just being lost in the dark is a terrible experience for a child!"

"Let's go on up to the house, fellows, and figure out what we're going to do," Dad suggested. "At least that way Dell can be a part of what we decide on."

As everyone started filing into the house through the back door Mama and the girls were busy setting up the kitchen table for a quick coffee stop.

"All you guys who want coffee, get around the table," Mama said— "looks like this is going to be a long night."

"I don't understand why Waldo can't isolate the trail," the sheriff said. "Usually with this much time he would have nailed it down easily. He seems to be hung up on the ladder leading to the loft, but we've already determined there's nothing up there."

"Girls, I want you to get your thinking caps on and try to remember if there's any place where Hoyt could be hiding," Dad said, motioning the girls over to the table. "The dog seems to think he's somewhere around the barn, but we can't find a thing."

Suddenly Dorothy's jaw dropped as she and Nellie made eye contact. "Oh my gosh, Nell!" Dorothy exclaimed. "I wonder if he could be hiding in the secret place!"

"What secret place?" Mama questioned, moving quickly toward the girls.

"We made a little room under the hay bales," Nellie volunteered.

"Yeah, we slid out four bales and used boards to hold up the other hay," Dorothy added.

"Good grief—it's a wonder that haystack didn't fall and crush the life out of you kids," Dad responded, with a shocked look on his face. "There's three tons of hay there."

"Oh, Lord, Dave, that's got to be where he is," Mama said, with renewed hope in her voice—"it's just got to be!"

"Alright, now we've got something going," said the sheriff. "That's why the dog was coming back to the ladder. He's been telling us all along that's where the boy is, but we just wouldn't accept it. Let's get all the light we can rustle up and go check out that secret spot," he said, nodding his head affirmatively at the girls.

Within minutes the search entourage was headed for the barn with a multitude of kerosene lamps, lantern and flashlights, and Mama and the girls were hurrying along out in front of the group.

* * *

Having no way to know that everyone was out looking for me, I was gloriously returning home with Old Trailer bounding along at my side. I had looked so hard all afternoon—running through woodlands and meadows calling his name with my heart in total despair then suddenly like magic—there he was—he seemed to appear out of nowhere. I fell to my knees and grabbed him around the body and we romped and loved on each other with total abandon—him licking my face and me holding on for dear life, sobbing tears of delight into his black and white coat. Suddenly I thought of the time and how late it must be getting, and I jumped to my feet and yelled, "come on boy; let's go." I knew it had taken me a lot longer to find him than I figured on, and I was really hurrying, trying to get back home as quickly as I could. We were running across a beautiful sunlit meadow with Old Trailer running along out in front of me, and I was so happy and full of joy—I had my dog back! I figured our house was probably just up over the next hill, and I was going just as fast as I could. Suddenly I began to hear voices calling to me from the distance—it sounded like Nelly, Dorothy and Mama, and I was trying really hard to hurry but something was holding me back. My leg was caught on something. All of a sudden I was thrashing around on the ground and it was all dark and Old Trailer disappeared from right out in front of me. "What's happening to me!" I cried out in despair, and

I began kicking desperately trying to free my leg. "I've got to get home; Mama will be worried!"

"Hoytie, are you in there?" I heard Nelly calling to me, then I could hear Dorothy's and Mama's voices too but they were far away in the darkness, and other people were talking.

"He's in there alright!" Daddy exclaimed, reaching through a crack between the bales. "I've got him by the foot. Boy, he's kicking like fury. Boys, let's gently start moving this hay and I'll try to pull him out."

"Mama! Mama, where are you!" I cried in desperation. "My foot is hung and I can't get loose."

"It's okay, Little Man! You're alright now," I heard Daddy's reassuring voice.

Suddenly my foot came loose and bright lights were shining in my face and I couldn't see anything, but I heard Mama's voice saying, "Oh thank God you're alright my little man."

"Mama—Mama I found Old Trailer," I cried out jubilantly. "He was right here just a minute ago. It took me all day, but I found him!"

"Oh My God, Honey," Mama sobbed, cradling my head in her arms. "You're just dreaming. Wake up Baby; please wake up!"

"Hoytie—Hoytie, wake up," Nellie repeated, putting her hands up around my face. "You've been asleep in the secret place. Everyone's been looking for you."

"No—no Sissy, I found Old Trailer. He was here just a minute ago!" I insisted fervently.

"Son, you've been asleep," Daddy said, in a stern but gentle voice. "Now, come on—wake up."

"No—Daddy, I found him; I really did," I said, as I began to sob uncontrollably

"I wish it was true, Little Buddy, but you've just been dreaming," Daddy said, starting to lift me underneath the arms. "Come on now, stand up and let's get you down this ladder and into bed."

"I don't want to go to bed!" I protested, as Daddy began walking me toward the ladder. "I want my dog."

HOYTIE'S GONE! AND DOCTOR CEDRIC'S WARNING! **191**

"Yeah I know, Little Man; we'll find him," Dad replied, turning me around to start me down the ladder. "Right now though, we've got to get you out of this loft. Here Ike, hold onto him," Dad said, to Uncle Ike standing halfway down the ladder.

"I've got him, Dave. Give me a hand here, Bud."

"I'll give him a sedative to help him settle down as soon as we get him to bed," the doctor said to Mother as they descended from the loft. "He'll probably sleep it off and be fine by morning."

CHAPTER TWENTY-ONE—Dad Locates Old Trailer and the Secret of Night Screams

I slept for the best part of two days and nights, with Mama constantly at my bedside trying to get me to eat or drink something as intermittent bouts of waking would occur. Whatever the doctor had given me really turned the lights out. On the morning of the third day I awoke to find Doctor Cedric stooping over me with his stethoscope up under my night shirt, and Mother and the girls standing around him looking down at me.

"Hey, look who's awake," said the doctor as he slid his stethoscope to the other side of my chest.

"Hi Doctor Cedric. I think I've been asleep," I said in the middle of a big yawn.

"You certainly have, and off hand, I'd say you needed it, Son. Dell, his heart is strong, and his overall condition seems to be good. I'd say all he needs is some of your good cooking and he should be as good as new."

"Well, son, if sleep was what you needed, you ought to be fit as a fiddle now," Mama stated, sitting down beside me and taking me by the hand. "You slept for two full days."

"Hi, Hoytie, how are you feeling," Nellie asked, as she and Dorothy dropped to their knees next to the bed.

"Okay, I guess, but I still feel sleepy. Sissy, has Old Trailer come home yet?" I asked hopefully.

"No, he hasn't, Son," Mama quickly interrupted, "but you just put your mind at ease now. Your dad and the guys are already planning on how to get him back. We're not going to let those thieves keep your dog."

"I dreamed about him a lot when I was asleep. I could touch him and I could pet him. It was so real, Mama! It almost makes me want to go back to sleep."

"Dell, I think you need to get this lad up and get him moving," said the doctor. "I prescribe a good breakfast then a brisk walk of a mile or two, to get his blood flowing. Maybe you young ladies could help your mama with the second part of that prescription."

"We sure can," Nellie replied enthusiastically. "Get up, Hoytie, we've got to do what the doctor says. He knows what's best."

"Come on in the kitchen, Son; Mama's going to make your favorite breakfast. How about a warm-up on your coffee there, Doc?

"I would certainly appreciate that, Della."

Within minutes, Mama had me fixed up with my favorite breakfast—one fried egg, sunny side up, sitting next to a flaky buttermilk biscuit covered in what I called thicken gravy. Mama's sweet cream gravy was a delight to my taste buds. "Dorothy, get him a glass of sweet milk," Mama said, as I slid into my favorite eating spot behind the table. "We've got to get this boy ready for the day."

"Mama, where's Daddy at?" I asked, talking around a mouthful of biscuits and gravy.

"He and the guys are with Sheriff Dan, Son. They're down at the Sloyd place with the bloodhound trying to locate their hideout."

"They're hunting for Old Trailer, Little Brother!" Nelly said, sliding in beside me on the bench. "They'll find him too; you just wait and see," she said, putting her arm around my shoulders.

"I sure hope so, Sissy," I mumbled, choking up a little. "I miss him something terrible."

"Yeah, me too," Nelly replied, hugging me a little closer. "Maybe Daddy will find him and bring him home or maybe he'll just get away from those mean people and come home by himself."

"Hurry up and eat, Hoytie," Dorothy encouraged, trying to speed up the process. "Let's go out and look around for him. Who knows, maybe he's on his way home right now and we might find him!"

"Girls, give him time to eat, please," Mother insisted. "As soon as he's finished you can have all the time you want."

"I'm sorry, Mama" Dorothy replied. "I'm just anxious to get outside."

"I know, Honey," Mama answered, "and I appreciate what you're trying to do, but we need to follow the doctor's orders. When he gets his breakfast eaten he'll be ready to go."

* * *

The next two days and nights were terrible for me because Mama and the girls were so eager to keep me occupied and not give me time to think, that they pretty much wore me out, and when night came and sleep wouldn't I was left all alone through the long hours of darkness tossing and turning with my mind locked in a never ending battle of what life was going to be like without my soul mate. Seeing daylight start all over again was almost too much for me to bear, and after the second night it was evident to Mother and the girls that their little plan wasn't working. I was visibly becoming lethargic and unresponsive to their efforts. Because of Doctor Cedric's early warning Mother and Dad had been watching me like a hawk, and when they saw the stress start building up in my face and darkness developing around my eyes they both responded as could be expected—imploring Doctor Cedric to please do something before the condition gets any worse.

"I can give him a sedative to make him sleep," said the doctor, "but as you both know that's only a temporary fix. The problem will still remain."

"My God, Dave, what are we going to do?" Mother sobbed, suddenly wiping tears with both hands. "I just can't lose my boy over a stupid thing like this. There's got to be some way to stop this nightmare."

"Folks, getting that dog back is the only sure cure for this malady," Doctor Cedric reminded, "and the quicker the better. Just as I predicted, the boy is starting to lose ground."

"I feel so damned helpless," Dad said, shaking his head and pulling Mother into his arms. "We've looked high and low for that bunch of scum, and we can't find a trace of them. They're like some kind of evil force that can reach out and touch you at any time, and you're helpless to defend yourself."

"I understand how difficult this is, Dave, but you need to understand what I'm saying too—sleep aids are for short time use only. The body quickly develops immunity to the medication, and it takes more and more to do the job—if continued, drug dependency is certain. That's no way for a person to live—especially a child."

"Then there's no choice," Dad conceded. "I'll get just as tough as it takes to find his dog. I'll take camping gear and food and go down there and just stay with it until I locate where they are."

"It's pretty obvious they're only moving around at night," said the doctor. "In reality that's the only time you would need to be there, Dave. You could stay at home and rest through the day and slip off down there when it gets dark."

"That sounds like the commonsense thing to do, Dave," Mother agreed, looking seriously into Dad's eyes. "We don't want to make this thing harder than it already is."

"Yeah, I understand where you're both coming from, but being rational and doing the expected has gotten us where we are right now. No—what I'm going to do now is the unexpected! I'm going down there and sit right on top of those bastards until I locate them—and God help them when I do! They're going to learn the hard way—they shouldn't have messed with my family!"

"All I'm going to say, Husband, is—you've got to live through what happens down there, and then carry on afterwards, and I'm counting on you to come back to us the same man you are right now. Use that good family man brain you've got and everything will be alright."

"I'll be doing my best. This mission is starting right now. Dell, only in an extreme emergency do I want anyone to know where I'm at. Now, let's start getting me some gear and food stuff together. We'll have to keep it light enough for me to pack. I'll cut across the pasture land to the bottoms and get me a lean-to set up before dark."

"Dave, I'll hang around here and keep an eye on the boy for a couple more days, but by Friday I've got to be back in Reveille. I'd sure like to see you back here with that dog before I have to leave."

"If it's within my power, Doc, you can count on it."

In two hour's time Mama was loading Daddy up with everything they could think of that he absolutely had to have and getting him ready to leave.

"You did put in those extra flashlight batteries, didn't you?" Dad questioned. "That's the one thing I can't possibly do without."

"Yes, and I put that other partial box of Winchester shells in too," Mother replied. "I want you to be safe and come back home to us. Life without you or the children would be unthinkable for me."

"That's exactly how I feel," Dad answered, taking Mother in his arms. "All we have in this world is each other and our family—I'll be damned if I'm going to let that low life bunch of thugs take it away from us. If they want to play hard nosed games, I'll get right down to where they live."

"The kids are in all in Hoyt's room playing Jacks," Mama said. "The girls are really trying to keep him busy."

"Well, you tell them all bye and hug them for me," Dad suggested. "I can't stoop over with this pack on anyway. Doc, you can never know how much we appreciate your knowledge and medical understanding. Without you helping us we would've been beaten already."

"Dave, that little boy we're conspiring to help is one of my favorite people. He needs to grow up to be a fine strong man like his daddy, and I'm very committed to that end," said the doctor, nodding his head and reaching for Dad's hand. "Good luck my friend and Godspeed."

"Thank you Doc. I hope to be seeing you both again real soon."

The old Sloyd home place was a bit of a shock to Dad, as he poked his head out of the woods for a look around. "Good Lord!" he uttered in disgust. "I just can't understand people who would drop out of life and allow a fine old place like this to go to ruin—what a waste!"

He had crossed Sugar Creek down at the Bentley bottoms and came in on the backside of the Sloyd farmland which was now grown up in saplings as big as your arm and covered in possum grape and black-berry vines. There was an eerie silence over the old house and out buildings as the long shadows of evening were starting to settle in. The barn, which had only about half of the roof left, was some 50 yards away standing stark against the adjoining forest. "What a sadness there is here," Dad thought, as he walked past the large ramshackle house toward the barn.

In the next two hours he was busily engaged in building himself a shelter to protect him from summer thunderstorms and a place up off the ground to sleep. He had brought his best hatchet and half a roll of binding twine to aid in the chore. He selected a spot out in the edge of the forest just far enough that he couldn't be easily seen from the house area, but still within earshot. First he went about gathering all the dry poles he could find that were about the right length or that needed only a little trimming, then he began lashing them together against a large oak tree to build a bench about four feet wide and three feet high. After the bench was finished he started tying more poles together to form panels to make the ends, back and front of the shelter which he covered with green cedar boughs and lashed them together. He covered the shed type roof with a double thickness of boughs to make it shed water. He also put a thick layer on the bed area to make it comfortable. The front part was fitted with binding twine hinges where it could be lifted up for entrance and exit. With that done he stepped back and said, "There—if I do get a chance to do any sleeping the bugs and snakes aren't as likely to cause me a problem. Right now though, I need to check my guns and get my lights ready to do what I came here for. This is going to be a long night."

With his hunting knife and his .38 special strapped on and carrying his Winchester rifle, Dad began slowly moving around from one location to another, standing quietly in the darkness and listening for long periods of time for sounds that might betray the whereabouts of his quarry. Since he didn't know the terrain, he re-traced his footsteps a lot, making sure he didn't lose track of exactly where he was in relation to his shelter. He was used to being in the woods at night, possum and coon hunting so he wasn't afraid of getting lost, but the time element was critical and he didn't want to lose time searching the same areas. "This hunt can't end in failure like some of my other hunts," He mumbled to himself, as he went about his unpleasant task. "No matter how long it takes or how hard it is. I'm staying right here until I get that dog back."

Along towards midnight a thunder storm blew in over the area, and Dad was forced to hurry back to his shelter for about two hours while Mother Nature dropped about a half inch of rain in a sudden downpour. "Well, there's one thing I can say for sure," he said, shining his flashlight around inside the shelter—"it's watertight, and it's quite comfortable," he added, stretching the full length of his body out. "Man, I didn't know how tired I was," he thought, with a big yawn. "Maybe I'll sleep for a couple of hours, then get up and go out again."

Within minutes he was dead to the world and remained so until the storm had completely blown past.

Suddenly he sat straight up in bed and grabbed his pistol out of the holster as the garbled sounds of people talking seemed to be coming from all around him. He laid there as quiet as a mouse with his pistol cocked and his heart racing, expecting at any time to be called upon to come out, or have a shotgun blast rip through his shelter, but as a minute passed then two—and still nothing happened he began to wonder if it had just been his imagination. "Man, that was strange," he thought, shaking his head. "I could have sworn there were people out there. I've got to get hold of myself!" he thought, lowering the hammer on his gun and sliding it back into its holster.

Being fully awake and a little bit rattled, he decided it was time he got back on the job, so he gently pulled aside the cedar branches and stuck his head out. "There's definitely nobody out here," he mumbled, peering around in the darkness. "Man, that's the weirdest thing I've ever done!"

He knew the creek had to be off to the right of his shelter about a hundred yards, so he decided to use a trail he had found earlier and see if it would take him down to it. That way he would know one of the outside boundaries of the Sloyds' property. He had ventured only about 50 yards when he became aware of a soft whining noise coming from somewhere. At first he just dismissed it as probably the wind in the trees, but as he got closer to a large oak standing near the side of the trail the noise began to intensify and take on the definite sound of a woman crying. "Good grief—what in tarnation is that?" he asked, under his breath, as he came closer to the big tree. "This has got to be what Maxy's sister has been telling everyone about," he thought to himself, looking the old oak over with his flashlight. Could there possibly be a real person connected to this somehow? he pondered. "Naw—surely not!" he thought—not out here in the middle of the forest at this time of night. On second thought, if there was a real person involved—where are they, and what's this oak tree got to do with it? "Man, it darned sure sounds real to me," he said, shaking his head in disbelief, as the soft tones became a bit stronger. "Maybe I'm finally meeting my first spook, or maybe I've found the world's only haunted tree. Whatever it is, it's sure got the short hairs on the back of my neck standing up."

The soft weeping sound seemed to be centered around the oak tree, yet when he would put his ear up close he couldn't hear anything at all. "That's a strange one," he thought, backing off some 20 feet and shining his light upwards along the trunk. "Out here I can hear it but not up close. Hey, it would appear that noise is coming out of that broken off hollow limb up there. I just wonder if I could climb up there and

A FUR COAT FOR MAMA

have a look. I don't know though that's got to be ten or twelve feet, and there are no other limbs around it to hold onto. "Maybe when it gets daylight I'll give it a try. Right now though I'm looking for a little boy's dog, so I'm just going to slip quietly on down this trail and keep my eyes and ears open."

As he made his way cautiously along the creek bank, at times he could still hear the weeping sound, and once he even thought he heard the garbled speech again, but it sounded like it was coming from the bamboo thicket across the creek. "This is getting me nowhere," he commented to himself, stopping and shining his light around. "What I need is to find something concrete—something that will betray their little secret and help me locate the entrance to their bunker. Maybe when daylight gets here I'll have better luck. It's probably about four in the morning," he mumbled, looking at the dim glow on the horizon to the east. "I think I'll go back and get a little rest and think things over. Maybe there's something I'm overlooking. Right now I'm too tired to even think."

Dad noticed the oak tree had fallen silent as he passed by on his way back to his shelter. "Well, I guess even spooks need to rest sometime," he commented, quietly. Passing the old tree even without the eerie sound was still an unsettling experience; there was a dark secret centered there and Dad didn't like things he couldn't understand.

The comfort of the shelter was even more endearing this time as he went about settling in. The fresh earthy smell of the cedar boughs and the softness of his sleeping covers made him feel like a field mouse tucked away in a fur lined burrow somewhere deep beneath the earth. Within minutes all the cares of the day as well as all the hard thinking he was planning to do were history, being left to a day that had run out of time. Unfortunately some days just won't give it up because somewhere in the wee hours of morning the tranquil scene was disturbed and the cares of yesterday came rushing back again. "Now, wait just a dad-burned minute here," he said, grabbing his pistol again. "I'm positive I heard voices that time and they're coming out of this danged oak tree," he said, illuminating the huge trunk with his flashlight. "What kind of

DAD LOCATES OLD TRAILER AND THE SECRET OF NIGHT SCREAMS

damned forest is this anyway?" he questioned, as more garbled verbiage began coming from within the tree. Suddenly a familiar voice rang out, and Dad's heart leaped with joy. "Now that answers a lot of questions," he said to himself as the sounds continued to emanate from the tree trunk. "That's just the break I was hoping for."

* * *

"Shut that damned dog up, Wag, or I'm going to knock both your brains out," came a garbled but familiar voice.

"Well, hello there Scorpion Boys!" Dad said, with a sigh of relief. "I do believe I've found your secret place. I may have to dig you out with pick and shovel, but at least now I know where to dig!"

It couldn't have been more than an hour that Dad lay there in his comfortable spot gloating over the fact that he had made such a dynamic discovery until he started hearing vehicles coming up the dirt road from the highway. He had just managed to get out of the shelter with his Winchester when the area around the old house and barn had lights shining all over it. "Man, I wonder what's going on here?" he questioned, jacking a shell into his rifle.

"Hey, Dave, are you around here somewhere?" came the unmistakable voice of big Dan.

"Yeah, I'm right over here," Dad replied, turning his flashlight on and shining it on himself.

"Hey, there he is over there," Ike yelled—"over by that big oak."

"What's this all about, boys?" Dad hollered, as he began walking toward the group.

"My sister said there's been strange activity out here tonight," Maxy yelled. "Have you heard anything?"

"Yeah, I've heard a lot of things. Let me get on over there where you are and I'll fill you in on what I've found out."

"What are you doing down here all by yourself, Dave?" Dan questioned. "We had a tough time getting your wife to even tell us where you were."

"Yeah, that's my fault," Dad answered. "We got a little bit shook up and didn't know what else to do. The doc told us that unless we get the boy's dog back fast we were in for real trouble. He can't sleep, and he's almost stopped eating. The shock of losing his dog is about to destroy him. I just figured I'd come down here and camp on top of these damned thieves and wait for them to make a mistake."

"My Sis called me earlier in the night and said she could hear moaning and crying coming from over here. I've spent most of the night getting the crew together. Did you hear anything?"

"Yeah, I heard it too a couple of hours back—strange thing—the sound seems to be coming out of a big oak tree about fifty yards down toward the creek."

"Coming out of an oak tree!" Dan replied, a bit skeptically.

"Yeah, I know it sounds screwy, but what I've learned since then causes it to make a little more sense. I've located at least part of their hideaway from sounds that are coming out of the ground."

"Well, lay it on us Dave," Dan insisted shaking his head. "I'd certainly like to hear something in this danged case that makes some sense. Lay your gun up on the hood of my car and tell us about it."

"If my calculations are right, their bunker runs at least from that big oak where I was when you guys got here, down to the other big oak where the crying was coming from. That's at least fifty yards down towards the creek, and I wouldn't be surprised if it doesn't go all the way."

"Now, wait a minute, Dave," Dan questioned. "How do you know those points are connected? How can you be sure?"

"Well, I'll have to admit it's only speculation, but I know definitely their voices were coming from the oak tree out to the left of us here, so that places them at that location for sure. The fact that there are no outside entrances to their tunnel means only one thing to me; they have a hidden entrance somewhere that gives them access to the whole thing. I just figure wherever you hear underground noise coming up is another part of the bunker."

"Man, if that's true those bums could have stayed down there forever," said Ike—"just coming out at night to pillage and plunder. They've probably got this whole place honeycombed with tunnels."

"I would almost guarantee it," Cowboy agreed. "They've probably spent their whole no-account lives working on it."

"The best I can figure is they've targeted the large hollow oaks as vent systems and dug right on up through the center of them," Dad said. "That's the only way the trees could be picking up sound from inside the tunnel. I heard the crying noise at the one down towards the creek then later on I heard them talking, and I also heard Old Trailer barking from the one over there where I built my shelter. Both of those have big broken off hollow limbs, ten or fifteen feet up that would suffice just fine as air intakes—that's also where the sound is coming out."

"You know—that's pretty ingenious," said Maxy, with a slight chuckle. "I didn't think they were that smart."

"Yeah, me neither," Cowboy agreed. "We may have to rethink my old school chums. By using a natural part of the landscape they've eliminated the need for outside air vents that could give away their location."

"Dave, if your hypothesis is right it can mean only one thing," said the sheriff, looking sternly at the rest of the group. "The wailing noise is a real person, just like we were afraid of, and the poor wretch's only connection with the outside world has been crying out to us through the trunks of dead oak trees. God, what a horrible thing! If I ever get my hands on that bunch of scum they're dead meat."

"That also explains why the sound could never be pinpointed," Dad said. "It was coming from all over the area. There's no telling how many of these old oaks have vent holes up through them."

"Dave, I'm confident you've got this thing worked out," said the sheriff, with a positive nod of his head. "God only knows what we're going to find down there! One thing for sure though, if we want to rescue this poor wretch and not get her killed, we're going to need a foolproof plan."

"That's what I was thinking" Dad replied. "If they know they've been discovered they'll do away with her post haste and probably the dog too."

"Well, we're not going to let that happen if it's in our power," Dan replied. "What we're going to do is pull out of here and leave everything just the way it is. We want them to think they've fooled us one more time. Then I suggest we go to your house, Dave, and go through as many pots of Dell's good strong coffee as it takes to hear everybody's opinion. It's imperative we do this thing right the first time."

"Yeah it's starting to get good daylight now, so Dell will be up cooking breakfast, but I would highly suggest we all take a silent tour out to the oaks and let everybody have an understanding of as much as I've found out. The ground's good and wet so if we walk quietly it shouldn't cause any disturbance."

"That's a great idea, Dave, that way we'll all have the same thoughts," Dan replied; "that's a good first start."

After a very quiet walk along the soggy trail past the oaks in question soon the posse was headed back to the Walker house to do some heavy thinking.

* * *

"Mama, the Sheriff cars are coming back," Nellie yelled looking out the front window—"Daddy's with them too."

"Oh thank goodness," Mama said, hurrying in from the kitchen, drying her hands on her apron. "Does he look alright, sweetheart?"

"Yeah, he looks just fine, Mama," Nellie replied, as Mama and Doctor Cedric came toward the front door.

"Do you see the dog anywhere?" the doctor questioned.

"No—I don't think so," Nellie answered hesitantly. "At least I can't see him."

"That's very unfortunate," said the doctor. "I was hoping this could all start resolving itself before I had to leave. That young man in the other room could sure stand a break right now."

"Oh Lord, Doc, what's going to happen to my little boy if we can't get that dog back? We can't just drug him forever," Mama cried, as the door opened and the guys started filing in.

"Well, we didn't get the dog, but we did locate their hideout, and the dog's there," Dad said, taking Mama by the hand. "I heard him bark two or three times."

"Oh, thank goodness, at least he's alive—maybe this is the beginning of the end to this nightmare. I'm sure glad you're home safe, Dave."

"What we need now, Dell," said Sheriff Dan, "is a few cups of that hot black brain stimulator that you serve, and a little time to let it work. We've got to figure out how to go about extracting those rats from their hole without getting killed ourselves."

"If that's all you need to fix the problem," Mama said, with a slight smile, "we're in good shape. I'll put a pot on right now and keep them coming as long as needed. You fellows all take a place at the table. I'm also going to start fixing you some breakfast, and I won't take no for an answer."

"Doctor Cedric, I'm sure glad to see you're still here," said the sheriff, as the doctor took a seat at the other end of the table.

"Well, I was intending on leaving later today," said the doctor. "How can I help you?"

"As you heard Dave say, we have located the general whereabouts of the Sloyd gang, and there's likely to be people hurt before we're finished taking them into custody. As the sheriff of this county and therefore responsible for the welfare of its citizens I would sincerely like to solicit your help in the matter. The county will pay you whatever your usual fee is just to stand by and be available, but I'll warn you up front—things may get messy before this is over. We believe there is a highly traumatized female being held in bondage by the Sloyds. Is there a chance you could accommodate us?"

"I'd be proud to render assistance in any way I'm capable of, sheriff. I would very much like to see this matter resolved. I have a patient whose life may depend on it, but I'd like to remind you I'm only a general practitioner. There are things I'm not qualified to handle."

"Doctor, you're as close to what we need as there is available. If you're willing to give it a try you've got the job."

"I'll give it my best efforts then," Doc Ced agreed.

"Alright then—the first step is out of the way," said the sheriff. "Gentlemen, this investigation is now open; does anybody have a suggestion?"

"Well, it seems to me that we're still pretty much in the dark," Ike said. "Finding out where they are was a major break-through there's no doubt, but the hard questions still remain; how do we get into the bunker, and how do we protect the woman—how do we get Old Trailer out of there?"

"Yeah, that's a fact," the sheriff agreed. "All those questions have to be resolved before we make our move, but there's one thing I'm confident of gentlemen, if we all put our heads together we will come up with a solution. Does anyone else have thoughts on the subjects—like how do we get in there? What are your thoughts on it, Dave?"

"There's no doubt in my mind those two big oaks both have holes up through them that go directly into the bunker, but only by cutting them down would we be able to gain access, and they're certain to hear the commotion which takes away the element of surprise."

"It's too danged bad we can't just cut those trees down and heave about a tubful of dynamite down through each of those holes," said Cowboy. "That would settle this thing once and for all without getting ourselves killed."

"At this point in time I'm just about that frustrated," said the sheriff, shaking his head, "but all of us know we'll have to do it the hard way."

Suddenly Dorothy rushed into the kitchen and said, "Daddy, there's a man coming up the walk! I don't know who it is!" Just about that time came a loud knock at the front door.

"I'll check it out," Dad said, getting up from the table. Within minutes Daddy was back with the man in tow. "Dan, this gentleman would like to speak with you on an urgent matter."

CHAPTER TWENTY-TWO—The Sloyds Are Discovered and They Take It on the Lam

"Sheriff, you probably don't remember me, but I'm Joe Jackson. I reported my boat stolen last fall."

"Yeah, Mr. Jackson, I do remember you. I'm very sorry we weren't ever able to recover your boat."

"Well, that's what I came to talk to you about. I was almost sure the Sloyd brothers were the ones who stole it, so I've been keeping a close eye on their place. Well, this morning I finally found my boat. They had it hidden down along the edge of the creek where it borders their property."

"If you're certain it's your boat Mr. Jackson, you just go ahead and take it home."

"Thank you Sheriff, but I've already done that. The reason I'm here is because I know you're after them for all the skullduggery that's been taking place around the area, and I think I've found something that might be of interest to you."

"Here, Mr. Jackson, have a seat," Mama said, sliding another chair up to the table. "Do you drink coffee, sir?"

"No thank you ma'am, but I will have a glass of water if you don't mind."

"You were saying you may have found something I'd be interested in. Would you please elaborate on that?"

"Like I said, I've been keeping a close eye on the Sloyds' property from outside the boundaries without actually going onto their land, and this morning as I was rowing along the creek I spotted something that caught my eye. There seemed to be an awful lot of wood drifted up in one spot along their bank that just didn't look natural, so I decided I'd stop and have a look. Well, back up under the bank behind that big pile of driftwood I found my boat, but it's what else I found that I think you'd be interested in. There was a tunnel that started back under the bank beneath the roots of a huge maple tree that was quite well used—in other words if you're looking for the Sloyd boys I'd give you better than even odds that's where they're hiding out."

"Mr. Jackson, I certainly want to thank you for your conscientious effort. You have probably given me and my friends here—well, this whole community, just the break we've been looking for! If there's ever any way I can be of assistance to you, just let me know. By the way, just where is this woodpile located?"

"It's on the upper corner of their property about a hundred yards upstream from the Killian spring."

"I know right where it is, Dan," Dad spoke up. "I passed it just yesterday. It looked a little strange to me too. It's only about a half mile from the Bentley bottoms, where I crossed the creek."

"You won't have any problem finding the tunnel," Mr. Jackson said assuredly. "It's right behind that woodpile. Well, I've got to be going now. Good luck to you fellows. I hope you nail those bums. They've been a pain in the rear to this community long enough."

"We're going to give it our best try, Mr. Jackson," said the sheriff. "Thanks again for the information."

"Well now, wasn't that a timely little happening," said Ike. "Just when we were about to starting knocking ourselves out trying to figure how to get in, it was dumped right in our laps."

"Yeah," said the sheriff, with a crooked grin, "wasn't it? Your hunch about the bunker going all the way to the creek turned out to be absolute fact, Dave. Now we've got something to work with. There's a chance that if some of us guarded that tunnel and the others went up to that first Oak tree and let them know we've found them—like start sawing the tree down—they might run right out of the tunnel into our arms."

"I suppose that's a possibility," Dad replied, "but it's highly unlikely they wouldn't have more than one entrance—and there's still the woman and the dog. How do we guarantee their safety?"

"Yeah, this is still going to take some real thought," the sheriff replied, scratching his head.

"You know—that dynamite idea might not be as far fetched as it sounds," said Maxy, looking around at the other guys. "Part of us could sneak into the tunnel as far as we feel is safe and wait while the others on the outside dynamite those two oaks to open up other entrances—in the confusion the people on the inside might be able to get the woman and the dog out of harm's way. We will definitely need to coordinate our plan where we all act at the same time."

"That might be our best hope," said the sheriff. "If we can rattle them bad enough we just might be able to pull it off. Dave, what do you think?"

"That's the best options we seem to have," Dad replied. "There are no easy answers here."

"Boys, when we go into that bunker," said the sheriff, with a stern look on his face, "we're going to do whatever is needed. If they try to fight us—which they probably will—drop them in their tracks—don't take any chances!"

* * *

"Dave, there's somebody out front," Mama said, coming in from the front room. "I don't know who it is!"

"Yeah, and he's acting really funny, too," Nellie added.

Instantly the gang began scrambling to their feet and heading toward the front room, with Dad and the sheriff in the lead. "You other folks stay in the house please," Dan asserted, unsnapping his holster and closing the door behind Dad and himself.

"Sheriff Shipley, I need help!" yelled the small, balding little man.

"That's Harmon Reynolds, the Sugar Grove store owner!" Dad said. "I wonder what's happened!"

A FUR COAT FOR MAMA

"Yeah, I recognize him now," Dan replied, as the store owner finally made it to the front yard limping really bad on his right leg.

"What's wrong, Mr. Reynolds?" The sheriff questioned, reaching out to steady the distraught little man as he came stumbling up onto the porch.

"Here, sit down Harmon," Dad said, shoving a chair towards him.

"Thanks Dave," he replied, dropping his exhausted body onto the chair.

"What's wrong, Mr. Reynolds?" the sheriff repeated, anxiously. "Is there some way I can help you?"

"Give me just a minute to catch my breath, Sheriff," Harmon wheezed, breathing hard and putting his hand up around his throat. "I've got a heart condition and this has just about done me in."

"Well, everything's going to be all right now," the sheriff replied. "You take all the time you need."

"One of you girls bring Mr. Reynolds a glass of cool water," Dad said.

"I was robbed and my car stolen," the store owner finally managed to get out between long labored breaths. "I've been tied up in my store room since late yesterday evening. I finally got loose about an hour ago. Oddly enough there wasn't a soul around to help me, so I hitched a lift from the first car that came by to come in and report it. I just happened to spot your car in the front of Dave's house here."

"Let me guess—the Sloyd brothers!" the sheriff responded, with a disgusted look.

"That's exactly who it was," the store owner replied. "They took every last dollar I had, filled my car up with gas at my own pump then they tied me up and threw me into the store room. The big mean one came in just before they left and kicked me in the leg—said he never did like me even from the time he was a kid."

"Dang it, they're cutting out!" said Cowboy.

"Yeah, I was afraid of that," Dad said, shaking his head. "Somehow they figured out they'd been discovered."

"Did you hear them say anything about where they were heading?" the sheriff asked, looking intently into Harmon's face.

"I heard one of them mention—some place called Mission Point—I believe that's what they said! I was pretty shook up about that time."

"I can certainly understand that," Dan agreed. "Was there anyone else with them—possibly a woman?"

"No, I didn't see anyone," the store owner mumbled between gulps of water.

"How about a black and white dog?" Dad asked.

"Yes, they did have a dog with them. They had him muzzled, and on a leash, and the younger one was dragging him around. It was easy to tell the dog wasn't a willing participant."

"They stole my son's dog awhile back, and the boy is really taking it hard—them leaving like this is a real setback for me and my family. God only knows where they're taking that dog."

"God and Walter Cedric!" the doctor mumbled, with a sarcastic chuckle.

"What's that Doc?" Dad questioned.

"Mission Point is in Louisiana, Dave. I know right where it is. You've heard of Bayou Blanc."

"Yeah, I definitely have," Dad replied, "but what's that got to do with this?"

"Well, that's where Mission Point is—right next to Bayou Blanc, and as you probably recall that's also where our late nemesis Bojoc Breen was born and bred. Some of the worst scum in the world lives there. Hey, now I remember where I've heard the name of Sloyd before!" the doctor said, with a sour look on his face. "They're cousins of the Breens. No wonder they're such despicable rogues."

"Good Lord, what am I going to do now!" Dad said, groaning and rubbing his face—"just when I finally thought I had a break!"

"Hell, Dave, if we can find out right where they are," said Cowboy, "we'll go down there and pay them a surprise visit."

"Yeah, Louisiana isn't all that far," Ike commented.

"That's a fact, Dave, and they're not going to be expecting anyone to follow them," said Maxy. "We can be on top of them before they can get settled."

"I suppose that's a possibility, boys, but right now we need to help Dan straighten this thing out with the bunker."

"I sure would appreciate it fellows; God only knows what we're going to find in there, and it's high time we get it over with. Mister Reynolds, I'm going to give you a ride back to your store and I'll put out an all points bulletin on your vehicle, but I'll need the license number and complete identification on it before I do."

"That will be fine, sheriff," said the store owner. "If you don't mind though I think I'll have you take me home. I'm going to need some time to get over this roughing up I've taken. I live about five miles from the store."

CHAPTER TWENTY-THREE—Wahrayah and Big Dan and the Bear Trap

Within an hour an A.P.B. had been put out on the Sloyds, and the whole crew including Doc Cedric, the sheriff and his two deputies were unloaded and ready to find out what lay beneath the mystery forest on the Sloyd lands.

"Gentlemen, my deputies and I each have a backpack battery powered sealed beam hand light that will provide us ample lighting, so breaking up into three teams—each with a light of its own—would seem to be the logical thing to do."

"Dan, this is definitely your call, but I would suggest that one group of us take down that big oak and make an opening directly into the area where I heard the woman," Dad suggested, "and the other two teams go in through the tunnel. If that bunker system is really extensive it might take hours to locate her exact whereabouts. What do you think?"

"That sounds like a wise idea to me, Dave," said the sheriff. "Boys, bring those tools and follow me."

"If it's alright with you, Dan, I'll help with the tree excavation," Dad said. "I feel like I can be of more use in that respect. You're going to need some young blood in the bunker group."

"Yeah, I think I'll stay up here too and give Dave a hand," said the doctor. "If we unearth the lady in question I'll be right here to treat her. If I'm needed elsewhere send one of the boys back to fetch me."

"I'll stay up here with you boys," said Maxy, looking at Dad and Doc. "I don't do well in small dark places."

"Gentlemen, good luck to all of you," said Sheriff Dan, nodding respectfully to the tree crew. "Boys, let's get this distasteful chore over with," he said, turning to the others. "We need to get on with our lives."

"The same to all of you," Dad replied. "With good luck this should all be history in a couple of hours."

No sooner had the other guys disappeared from view down the trail than suddenly the tree crew froze in their tracks as a low mournful wail started emanating from the giant oak. "Well, there it is, boys," Dad said, as Doc and Maxy stood looking dumfounded at each other. "I'm really glad to hear that. I was afraid they would do away with her when they left."

"Holy mackerel," Maxy breathed out. "It's still hard for me to believe there's actually a real person down there."

"Well, evidently there is," said the doctor, walking up and putting his ear against the tree.

"Doc, the sound seems to be coming out of that broken off limb up there," Dad said, backing away from the tree.

"It does for a fact," the doctor replied, as both he and Maxy backed up to view the broken limb. "Dave, did you try pecking on this tree to see what would happen?"

"No I didn't, Doc. It was in the middle of the night and I wasn't actually sure if the sound was real or not—truth is, I was just a little bit spooked with the whole thing."

"Well, that's understandable; suppose we just do ourselves a little test here and see what happens," said the doctor, picking up one of the axes and using the blunt end to pound on a large root down next to the ground. Instantly the groaning stopped and there was dead silence. "Well now, I'd say we got somebody's attention wouldn't you?" About 30 seconds went by without so much as a whisper, but when the doctor began pounding on the root system of the giant tree again, suddenly there were new sounds coming from within—instead of the moaning, there was screaming and crying intermingled with words that Dad couldn't understand. *"Ayuda me—por favor—en el nombre de Dios—ayuda me. Oh Dios mio. Et me ket no le ha kah!"*

"Doc, you're the educated man here; what do you make of that?" Dad questioned, shaking his head and looking wide eyed at the doctor.

"What we have here, Dave, is a woman who is speaking part Spanish and possibly an Indian dialect thrown in for good measure," the doctor said, "and she's crying out—'Oh please help me—In the name of God please help me.'"

"Holy moley!" Maxy exclaimed, shaking his head. "This is getting more bizarre by the minute."

"Boys, how about chopping a good sized hole in this tree up here high enough that I can speak and hear through," said the doctor. "I want to try and communicate with the poor thing."

It took about 10 minutes of Dad and Maxy swinging sharp double bitted axes simultaneously into the big oak tree to open a hole large enough for the doctor's use.

"I think that will be sufficient, Gentlemen," said the doctor as he viewed the rectangular hole about 18 inches in width. "I believe I might be able to even get my head in there," said the doctor, stepping up on the root of the big tree to reach the hole. As soon as the doctor got his head inside the hole he yelled—*hola* (hello, in Spanish) and instantly the sounds of a liberated soul began to flow forth. The most pitiful crying moaning and sobbing sounds ever heard by human ears began pouring out in a very relieved heartrending female voice. *"Oh Dios Mio—Me han encontrado!"*

"Thank God they've found me"—the doctor relayed, looking back at the guys exuberantly. "She knows she's got help, boys. Now I'm going to inform her of what's happening and then we'll start sawing this tree down. *Senora—somos amigos—estamos con la policia. Vamos a sacar te por alli, pero primero vamos a cortar este arbol para tener entrada. Me puedes echucar?"*

"Si senor, te puedo eschucar bien. Por favor con prisa—no quiro morir aqui. Gracias al Dios Y gracias a ustedes tambien!" she cried.

"Yes sir; I hear you very well," the doctor repeated. "Hurry, I don't want to die down here!"

"*Senora como se llama ustead?*" (What is your name, the doctor asked.)

"*Me llamo Wahrayah.—Yo vivo en Bayou Blanc!*"

"Her name is Wahrayah—her home is in Bayou Blanc." Repeated the doctor. "Wouldn't you just know it; those degenerates brought her here then just left her down there to die!"

"Her name sounds Indian doesn't it?" Maxy commented, looking at Dad and then Dr. Cedric.

"It does," the doctor affirmed, nodding his head at Maxy. "Her voice also has an Indian accent to it. Gentlemen, let's get Wahrayah out of this mess she's in. We can talk to her later."

With those words Maxy and Dad grabbed the long crosscut saw and went to work. It took about 45 minutes of intense labor to bring the huge oak crashing to the ground, but after the dust settled, it was easy to see their objective had been reached—a large dark hole leading into the darkness below.

"Alright, now we've got access!" said the doctor, looking down through the big tree stump down into the tunnel. "Oh man, we've got something else too," he said, taking a step back from the hole."

"What is that smell?" Maxy questioned, putting his hand over his nose.

"Yeah, that's pretty rough," Dad acknowledged, moving back a ways.

"That's the smell of death gentlemen," Doc Cedric replied. "It's a terrible offense to the olfactory senses, but somehow we're going to have to deal with it."

"I'll take care of it," Dad replied, taking his big red handkerchief out and tying it loosely around his neck. "Help me get this light strapped on, and let's get that poor lady out of there."

"Dave, we've got another little problem—how are you going to get down there and not kill yourself in the process?" Maxy questioned.

"Maybe there are some roots I can hang onto," Dad said, walking around to the other side of the stump and looking down inside. "You're not going to believe this!" he remarked with a chuckle.

"What is it Dave—what do you see," Doctor Cedric questioned.

"The Scorpion Brothers threw us a curve ball," Dad said, continuing to scrutinize the dark interior. "We struck out and didn't even know it."

"Dave, what the cat hair are you talking about?" Maxy asked, walking around to where Dad was standing.

"This old tree wasn't just a vent hole; it was also a lookout where they could climb up into it and check things out. There's a ladder right down there."

"Well, now isn't that convenient," the doctor said, walking around to the viewing spot. "That's how they knew they had been discovered."

"Yeah, and that's also how they evaded the police so long. There's probably viewing spots in a lot of these old trees. From one or the other of them they could hear and see everything that was going on. They may be an ignorant bunch of clods, but when it comes to keeping a low profile they're right on top of their game. Give me a hand here, Maxy; I need a little help getting down to the top of that ladder."

"*Senores, endonde estan ustedes?*" came a weak but still hopeful voice. "*Por favor no me dejan. Quiero regressar a me familia a Bayou Blanc!*"

"What did she say, Doc?" Dad asked as he began to descend into the darkness.

"She's afraid we've forgotten about her, and she wants to go home to Bayou Blanc," the doctor explained, shaking his head.

"Tell her there's no need to worry. I'm coming to get her right now."

"*Wahrayah no tenga miedo. Un hombre bueno, nombrado David esta veniendo.*"

"*Daveed*", came an almost inaudible whisper—"*Mi salvador.*"

"Well, I'm down," Dad said, stepping off the ladder, and looking back up at the guys. "Now I'll see if I can find where she's at. Doc, how about having her make some kind of noise so I can locate her."

"Okay, Dave. *Wahrayah, hace ruido para que, David te puede encontrar.*"

Instantly Dad could tell he was some distance from where she actually was because she quickly broke out into what seemed to be an Indian chant or song. "This tunnel is running about east and west," Dad said. "The best I can tell she's probably back in the eastern part a ways; that's also the direction that bad smell seems to be coming from."

"Dave, you be real careful in there," Maxy cautioned. "When those guys found out their little safe haven had been compromised it's a good possibility they may have booby trapped it some way."

"That's a fact, Dave—keep your eyes wide open," said the doctor.

"I'll give it my best shot. If I have problems, you boys will be the first to know," he said, heading up the tunnel leading back towards the barn.

He had covered only about 50 yards back into the eastern part of the tunnel when he encountered a branch leading off to the right. "This has got to be where she is," he said, "noting the intensity and change in direction of her voice." Working his headlight all around him slowly and methodically he began to move forward, and within just a few seconds he was standing in front of two heavily barred rough wooden doors that stood side by side in the clay bank of the tunnel. He knew for certain the first one was Wahrayah's place of captivity because it had a strange, almost child-like voice emanating from behind it. Remembering the advice of his comrades about watching for booby traps he noted the area in front of the door had no foot prints and was unnecessarily smooth. "Huh—looks something like a set I would make for mink," he thought—but not as good. Picking up a large dead tree root laying back against the far wall of the tunnel, he began punching around in front of the door. Bam—instantly out of the dirt jumped a large double springed bear trap and sunk its brightly sharpened steel teeth deep into the big root. "Wow, if that was my leg I would be a very unhappy boy right now! I just wonder if there are any more of those around here," he thought, shoving the steel trap, firmly attached to the end of the big root around the area to further check it out. "I guess that was it," he mumbled heaving the big root and heavy trap to the side.

"*Es usted, Daveed?*" came the child like voice from behind the door.

"Wahrayah—it's Dave; I'm here to take you out of this terrible place," Dad said, cautiously stepping forward to remove the wooden bar.

As the door swung open the smell from inside the room was overwhelming. There in the light stood a very thin young woman about 5 feet tall with her long black hair terribly matted and tangled. Her torn one piece dress was the epitome of filth and degradation, and was stuck to her body in several places. She had her eyes closed with her hands partially covering her face. Realizing what he had done Dad quickly flashed the light to the side. There was nothing in the room but an old mattress and two or three old blankets. The humid air was heavy with the smell of mold and human feces. The room was like the rest of the tunnel Dad had seen—just a hole dug from the clay earth.

"Come on lady," Dad said, reaching out and taking her firmly by the hand. "Let's get you out of this hell-hole."

"Bobbi Jo" Wahrayah said, stopping and pointing to the other door, then putting her hand over her nose. "*Esta* muerta!"

"Yeah, I don't think we're going to be able to do anything for Bobby Jo," Dad said, taking Wahrayah's hand firmly and heading back towards the ladder. "Let's get you out of here!"

When they were about 50 feet from the ladder, Dad hollered, "boys, get ready to help us out of this stinking place!"

"You just get here," Maxy replied. "We're as ready as we'll ever get."

"Doctor, I think you need to explain the situation to her, so she understands what I'm doing." Dad said, as he and Wahrayah appeared at the foot of the ladder. "I'm going to tie my handkerchief loosely over her face to protect her eyes, and it's liable to scare her worse than she already is."

"That's good thinking, Dave," the doctor replied. "The poor child has to be terrified, and God only knows how long it's been since she's been exposed to sunlight."

It took about ten minutes for the doctor to explain the situation to Wayrayah and for the guys to get her up the ladder and seated on the big stump so the doctor could check her out, but just when they thought they had things starting to shape up a new development popped up. Suddenly from within the tunnel came a tirade of screaming and yelling with masculine voices all mixed and mingled together, and above all the noise and confusion one could make out the extreme pain conveyed in one of the individual voices.

"What the cat hair was that?" Maxy asked, looking down through the old stump.

"Gentlemen, that sounds to me like our crew," Dad replied, listening intently to the clamor taking place below.

"That's definitely them," the doctor agreed—"sounds like they've run into some serious trouble. That first yell sounded like Sheriff Dan."

"Oh my God," Dad exclaimed, "I hope he didn't step into one of those damned bear traps. Come on, Maxy," Dad said, grabbing the light. "Help me get this thing back on. We've got to get down there fast."

"Dave, I think I should be going along," the doctor stated firmly. "If somebody's hurt down there I need to be there."

"Doctor, it's a certainty we'll have to bring him out of the tunnel anyway—besides you already have a patient. We'll be back as soon as we can," Dad said, as he and Maxy descended into the tunnel.

"It sounded to me like the noise was coming from back to the right—what do you think, Dave?"

"It was definitely to the right," Dad agreed, striking out in a brisk but very cautious walk. "You walk directly behind me now," Dad cautioned. "When you guys warned about traps you had it right. There was a big double springed bear trap set in front of where I found the girl. They're not very good at trapping or I would be in bad shape right now."

"That's what you think has happened to Dan, isn't it?" Maxy stated.

"It's a very good possibility. If he stepped into one like I found, he's in bad trouble. Hey, there they are; I saw a flash of light come out somewhere down there ahead of us."

As Dad and Maxy made their way forward, suddenly they rounded a bend in the tunnel and there came their desperate friends half carrying and half dragging their ailing comrade.

"Hey boys we need your help bad," said Ike. "Our captain here has a big bear trap latched on to his ankle."

"Oh no—I was afraid of that," Dad replied soberly.

"Damn those dirty bastards," Dan groaned. "They better hope I never catch up to them. I sure wish I was out of this danged gopher tunnel."

"Just hang in there, big buddy," Dad said. "The doctor is just about two hundred yards back the way we came. We'll have you out of here before you know it, but the first thing we've got to do is remove this trap."

"Oh, I don't know about that, Dave!" Dan replied apprehensively. "It feels like those damned teeth are imbedded in my ankle bones."

"They probably are, big guy, and that's even more reason to get it off of you."

"Dave, I could take one of these other boys back to stay with the girl and bring Doc back," Maxy suggested.

"Actually that's just a waste of time, partner, because the doctor can't do anymore about getting this thing off than we can—in fact not as much. We're trappers and we understand how traps work. It's a tough situation, fellows, but we can handle it," Dad said, looking at Ike and then at Cowboy. "We'll have it off before you know it, Dan. Trying to move you with it on is going to cause you more pain and more damage."

"Let's get after it then," Dan replied. "I want out of this stinking hole."

"Cowboy, you and Ike get on either side and get set to depress the springs, and I'll handle the jaws. You deputies hold onto Dan, and stabilize him. Maxy, you can just stand by in case we need extra help. As soon as I get the jaws starting to release I want you guys to grab hold from each side and pull until the trap snaps open. I'll count to three then we'll all start the process—one—two—three!"

The process was over and done with in about ten seconds, but the large steel teeth left huge gouges in the sheriff's leg through flesh, tendon and bone.

"Well, now, that was as smooth as a calf sucking without half the bucking," Big Dan said, with a grimace, as the big trap snapped open freeing his leg. "Gentlemen, I'll express my gratitude at a later date; right now let's just get the hell out of here. You lead the way and my boys and I will be right on your heels."

"Just one more thing, Dan, and we'll get going," Dad said. "Ike, give me your big handkerchief. I'm going to tie it just below his calf to stop some of this blood loss. There, that should slow it up some. Now let's get out of here. Walk directly behind me and I'll take it at a pace you can handle. There's no telling how many of those darned traps they set."

It was a tough job getting Big Dan up that ladder with the guys pushing and pulling on him, but they finally got him out. "Oh Man, you got her!" he said, between groans, as he spotted Wayrayah seated on the stump. "Man, that takes a burden off me!"

"Now, hold still Dan, I'm going to knock that pain down a little for you," said the doctor, as he drew a syringe full of morphine. "It'll be a few seconds before it takes effect.

"It can't be too quick to suit me," said the Sheriff with a grimace "Aww—that's starting to feel better already, doctor—thank you."

"You're very welcome, Sheriff," the doctor replied. "That's a grievous wound you've sustained. Folks, let's get this man to the car as gently as possible. We've got to get him to the hospital."

Wahrayah, for the most part, had sat on the stump patiently and without too much emotion as everything was happening around her. One could tell that she was still having a problem with her eyes, but it was also obvious that she had put Dad's voice and his image together because she was watching him like a hawk—every time he moved, her eyes followed, and when everyone started leaving to go to the cars she quickly ran over and grabbed him firmly and decisively by the hand, just like he had done to her in the tunnel. "*Quiero ir con usted, Daveed*" (I want to go with you,) she said, looking hopefully up into Dad's face.

"What happening, Doc?" Dad asked, looking down at the smelly little waif clinging to his arm.

"She's insisting on going with you, Dave," the doctor explained. "It's a natural reaction. You saved her life and she feels safe with you."

"Well, I suppose that's the way I'd feel too—under the circumstances," Dad replied.

As the doctor was crawling into one of the sheriff's cars to go to the hospital, Dad was getting just a little bit nervous about what was starting to take place. "Hey Doc, what am I going to do here?" he questioned. "I can't communicate with her, and she's clinging to me like glue."

"The poor child is scared to death Dave, and you're the only one she trusts. I'd suggest you take her home and have your missus and those two lovely daughters of yours give her a bath. That and the loan of one of your daughter's clean dresses and something decent to eat would probably solve a lot of her fears. When she finds out she's among friends she'll be a different little girl—you'll see. I'll be back as soon as I get Sheriff Dan settled in, and we'll have a good talk with her."

"Dave, my office will file a missing person's report on her, and in a few days they'll contact you," the sheriff yelled, as the car carrying him and the doctor pulled away.

"You get in the backseat with the girl, Dave," said Maxy, opening the back door. "The boys and I can all fit in the front."

* * *

The next two days at the Walker house was a real ordeal for Mother. Not only did she have the worry of a sick child, but now she had another woman in the house that she couldn't communicate with that insisted on never being more than ten feet away from Dad. Mother had to make her a pallet in their bedroom to even get her to go to bed—plus she whimpered and cried so much in her sleep that neither Mother nor Dad could get any rest.

The doctor tried several times to get her to open up and talk but to no avail. He hoped to get her to talk about her family and her ordeal with the Scorpion Brothers—trying to reduce her mental anguish—but about all she would ever say was—"*Quiero ir a casa en Bayou Blanc*" (I want to go home to Bayou Blanc) in a sullen tone. It became obvious to the doctor that she was not going to cooperate with him. The second morning at the breakfast table after another sleepless night, it all started coming to a head.

"Folks, I don't know what to tell you," the doctor said, shaking his head—"this just isn't working out. She won't say anything except I want to go home. Dan said he was going to send the state Missing Person's Agency to pick her up, but she's so insecure it would probably kill her to take her away from where Dave is. I'm at my wits end on how to handle this situation."

"Well, maybe we should try to kill two birds with one stone, Doc," Dad said, in a contemplative tone.

"What do you mean, Dave?" the doctor questioned. "I need to hear what you're thinking."

"Since you say you know where those thugs have gone, why don't we get the guys together and go hunt them up; maybe we can get the boy's dog back, and take her home at the same time. That's the only way I see out of this mess."

"That's the only answer there can be, Dave," the doctor replied, nodding his head—"so far though, she won't tell me anything about her people—she's a strange one! I suppose she would tell us when we get there."

"If we start getting things together right now—at best—it's going to take us a couple of days to get everything ready to go," Dad speculated.

"I'm going to need at least that long to catch things up in Reveille and get someone to stand in for me. I can also have him check in on Hoyt every few days, but after I get that done, I'm ready to go."

"Dell, how does that sound to you?" Dad asked. "We don't have too many options here!"

"I don't see any options," Mother stated, soberly. "Right now having my family back to normal is all that matters to me, and this girl is just another millstone around our necks. For all purposes the Sloyd brothers have destroyed our family, Dave!"

CHAPTER TWENTY-FOUR—Mama Gets Mad and Dad Calls in the Crew

"Well, we are between a rock and a hard spot, Mama," Dad said, taking Mother by the hand, "but we're not licked yet."

"I've tried all my life to be a fair person," Mama said, wiping tears that quickly began flooding down her cheeks, "I've never wished trouble or bad luck on anyone in my whole life, but if I had the power to erase that bunch of bums from the face of the earth and get my family back the way it was, they would no longer exist! I'm frustrated and I'm mad," Mama said, "and I don't care who knows it!"

"Sometime life bares us to the bones, Dell," the doctor grumbled, stroking his handlebar mustache with a far away look in his eye. "You've got every right to feel the way you do. People like that need to be erased. They're an irritant that the rest of us have to put up with—like mosquitoes sucking your blood and there's nothing you can do about it! The only problem is, we don't have an eraser that will do the job," he said, in a contemplative tone.

"Dave, the life of our family has been disrupted and ruined by that bunch just because they felt like doing it! It was just a game to them!" Mama said, with a vengefully tone to her voice. "Well, I'm not willing to let them get away with it. I want my little boy back the way he was—growing up happily with his dog and his sisters. You're the only hope I have of ever having it that way again Husband," Mama said, looking up at Dad with tears streaming down her face. "So whatever it takes I want you to make it happen for me and for your family. I want you to do it as quickly as you can and get back home."

"I believe that about sums it up!" Dad said, getting up and taking Mother into his arms. "I'll find the boy's dog, Mama, whatever the cost. Doc, the quicker we start, the quicker we can head for Louisiana. Let's get the gang together."

* * *

"Dave, I hope I didn't wake you," Maxy said, as Dad opened the door in the pre-dawn light the following morning. "I've been awake most of the night thinking on the problem you've got here, and I think we need to talk it over."

"Come on in, Maxy," Dad said, swinging the door open. "The wife and I have been up most of the night too."

"Dave, the only hope I can see to end this dilemma you and Dell are caught in is to go get that dog," Maxy said, as they headed for the kitchen.

"Yeah, that's the same conclusion we've come to, Maxy. We talked to Doc about it last night and he feels the same way. We were hoping to solicit your help in getting the gang together and trying to arrange transportation for the trip. The doctor says he's going to need a couple of days to get his affairs in order, so that's sort of the time line for now."

"That sounds fine to me, and transportation is no problem. We can take my six seater Model A, and I also have a double axel trailer we can haul all our gear in. Why don't I go pick up Ike and Cowboy and let's talk it out?"

"Thanks, Maxy, I don't know what we'd do without your help; while you're doing that I'll get the wife up and she'll get breakfast going for everybody."

* * *

Within the hour the entire gang was once again gathered around Mama's kitchen table and the conversation was hot and heavy about how to take the Scorpion Brothers down and retrieve Old Trailer when a surprise visitor appeared at the front door. "Hey, are you folks up yet?" came a familiar voice followed by a determined knock.

"It's Sheriff Dan," Mama said heading for the front room.

"Hey, look who's up and around," said the doctor as Dan followed Mama into the kitchen, sporting a new pair of crutches and a walking cast.

"Yeah, I'm not moving very fast," Dan replied, with a half way grin, "but at least I'm moving."

"Sit right here, Dan," Mama said, putting another chair between Dad and the doctor.

"Man, it sure is good to be out of that bed. You never know how well off you are, gentlemen, until something like this comes your way. I'm sorry I haven't gotten back to you folks. There are a lot of things I need to catch you up on. First of all, there's now a 100 dollar reward on the head of each of the Sloyd gang, payable dead or alive. My people and the county coroner went back into the tunnel and they found the desiccated remains of Bobbi Jo Wilcox right where you told us, Dave. They also found the remains of another, as of yet, unidentified female in the same room. I am humiliated and ashamed that such a thing could happen in my jurisdiction without me suspecting anything."

"You had no way of knowing what was going on down there, Dan," Dad said.

"You did say—dead or alive—didn't you, sheriff?" Cowboy questioned, with a cold look in his eyes. "I want to make absolutely sure of that!"

"Yeah, you heard me right—dead or alive—preferably dead, for my benefit," said the sheriff, shaking his head. "That bunch of rotten thugs turned our peaceful little community into a horror story. Dave, the state people should be here tomorrow afternoon to pick up your boarder. You will receive compensation for the time she's been here, of course."

"Dan, I don't know if that's such a great idea," Dad replied. "Doc, why don't you tell Dan what you told us?"

"Sheriff, the girl's mental condition is very unstable—trying to move her right now might be a big mistake. Her only security seems to be staying close to Dave. If you take her away, God only knows what's going to happen."

"Well, what are we going to do? You folks can't keep her forever!"

"The crew and I are on the verge of going after the boy's dog, and we thought we could just take her with us."

"Could you do that?" the sheriff questioned. "That would certainly solve everybody's problem—including the state of Arkansas, but God only knows what you're going to get into down there!"

"That's where she came from," the doctor replied. "There shouldn't be any problem taking her back where she belongs."

"All right then! I'll just inform the missing persons people that the problem has been taken care of. She is now your responsibility. When are you guys figuring on taking off?"

"As soon as we can get around to it," Dad replied. "We're actually in the process of talking it out right now."

"God—I wish I could go down there with you boys," Dan said, looking down at his injured foot—"Damn those bastards anyhow. You know—for all purposes you guys are duly deputized people that could represent me and my office. You have been working on this case with me all along, and you're going after fugitives with a bounty on their head, offered by this county, so in every respect, you could be working within the framework of the law. If you want to cooperate with my office I could make out the necessary papers and have them back to you by this evening."

"Dan, next to having you go with us that would be the most helpful thing you could possibly do," Dad said. "This is a very distasteful thing for honest men to be involved in, and it would certainly give us comfort to know we're on the right side of the law."

"I will have a court order drawn up and signed naming each of you as my deputies, and naming the fugitives you are there to deal with. If there should be any authority down there—get them to sign it; that will satisfy our needs up here."

"It's my estimation that our fugitives from justice are down there specifically because there is no law presence!" Doc Ced ventured. "It's a very primitive area."

"Well, it won't hurt to have it anyway. If there is any authority, get them to verify the bodies are who they're supposed to be, and sign the court order. It will help me close the file on this terrible mess. As far as I'm concerned you can leave the scum down there. Just bring me proof they are deceased. By the way, Doctor Cedric, are you going with them?"

"I certainly am, sheriff. I'm not about to let these boys go off down there into that snake infested swamp alone—besides I know the terrain. That's where I grew up."

"Well then, do you want to be named in my bounty hunter list?" the sheriff asked.

"Absolutely, I'm their personal physician and I'm riding shotgun to boot."

"Then stand up and raise your right hand. These other boys are already sworn in. Do you swear to uphold the laws that will be named in the court order from the county of Logan and the state of Arkansas that you will be working under?

"I do," the doctor replied.

"Then you are deputized, Sir. Gentlemen, I need to be heading back. As far as I'm concerned the Sloyd gang is history. All that is needed is to finish the paperwork when you fellows get back. Be very careful; I want to see every one of you back here alive and well when this is over. Thanks for taking the girl back. That's a big help to this county."

"You're very welcome, Dan," Dad replied, as the sheriff went hobbling toward the front door. "Take care of that foot!"

CHAPTER TWENTY-FIVE—Grandpa Cedric's Sloyd Eraser and the Crew Heads for Bayou Blanc

As the planning committee continued on into the afternoon, suddenly, Doctor Cedric garnered everyone's attention with a somewhat strange statement. "Boys, I was just thinking," said the doctor, in a contemplative tone. "I've got an old Sharps rifle at home in the closet that belonged to my grandpa. It's a cartridge firing long distance buffalo gun—a .45–70 caliber, and there are two full boxes of shells still left for it. If those old shells would still be usable—well, I was just wondering what you boys would think about looking that old gun? It might be something we could use."

"I don't know, Doc," Dad, said, shaking his head. "I think you'd be asking an awful lot of ammunition that old."

"That's a certainty, Dave. They've got to be 50 or 60 years of age, but for as long as they've been in my possession I've kept them high and dry, and Granddad was a meticulous man also. That leaves me to believe they might still be alright—at least part of them."

"Man, with a gun like that, Doc, especially with a modern telescopic sight mounted on it, we might be able to deal those boys the misery without getting ourselves shot in the process," said Maxy, looking around at the other guys.

"Hey, I hold that idea in very high esteem!" Ike replied enthusiastically. "Getting shot up or killed is something I'd like to postpone if it's at all possible."

"I'm with you there, Pal," Cowboy agreed. "We're not going down there to show what nice fellows we are. If luck should smile on us and we get a chance to distance shoot that scum—I'm for it!"

"We'd have to make absolutely sure of who we're firing on," Dad declared, with a bit of uncertainty.

"Yeah, that's a fact," the doctor replied. "Once they're shot with that weapon, the deed is done, but who knows, there might be a situation come up where that old buffalo stick would be the right tool for the job."

"I've got that big pair of binoculars," Maxy proposed. "We could use those to thoroughly scope things out before we commit to action."

"Hey, I remember those glasses," Dad spoke up. "That might just give us the edge we need; those were really powerful things."

"I'll say!" Cowboy chimed in. "You can see a grasshopper munching a blade of grass a hundred yards off."

"You know, I'm beginning to feel better about your idea," Dad said, nodding his head at the doctor. "Solving this problem and being able to walk away from it is all this thing is about."

"That's an absolute fact, Dave," Maxy replied. "This fight is something that none of us want to be involved in, but it has fallen squarely on our shoulders. The biggest problem I can see with that old gun though—it was designed for open spaces. All the bayous I've ever been around were full of trees and underbrush."

"For the most part, you're right," said the doctor. "Bayou Blanc does have lots of trees and vegetation, like most bayous, but it also has plenty of open waterways where that weapon might give us the edge. It was said that in the hands of a skilled marksman a 45-70 could knock a buffalo down at up to half a mile, and that was done using regular iron sites. If we did what Maxy suggested—hey, there's no telling what we might accomplish!"

"Man, I'm already getting excited," Cowboy grinned, shaking his head. "I can't wait to see that gun!"

"Me neither," Ike spoke up. "I've always wanted to get my hands on one of those old Sharps."

"It's a big heavy thing, fellows," said the doctor. "I believe it weighs 12 or 13 pounds and it shoots a huge 500 grain bullet. Needless to say it takes a very heavy charge of black powder to move that hunk of lead."

"Small artillery is what it is," Maxy added. "I've done considerable reading on the old Sharps rifles, and the model 74 cartridge gun with rolling block action was the choice of most serious buffalo men."

"That's what Grandpa said. He also told me, you'd better be ready for a real wallop when you slip off that second trigger because it kicks like a young mule. So boys, if it does work, I'm leaving it up to you young bucks to do the shooting," said the doctor, with a sideways grin.

"Hey, if it's a gun, Bud and I will shoot it, won't we?"

"You know we will!" Cowboy replied, enthusiastically, "especially if it's aimed at one of the Scorpion Brothers."

"Grandpa said shooting that old rifle was an unbelievable experience," Doc Cedric mumbled with a bit of nostalgia in his voice.

"How's that Doc?" Dad questioned. "What do you mean—unbelievable?"

"Well, he said you could make your shot—stand up and brush the dirt off your clothes—and use the gun to lean on and still have time to watch the buffalo fall, over on the next ridge—that is, if you hit him!"

"Holy mackerel," Ike breathed out with a soft chuckle. "I'd sure like to see one of those old guns in action!"

"Hey, if it turns out those shells will fire, we can use a shotgun stock shoulder protector to help reduce some of the recoil—maybe even by half," Dad said. "Boys, we may have found ourselves a new gimmick of our own!"

"Yeah, a Sloyd eraser," said the doctor, catching Mother's eye with a sly grin. "I guess that's it then," the doctor concluded, looking around at the rest of the gang. "The whole thing hinges on whether those old shells will fire. How about we all meet back here tomorrow morning around nine o'clock and I'll bring the gun by. If it's usable, I'll run on into Boonville and pick up the heaviest shoulder guard they have at the hardware store, and I'll also check out what they might have in the line of optical sights. I've got to make some arrangements with a Doctor friend of mine there anyway, so I'll take care of everything at the same time."

"That sounds like a winner to me, Doc," Dad said. "What about you other boys?"

"Oh yeah!" Maxy agreed heartily "Now that we know what we've got to do; I'm for getting it done the best way we can."

Cowboy and Ike instantly added their blessing to the plan, and suddenly the buffalo gun issue was put on hold until the next day, and the doctor stood up and said, "Boys, I've got to be getting on home—I've got things to do."

"Yeah me too," said Maxy. "I promised to take June to the Market to get a big bill of groceries this afternoon. I'll see all of you in the morning."

"Holy cow, I can hardly wait for tomorrow to get here now," said Ike, with a lusty chuckle.

"Yeah, that's the way I feel too," Cowboy professed, as Maxy passed by on his way out.

"You guys may not be so chipper about the whole thing by this time tomorrow," said Maxy, leaving the boys with a little touch of sarcasm. "What I've read about those old guns says they're just about as brutal on the rear end as they are on the front!"

* * *

The next morning about seven o'clock the gang started filtering into Mama's kitchen for their morning coffee ritual. First it was Cowboy and Ike showing up just after Mother had her first pot ready, then Maxy came in about 7:30 and joined the group. As 9:30 and then 10:00 rolled around the whole group was starting to get fidgety—wondering what had happened to the doctor. Finally about 10:30 the good doctor's Model A came pulling up into the drive.

"It's about time that old scamp got here," Mama said, as the whole crew started getting up to go greet the doctor. "You guys just stay put," Mama said, motioning with her hand. "He's coming up the sidewalk right now. Well, it looks like he brought that old gun you guys are all dying to see."

"Hot dang, I'm finally going to see a buffalo gun," Ike said. "It's been a long time coming."

"I'll bring him on in," said Mama, heading for the door. "Doc Ced, where in the cat hair have you been?" Mama scolded. "You've had all these knot heads hanging around here underfoot since 7:00 this morning."

"My apologies sweet lady. I got hung up on the telephone, but I think in the long run it'll all be worth it," he said, reaching out to give Mama a one armed hug. "Well, boys, there she is," said the doctor, holding up a large hexagon barreled rifle with an oversized hammer—"the famous Scepter of the Plains. The 45-70 rolling block action buffalo gun."

"Hot damn, Doc, let me look at her first," said Cowboy, reaching toward the doctor. "These other guys can see it later!"

"Hey, you bum—who elected you president?" Ike protested, as Cowboy took possession of the big gun.

"Gentlemen, I'm sorry I'm late. I was on the phone longer than I meant to be, but I think I've turned up something really worth while," said the doctor.

"Tell us about it, Doc," Dad insisted, as Mama began pouring the doctor a large mug.

"Well, I had a brilliant idea last night while I was trying to go to sleep," said the doctor, raising the steaming mug to his lips. "I happened to remember an old friend of mine that I hadn't seen in about 20 years, and it flashed through my mind that he was a collector of ancient guns. Well, this morning as soon as I got up and around, I chased him down in the Booneville phone directory and we had us a long chat. I'm on my way up there right now. I'm taking both boxes of those old cartridges, and he's going to outfit them with brand-new caps and load them up with modern smokeless powder. Not only is he a dealer and collector of guns, he has all the equipment to reload the old shells."

"Holy mackerel, Doc," Maxy exclaimed. "That's going to give our project a major boost!"

"You bet it is. Hey, I forgot to tell you; he also has a fine line of optical sights," said the doctor, "and he's agreed to mount whatever type we want. All we'll have to do is sight her in and we're ready for action. What we need to do right now is decide how powerful a scope to put on her and we'll be that much closer to ridding the world of some unnecessary filth."

"Doc, I would say that between you and your friend—you knowing the terrain down there and him knowing optical gun sights, you should be the ones to make that decision," said Maxy.

"That sounds like good advice to me," Dad agreed. "I've never had any dealings with optical sight before."

"That makes two of us," Ike agreed. "Hey, give me that dadburned gun, Bud! Are you going to hog it all day?" Ike protested.

* * *

Well, the doctor made his connections in Booneville with the gun dealer and his doctor friend, and in the afternoon the gang took the Scepter of the Plains out and adjusted the brand new scope down to a gnat's eyebrow. Everyone was amazed with the accuracy of the big gun, and the distance it would shoot, but they were a little put off with the recoil it had even with the best shoulder protector the doctor could find. "There's no doubt your collector friend put a bumper load of powder in those shells," Ike, said rubbing his shoulder—"she kicks like a young stallion."

"Yeah, it's a little rough, alright," said Cowboy, "but that just adds to the excitement for me!"

"Well, as far as I'm concerned you boys are the elected shooters," Maxy stated. "I'll be very happy just to stand back and watch."

"That makes two of us," Dad agreed. "I've shot a lot of guns in my day, but that one's just a little too tough for me. Boys, this chore is finished; let's store this weapon with our other gear, and get as much sleep as we can. Tomorrow, about four in the morning, we're heading for Louisiana."

CHAPTER TWENTY-SIX—Wahrayah Takes a Powder and the Ghost of the Night Appears

After another almost sleepless night of keeping a vigil on the clock and listening to Wayrayah's sleep noises, seeing 4 a.m. roll around was a definite relief for Mama as she reached over and pushed the alarm button down before it went off. "Dave, it's four o'clock," she said, gently shaking Dad to wake him up.

"Man, it seems like I haven't even been asleep!" Dad replied, yawning and rubbing his eyes.

"Yeah, I can certainly vouch for that," Mama agreed. "Sleeping in this house nowadays is just about an impossible chore. I sure hope you can make short work of this and get back home, Husband. I'm truly fearful of what's happening to us and being left alone makes it ten times worse—I'm really scared, Dave!"

"Yeah, I feel the same way, Hon," Dad said, rolling over and putting his arms around Mama. "I'll do everything in my power to find that dog and get right back. One day this will all seem like a bad dream. We'll just have to take it one day at a time. I'll get the guys up and around, if you'll wake Wayrayah and get her dressed.

* * *

All day long the voyagers rolled through lower Arkansas—entering one small town after the other—traveling through huge expanses of rolling wooded hills with small farms dotting the country side here and there. Late in the afternoon they finally crossed the Louisiana border where they promptly stopped at a small diner to get something to eat.

After having their supper they walked around the area to get some of the kinks out of their tired bodies then resumed the trip. They drove for another three hours with the intention of stopping somewhere and renting rooms for the night, but before they could find a place Wahrayah showed them just how uncooperative she could really be. She asked to stop along the road side in a wooded area that Doctor Cedric determined was the beginning of the Bayou Blanc marsh system. The crew just figured she needed a private moment, but after 15 minutes had passed they decided she was taking entirely too long and went looking for her—only to find that she had vacated the area. For the next two and a half hour the crew did a frustrated mind boggling search of the whole area but to no avail. Finally after regrouping back at the rig they decided there was nothing else they could do but leave her behind.

* * *

As the vehicle continued on into the Louisiana darkness with everybody airing their frustration over losing the girl and what they could possibly have done, suddenly another startling event brought the weary travelers back to full attention, as a tall dark figure went dashing across the road, 30 yards in front of them and disappeared into the underbrush. "What the holy hell was that?" Ike questioned, leaning forward from the backseat.

"Man, you've got me!" said Maxy, shaking his head and looking over at Dad. "It looked like some kind of man to me; didn't it to you, Dave?"

"It definitely looked human, but what kind of person would be out here in the middle of the night with no light? You can't see your hand in front of your face out there!"

"I think we need to check this thing out a little closer, boys," Maxy said, as he began pulling the car to the side of the road where the figure had disappeared.

"Man, that's a thicket down there!" Ike said, stepping out the back door of the car and shining his flashlight down the slope toward the marsh. "I don't know how he got through that—but he did!"

"Doctor Cedric, what do you make of what we just saw here?" Dad asked, as they all began crawling out of the car.

"Gentlemen, we are in a part of the world where strange is commonplace," the doctor replied. "There are people living in this swamp that can barely be classified as people. They know every trail in their neck of the woods just as good as the animals that live there, and when they decide to go somewhere they take the closest route, day or night. Some of them probably have never heard of a flashlight."

"You're kidding!" said Ike, with an astonished look on his face.

"No, I'm afraid not, Ike. Some residents of this swamp are unbelievably backward. They live in small groups here and there, and some of them have virtually no contact with the outside world."

"So, you figure this was probably just some local resident then—huh Doc?" Dad questioned, searching the doctor's face for answers.

"Well, I'll have to admit that was a bit strange even for here, Dave, but I can't think of any other reason he would be out here in the dark unless he was going somewhere."

"It's for certain he had to know exactly where he was heading," said Cowboy. "He didn't waste any time getting gone."

"Yeah, and he didn't even take time to acknowledge we existed," Ike replied, shaking his head.

"I guess that's what's bothering me about the whole thing," Dad pondered, removing his hat and rubbing his forehead. "Although it certainly appeared to be human, its actions were strange; that's a bit unsettling to me!"

"Yeah, I definitely understand where you're coming from there, Dave," Maxy agreed. "If that's the norm down here, we're in big trouble!"

"I highly recommend we keep our eyes peeled and get moving," said the doctor. "This whole trip is starting to take on a strange feeling. Having that Indian girl run off from us like that really bothers me. I guess she was just too rattled to understand what was going on. I wonder where that poor thing is going to end up."

"It's a heart wrenching situation, Doc," Dad acknowledged, "We did everything we could though—for whatever reason, she didn't want us to find her."

"Yeah I know, Dave; It's pretty obvious she had us stop for that very purpose—the question is why? We can't be that far from Mission Point."

"Maybe that's it, Doc," said Maxy. "Maybe she knew where she was, and for some reason she wanted to go home on her own. What she went through was a terribly humiliating ordeal. Maybe she wanted to explain it to her people in her own way."

"I suppose we'll never know," the doctor mumbled. "There's one thing I know for sure though—stomping through that dadburned swamp for two hours hunting her sure tuckered me out."

"Oh well, I guess we might as well load back up," said Maxy. "Standing out here in the middle of the boondocks is certainly not getting us anywhere."

"Yeah, we need to get to some kind of civilization where we can rent a place for the night," Dad said. "Maybe all of this will look better in the morning."

"Boy, I sure hope so," Maxy said. "What I've seen so far hasn't impressed me much."

Within the space of another 30 minutes—after packing themselves back into the vehicle, suddenly Maxy leaned forward and peered intently into the darkness.

"Boys, I think we're coming up on something here."

"Yeah, I see it too," Dad acknowledged. "The moonlight is finally punching a hole in this bushy timber we've been running under.

"Possum grapevines," said the doctor, with a bit of nostalgia in his voice. "When you get close to the bayou like this they grow over the top of everything. They can be a real pain, but in the late fall when they're dead ripe those little black clusters are sure delightful to encounter— they make awesome jelly too."

"It feel's just like you're in a jungle," Ike volunteered. "It's darker than the inside of a cow's belly.

"There should be signs at a crossroads this big," Maxy suggested, as the vehicle rolled out of the wild grape jungle into the bright moonlight.

"Okay—now were getting somewhere!" Doc exclaimed, as a large road sign started coming into view. "Mission Point—Bayou Blanc. There it is, gentlemen. Take the right turn, Maxy, and I believe it's only two or three miles down to the Point, right next to the bayou. I haven't been there in many years, but it's a better than average chance they'll have some kind of cabins for rent."

"What about Bayou Blanc, Doc? Isn't that where we're going?" Cowboy questioned.

"It actually is, Cowboy, but we won't be going out there tonight. Bayou Blanc is a huge shallow lake basin or marsh, filled with all kinds of trees and vegetation. It spreads out over half of this whole parish—hundreds of square miles. It has lots of little islands inhabited by small communities of people and a lot of waterways connecting them all. Mission Point is just the closest land based settlement to it. It gets its name from the Spanish mission that's been there since the 17th century. The Spanish people were Canary Islanders who were forced to come here by the Spanish Crown to prevent the French from claiming the land. Those poor people suffered horribly. The Spanish Government promised to give them enough money to get themselves settled, but for the most part they were just left to live or die. Unless it's changed a lot since I've been here it's a very primitive place—just the type of spot the people we're looking for would want to hide out. The marsh gets its name from the thousands of white birds that migrate in to nest here every year. Bayou Blanc means 'White Bayou.'"

"So, what you're saying here, Doc, is we're going to have to have some kind of boat to get out to where those guys are," Dad speculated.

"That's an absolute fact, Dave. We're just going to have to take this thing one little step at a time and try to figure everything out as we go. The first order of business is finding us a place to stay for the night and trying to get rested up a bit. Then we'll see what tomorrow brings."

"That sounds about right," Dad agreed. "I'm bushed!"

"Alright!" Ike exclaimed loudly, with relief in his voice. "Frenchy's—Mission Point Market and Marina, Cabins and boats for rent—full line of groceries and sundries. Hey, what's that other writing, Doc? I sure can't read that!"

"That says the same thing in Spanish, Ike. That sign is a good indication that English and Spanish are still the dominant languages here. That's great news because my French is terrible. I can read it pretty well, but speaking it is a different story."

"Hey, this is a decent sized little village," Maxy remarked. "They've got a post office and a half dozen little shops plus a general store and a gas station—not bad. That must be the cabins and the Marina off down to the left there where all the lights are. I'll bet the electric bill for all that is a pretty penny."

"If I were you Maxy, I'd pull this rig right up there in front of the store in the light where we can keep an eye on it." Doc Ced suggested. "We've got too much gear in that trailer to have it sitting out in the dark."

"I think you've got something there, Doc." Maxy replied. "We sure don't want to lose our equipment. That would defeat us before we even get started."

"Man, it's been a long time since I've been in this part of the world," the doctor said, rolling down his window and taking a long breath of the night air. "Bayous all seem to have their own distinctive sounds and smells. The smell of this one reminds me of when I used to gather eggs from Mama's hen house when I was a kid."

"You mean it's kind of foul smelling," said Ike, with a chuckle.

"It does have a distinctive bird odor, Ike," the doctor agreed. "Not enough to be offensive, but it's definitely there. The smell is the same as I remember it, but I can't ever remember the crickets and frogs being this dadburned noisy before."

"Man, they are revved up," Maxy agreed, rolling his window farther down. "Sounds like there's a jillion of them."

"Well, I've never tried me any fried crickets before," Ike said, wiping his big hand across his mouth, "but as far as I'm concerned fried bullfrog legs are some of the finest eating a man can ever set his teeth into. There can't be too many frogs to suit me."

"Yeah, there's nothing I like better than a good mess of fried frog legs," Cowboy added, smacking his lips. "In fact before we leave here, Ike, I'd almost guarantee you there's going to be a lot less croaking going on out there than there is right now."

"That's the way I figure it," Ike agreed, with a big grin—"my thoughts exactly."

"Fellows, all this chit chat about frog legs is starting to bring back some fond boyhood memories on the subject. It seems like an eternity since these old taste buds have savored that mild delicate flavor," Doc Cedric, reminisced. "I'm getting seriously hungry just thinking about it. Golden brown frog legs dipped in light garlic butter, with a side order of fried potatoes!"

"Don't forget the warm bowl of pinto beans with bacon floating on top, there Doc," Ike said, with a mischievous chuckle.

"Oh God, boys, we've got to stop this!" said the doctor, as his belly let out a noisy rumble. "I just hope this store carries an ample supply of fresh garlic."

"I think we've got the first couple of batches covered, Doc," Dad interjected. "I remember seeing the missus throwing 4 or 5 heads into our grub box."

CHAPTER TWENTY-SEVEN—New Friends and a New Home for Dad and the Crew

"Hey what's going on in there?" Maxy questioned, sticking his head out the window and looking intently at the front of the store. "Suddenly there's an awful lot a racket coming out of there!"

Instantly the big double doors flew open and three men came rushing out with burlap sacks slung over their shoulders, heading towards the marina.

"Hey boys, this doesn't look good," Dad said, in a guarded tone, as the men went running off the porch. "Those men are heavily armed!"

"You're not kidding about that, Dave!" Cowboy agreed. "They were all wearing side arms and that big chunky one had a sawed off shotgun."

"I'll have to admit they didn't look like casual shoppers!" the doctor grumbled, watching the men disappear into the night.

Just about the time the guys had it figured out there was something seriously amiss, the doors shoved open again and out stumbled a heavy set man with an apron on that promptly collapsed on the front porch.

"Doctor Cedric, it looks like you're just about to have your first patient," Maxy exclaimed. "That's probably the owner of this store, and I would say without a doubt, he has just been robbed. Let's get out there and see what we can do."

"Fellows, I'm going to strap on my pistol," Dad said, heading for the back of the trailer. "Things are moving just a little too fast here to suit me."

"Good idea, Dave!" the doctor replied. "We can't afford to take anything for granted, down here. Boys, would one of you grab my medical bag out of the trailer? I'm going to see what I can do to help this man."

"*Bandidos—bastardos,—*" (Bastards—Thieves) screamed the injured man as the crew started up onto the porch.

"*Senor no somos los bandidos,*" (We are not the bandits), said the doctor in Spanish. "Do you possibly speak English?"

"Yes, I speak English among others," the injured man groaned, slinging his head as if trying to focus his eyes. "How can a man run a business in a hellhole like this? Who are you people anyway?"

"We're from Sugar Grove, Arkansas, and we're here on business," Dr. Cedric replied.

"We're looking for the Sloyd brothers," Dad stated. "Do you know them?"

"If you're friends of those filthy pigs, get the hell off of my property!" yelled the would-be patient, flailing his big right arm and knocking the doctor backwards.

"Hey man, I'm trying to help you here," the doctor complained, trying to regain his balance.

"This is the second time this month your friends and their cousins have robbed me."

"With God as my witness sir, they are no friends of ours!" said the doctor. "I'm Dr. Walter Cedric, and as soon as my friend gets here with my medical bag I'd like to check you over before you move around too much."

"I can't see very well! It seems like my eyes don't focus right."

"That's a pretty sound indication you may have a concussion. Please stay calm and as still as you can," said the doctor. "You've got a major lump on your forehead here."

"Yeah, that fat one punched me with the stock of that shotgun he was carrying—the pig! The next time they come back, I'm going to be ready, and I'll do my level best to kill every last one of them!"

"Here you are Doc," said Ike, handing the doctor his bag.

"Okay, be as still as you can, and let me have a look at you," the doctor insisted, unzipping his big leather bag. "If we would have gotten here a few minutes sooner we'd have given you some help. In fact we'd have shot the sons a bitches dead if we would have known it was them," said the doctor, looking into the store owner's eyes with his optical light.

"That chunky one with the shotgun was old Dud, I'm almost certain," said Cowboy. "I couldn't get a good look at his face, but his movements were right."

"If you guys are from Arkansas, how do you know this bunch of trash?"

"This bunch of trash—at least the Sloyd part of it, lives only about 5 miles from where I do near Sugar Grove," Dad replied. "That's the reason we're here. We've taken all of their abuse we're going to. They've been doing the same thing to us up there as they've just done to you. We're here to see to it they don't come back to Sugar Grove no more."

"The Breens, and the Sloyds—they're cousins you know—they're the bums that just robbed me," said the store owner.

"Yeah we know; we've had dealings with the Breens too," Dad replied.

"You fellows wouldn't be the ones who nailed old Bojoc, would you? We heard someone from Sugar Grove did it!"

"We were there when it happened, but federal officers actually killed him," Dad answered.

"They couldn't have applied their efforts to a more deserving piece of crap," said the store owner. "He was the worst of the bunch. I just wish they would come on down here and finish the job. These bums have us trapped here like catfish in a barrel! I don't know what we're going to do!"

"Well, we've got to get Dave's dog back before we do anything rash," said Maxy, "but after that we intend to put an end to their lineage—at least the Sloyd part of it."

"Man, that must be some dog—to bring you guys down here in that frame of mind."

NEW FRIENDS AND A NEW HOME FOR DAD AND THE CREW

"The dog is just part of the problem, sir," Dad replied, "That bunch has disrupted my whole way of life. They attacked my wife, killed half my livestock, stole my furs, and the straw that broke the camel's back was when they took my son's dog. The boy has fallen into a deep state of depression that's threatening to take his life. He and that dog are inseparable. Unless I get the dog back I may lose the boy and the dog, all because of a bunch of degenerates that don't deserve to exist. My friends and I have come down here to do whatever it takes to solve the problem."

"I want you to come up to a sitting position, now," said the doctor, "but we're going to be helping you. Maxy, how about you get him by the other arm and we'll both lift at the same time. You don't seem to have any bleeding in your eyes, but there's a good possibility you may have suffered a skull fracture. Your eyes are a little bit dilated. You need to refrain from stooping or doing any heavy lifting for a day or two. How many fingers am I holding up?"

"I can see you've got three fingers up, but it's all blurred and I've got a terrible headache."

"Well, you've got a good reason, my friend. You took one heck of a wallop. We're going to help you stand up now," the doctor stated. "Put all the weight you can on us, and get your feet under you."

"I really don't know how to thank you folks for the kindness you're showing me. I'm ashamed of how I treated you awhile ago, but I thought you were part of that bunch of thieves. I'm the owner of this place, François Gateau. Most everybody calls me Frank or Frenchy."

"Frank, we're actually very proud to run on to you because we feel the same way about that bunch. Your enemy just happens to be our enemy. My name is Walter Cedric, and these are my good friends, Dave and Ike Walker, Cowboy James and Johnny Maxwell."

"I am so very proud to make all your acquaintances," Frank replied, shaking hands meticulously with each individual. "If there's any way I can help you boys out just let me know. If you need supplies just come on into my store and take what you want."

"We're going to be needing a lot of stuff, off and on, Frank," Dad replied, "but we'll pay for everything we get. What we need right now though is a place to stay. Your sign said you have cabins for rent. We're going to need one big enough for all of us with a place to cook, and we're probably going to need it for a month or more. As soon as we get a good night's sleep and rest up a bit we'll also need to rent two or three boats to get us out there where the Sloyds are."

"Well, the cabin and the boats won't be any problem, but finding out right where the Sloyds are hanging out, will be. The whole area back there in the south part of the Bayou is mostly riffraff and people who are too poor to get out of there. The Breens and the Sloyds have lived in that dump for generations. They're actually descendants of old time pirates that had their base of operations there—although these live in the present day, they're still what they've always been—thieves and murderers. Everybody there is either kin to them or afraid of them. That's the reason they've been able to do this strong arm stuff and get away with it for all these years. They do their dirty work then run back into that bucket of slime over there!"

"Isn't there any law in these parts?" Maxy inquired.

"It's at least two hundred miles to any law, and they never have enough personnel to really do anything. Twice now, they've made a token response trying to solve our problem. They seem to think they can just go over there and arrest the bad guys and the problem is solved. Both times they sent a two man team over there and both times they went and never came back. Their big power boats are now the property of the Sloyds and the Breens. That's how they're able to move around so quickly and cause the problems they do. For individuals like you to go over into that mess is suicide. The best possible advice I could give you is to forget the dog and go back home. As bad as we want to be shed of that bunch of crud I just can't stand the thought of you guys ending up like those officers!"

"Well, Frank, there's only so much abuse a man can stand for and still call himself a man," Dad replied. "We've come down here with a mission to perform, and we won't be leaving until it's finished. We have families to protect, and allowing a gang of cutthroats like this to destroy us is just not our style. If we can find out where they're hiding place is we're going to make them pay the price. If it's in our power—they won't be going back to Sugar Grove!"

"Gentlemen, I can see that you are men of conscience and integrity," Frank said, looking at each member of the group, "First of all I would like to shake your hands all over again because I already feel a common bond with you. Then I would like to assure you of just where I stand. We want to be rid of this trash so bad there's nothing in reason I won't do to assist you. I will help you any possible way I can. You're right, Dave! There's a time and a place where every decent man has to say—I've had enough—and, by God, I'm saying it!—I've had enough!" he said, with his fist clinched and his face flushing bright red. "Now it's time to do something about it. I know the people—I know the languages they speak, and I know the lay of the land. Maybe we can change things around here where decent people can finally have a life. Since there's no law hereabout, how about we become the law until this mess is cleaned up? I know a lot of other good people who will want to be a part of the action. "

"That sounds like a fine suggestion to me," Dad agreed, looking around at the other members of the crew.

Within seconds everyone had given his nod of approval to Frank's proposal, and one could tell it was a feeling of accomplishment to all.

"Gentlemen, off hand, I would say we have just formed ourselves a citizen's committee for action," said the doctor.

Suddenly, Frank jerked his head around and said, "Oh, Lord, boys—I totally forgot," and went hurrying back into the store followed by all the gang. "Swamp Rat Charlie was in the back of the store helping me restock when those thugs came in! I sure hope they didn't hurt him. Hey, Charlie, where are you? How about you fellows spread out and let's look the store over real quick. If they've injured him he could be laying anywhere. I'll check in the back room to see if he's in there"

After the gang had thoroughly checked the store over, there still wasn't any sign of anyone else.

"Well, he was back here somewhere," Frank exclaimed, as the rest of the gang walked into the storeroom.

Just as everyone was about to give up the search, suddenly back in the back of the room a head appeared above a stack of grocery boxes, and a small bearded man wearing a custom made muskrat skin cap, complete with ears, eyes and protruding front teeth, stepped out.

"Oh man, Charlie, I'm sure glad you're all right! Those thieves bashed me on the skull and stole half the stuff in my store again."

"I suppose they took all the ammunition in the whole damned place just like they did last time," said Charlie, adjusting his muskrat pelt hat with a disgruntled look on his face.

"Well, I'm sure they would have," Frank replied, "but this time I threw them a little curve; I only put half of it out. Boys, I'd like you to meet a longtime friend of mine, Charles Raton—alias, Swamp Rat Charlie. Charles is an ex school administrator that gave it all up to live in the Bayou. We've got us some new allies, Charles. These boys are from Sugar Grove, Arkansas, and they're here to nail the Sloyds and the Breens. What do you say about that?"

"I'd say they're either suicidal or just don't understand what they're up against," said Charlie, looking around a bit nonchalant at the whole gang.

"Well, we didn't figure it was going to be easy," Doctor Cedric grumbled in a low soft tone, looking straight into Charlie's eyes, "but I'll assure you of one thing, there's going to be part or all of those ruffians missing when we leave here. This is a life and death situation with us, and we're not going to be put off."

It was easy to see that the doctor's statement had a profound impact on the little man because his glib attitude suddenly disappeared and he started acting more interested in what was going on.

"Charlie, these boys are specifically here to do a job on that bunch. They're not just passing through. I've talked to them already and we're

NEW FRIENDS AND A NEW HOME FOR DAD AND THE CREW   251

going to form a citizens committee. This is the best chance we've ever had to bring some law and order to Bayou Blanc."

"Frank, you know how bad I hate that bunch, but what these guys are suggesting is just wishful thinking. Those guys over there will kill you at the drop of a hat. You saw what happened when those dumb troopers went over there!"

"Charlie, you and I both know those officers were used to handling trouble where there was law and order—with law abiding citizens. We'll be approaching the problem with full knowledge of what's going on, and we can make plans on how to handle it."

"Boys, if I thought there was a prayer of eliminating that bunch, I would be the first man to stand up and say let's get our guns," Charlie said, "but they're dug in over there like ticks on a fat hound dog's rear. It would take an army to route them out of there."

"Charlie—it's our firm intention to make certain that the five Sloyds are either dead or dying before we leave here," Dad stated flatly—"that is, if we leave here! We intend to take care of that with or without local help."

"Well now, if you boys feel that strongly you can count me in. I just don't want to be a part of some abortive attempt that's going to get a whole bunch of people killed and still leave us in the same mess—or worse! Just so you fellows know up front," Charlie declared, looking around at the group—"there's likely to be part of you guys who won't be going back to Sugar Grove! This is a tough bunch."

"We know how tough they are, Charlie," Dr. Cedric asserted. "It's them or us, now—there is no going back!"

"Charlie here is friends with the Indian tribe that lives out there on Sabo Island. Those poor people have been horribly brutalized by the Sloyds and the Breens over the years."

"Yeah and it's still going on," Charlie said adamantly. "My friend Wenoch's wife was brutally raped and murdered less than a week ago. Now he's got three little children to raise all by himself."

"Our fight is basically with the Sloyds; we intend to make sure that problem is taken care of," Dad said. "We don't know if they had any

A FUR COAT FOR MAMA

part in what happened to your friend, but they've devastated us at Sugar Grove, and now they've run off down here into the swamp to try and hide. We know of the Breens, but our first concern is with Sloyds. If the Breens want to get involved that's up to them. We're sorry to hear about your friend's wife, but maybe the children will have a better place to grow up after this is all over."

"Gentlemen, I don't think there's anything else we can accomplish here tonight," Frank said, "but tomorrow morning when the sun starts rising over Bayou Blanc this little band of malcontents right here is going to start a revolution; right now though we need to concentrate on the present. Since you fellows need a boat and also a place to stay maybe we can kill two birds with one stone. I've got a large houseboat down at the marina that I think might fit your needs, and it's yours as long as you need it."

"Man, that sounds like a deal," Dad answered, looking around at the rest of the crew.

"I'll say it does," Maxy agreed. "Is there a way we can drive our rig down there? With things the way they are, we don't want to let it out of our sight."

"You bet there is! As soon as I get this place locked up, Charlie and I will walk down in front of you, and you can follow us with your rig. Charlie, do you need anything out of the store?"

"Naw—nothing that can't wait until morning. I sure hope your guest house is open for a man without a place to sleep."

"Anytime—old friend," Frank replied. "How about you boys; do you need anything before I close up?"

"We've actually got enough food in our grub box to hold us tonight, Frank," Dad answered. "I think all we need right now is a place to lay our tired bodies down."

"Okay then, let's close this joint and take you boys down and get you settled in."

* * *

NEW FRIENDS AND A NEW HOME FOR DAD AND THE CREW 253

"Well now, wasn't that a stroke of luck," said the doctor, as everybody started piling back into the car.

"Man, I'll say, not only did we come right straight to where the bad boys were doing their thing," Maxy exclaimed, starting the engine of the car, "but we probably made friends with two of the most outstanding men in the area, and got us a place to stay at the same time. Things are definitely starting to look up."

"Okay guys, just follow us," Frank said, as he and Charlie hurried down off the porch and took the lead. "This road is a bit bumpy but it'll get us there."

The lumpy blacktop and partially gravel road wound down the hill for about 200 yards before it made a hard left and turned down along the water's edge. There were about a dozen long wooden ramps connected by walkways with lots of boats of varying sizes moored alongside, and on the adjacent side of the road were 15 or 20 cabins of various shapes and sizes. The whole area was lit up quite nicely with electrical weather resistant lamps seated on tall sturdy wooden poles at various intervals. As Frank and Charlie hurried along in front of the vehicle suddenly a large dark shape started looming up at the very end of the dock system. "There she is, boys," Frank yelled as he and Charlie trotted up onto the dock in front of the houseboat. "Just pull your rig up along side the ramp here."

"My God, boys, look at that!" Doc explained. "This is a two or three bedroom house built on the water. I wonder what kind of flotation devices there are under this thing?"

"Hey, what kind they are doesn't worry me in the least," Dad exclaimed. "I just hope they're good ones! We're not even moved in yet and already I'm starting to feel like we've found us a home."

"Hey, Dave, look at that!" said Cowboy. "See that stovepipe coming out through the roof; she's even got a wood heater."

"Yeah, there's nothing better when you're trying to settle into a new place than to get it nice and warm," Dad added.

"Warm is definitely nice, gentlemen, but that little pipe sticking out through the wall back there in the rear is the one that's got my attention," said the doctor, pointing out the car window. "That's got to be the cook stove back there, boys," said the doctor, looking at Ike and Cowboy with a contented smile. "That's where we're going to fricassee those frog legs in garlic butter. Dadburn it, I hope I don't wake up and this is all just a dream!"

"Yeah, I know what you mean Doc, this is as exciting as all get out, to me!" said Cowboy, slapping his leg with an excited grin. "I've never been on a houseboat before!"

"Okay boys, enough chit chat," Maxy snapped. "Let's take possession of this craft before our new host changes his mind. Fall out, and let's start unloading!"

"Hey Maxy, before you get out, how about pulling her up just a little more," Dad said, "we need to get the trailer right up here even with the ramp."

"Hey Bud, look at this," said Ike, shining his flashlight down under the front of the boat. "There's two big bullfrogs sitting right there; Doc, come over here!"

"Man—this is frog heaven!" said the doctor, stooping over to get a better look. "I sure hope this craft comes with two or three frog gigs thrown in."

"You boys need to keep your eyes open pretty good around here at night," said Charlie. "There's been a big bull alligator hanging around here lately. Sometimes they can be a bit unpredictable."

"Hey, Charlie, are alligators good to eat?" Cowboy asked, with a little hesitation in his voice.

"Actually they're not bad," Frank chimed in, "but you don't want to start out with a full grown one. The smaller ones are the best—nice and tender—you know."

"Well, if I had a small tender one right now," said Ike, with a big grin, "I think I could eat him like a roasting ear. My belly's stuck to my backbone!"

"Come on boys, we don't need problems with no bull alligator tonight," Dad said. "We need to be getting this trailer unloaded, and get us a fire going to warm the place up."

"There's enough wood stacked on the back porch to keep you boys for a couple of days," said Frank, "but after that you're on your own. There's a crosscut saw and some axes out on the back deck. You're welcome to use anything you can find."

"Frank, we're certainly obliged for your generosity, and we will see that you are paid in full before we leave," Dad said.

"Don't worry about it, Dave. This old boat is just sitting here needing somebody to use it. A few years ago my wife and I would stay for days at a time out on the marsh, but now we've sort of lost interest in it. You boys can just consider it your home as long as you need to. Each bedroom has its own closet and there are plenty of quilts and blankets to take care of your needs. By the way, it's powered by a four cylinder Model A car engine. It usually runs pretty good but you might need to tinker with it a little. I've got the battery out right now charging it. I'll put it back in tomorrow."

"Holy cow, Ike, it's even got a motor in it!" Cowboy said, with a wide eyed grin.

"Man, this is getting better by the minute," Ike replied, in a half whisper.

"Like I said, Frank, we are truly obliged," Dad repeated. "Doc, why don't you come with me?" Dad suggested. "Let's leave the heavy lifting to these young bucks and you and I go on in and build a fire and see where everything needs to go."

"I hear that," said the doctor, following Dad up the gangplank.

CHAPTER TWENTY-EIGHT—The Voodoo Princess and Indian Sausage

"By the way, boys, there'll be a lady swamp dweller coming in early in the morning that I want to introduce you to," said Frank. "She always ties her canoe up to the houseboat here so you won't be able to miss her. She lives about five miles out in the swamp on her own boat. She comes in to shop at the store every Thursday; she'll probably be here about six o'clock."

"Well, then we'll be up and have the coffee on," the doctor replied, stopping midway up the gangplank. "In all my life I've never met a lady swamp dweller," he said in a very interested tone. "I'm already looking forward to the event."

"You'll never meet another one like this one; I guarantee you that," Charlie said, with humor in his voice.

"What's her name?" asked the doctor, "just so we can be prepared."

"She's known throughout the swamp, as Miss Hattie—the Voodoo Princess," Frank replied with a little chuckle. "We call her, Miss Hattie—or The Princess, but we'll wait until morning and introduce you properly. You'll like her; she's a real character."

"The Voodoo Princess," the doctor repeated, turning to look at Dad with an inquisitive smile. "Tomorrow could prove to be an interesting day, my friend," he said, with a nod and a wink. "I'll be sure to be up and have the coffee going when she arrives."

The boys worked until about two o'clock in the morning getting all their gear inside, and getting settled into their new home. The large half barrel heating stove gave off a tremendous amount of heat, and it wasn't long until everyone was pulling off his coat and getting busy with all the chores that had to be done. The beds were the last thing to get completed and the guys were so exhausted they literally fell in with their clothes on.

Neither the crickets, nor the frogs, nor the bull alligator crawling around the boat occasionally bumping into it was enough to keep the guys awake, but the night was entirely too short, and early the next morning right around six o'clock, Dad sat straight up in bed with his eyes wide open as a major case of thumping and bumping started happening out along side the boat. "Boys, I think the lady swamp dweller has arrived," he announced.

"*Francois, como a estado,*" came a shrill female voice from outside. "I have meesed you mucho!"

"Well, I see our lady of the swamp speaks a few languages," said the doctor. "She just used three of them in her opening statement. Frank must already be out there. It's a good thing I didn't oversleep like the rest of you bums, or we wouldn't have any coffee to entertain the lady."

"Hey, are you guys up in there? Get up—we've got someone we want you to meet," came the unmistakable high pitched voice of Swamp Rat Charlie.

"Give us just a minute folks," Doc Ced called back. "All these land-lubbers in here overslept."

"I sure wish we had time to wake up a little before we have to entertain," Ike complained, stumbling out of the bedroom, rubbing his eyes.

"Yeah, me too," Cowboy grouched. "My tongue feels like it's wearing an overcoat."

"Aw, you'll be alright!" the doctor replied excitedly. "Run your hands through your hair a couple of times, put on a big smile and get yourself a sip or two of coffee—let's do it! It's not everyday you get a chance to entertain a lady swamp dweller."

"*No no Gato—no te moleste.* Huevito is you friend," rang out a shrill voice just as the doctor began to open the door.

"Here, Princess, let me hold your monkey," said Swamp Rat Charlie. "One day that damn snake is going to have this little bastard for lunch."

"Oh, no, Swampy, they are very good friends," insisted the Princess.

"Friends my butt," Charlie grinned. "It's just a matter of time until this little bugger is snake food."

"Holy mackaroly!" Cowboy muttered unconsciously, as the door swung open with the visitors standing forefront. "What have we got here!"

"What we've got here is the biggest damn snake I've ever seen in my whole life," Ike whispered, backing away from the door with his eyes bugged out. "That thing has to be 8 feet long."

"Good guess," Frank chuckled. "He's 8 feet 3 inches, but as long as he's had a couple of rats in the last week he's actually harmless. I still don't know how the Princess carries that heavy bugger. He weighs about fifty pounds."

"He is mi Gato," the Princess replied cheerfully, adjusting the weight of the big python around her neck. "He catches all the big nasty ratas en mi casita barco."

"He is her house cat," the doctor translated with a smile. "He catches all the rats on her houseboat."

"I speak the good English, no?" said the Princess plainly proud of her communicative skill.

"You certainly do, Madame," the doctor agreed nodding his head graciously.

"Boys, I'd like to introduce you to our good friend, Miss Hattie La Rue—otherwise known as the Voodoo Princess," said Frank. "Why don't all of you come out on deck, and I'll introduce you individually. Yeah, that's good; come on around here by the rail. Hattie, this is Doctor Cedric, and this is Ike and Dave Walker, and over here we've got Maxy and Cowboy. They're down here from Sugar Grove, Arkansas, to hunt down the Sloyd brothers, and Swamp Rat and I have agreed to give them all the help we can!"

"I am so very please to meet all of you, Señores," the Princess replied, with a gracious smile. "I hope to be you very good friend. If Francois and

THE VOODOO PRINCESS AND INDIAN SAUSAGE   **259**

Swampy like you, I like you too—very much," she said, with a deep curtsy. Instantly the guys could see the weight of the big snake had the Princess overbalanced, and everyone made a quick move in her direction.

"Get her Frank," Charlie yelled as Miss Hattie started to fall sideways.

"I've got you kid," Frank responded, quickly slipping his arm under her.

"Oh thank you so much, Francois!" said the Princess, trying to adjust the big snake's weight. "Gato—you almost make me fall; you bad boy!"

"I can't believe that damn critter has gotten that big, Hattie," Frank commented. "He was only about 2 feet long awhile back."

"Yeah, but that was two years and 10,000 rats ago," said Charlie. "There's no telling how big that thing is going to get. If I were you Hattie, I'd try to find a place in a zoo somewhere to put him. In the next few years he's going to start wanting bigger things to eat than rats!"

"Oh Swampy, you are so funny!" said the Princess, with a whimsical laugh. "Gato is mi very good friend; I could not send him away."

"I take it there are still plenty of rats in the old swamp," the doctor grumbled under his breath.

"There's every classification of damn rat known to mankind out there," said Frank, shaking his head.

"Yeah and probably a few varieties that haven't even been discovered yet," Charlie added. "It's a good thing we've got a lot of snakes too or we'd be in real trouble."

"I hope they're not all this danged big," Ike said, in a half whisper, "or I sure won't be getting much sleep."

"Yeah, rats running around on the floor in the dark, isn't very sleep conducive either," said Charlie, "but I'll take a couple of good house cats over a critter like that any day."

"Miss Hattie, let's take your pals around to the back of the boat and put them in their cages," Frank suggested.

"Yes, I think we should," the Princess replied. "I have many things I wish to buy at your store, Francois, and they would be very much be in the way."

"We've got a couple a cages around the back of the boat where she stashes her critters when she comes to the settlement," said Frank, as everyone began walking along the rail to the back of the boat.

"That's good," said the doctor. "As soon as you're finished with that we would like to invite all of you in for coffee.

"Yeah, we would like to have you in for breakfast, but we're suddenly all out of grub," said Maxy.

"This man right here owns a grocery store, gentlemen," Dad reminded, pointing to Frank. "As soon as he gets time we can take care of our problem, so you're still invited. We just need to buy some groceries first."

"Oh please, permit me to make breakfast for everyone," said Miss Hattie. "We can use the Indian sausage I brought to you, François, and we can cook some huevos, and we will have fried bread like they make in New Orleans. It will be wonderful! I have not cooked for so many handsome men in such a very long time," she said with a very pleased smile.

"That sounds just fine to me, kid," Frank replied, turning to face Miss Hattie. "The Princess here is a very fine cook, gentlemen. She was a well-paid chef down in New Orleans before she changed occupations."

"Yeah, for my two cents she should have stayed a cook!" said Charlie, adamantly. "All that witchcraft mumbo-jumbo gives me the creeps."

"It's not witchcraft, Swampy! It's Voodoo!" the princess promptly corrected, showing a definite irritation with Swamp Rat's analogy. "There es a big difference!"

"Well, whatever it is it still gives me the creeps!" Charlie said smugly. "I like you much better as a chef, Sweetheart."

"And I like you very much too Swampy, but I'll have to admit, that hat you always wear bothers me. It *es* so *feo*! How do you say en Engles? Yes— it's ugly! It gives me the creeps," she said with a little giggle. "Those pointy teeth, and those ugly dried-up eyes—yes, you must have a new hat."

"Hey, I've had this hat a long time!" said Charlie. "I made it myself."

"Yes, I can tell, it's ugly, and you know it," she declared. "He definitely needs a regular hat; doesn't he, Francois?"

THE VOODOO PRINCESS AND INDIAN SAUSAGE

"Hey, you're not dragging me into this cat fight," Frank replied. "I'm more interested in that Indian sausage fried bread and egg thing you told us about. Let's all head on up to the store. We need to get back and have breakfast as quick as we can. I need to open the store at 9 o'clock."

"Since we're going to buy a full bill of groceries," said Maxy, "I guess we better take the rig. I'll haul as many of you as I can in the car, but somebody's going to have to ride in the trailer."

"Bud and I are going to stretch our legs," said Ike. "We'll meet you up there."

"Yeah, I think I'll go with you boys," Dad replied. "We'll probably be there before they will anyway, since they've got to turn the trailer around."

"Oh, wait! Señor Maxy," said the Princess. "I must get the chorizo out of my canoe and put it in the houseboat. I do not want some animal to eat it."

"Yeah, we certainly don't want to lose our sausage," Frank agreed. "I'm really looking forward to that. I just wonder what kind of meat went into this batch."

"*Me amiga*—oh, I mean my friend—" she said, "it was almost all tortuga, and alligator, but it also has some other kinds of animals they caught."

Instantly all the guys started discretely looking around at each other with definite question marks in their eyes.

"What's tortuga, Doc?" Ike whispered.

"Oh, that's the big swamp turtle," Charlie quickly replied. "They can weigh up to two hundred pounds."

"Don't ever turn down alligator snapping turtle, Ike," the doctor advised. "Those ugly critters, next to garlic frog legs, are probably the most succulent eating in the swamp."

For about an hour with Françoise's market still closed, Miss Hattie and the Sugar Grove Boys continued to gather all their necessities, working hard at remembering everything they would be needing. "Well, fellows, look around and see if there's anything else you want," Dad suggested. "That's just about everything I can think of."

"Yeah, I think that's pretty well got it covered, Dave," said Maxy. "At least we've got all the staples. We'll be around here for another few days anyhow; if we think of anything else we can still pick it up."

"We bought nearly all the garlic and onions you had out," the doctor said to Frank. "You might need to stock some more."

"Did you get enough?" Frank questioned.

"Yeah, we probably got enough to last us as long as we're going to be here. The boys and I are scheming on the abundance of bullfrogs you've got down here, and I'm looking forward to our first big pan full of garlic bullfrog legs."

"Oh, doctor, you must permit me to make them for you!" Miss Hattie insisted passionately. "That was one of my specialties when I cooked in New Orleans."

"That would be most delightful, my dear. You just inform me of where and when the event is taking place, and I'll be there with bells on."

"*Bueno*—how do you say—it es a date, senor," said the princess, with an elegant smile. "We will have an afternoon fiesta for everyone at mi casita barco."

"Okay. Do you folks think you've got everything you're going to need?" Frank questioned.

"It's probably as close as we're going to get for now, Frank," Dad replied. "We may need to pick up a few things a little later on."

"Princess, do you have everything you need to make breakfast?"

"Si, I believe I do, François. Please put this on me cuenta; Oh, I mean—my bill," the princess corrected. "I will be paying you very soon now."

"You've always paid me sweetheart, and I know you always will. What I'm looking forward to right now is getting my teeth into some of that Indian sausage; man, am I hungry."

"As soon as you are finished with your counting, and I can get some of these handsome young men to help me carry it to the *caro*, we will be ready."

Within minutes, with everyone loaded into the car and trailer, the breakfast parade left the store and headed down the hill, but it didn't take long for them to realize there was something very wrong. "What the hell is going on here?" Frank blurted out, as they pulled up in front of the houseboat mooring.

CHAPTER TWENTY-NINE—Revenge from out of the Past and the Bully Boys Bite the Big One

"*Que pasa?*" the Princess shrieked. "*Me gato Y Huevito.* Where did the boat go, Francois?"

"Yeah, what happened to our new home?" Dad questioned, looking around at the other guys.

"Evidently, someone took it upon themselves to move it," Frank replied adamantly—"but who—and why! Hey, Marco—who took my houseboat?" Frank yelled as a man quickly approached from across the road carrying a .30-30 rifle.

"It was Elmer Breen and that tall Sloyd brother and Jhondoc. I came out here to check on what they were doing, and they threatened to blow my head off if I didn't get back where I belonged. I couldn't tell who they were until I got here, but I definitely knew they didn't have permission to be taking your boat."

"Hell no—they didn't have permission to rob my store either, but the Sons a Bitches did it anyway!" Frank yelled, with his face flushing a bright shade of red. "This is the last damned straw, boys," he said, looking around at the gang with his eyes glaring and the muscles in his jaw clenched. "I'm going to destroy that bunch of thugs if it's the last thing I ever do."

"Well gentlemen—looks like somebody has decided to change our plans," said the doctor.

"Damn, this is a devastating blow," Maxy said, shaking his head. "Those bums either got very lucky, or they're smarter than we give them credit for. I don't know how we're going to overcome this kind of setback."

"Yeah, no guns—no place to live and no way to sustain ourselves," said the doctor. "The money we all got together for the trip was in my medical bag."

"Just off hand, I'd say we've pretty much hit the end of the line, fellows." Dad confessed, with the stress of the situation showing in his face. "Being out maneuvered this early in the game indicates we may have bitten off more than we can chew—the only problem is, I can't let it end this way—I've got too much at stake!"

"They're not that smart, Dave!" Frank shouted with rage in his voice. "They're not thinkers and planners; they're a bunch of inbred dysfunctionals. The only game they know is brute strength and awkwardness, and shoving a sawed off shotgun in your face. They just lucked out this time, but they're never going to win as long as there's one breath of life left in this carcass of mine—buck up boys, we're not beaten. We just haven't started to fight!"

"Hey Marco, how long have they been gone?" Charlie asked, scanning the huge inland lake.

"Just about 10 minutes. They've still got to be out there somewhere," he said, pointing at an island about a mile off to the left. "They hooked onto that houseboat with one of those big power launches and just took off with it. I had just gotten my .30-30 and was heading up to the store to tell you what was going on when you guys showed up."

"Damn the luck," Frank said, looking out across the open waterway to the island. "I sure wish I had a fast motorboat right now."

"Hey, there they are!" Cowboy yelled, pointing out towards the island—"looks like they're heading back in this direction."

"That's just what I figured they'd do," said Marco. "They've parked the houseboat on the other side of the island where it's safe, and now they're coming back to mess with us some more."

"They're definitely heading in this direction," said Maxy.

"Man, I sure wish we had that old Sharps right now," the doctor lamented. "This would be a perfect time to put it into action."

"Hey, unless some of you guys took it out of the back of the car it's still in there!" Maxy yelled excitedly. "Remember, the trailer was full, and we put the Sharps and the ammo in the trunk!"

Suddenly everyone looked at each other with a blank stare, and Ike and Cowboy leaped off the dock, and headed towards the car on a run.

"Man, I sure hope that thing is in there," said the doctor, glancing nervously at the motor boat off in the distance.

"If neither of you guys moved it, it has to be," Maxy replied, looking at Dad and the doctor. "I didn't, and it's for sure the boys didn't—right?"

"The way I see it folks, we better start removing ourselves off this dock," said Frank. "Those guys are probably going to start plinking at us as soon as they get in range,"

"Well, there's going to be somebody plinking back this time," said Marco, jacking a shell into the chamber of his rifle.

"Come on, Miss Hattie," Charlie said, taking the Princess by the hand. "Let's get closer to the car."

"Oh man, it is there!" Maxy yelled, as Ike and Cowboy slammed the trunk and headed for the dock. "Now we'll give those thugs some of their own medicine."

"Hey, do you want to shoot or do you want me to?" Ike yelled, as he and Cowboy came hustling up where everyone was standing.

"I'd like to have the first crack at it, if it's all right with you!" said Cowboy.

"Go for it then!" Ike said, shoving the heavy rifle into Cowboy's hands. "Get yourself a rest off the top of that post right there."

"Okay, you slime balls," Cowboy scowled, laying the big rifle over the top of the big flat topped post. "Now, we're going to see if you boys can take it as good as you can dish it out."

"They'll be getting into range real soon now, Son," said the doctor, as Cowboy slid a large lead pointed shell up into the firing chamber and closed the rolling block breach.

"Don't forget the double trigger, Bud," said Ike. "You're going to need a real smooth pull off to ever do any good."

"Holy mackerel!" said Cowboy, as he looked through the big scope. "It looks like those guys are right on top of us already!"

"They're still a little out of range, Son," the doctor cautioned, walking over next to Cowboy. "Just give it a few seconds more."

"Man, I can't believe this scope!" Cowboy exclaimed, looking at Ike with big wide eyes.

"Alright, now you can start thinking about taking a whack at them," said the doctor. "They'll be entering the half mile zone any time now."

"Hey, there are only two of them! I thought you said there were three," said Cowboy, quickly removing his eye from the scope and looking over at Marco.

"There are three—that means there's still one on the houseboat."

"All right then," said Cowboy. "Let's get down to business here. That one right there has to be old Wag; he's at least a foot taller than the other guy."

"What's the other guy look like?" Marco questioned quickly.

"He's sort of dumpy looking with a big black beard."

"That would be Elmer Breen. He's one of the sorriest men on the face of this earth," Marco replied.

"Bud, you need to be doing something here real soon," said Ike. "They're well within range now."

"Okay then this is it," Cowboy, said, pulling back the big hammer and nestling his face into the scope. "We came here to rid ourselves of the Sloyd brothers and I've got one of them dead in my sights."

"Then kill that slimy bastard," Swamp Rat yelled out. "I wish I was pulling that damned trigger!"

Suddenly the muzzle of the big gun exploded upwards and back and a major thunderclap hit the dock area as Cowboy went running backwards two or three steps trying to hang on to the heavy weapon. Everybody had taken the liberty of placing both hands firmly over their ears, but their eyes were firmly glued on the powerboat as it continued to race forward completely undeterred. About two heart stopping seconds later though—just like grandpa Cedric had described—the buffalo went down. The boat swerved sharply to the left and appeared to almost turn over before it finally came to a stop.

"Holy cow, you nailed that sucker, Cowboy!" Maxy yelled ecstatically, viewing the scene through his powerful binoculars.

"Hey man, get another shell into that thing quick," said Marco. "If there's any chance at all get a bullet into that damned Elmer."

"Yeah, nail that pig," Frank squalled, with both fists clinched, and his face flushed a deep shade of purplish red. "He's one of the bastards that's been robbing me."

"Man, the impact of that big slug knocked old Wag ten feet off the back of that boat," said Maxy, still observing the scene. "Hey, Cowboy, you need to hurry it up; the other guy's heading back to the steering wheel. He's about to take off!"

Once again the thunder of the ancient rifle impacted the area, and about six point three stressed out heart beats later, Maxy said in a very calm voice—"Well, Frank, you said you needed a speedboat, there's one out yonder a ways that nobody seems to be using. Maybe no one would mind if you had it."

Suddenly the dock exploded with hoops, hollers and yells of pent-up emotions, as the committee for action reveled in its first major success.

"Both of those guys are in the water at least 10 to 15 feet away from the boat," Maxy observed. "I would say that Grandpa Cedric would be very proud of your marksmanship, Cowboy."

"Fellows, this game may not be over yet!" Dad yelled, with renewed optimism. "We may have just turned it around! Cowboy, that was one fine piece of work. I suggest we get out there and take possession of that craft immediately."

"You bet we will," Frank agreed. "We're going to use it to hunt up my houseboat. I want to pick up those two pieces of dirt too before they sink."

"Gentlemen, my skepticism was totally unfounded," Charlie said, shaking his head with an apologetic smile. "Bayou Blanc still may have a future."

"Hot damn, what a gun you've got here, Doctor!" said Cowboy, holding the old hexagon barreled Sharps up in both hands. "That was as easy as shooting catfish in a barrel. Now as soon as the feeling comes back into my shoulder again we'll be all set to do it again," he said, with a bit of a grimace.

"Bring that relic from the past and follow me, boys. I've got a canoe down there that will haul at least three of us," said Frank. "We need to get out there and latch onto that craft. If possession is nine points of the law and we have possession, that means one thing—the committee for action has just acquired its first naval vessel."

"Ike, it's your turn to shoot, so you get in front of the boat and take the gun," said Cowboy; "Frank and I will do the paddling."

"Oh, François, I must go with you," said the Princess. "*Me Gato Y Huevito*. I am so afraid for them. I really must go!" she said, with determination in her voice.

"It's all right, Princess, but you'll have to come in another canoe; this one is full. Hey, Marco, how about getting another crew together and bring the Princess? Hell, bring anybody that wants to come! The way these guys shoot we're the kings of this damned swamp, and from here on out, everybody in Mission Point and surrounding parts is going to know it."

Within minutes, there were three canoes heading away from the dock towards the power launch which was freely drifting on the waves. Ike, Cowboy and Frank were out in the lead, with Dad, Marco and the Princess close behind, and bringing up the rear a few yards back came Maxy, Doc and Charlie.

"Man, look at that!" said Ike, pointing to the launch some 20 yards away, with two major holes adjacent to each other in the windshield.

"That is unbelievable," yelled, Swamp Rat. "I suddenly feel foolish as hell about doubting you boys' capability."

"I told you they meant business," Frank yelled back. "This show of force will go a long ways in helping bring this community together. We're finally in the presence of honorable men that won't be pushed around."

"I can certainly vouch for that," Charlie replied, "and I'm darn proud to say, I'm on their side."

"Hey, the motor is still running," Ike yelled, as the lead canoe pulled up alongside the launch. "Bud, take this gun, and I'll crawl over the side and check everything out."

"There's a bit of blood splashed around here and there," said Cowboy, looking over into the launch, "but other than that and a couple of holes in the windshield, she looks to be in perfect shape."

"You boys bring that canoe on around to the rear and crawl in," said Ike, checking over the working mechanism of the boat. "We need to get after that houseboat—pronto—that is, if we want a place to sleep tonight."

"That's a fact," Dad agreed. "I'm a man that likes to go to bed early, so let's get after it."

"What kind of setup does it have, Ike?" Cowboy asked, as he and Frank started climbing over the stern.

"It's just about like a car. It's got a clutch and a gear shift on the floor and a throttle on the dash. We're just lucky old Elmer had it out of gear when you whacked him, or we might never have chased it down," Ike said, shoving the throttle forward to idle the engine back.

"Speaking of Elmer," said Frank, visually scouring the area around the boat. "Where is that piece of human dung, anyway?"

"As far as I'm concerned," said Charlie, as the other two canoes came alongside, "I'd just let the sucker fatten up the crawdads. That would probably be the only positive thing he's ever done in his whole entire life anyway. You wouldn't want to cheat him out of that now would you?"

"I think Frank's right, in this case, Charlie," Dad said, grabbing onto the side of the launch to stabilize the canoe. "We need to retrieve both of those guys. Letting everybody see that the bad boys have finally met their match is going to strengthen the resolve of this community, and it will also help to erode the power structure of the others over at South Bayou."

"My thoughts exactly," Frank agreed, "You guys spread out now, and let's cover as much area as we can in the direction this boat has been drifting. Then we're going to hunt up my boat, and maybe we'll get a chance to clobber that damned Jhondoc. If we can nail him too that would really be a feather in our hat—we'll have recruits running out our ears."

"Francois, please help me into the boat with you," said Miss Hattie. "We must hurry and go find Huevito and Gato. I am terribly afraid those bad men will hurt them."

"Well, good lady, there's only one of those bad men left," said Frank, with a facetious smile, "and his life expectancy right now is in the minutes. If your critters haven't been harmed by now they're probably going to be all right."

"Here, Frank, grab onto her," Dad said, holding the canoe firmly up against the boat.

"Take it easy, now," Frank cautioned, as the Princess collected her skirts and began climbing into the launch. "Sit right here on the side-seat for now, Kid. Okay, boys, let's get on with it!"

"Hey, fellows, we've got one over here!" Maxy yelled.

"This is Elmer," Marco yelled. "I see the top of his bald head. He was the last one we whacked, so that means the other one should be a little ways over there. Hey, I think that's him about 20 yards out there," he yelled again, standing up cautiously in the canoe and pointing off to the left. "I'm pretty sure that's his hair sticking up."

"Hey you guys, rather than wasting time getting those bums on board, let's just secure them to this empty canoe so we don't lose track of them and go take care of the rest of our business," Frank said, as Ike started turning the launch toward their position. "We've got lots of rope under the dash here."

Within minutes the two former bad boys of Bayou Blanc were secured one on each side of the canoe with a short piece of rope and left to drift. "Boys, pull those canoes up here by the launch," Frank suggested. "Let's talk a bit on how we're going to go about this thing."

"Well, I think the logical approach would be to come at him from both directions," said the doctor. "Why don't we just use one canoe and the launch and send one around each end of the island."

"That sounds like the right idea to me," Maxy replied. "I would suggest that Ike, Cowboy and I take the canoe around one end and stay hidden along the brush just as much as we can while the launch goes around the other end in full view."

"Yeah, then maybe he'll get careless and I can get a clear shot," said Ike.

"That sounds like the right way to do it," Frank agreed. "Does that sound okay to everyone?"

"That sounds fine to me," Dad concluded, as everyone else nodded their heads in agreement.

"Alright then, let's get everyone else in the launch and get on with it," Frank agreed. "Let's tie the other canoe off with a fairly long lead rope and keep it with us. We may need it again. We'll give you boys a tow to the island then we'll coordinate and go our separate ways."

CHAPTER THIRTY—A Close Call and Jhondoc—the Supreme Bad Guy—Is Trapped

In no more than 5 minutes the preparation was over and Frank began easing the throttle forward and turning the launch toward the island a couple of miles away.

"This is a mighty fine craft, folks," the doctor commented as he sat down next to Dad, across from Marco and the Princess. "It's got to be 20 or 22 feet long, wouldn't you say, Dave?"

"It's at least that. I'm amazed how much room there is in here."

"It sure has nice upholstery," Miss Hattie commented, running her hands over the red leather seat covers.

"Yeah, it's too bad the former owners didn't take better care of the windshield," Swamp Rat quipped, "or this boat would be in perfect condition."

"You knot head," Frank replied, looking over at Charlie in the passenger seat. "Don't you have any respect for those poor old boys all dead and blown apart like that?"

"I'll have to admit my compassion has run a bit thin," said Charlie, shaking his head. "The only possible thing I might be persuaded to do that could benefit them would be to help send old Jhondoc to hell with them. He is their captain, you know, so I'm sure they'd appreciate that."

"We're going to give it our best shot!" Frank stated. "Boys, I think this is just about as close as we dare get," he said, looking back at the guys in the canoe, and throttling down the engine.

"Yeah, since we don't know just where the houseboat is we need to take it slow and easy," said Maxy.

"We're going to need at least 10 to 15 minutes—maybe more, to paddle to the other end of this island and get into position," Cowboy estimated, as he picked up his paddle. "You'll need to hang around here awhile until we get there."

"How about we time it and give you a full 30 minutes?" Dad suggested, taking out his pocket watch. "That way we'll be sure you're where you need to be."

"That'll work," Maxy agreed.

"Your houseboat is almost certain to be tethered up against the side of the island," Ike projected, looking directly at Frank, "so when you come around the other end, stay away from the island at least 50 yards. I don't want to shoot somebody I'm not aiming at."

"I get you," said Frank. "We'll get the houseboat spotted then we'll back off and give you time to get into position before we make our move, and we'll definitely steer clear of the thunder stick. Good luck, gentlemen; let's get to it," Frank said, as the canoe carrying the small artillery started heading off toward the other end of the island.

"Folks, just to be on the safe side," the doctor said, "I think we should start moving this boat slowly and quietly into position then when we get close enough we can tie it up or anchor it and use the canoe to slip around the end of the island and check things out."

"That's a very wise idea, my friend," Frank said, as he gently started turning the big boat towards the end of the island. "We'll just cruise up there nice and slow and no one will be the wiser."

In 10 minutes or less the launch crew was dropping anchor off the point of the island just far enough back so it couldn't be seen from the front. "Marco, how about you and Charlie take the canoe and have a peek around the front side and see where my houseboat is, then as soon as the time is up we'll pull anchor and go to it. How many minutes do we have left, Dave?"

"22," Dad replied, looking closely at his watch.

"That's plenty of time," Marco replied, as he picked up his .30-30 and followed Charlie to the canoe. "It shouldn't take us any more than 10 minutes or so to check things out and get back here."

As the boys in the canoe headed for the end of the island, Frank turned around to face the group. "You know, I've just been thinking on how we should go about this thing. Should we make our entrance with the boat revved up to top speed and come roaring into view to draw Jhondoc's full attention, or should we come around the end of the island slower and hope he will think we're his friends coming back and let us get closer?"

"Doc, what would be your thoughts on the matter?" Dad asked.

"Well, since Ike is going to be the one to administer the coup de grace, I think we should draw just as much attention to ourselves as possible. Let the thug know we're not his friends and get him just as shook up as possible. If we rattle him bad enough he's more likely to make an error that can be taken advantage of."

"Yeah, I agree with that concept," Frank said. "If we can get him concentrating on us heavy enough—even firing at us, then maybe Ike will have a chance to lay one on him, but we'll try to stay just out of range and not give him any more to shoot at than we have to."

"That sounds like the way to go," Dad replied. "Firing that big rifle accurately from an unstable situation like a canoe isn't going to be easy, and we need to give Ike every possible chance to get the job done."

"Oh, look, Swampy and the other man are coming back," said Hattie, standing up and pointing towards the end of the Island.

"That's good," Frank replied. "Now we'll know more about our situation."

In another five minutes the canoe was pulling up to the end of the launch, and Swamp Rat and Marco were crawling in. "What's the news, gentlemen?" Frank questioned.

"It's just about like we figured; your boat is tied up to the brush about halfway down the island."

"We've got another 8 minutes left, folks," Dad said, sliding his watch back into his overalls pocket.

"Alright, that gives us just enough time to get the anchor pulled and get ready. By the way, while you boys were gone we decided we're going to make a grand entrance at top speed around the end of the island. We're going to swing wide and try to stay just out of rifle range. Dave, how much time have we got now?"

"Six minutes."

"That's close enough," Frank said, starting the engine. "Charlie, how about you pull the anchor, and we'll get this show on the road. Marco, I want you to ride up front with me, and when I tell you to, start firing towards the houseboat, but don't try to hit it. I don't want any unnecessary holes in it—especially the pontoons. We just want to rattle him and let him know he's under attack. All right everyone, this is it! I'm going to head down the back side of the island a little ways to pick up some speed and then we'll turn back and whip round the horn."

As the big boat started picking up speed it was easy to see the adrenaline rush that was starting to go through the crew. "Man, I've been waiting on this day for a long time," Swamp Rat Charlie yelled, waving his homemade cap in the air and looking excitedly at the rest of the gang.

"Yeah, it's been a long time coming, pal," Frank agreed. "Now if we can just nail this other piece of scum we'll take them all back and let everybody in town know that Bayou Blanc still has a future."

"Hey, this thing's doing 30 miles an hour," Marco yelled, looking down at the speedometer.

"Here we go!" Frank said, as the big launch went roaring around the end of the island. "Good luck to us all, and may we all live to fight another day. This is the first day of the war for Bayou Blanc. All right—there's my boat!"

"Our boys are all set," Dad exclaimed, pointing down the length of the island. "They're behind that first clump of brush down there."

"Yeah, I see them," Frank said observing the situation. "They've got themselves a good spot there. Marco, fire a three or four round salvo into the brush right next to the houseboat and let's see what happens."

"Hey, there he is!" Marco yelled, looking down the barrel of his rifle. "He just ran out onto the deck with his gun."

"Well, take a few whacks at him!" Frank yelled, "but try not to hit the pontoons."

"I probably can't even come close to him," said Marco, "but at least he'll know he's being shot at."

"Folks, I would suggest that everyone get down on the floor. We're taking this tub into the danger zone right now!" said Frank, turning the big boat directly into the island.

Just as the last of Marco's four round salvo ended, suddenly a small thunderclap, from the south, greeted the ears of the crew. "Did he get him?" Doctor Cedric yelled from the bottom of the boat.

"No, dammit," Frank replied, "but he damn well knows he's been shot at," said Frank. "He's hiding on the opposite side of the houseboat, looking around the corner in the boys' direction. Evidently our little surprise didn't work, gentlemen, so how do we play the game now?" Frank questioned, as he began throttling back.

"Maybe we need to come at him from both sides at once, so he doesn't have a place to hide," Dad speculated, "but first, I'd say we need to go down and coordinate with the other guys."

"Fellows, what I see about to happen here is not good," the doctor spoke up with urgency in his voice. "If we don't nail this guy right now, he's got no choice but to jump ship and get lost on that island, and we'd probably need an army with bloodhounds to ever find him."

"Hey, look Frank—there he goes!" Marco yelled, pointing at the houseboat.

"Oh Man!—Doctor, it appears you're not only a fine physician you're also a prophet," said Frank, shaking his head. "Unfortunately your warning came just a hair too late. Our quarry just made a flying leap off the front of the houseboat and disappeared in the underbrush."

"Dad blast it!" Charlie yelled, in frustration. "That's going to complicate the dickens out of things, Frank!"

"Yeah, it does sort of spoil our plans for the present," Frank agreed. "I sure wanted to take him back to town with his buddies. The whole fact is though he's trapped with no food and no way to survive. It's just a matter of time until he'll have to give it up, and guess who's going to be waiting on him!" Frank said, with a sadistic grin.

"Yeah, and for once in his life, Jhondoc is going to be the one having to do all the suffering," said Charlie, "there's nobody there for him to push around. Every citizen in Bayou Blanc would be cheering if they knew about this—well, most of them anyway!"

"They're going to know it soon enough," Frank said. "What we've done here today will spread like wildfire—meantime, what's our next move? We need to get our brains together, so we don't mess up again."

"I suggest we get the rest of our crew up here," Dad said. "They can sit a ways off shore with their binoculars and that big gun and guard us while we go in to retrieve your houseboat."

"That's a plan," Frank agreed, revving the engine up and turning the launch toward the east end of the island.

"How large would you say this island is?" Doctor Cedric, questioned as Frank brought the big launch up to a full plane.

"Aw, it's probably about a mile long and half a mile wide," Charlie spoke up. "The problem's not the size, it's the terrain. The interior is nothing but a bramble patch of tall swamp grass and thorn bushes. You called it right when you said it would take a small army to rout that bum."

"Yeah, and probably get a half dozen people killed in the process," said Frank. "We're going to have to think on this a while."

"Hey, brother, maybe you should've let Cowboy shoot," Dad yelled, as the launch came gliding towards the canoe.

"Dadburn it, I missed him!" Ike gestured in frustration with his fist closed. "Firing this miniature cannon without a stable position is a real challenge."

"Not only that—the recoil darn near capsized us," said Maxy. "Using that weapon successfully from a canoe is going to take some practice."

"Yeah, either that or we're going to be picking ourselves out of the water a lot," Cowboy commented, looking at Ike with an ear to ear grin.

"Aw, don't sweat it boys; this is just a minor setback," Frank replied, with a very upbeat attitude. "In time, we'll get the bugs all worked out of our plan, and then we're going to rid this area of this stinking criminal element for good, and we'll probably find your dog in the process, Dave. If we can just hook onto my houseboat and pull it out of rifle range without getting shot, I'll think we've done exceptionally well. Then we need to talk about our next move."

"Well, for my two bits, I'd say we need to get on with our breakfast plans," Doctor Cedric grumbled. "My stomach is feeling mighty lank."

"Oh, yes, François, I agree with the doctor, and I have to see if my little friends are all right too," said Miss Hattie. "I hope those bad men did not hurt them!"

"Yeah, me too, Princess," Frank agreed. "Okay, boys—tie that lead rope off firmly; we're heading back. We're going to put you back out of rifle range to guard us when we go in to retrieve my houseboat."

"Man, I sure hate seeing that bum get away like that," said Ike.

"Aw don't sweat it, Ike," Frank replied.

In 5 minutes or less the canoe carrying Ike and the small artillery crew had been deposited back out of rifle range in a rear guard maneuver and the launch was slowly gliding towards the end of the houseboat with all the occupants, except Frank and Marco keeping a low profile on the floor of the boat. "Marco, if I stay directly behind the houseboat for protection, do you think you can sneak out there and tie the tow rope to that big iron hook on the back deck?" Frank questioned.

"You bet I can," said Marco, climbing out on the front of the boat.

"Hey, you've got it!" Frank said in a subdued yell as Marco slid the rope over the hook. "Now can you see how she's tied up without exposing yourself?"

"It's just tied loosely to some dry brush," said Marco, sneaking a peak around the side. "It should break right off with a good tug."

"Alright then, get back on board and let's get this tub out of here."

Just as Marco made a running leap from the houseboat to the front of the launch suddenly two gunshots exploded from the underbrush and Frank hit the deck as another bullet hole suddenly appeared in the windshield right next to him. "Man, that one just about took the fun out of my day!" Frank said, looking at the group down on the floor and brushing the shattered glass off his shirt.

"Hey, Frank—I'm hit!" Marco yelled, crawling up the front of the boat on his stomach.

"Keep coming this way, Marco," Frank yelled, as he slammed the launch into reverse and gunned the big engine. "I'm getting us out of here."

In about 60 seconds the houseboat was jerked free of the island, and the thunder of the buffalo stick could be heard as Ike pounded a few rounds into the area where the shots had come from. "Come on in here, pal," Frank said, grabbing Marco by the arm and jerking him on board.

"Let me have a look at him," said the doctor, as Marco dropped down into the boat.

"I don't know if he's wounded anywhere else, Doc," said Frank, "but he's got a major gouge right above his right eyebrow."

"I think that's the only place I'm hit," Marco mumbled, putting his hand up to his head with a grimace. "Man, does that sting!"

"I'll guarantee it does," said the doctor, looking at the bloody groove in Marco's forehead. "Does anyone have a clean handkerchief we can borrow to make a compress out of?"

"Si, I have one," Miss Hattie replied, reaching into her pocket.

"Keep this doubled just like it is and apply a little pressure," said the doctor. "As soon as we get on the houseboat I'll disinfect the wound and apply a bandage for you, and you'll be as good as new. He just barely got a piece of you—another inch to the left though and you would be in a world of hurt!"

"Damn, that was too close for comfort!" Frank mumbled, shaking his head and continuing to accelerate the launch backward towing the houseboat farther out of range.

"Thanks Doc—thanks Miss Hattie," said Marco, putting the hand-kerchief gently over the wound.

"You are very welcome, señor. I hope it does not hurt too much!"

"Naw, it's just a scratch, ma'am, but it stings like fury."

"All right, this is well out of rifle range," said Frank. "We'll stop right here and let our buddies catch up then we'll talk things over."

"Oh, François, I must hurry and go see that my little ones are all right," said Miss Hattie. "Oh, I pray they did not get hurt!"

"You stay right here, Princess, and I'll check things out," said Charlie, showing serious concern for the welfare of the animals.

"Oh, thank you so much, Swampy," said Miss Hattie, patting Charlie on the shoulder as he passed. "You are to me such a good friend."

"You are to me such a good friend also, Sweetheart," Charlie smiled, grasping her by the hand. "I'll be right back."

"Man, I thought you guys weren't ever going to stop," Cowboy yelled, as the canoe came alongside.

"Yeah, I was making sure we were well out of gun range," Frank said. "Jhondoc is very angry with us right now."

"Hey, did anyone get hurt when he fired on you?" Maxy asked.

"I got nicked a little," Marco said, standing up where the guys could see him. "It could have been a lot worse," he said, putting his hand to his forehead.

"A lot worse is an understatement, young man!" Dr. Cedric exclaimed. "You came within an inch of being killed. I think we ought to celebrate our good fortune by having that exotic breakfast Miss Hattie offered to cook for us."

"I'll second that motion," said Ike. "That make-do supper we had last night is really starting to wear thin."

"That's a first class idea," Frank agreed. "We'll have a liberation celebration; today is a special day for every honest person in this area; let's anchor right here and do it. You boys and the Princess can start getting set up to make our meal while Charlie and I go back and take care of some unfinished business and bring our groceries out. We'll also bring the battery for the houseboat back, and you boys will be mobile."

"Let's get after it," Dad said, starting to climb onto the houseboat. "I'll get a fire going in the cook stove."

"I'll do the back anchor," said Ike. "Bud you drop the front one."

"I'm going to leave a sign on the door of the market that it will be closed for the rest of the day, and that anyone who wants to join our celebration is welcome to do so," said Frank.

"Oh that is so wonderful, Francois!" the Princess cried out enthusiastically. "We will have a gran fiesta. I will make enough food for everyone. Please bring a block of ice and some rum and the usual things to make my rum punch. You do remember them all don't you?"

"There's no way we're going to forget your punch recipe, Sweetheart," Frank said, smiling and shaking his head. "We might forget everything else but not the punch ingredients."

"Rum punch"—the doctor said with a soft pause in his voice. "That was the only alcoholic drink my late missus would ever indulge in. I might just have a few extra in her memory—yes—yes, I think I shall!" he said, nodding his head affirmatively. "This is a very special day."

"Hey, Princess, look what I've got," said Swamp Rat, as he came walking up to the end of the houseboat.

"Oh, Huevito—my little one—you are all right!" Miss Hattie uttered softly with relief in her voice.

"The big guy is okay too," said Charlie, starting to climb down to the launch. "For obvious reasons I left him in his cage. This little bugger is really scared; he's shaking all over."

"Oh, bring him to me, Swampy," said Miss Hattie reaching for the little spider monkey. "My poor baby—it's all right now—Mama's got you! Did those mean men scare you?"

"All right—everybody get on the houseboat," said Frank. "Charlie and I have work to do. We'll be back just as soon as we can."

"I think I'd better go back with you," said Marco. "My wife doesn't even know where I am."

CHAPTER THIRTY-ONE—Indian Uprising and Doc and Miss Hattie Touch Heart Strings

It was obvious very quickly that the Voodoo Princess was much more than the image she had been portraying. She was a very talented individual who was used to working with people. Even before she had the chance to show off her culinary skills she had all the guys lined out on special jobs that she needed to get done before she could produce her gran fiesta, as she called it. As she entered the kitchen her demeanor changed immediately, and she was all business. The monkey was put away in his cage on the back deck and she scrubbed her hands and arms thoroughly with soap and hot water and insisted that everyone else follow suit. It may have been because they were all as hungry as a bunch of wolves or because she was an elegant lady that knew how to handle people, or maybe a little of both, but every man there quickly became involved in her process, and within the hour, Miss Hattie had transformed a kitchen she had never seen before into a suitable work place and men who knew nothing about cooking or kitchens into willing helpers. By the time Frank and Charlie finished their duties ashore and got the groceries back to her she was ready to go.

"François, could you and Swampy please hurry with the chorizo and all the other groceries?" she called out, from the back end of the houseboat. "The stove is almost ready and I need to start cooking. Señor Dave, could you please make the stove just a tiny bit hotter?" she asked, politely, as she passed Dad on the way back into the kitchen. "Señor Maxy, would you and Señor Ike please peel potatoes for me?" she asked. "I will need a large bowl full. Francois is bringing them right now."

"Miss Hattie, we are all your friends and as of now we are all your willing helpers," said the doctor. "In my opinion we would get a lot more done if we just relaxed and called each other by our first names. My name is Walter—I seldom hear it nowadays, but at least that what's on my birth certificate."

"Oh yes, Doctor, I think that is a wonderful idea," Miss Hattie agreed. "Walter—that is a very nice name. Everyone can call me Miss Hattie—that's who I really am," she said with a shy grin. "The Voodoo act is just for touristas."

"Yeah—now that's the woman I love!" said Charlie, walking in the door with a big bag of groceries in his arms. "Boys, this lady right here is the finest cook this side of New Orleans; you haven't lived until you've had her shrimp gumbo."

"Oh, Swampy, shrimp gumbo is such an easy dish," said Miss Hattie, nonchalantly. "All you need is fresh shrimp, some good swamp sausage like this I'm about to cook and some different kinds of vegetables—but, getting the roux exactly right—it does take a little practice."

"It'll be forty-five years next spring since I've had shrimp gumbo," the doctor reminisced, rubbing his handlebar moustache. "In fact, it was the first and only time I've ever had it," he disclosed. "My late missus and I were in New Orleans on our honeymoon. You know, for the life of me," he chuckled shaking his head, "I can't remember what that gumbo tasted like."

"You probably had other things on your mind, Walter," Miss Hattie said, with a sheepish grin and a definite blush to her cheeks. "If you would like, I could prepare it for you the same time I cook your garlic frog legs," she volunteered. "It would please me very much to make it for you."

"Hey, now, Princess, I was the one who praised your shrimp gumbo," Charlie protested—"remember me!"

"How could I ever forget you, Swampy?" Miss Hattie said, looking at Charlie with an endearing smile. "You are my very good friend. You too are invited—you are all invited. I so much enjoy cooking for people who like to eat good food."

"I can see right now, you and I are going to be great pals," the doctor replied, smiling at Miss Hattie and rubbing his tummy. "Food that has been properly prepared is one of the finest things there is in life."

"When I was a young girl my family was very poor, and there was little to eat," said Miss Hattie, "but then we moved to New Orleans where there was lots of work, and I swore that I would never go hungry again. There were wonderful foods being prepared everywhere I went. When I saw someone doing a dish that I wanted to learn I would watch them very closely, and then I would go straight home and write everything down in my little book. I would practice it over and over—making it for my family and friends until I could do it absolutely perfect. I had my first full time job when I was only 14 years old, and I have never been hungry since."

"That is a beautiful success story, Missy," said the doctor, with a definite look of humility on his face. "There is nothing more inspiring than to see someone succeed in life after rising from humble beginnings. What I would like to know right now though," said the doctor, savoring the intense aromas emanating from Miss Hattie's skillet—"can that sausage actually taste as good as it smells? I swear, good lady—I've just got to know!"

"In just a few minutes you can find out for yourself, Walter," Miss Hattie said, dumping the first skillet full of fried sausage onto a large platter. "I need to make a skillet full of fried bread to go with it."

"All I can say, sweetheart, is you'd better step it up," the doctor added, looking at the gang with a crooked grin. "We're all on the verge of slobbering on your kitchen floor."

"Amen to that," Ike agreed.

"Oh Walter, you are so funny," said Miss Hattie, with a little giggle, looking the doctor square in the face—"yes—yes, I will hurry!" she said, quickly pouring the batter into the hot skillet. "As soon as I finish the bread I will start cooking a full meal for everyone and we will all eat together at the big kitchen table. After that I will start preparing special snack foods for our evening fiesta—later on I will make us a bowl of my special rum punch and we will enjoy the evening together."

"Lady, I am truly looking forward to that," Doc Cedric, replied, smiling endearingly at Miss Hattie. "You're a woman after my own heart,"

One could easily tell that Miss Hattie was quite taken by the doctor's attention.

"If that sausage is half as good as it smells," said Ike, shoving in closer and eyeing the platter of golden brown patties, "alligators and swamp turtles are likely to become very scarce in this neck of the woods—right, Bud?"

"That's a fact," said Cowboy—"right after bullfrogs."

"Walter, would you please take the chorizo to the table and I will bring the bread," said Miss Hattie. "Remember this is only an appetizer, so do not eat too much, and spoil your supper."

"Too much my butt," the doctor grumbled. "I could eat all this by myself, and still have room for a five course meal."

"There is more food there than you think, Walter," said Miss Hattie. "There is one good sized piece of chorizo for each of you, and I will give you a nice piece of hot bread to eat with it. That will take away the hunger pains until I can cook."

"Now comes the moment of truth," said Ike, holding a piece of hot bread with a sausage patty on top of it up to his mouth; do turtles and alligators cease to exist as we know it or do they always remain?"

"Good Lord, Missy, this sausage is awesome," said the doctor mumbling around a mouthful of hot food. "Boys, let's hope there are some of these critters smart enough to hide where we can't find them. We definitely want to leave enough to keep the species going, but anything that tastes this good is in mortal danger around me."

"You can say that again," said Cowboy. "I just wonder what other variety of critters went into the mix, and what kind of herbs and spices they used."

"This is really good stuff, Miss Hattie," Ike agreed, with a wide smile. "My skepticism was truly unfounded. How do we get this recipe?"

"I wish I knew," Miss Hattie replied, shaking her head. "My friend Wynoka will never tell me everything it is made from, or the wild herbs they put into it. I can only get it by trading with them."

"Well, that's a real downer," Doc Ced replied, looking around at the guys.

"What do you trade for it?" Ike asked

"*Huevos salvajes*," Miss Hattie replied, cheerfully.

"Well, how do we get some of them Huvoes salvajes?" Ike asked, with a confused look on his face.

"Yeah, and what is it?" Cowboy questioned; "I've never heard of nothing like that before. Man, I'd like to get a bunch of this stuff."

"That's Spanish—for wild eggs, boys," the doctor replied. "I suppose you're referring to eggs from the wild birds that nest in the swamp, Miss Hattie."

"Yes—the Indians prefer them much more than eggs from chickens."

"Do you eat the wild eggs yourself," the doctor questioned.

"Yes, now I do, but when I first moved to the bayou I did not like *huevos salvajes* at all. They take some getting used to. Now I am like the Indians; I prefer them over the regular ones. They have a mild fish flavor. Huevito gathers them for me."

"Your monkey gathers wild bird eggs for you?" the doctor questioned—"or did I misunderstand you?"

"No, you did not misunderstand," Miss Hattie answered. "He loves doing it. When we get time I will let you watch him. It is really funny—but now I must get busy. I have lots of handsome men to feed."

"Princess, you may have at least one more person for your afternoon fiesta," said Frank, coming in with another sack of groceries.

"Oh, that is wonderful, Francois" Miss Hattie replied. "Who is it?"

"Father Juan Gomez."

"Oh—Padre John! That is so nice. Maybe he will ask the blessing for us."

"Oh, I'm sure he will," Frank replied. "He came over to the undertaker's house to give those thugs their last rites, and Charlie and I told him everything that's been going on. He is thoroughly delighted, and he wants to meet the boys from Sugar Grove. He says they have to be instruments of God to be so successful already."

"Wenoch is also coming by," said Charlie. "I saw him and told him what has happened. Boy was he excited. He said, maybe The Great Spirit is finally going to free his people from the evil that has plagued them for so long."

"Oh Lord!" Dad said shaking his head and looking around at the gang—"and just to think—we're only down here looking for a little boy's dog. I sure hope this thing doesn't get out of hand."

"Don't knock it, Dave!" Doc Ced remarked, in a very upbeat tone. "You know what they say—the Lord works in mysterious ways."

"Yeah, I've definitely heard that one a few times. That was my mother's favorite saying. I suppose anything is possible," Dad replied, with a troubled look on his face. "I just don't want to get bogged down and lose track of why we're down here; my boy's life is on the line."

"Well, who knows," the doctor replied. "Maybe it took your little boy's life on the line to start the march of freedom for these people—stranger things have happened. I think we ought to be open to help from any direction. Let's just relax and see where it takes us."

"I guess that's about all we can do," Dad agreed.

"Oh, my goodness, I must hurry," said Miss Hattie, suddenly finding herself engrossed in the conversation. "I must get back to work."

"Well, it would seem that your grandpa's buffalo slayer has made an instant hit with the locals," said Maxy, looking over at the doctor with an approving grin.

"Yeah, sometimes people can get too carried away with instant success though," said the doctor. "I just hope they have the resilience to hang in there when the going gets tough. This bunch of scum is not going to be displaced easily."

"That's for sure," said Swamp Rat—"they've been here too long! The only way to get rid of the hard core ones is like the two we just left at the morgue. Padre John didn't seem to have any problem with that concept of action though—did he, Frank?"

"No he certainly didn't. The Padre is a patient compassionate man, but he's tired of seeing the innocent in his parish constantly being abused—especially the Indian tribe—he'll be behind us all the way."

* * *

As the celebration of independence wore on into the evening and the second bottle of rum met its fate in the punch bowl, the partiers became aware of an unusual event taking place back toward the east end of the island. "Hey Dave—Frank! You fellows might want to come out on deck," said Cowboy, sticking his head in the door of the houseboat. "There's something going on here that we don't understand. I'm going to take the thunder stick here just in case," he said, picking up the Sharps from the corner.

"What seems to be wrong, Cowboy?" Dad questioned, as he and Frank walked out the door.

"There's something happening down at the east end of the island there," Cowboy said, pointing in the direction. "We've been watching them now since a little before dark. At first there were only two canoes, but in the last few minutes three more have joined them and they've lit those big torches they're carrying; so far we can't figure what they're up to."

"Well, it's not Jhondoc's bunch because they'd be coming from the south, and they'd definitely be in that big power boat," said Frank. "If those guys start paddling out towards that island though, we'll take the launch and go see what they're up to; nobody's going to give that degenerate aid if I can help it!"

"Man, look at all that light back in there!" said Maxy. "Suddenly the whole neck of the woods back where that channel comes out is all lit up."

"That's got to be the Indian tribe," said Swamp Rat. "That's the channel that leads back to Webo Island where the village is. There's definitely something big going on here! I didn't know there was that many canoes on the whole reservation."

"What do you think would bring them all out in force like this, Charlie?" Frank questioned, continuing to observe the mass of torch lit canoes coming through the wooded channel.

"Jhondoc,"—said Charlie, looking at Frank with a stunned look on his face. "That's all it can be! Wenoch didn't waste any time letting the Chief know his arch-enemy is trapped on that island over there. I don't know the ins and outs of it all, but the Chief has a real hatred for Jhondoc!"

"It appears he wants in on our action, boys," Frank said, looking around at the crew.

"Yeah, it's got to be him," Charlie acknowledged. "Nobody else could possibly mobilize a response like this. If those people take Jhondoc captive, he will wish a thousand times that Ike was a better shot," said Swamp Rat, looking at Ike with a devious grin.

"Well, I was trying as hard as I could," Ike replied, rubbing his right shoulder with a disgruntled look on his face.

"What did you say the chief's name is again, Charlie?" Dad asked.

"Wacanabbi-Min-Coto," Swamp Rat replied. "He's been Chief now for about 20 years. He's a good honest old man. It appears he's come to the same conclusion we have—it's time to put Jhondoc out of business."

"Well then our fledgling revolution has just gained a powerful new ally," Frank said. "I don't know just what the Chief has in mind for Jhondoc, but that string of canoes heading out towards that island tells me one thing—he is no longer our concern, and that Gentlemen, clears the way for us to move on to other things."

"Like South Bayou," said Swamp Rat, looking at Frank with a resolute scowl on his face.

"Exactly," Frank replied, with a nod. "There's a whole bunch of backwater scum over there that needs our attention. Fellows, this has been a long worthwhile first day and even though I hate to—I'm feeling like it's time to start closing her down," Frank said, with a big yawn. "Charlie, let's get the Princess and her critters aboard the launch and take them home. Boys, if you'll be up around 6 o'clock in the morning

Charlie and I will bring the battery and we'll fire up the engine on this thing and you boys will have transportation. I have to open the market at 9 o'clock."

"We'll definitely be up," Dad answered—"at least I will."

"That's makes two of us," Doc replied. "Maybe we can look this old swamp over a little. It's been a long time since I've been here. I'd even like to see the old place where I grew up if we have time."

"We definitely need to explore the whole area," Dad replied— "accomplishing what we came here to do may depend on it. We need to learn where everything and everybody is situated."

"Hey, if you fellows would like I could spend the day with you and show you around a little," said Charlie. "I don't have anything better to do."

"I think that would be very helpful, Charlie," Dad replied—"how about the rest of you guys? Then it's settled," he announced, after observing the positive feedback. "We'll see you boys in the morning."

Throughout the night the flotilla of torch bearing canoes continued to expand until the entire island was circled by light. There was no doubt that Wacanabbi-Min-Coto did not intend for Jhondoc to have any avenue of escape. It soon became apparent to Dad and the crew that this was something more than just an outlaw being apprehended. For some reason there seemed to be a vendetta of deep anger aimed personally at Jhondoc.

CHAPTER THIRTY-TWO—The Mystery Thickens and the Crew Tours the Bayou

"Good God Almighty, can you believe that?" Dad said to the doctor, as they came out on deck about 5:30 a.m. the next morning. "Either these people take their work extremely serious, or there's a lot more to this story than we know about."

"Yeah, that's just a little bit unreal," the doctor agreed, stroking his handlebar mustache and observing the hoard of lights around the island—"talk about overkill! Off hand though, I would say Frank had it right; we don't have to worry about that reprobate anymore. Let's get us a fire going and make us some coffee, Dave."

"Yeah, we need to get the rest of the guys up too. Frank and Charlie will probably be here pretty quick."

"You know, I'm really looking forward to our houseboat excursion today, Dave—I sort of feel like the prodigal son returning home. I spent a lot of my youth exploring this old swamp, and it's still a job unfinished. I think it'll be good for us to take a day off and relax a little—you especially my friend! You can't help your boy if you don't take care of your own health."

"Yeah, you're probably right, Doc," Dad agreed. "I'm wound up tighter than an eight day clock!"

"I know you are, Dave; what you're going through is a natural occurrence in a horrific matter of this sort, but you need to pace yourself a little. We'll give it hell again tomorrow, but today we're going to take a breather, and that's an order from your family physician—alright?"

"Alright Doc—I'll try to let it go. I'll get the fire started if you'll take care of the coffee."

"That's a deal," said the doctor, as they entered the back door. "Hey you landlubbers, start waking up!" he yelled. "We've got a day of exploration ahead of us."

"Yeah fellows—hit the deck, our host will be here any minute now," Dad called out. "Let's get up and around."

"Is there any coffee yet?" Cowboy mumbled, stumbling out into the kitchen rubbing his eyes. "I woke up with a extreme case of coyote breath."

"I hear that," said Ike, following Cowboy into the kitchen—"tastes like I ate a piece of rotten jack rabbit."

"Yeah, or something worse," Cowboy agreed, with a smirk.

"That's a common occurrence when you've had too much rum the night before," the doctor chuckled. "I'm afflicted with the same malady. All in all though, it was a marvelous evening, don't you boys think so? Here Dave, sit this on the back of the stove, over there," said the doctor, handing Dad the pot.

"All in all, Doc—I'd say you and Miss Hattie were doing some mighty heavy sparking there," said Cowboy, grinning from ear to ear, and winking at the other guys.

"It's a good thing Frank only brought two bottles of rum or you might have waked up a married man this morning," Ike teased.

"Yeah, I did let my hair down a little, didn't I?" the doctor said, grinning and shaking his head. "I haven't done that in many a moon."

"Now, you boys leave the doctor alone," Dad intervened, with a slight grin. "We've got more important things to be talking about."

"Oh, it's alright, Dave—in fact, it feels kind of good," said the doctor, with a pleased look on his face. "I haven't felt this much like a man in a lot of years, and I think I like it! I do find Miss Hattie quite captivating."

"Well, it was easy to see she found you appealing too, Doc," Maxy added, jumping into the conversation. "The only person who didn't seem pleased about the whole affair was Swamp Rat Charlie. It was quite obvious he wasn't keen at all about Miss Hattie showing you that much attention."

"Yeah, I'm sorry about that too," the doctor replied, shaking his head. "Charlie is a fine fellow—unfortunately—in the affairs of love and war—it's every man for himself. I just hope this doesn't cause a rift in our alliance."

"Alright fellows, I believe our coffee should be ready," Dad said. "Get your cups, and line up."

"Hey, here comes Frank and Charlie," Maxy announced, looking out the side window. "I'll go help them tie up."

"Today you boys get motorized," Frank hollered, throwing the bow line up onto the deck of the houseboat. "We brought your battery, and we also brought you 2 five gallon cans of gas. That ought to let you fellows do all the looking around you want to. How about tying us off and dropping the ladder, Maxy."

"Hey Ike—Cowboy—give me a hand out here," Maxy yelled.

"Charlie, if you'll stand up on the back of the boat there, I'll pass everything up to you and you can hand it on up to Maxy," Frank suggested.

"Hot Damn, we've got power," Cowboy said excitedly, as he came out and saw the gas cans and the battery.

"Don't forget the funnel," Charlie reminded, looking back at Frank.

"Here, let me give you boys a hand up," said Maxy, bracing himself and reaching down.

"Gentlemen, coffee is being served inside," the doctor announced, stepping out the back door. "Let's get it while it's hot."

"We'll just leave this stuff here for now boys," Frank suggested, heading for the door. "We'll take care of it in a little while."

"Man, can you believe that Indian build-up?" Doc said, coming in and sitting down at the table. "That whole dadburned island is surrounded."

"Yeah, that's unreal," Frank said, shoving his cup out towards Dad. "We made certain to stay well out of rifle range as we came over. You know—I've heard rumors for years that Jhondoc is somehow connected to the Indian tribe. I just wonder if he's part Indian."

"Well, whatever his connection is, it doesn't seem to be serving him too well," said the doctor. "It's obvious they want him bad, and it doesn't appear they want to pin a medal on him either."

"Wacanabbi-Min-Coto hates the very ground he walks on," Charlie stated, "and it's not just because he's one of the bad boys—it's something more. When they get their hands on him he's in for real trouble. Sometimes Wenoch will make references to how bad the Chief loathes Jhondoc, but as soon as I start asking questions about it he clams up. There's definitely a silence about it in the Indian community, and as of now I haven't been able to get the skinny on it."

"Gentlemen, we have a bit of a mystery on our hands also," Dad said, pouring himself a mug and sitting down at the table.

"What's that, Dave?" Frank asked. "Is there something we can help you with?"

"Well, it's not actually something we need help with," Dad answered. "It's just something we saw as we were coming into this area."

"Yeah, that was strange," said Maxy, shaking his head. "With all the excitement we've been having I had forgotten all about that."

"What did you see, Dave?" Frank questioned.

"It sounds dumb as heck to even talk about it," Dad said, with a sour expression.

"Well, what was it?" Frank repeated, a little more intently.

"A tall manlike creature went rushing across the road in front of us in absolute darkness. It looked like a man about six foot four, but it acted strange, and it didn't seem to need any kind of light to see where it was going. It was just far enough away that we couldn't tell if it wore clothes or not."

"Yeah, it just plowed off into the underbrush and was gone," Ike added, dramatically. "It seemed like it was right at home out there in the darkness."

"Gentlemen, you'll be pleased to know this weird account doesn't sound out of the ordinary to Charlie and me—right Charles?"

"Not at all," Charlie quickly replied. "Strangely enough, you've hit upon another touchy subject among the Indians. We call the thing you're talking about—The Ghost of the Night. The Indians call it—Me Watha Min Chato—roughly translated—He Who Walks in Shadows, or in Darkness, and they are very reluctant to speak of it. It's a local phenomenon that is yet to be explained. We know it's not our imagination, because we've watched it grow."

"Yeah, fifteen years ago it was only four feet tall," said Frank, "and it's gotten bigger and bigger. We can never seem to get a close look at it—it's now you see it—now you don't!"

"Well, that makes me feel a little better," Dad said, looking around at the rest of the gang. "At least we know we're not all losing our minds; It's really strange how something out of the ordinary like that can rattle your cage!"

"That's a fact," said the doctor, nodding his head in agreement, "but it also reminds me that I have a minor degree in anthropology that I've never had the time to entertain. Suddenly my scientific interest is peaked at white hot. This might be the find of the century, gentlemen. Is it possibly a wild man still exists out there?—incredible!" he said, shaking his head.

"Boys, in order to get this day moving forward," Dad said, "I suggest we set all that left-over food from yesterday's celebration on the table and fill our bellies."

"Hey, I agree with you," said Swamp Rat. "We've still got to install the battery and fill this tub with gas before we can get going, so that'll help speed things up."

"Yeah, and I've got to get back and open the store," said Frank. "By the way, Padre John said to tell you boys he's really sorry he couldn't make it to the independence celebration, and he wants to meet with you at the earliest opportunity. He was called out to the Indian community to administer last rites to an old person who was about to pass."

THE MYSTERY THICKENS AND THE CREW TOURS THE BAYOU   **297**

"Your priest sounds like a fine human being," Dad said, nodding his head at Frank.

"Padre John is the life's blood of this community gentleman. He's there when our babies are born and he sends our old folks to their final rest—he's our friend and inspiration—and whether you fellows like it or not, he's making you boys local heroes. Everybody in this area is going to know your names. He even wants to put his blessing on the buffalo stick—he calls it the wrath of God," Frank said, slapping his leg with a boisterous laugh."

"Oh my Lord," Dad groaned, rubbing his face and glancing discretely over at Doctor Cedric.

"Dave, just relax," the doctor whispered. "This could be very good for our cause. The more people we can get on our side the better."

"Gentlemen, have a great day, but be careful," Frank cautioned. "The bad boys are going to be looking for revenge."

"Let them look!" the Doctor grumbled, with a sarcastic smile. "The Wrath of God will be sitting right there in the corner. If anyone gets too pushy we'll lay a thunderbolt or two on them."

"Hey, that's a good one, Doc," said Cowboy, grinning and shaking his head. "I'm just glad it's Ike's turn to do the lightening. My shoulder's still hurts from the last time."

After 30 minutes of stuffing their faces with leftovers, Dad spoke up—"fellows, how about Doc and I put everything away, and straighten things up a little while you guys get our excursion vehicle ready to travel."

"Yeah, I'll second that motion," said the doctor. "I'm anxious to get on with our day."

"That sounds good to me," said Maxy—"let's get to it."

"Gentlemen, the fuel tank and the engine access are both on the back of the boat," said Charlie, as they walked outside.

* * *

A FUR COAT FOR MAMA

Within 15 minutes the newly charged battery was in place, the gasoline was in the tank, and the model A engine had been fired up and was running smoothly at idle. "Boys we're ready to go," said Charlie. "If we can find some volunteers to pull the anchors, we'll get this scow under way."

"Man, I'm just about as excited as old Doc," said Cowboy, shaking his head and looking at the other guys.

"Yeah, this is definitely something I never expected to be doing," Maxy agreed. "If the circumstances were different this would be a real kick in the butt."

"Gentlemen, the circumstances are different," the doctor announced as he and Dad came walking up behind the others. "This is our day to let our hair down. Dave and I have talked it over, and we are both in agreement—we need to back off a little. Working under this kind of pressure will burn us out. We're trying to do too much too fast."

"Yeah boys, I want all of us to just let it go for now," Dad said. "We'll take up where we left off tomorrow, but today belongs to us. We're going to look this old swamp over."

"Hot damn," said Cowboy enthusiastically, "maybe we can even gig us a mess of frogs and fry them up for lunch,"

"Yeah, and do some fishing," said Ike. "There's two cane poles right around there that are already strung up and ready to go. I'd like to see what kinds of fish there are in this marsh. I just wonder what we could use for bait."

"Bait is everywhere, Ike," said Swamp Rat—"Minnows, little frogs, crickets—we'll pull up in a little cove somewhere out in the back country and stock up. We've got a long handled dip net and a minnow seine around back."

"That sounds like the makings of a fine day, boys," Dad agreed. "We're also going to visit Doctor Cedric's old home place. Other than that we're just going to look around and do whatever we darn please."

"Hey we could always go by and pay the Princess a visit," Charlie suggested. "She lives over behind White Bird Island in the bird zone;

THE MYSTERY THICKENS AND THE CREW TOURS THE BAYOU 299

it's about five miles from here. It'll be a tight squeeze getting this big boat back in there. But I think we can do it—by using the poles a little I know we can."

"The bird zone," the doctor pondered stroking his mustache as usual and looking off into the distance. "If I'm not mistaken that would be east of here somewhere in that direction," he said pointing back to the right of the channel where the Indians had come out.

"That's where it is alright," Charlie agreed, nodding his head at the doctor.

"That's where the old home place is too," said the doctor. "It will be doubtful if I can still recognize it after all these years, but I'd sure like to give it a try anyhow. Hey, let's get those anchors up and get her moving, boys! We're burning daylight here!" the doctor yelled enthusiastically.

"I'll get this one, Ike," said Cowboy, grabbing the big anchor line on the back of the boat. "You get the front!"

"Hey, which one of you guys want to drive?" Charlie asked. "I'll be the navigator and try to keep us from running aground."

"How about we all take turns," Cowboy suggested. "Do you want to go first, Ike?"

"You betcha!" Ike replied exuberantly. "Man, this is going to be a great day!"

The steering wheel and all the driving components were set up in the very front of the dining room where a large three sided garden type window of heavy plate glass protruded out onto the front deck.

"Hey Bud, this is something else!" said Ike, as he slid into the driver's seat and took hold of the wheel. "You can see everything from up here. Man, I think I'm going to like this," he said, with a big smile!

"Well, just remember," Cowboy reminded—"we are taking turns, so don't get too dadburned comfortable in there!"

"Ike, I'd like to caution you a little before we get going," said Swamp Rat. "As you can see it's pretty much the same as driving a car except you're one pedal shy down there on the floor. There are no brakes on this thing! If you get into a tight spot and have to stop or slow down in a hurry you have to use the reverse gear, and sometimes it's a bit tricky to get in. The best thing to do is drive cautiously and don't get into trouble."

"I'll keep that in mind." Ike replied.

"How much water does this thing need to operate?" Dad asked, "and how are we going to know when it's getting too shallow?"

"It needs three feet of water to float it," Charlie replied. "When you think you might be getting too shallow, someone has to stand on the front of the boat with a push pole and checks the depth every few yards. The poles have a 3 foot mark painted on them. This scow isn't built for speed, boys, but in open water she'll run up to 10 or 12 miles an hour."

"That's a pretty decent clip for a tub like this," said the doctor. "I'd sure hate to hit a solid object going that fast."

"Yeah, a fellow could find himself sitting on top of two very large pontoons with a whole pile of used lumber floating around him," Maxy quipped.

"I'm pretty well acquainted with this part of the lake, and most of the navigable channels in the back country," said Charlie; "we shouldn't get into any trouble we can't handle. When we get into shallow water or tight quarters we'll use the push poles. The channel at White Bird Island where the Princess lives—we'll definitely have to use them there. Okay Ike, put her into gear and let's get going."

"Here we go," said Ike as he pulled the gear shift down and pressed the accelerator. "Hey, this thing responds well; we're already moving. Whoever designed this thing did one heck of a job."

"I'll say," Dad responded, "we can sit right here at the kitchen table having coffee and see everything that's going on—that is if we had some coffee."

"I'll get some going, Dave, if you'll stoke up the cook stove," said the doctor.

"Head straight down to the east end of the island, Ike," said Swamp Rat, "but stay all the way over to the right side. The channel to the left goes to Webo Island, and Indian Territory—to the right goes into the back country and the truly wild part of Bayou Blanc. That's where the birds are. Most of the people back in that area live very primitive lives—hunting, fishing and gathering. They eat anything that's edible, and birds and bird eggs—in season, are definitely on the menu."

"I'm glad to hear it's still like it used to be," said the doctor with a melancholy tone in his voice. "Damn, it's been a long time—and there's been a whole lot of water under the bridge—but you know something!—being here with you fellows is starting to revitalize my old spirit—I'm starting to feel the pull of the old ways again—in fact, today I'm going to teach you guys how to weave a crawdad trap out of willow switches," said the doctor, with a vigorous smile and a nod of his head. "Man, there's no satisfaction like boiling up a bunch of crawdads you caught in a trap you made on the spot. What I like even better than boiling them is to get some real big ones and peel their tails and fry them in butter with a clove or two of crushed garlic—oh man that's good!"

"Darn you, Doc, you've convinced me already!" said Cowboy, looking intently into the doctor's eyes. "The quicker you can show us that little trick the better we're going to like it!"

"Amen to that," Ike agreed. "I want to do it right now! I've always loved crawdads, but I've never been able to catch enough at one time to have a real feed."

"That was always my problem too," Dad replied. "Catching enough to use for fish bait was about all I could ever muster."

"You're in for a real treat then, gentlemen," said the doctor, "there's an abundance of those tasty little crustaceans in Bayou Blanc. They're the food source people in the back country can always count on. I was the sole provider for my mother and two younger sisters, from the time I was twelve years old, and I knew this old Bayou like the back of my hand."

"Okay Ike, start pulling hard to your right," said Swamp Rat. "We want to stay in the deeper water right next to that bamboo thicket. You'll need to get up a little more speed to navigate this part. The confluence of two rivers are merging right here and it's going to be fairly swift. Yeah, that's better; just stay about 30 feet away from the cane and keep pushing on up stream. It won't be long until the water slows down and we won't need to fight it."

"Is this all fresh water right here, or is it partly salt?" Maxy inquired.

"This is fresh water," said Swamp Rat. "Bayou Blanc drains off to the south. You start seeing the salt water influence over around South Bayou—like mangrove forests and cypress trees."

"Yeah that's the reason I asked," said Maxy. "Bamboo certainly doesn't like salt water and there's definitely an abundance of it here."

"I sure appreciated that when I lived here," said the doctor. "One thing I never had to worry about was a fishing pole. Wherever I decided to go fishing there was always a cane thicket nearby. I would just take out my pocket knife and cut me one that suited my fancy. When I decided to give it up for the day I'd just break off about three inches of the tip to wind my fishing rig up on and slip it into my pocket."

"Man, what a life!" said Cowboy. "I'm not sure one day of this is going to be enough. Hey, can't this thing go any faster, Ike? The quicker we get there, the quicker we can get to fishing!"

"Fellows, you need to make a decision here pretty soon," said Charlie. "Do you want to go sightseeing and look around, and maybe go back to visit the Princess, or do you want to catch us a lot of good bait and go fishing? If we're going to go fishing, there's a little bay up here about a mile where we can get all the bait we need."

"Well, why can't we do it all?" the doctor questioned. "Maybe Miss Hattie would like to go fishing too. Why don't we go by and see if she wants to go with us?"

"Hey, I think that's a great idea," said Swamp Rat, looking around at the other guys. "We're liable to have one hell of a fish fry before this day is over, boys! The Princess is the best damn fish fryer there is. I'd suggest we get bait then go by her place; she only lives about three more miles up here. Hey—fishing off her houseboat is just about as good as fishing gets!"

"Does that sound alright with the rest of you fellows?" the doctor asked—"how about you, Dave?"

"That sounds just fine to me, as long as it's okay with the other guys," Dad replied.

"We just want to go fishing; that's all we care about—right Ike?" said Cowboy.

"That's it in a nutshell," Ike replied. "I want to catch something to fry."

"Man, there's nothing I like better than a good fish fry," said Maxy, nodding his head and smiling in agreement. "If Doc will show us how to catch crawdads we'll do up a batch of them too."

"Then it sounds like we're catching bait," said Swamp Rat. "Our cove is coming up right around this curve. This little bay is the beginning of Bayou Blanc's bird country, and you're going to see a dramatic change in the terrain also. The river turns into a shallow marsh system that splatters out in all directions from this point on. This is one of the bird's favorite feeding areas. Most of their nesting is done from this point on inland. Ike you might start throttling back a little, and hold hard to the left."

"Holy Moley, look at that!" Maxy exclaimed, standing up and headed for the door. "Talk about a change—that's hard to believe!"

"Wow, I'll say!" Dad agreed, shaking his head, and following Maxy out onto the deck. "I've never seen this many birds in one place in my whole life."

The little bay was 10 or 15 acres of extremely calm shallow water leading in from the river about two hundred yards. There were countless birds—large and small and a myriad of different species standing in the shallow water vying for a position to hunt from, and literally filling the trees of the thick brushy forest that protruded almost to the water line.

"These birds are in here for the same reason we are," said Charlie. "They're taking advantage of the schools of bait fish. There are a couple of different types of shiner minnows and large schools of threadfin shad that frequent the shallows here. All we have to do is find us a spot and get quiet and they'll surface all around the boat."

"How do we catch them?" Ike asked.

"There's a long handled dipnet and a small mesh seine about eight feet long on the back deck in the little shed—in fact, there's about everything we're going to need for fishing in there. Frank really has this thing stocked up," said Charlie.

"Pull toward the center of the bay and kill the engine, Ike; we're going to pole on in from here."

"Good Lord—now I understand what bird country means," Dad said, as hundreds of multi colored birds took to the sky. "That—is a beautiful sight!"

"Yeah it's hard to believe I gave this up for the real world," Doctor Cedric stated, with a nostalgic look in his eyes. "It's really strange how life twists and molds you, Dave. My late missus despised this place. We lived here two years after we were married, and she hated every minute of it. Her family were people of means—she wasn't brought up like I was. I'm actually grateful to her because I did go through medical school on her daddy's money, but somehow I just never seemed to be content with life outside the Bayou, and it's almost like I still hold a grudge against her—God forbid," he said, shaking his head! "I did love the woman dearly, but this is where I've always belonged."

"As you already know my friend, life can be cruel and terribly unjust," Dad replied. "A person is very lucky if he finds a spot where he can be reasonably happy and someone to be happy with."

"No truer words were ever spoken, Dave," the doctor replied, nodding his head. "We're born alone and we die alone. If we're lucky there's a brief interval we can reach out and make a grab for the brass ring."

"Boys, lets get those push poles and go in a little closer," said Charlie. "We need to be in about four feet of water. If you guys will take care of that I'll get the nets and buckets out. If we can't catch them out here we'll go on in to the bank and seine them. We can get all we want in

THE MYSTERY THICKENS AND THE CREW TOURS THE BAYOU   **305**

that shallow channel up in front—but that means getting muddy, and I'd rather not, if we don't have to."

"I hear that," Ike replied. "That looks like a real mud hole out there, plus it's covered in bird poop."

"Here, one of you boys take the other side and I'll get this one," said Maxy, coming up the left side of the deck with the push poles.

"I've got it," Dad responded, reaching for the pole.

"It looks like we're already in about 6 feet of water," said Maxy as he touched the pole to the bottom.

"We don't want to run aground, so go easy," said Charlie, coming back with the buckets. "Push in a little closer—four feet is about where we want to be."

"That shows to be about four feet right there," Dad yelled.

"That's what I'm reading too," said Maxy.

"Throw the anchors boys, we're going to catch some bait," said Charlie.

"Hey, give me that dip net," said Cowboy. "I already see a few coming up around the front of the boat here."

"Give me a second to get some water in these minnow buckets," Charlie said, tossing the two buckets overboard with a quarter inch cotton rope tied on each one.

"Hey, men, I've got bait," Cowboy yelled exuberantly, as he retrieved the long handled dip net hand over hand.

"Dump them right in here," said Charlie, laying the lid back on one of the minnow buckets.

"Hey, you got three, Bud," Ike yelled, excitedly as Cowboy walked forward with the net. "Man, those are pretty little guys."

"Yeah, you got two golden shiners and one silver," said Charlie, flipping the net over to dump the minnows. "All we need is a couple hundred more and we can go fishing."

"A couple hundred!" Cowboy exclaimed, "I thought I was doing good getting that many!"

"We might need to move around a little, but I believe we can get all the bait we need. In a pinch we can always get some fiddle worms to finish the day with."

"Fiddle worms," said Ike, looking Charlie straight in the eyes with a sarcastic grin. "I think you're pulling our leg now."

"No—actually I'm not," said Charlie. "You actually do have to fiddle for them. Here, give me a hand with this seine. Let's unroll it and get it in the water. Would some of you guys fetch us a piece or two of dry bread from the kitchen?"

"I'll take care of that," Dad replied.

"We need some bait to draw the minnows in where we can net a bunch of them at one time," said Charlie

"Hey, that's a great idea," said Cowboy, as they started lowering the seine toward the water. "We just lay the seine out on the bottom then draw the minnows over it."

"That's about it," Charlie said. "These two long poles with lead lines on them allow us to lay the seine out nice and flat then when the minnows get over it we quickly walk backwards in opposite directions to raise it."

"Now, I can see how we might catch two hundred more minnows," said Ike. "That's pretty slick!"

"Just roll the slack up and make it taut then prop the pole up on the rail like this," Charlie said. "Alright, Dave, let me have that bread and we'll get started."

"Holy cow—look at that!" said Ike, as Charlie began crumbling the bread onto the water. "There's a pile of those little buggers down there already!"

"Man—those bread crumbs draws them like flies to sugar!" said Cowboy with a wide grin. "We're going to massacre them!" he said, looking back at Dad and Doc.

"Gentlemen, get ready to bring in a pile of bait," said Charlie. "We've got a whole school of threadfin shad, and God knows what else over our seine. We need a couple of people to grab the outsides of the net and roll the fish together as we draw them up and someone else to guide them into the buckets. We may have our bait already caught. Ike, grab that other end and start backing up."

"Good grief—I have never seen this much danged bait in my whole life!" Dad chuckled, stepping forward to help direct the catch into the buckets. "This is unbelievable!"

"Now, you're getting the picture of life in the swamp, Dave," said the doctor, helping Dad direct the squirming mass. "A man can live down here without half trying. One of these little beauties right here can easily be turned into a five pound large mouth bass or channel cat, and then you filet the fish and use the carcass to catch a pile of crawdads. What could be easier than that?"

"I'll have to admit it's sure a lot different than where we live, Doc."

"Holy cow—I still can't believe it," said Cowboy, kneeling down to pick up several minnows that escaped the buckets. "There's more minnows here than I've seen in my whole danged life, and we caught them all in one scoop."

"Let's go fishing, boys," said Charlie. "We may not need fiddle worms after all!"

"Fiddle worms!"—Ike said, shaking his head. "I still say you're pulling our leg, Charlie."

"Well, you'd be wrong, Ike. There's a type of worm down in this country that's a little hard to believe even when you see it," said the doctor.

"Tell us more, Doc," Dad suggested. "I've never heard of nothing like that before."

"Me neither," Ike agreed with a suspicious grin. "I still say they're setting us up for a prank."

"Fiddle worms are a type of night crawler that is exceptionally sensitive to vibration," said the doctor—"the reason being—they are the favorite food of moles—so their defense is to crawl out of the ground when they feel a mole heading their way. The way you catch them is to drive a hardwood stake into the ground and saw across the top of it for a few seconds with an old dull handsaw to vibrate the ground. That's what we call fiddling. I know it sounds silly, but they'll come out of the ground for twenty feet around. You can just hurry and pick up what you need."

"Boys, I'm going to have to see that little trick," Dad said, chuckling and shaking his head.

"That makes two of us," said Ike. "That's sounds mighty suspicious to me!"

"You boys have a whole lot to learn about the swamp!" said Charlie, with a sly grin. "Life down here marches to a different beat—it's a bit strange to outsiders—right Doc?"

"That's a fact; it's truly a place of surprises, gentlemen. I didn't know how much I missed it until right now," the doctor replied, looking out across the serene little bay. "It sure feels good to be back. Hey boys, let's go fishing! Who's driving this pile of boards anyway? I know I'm not," he said heading around the side of the boat. "I'm putting dibby's on one of those fishing poles."

"Hey Doc, now that's not fair," Cowboy yelled. "You're taking unfair advantage here!"

"It's alright Bud," Ike said, in a conciliatory tone. "You're going to be busy driving anyway. The doctor and I can handle the fishing."

"Ike, you dog face—we're going to get you and Doc for this," Cowboy declared—"just you wait and see!"

"We've got plenty of tackle," said Charlie, grinning at Cowboy.

"Yeah, we'll cut us a new custom pole and they'll be fishing with those old second hand things," Cowboy said loudly—"cheaters never win!"

"Dave, I'll get the back anchor if you'll get this one," said Maxy. "We need to get this thing on the move—we're burning fishing time."

Thirty minutes later and three miles deeper on into the bayou, the crew observed a change in Doctor Cedric's demeanor, as he began twisting on his moustache and pacing back and forth from one side of the boat to the other, closely scrutinizing everything around them.

"Well, what do you think, Doc?" Dad asked, as he and Charlie walked up beside the doctor. "Is there something along here you think you might remember?"

"You know fellows," he said, putting his hand up to his eyes to block the sun, "I think there is—it's been fifty years or more since I've been here, but I'd almost guarantee you this waterway coming up is the entrance to the old home place channel—in fact—I know it is!" he yelled, looking at Dad and Charlie with excitement in his face. "I've spent many a day fishing off of that big old rock right there," he said, pointing to a house sized flat topped rock in the mouth of the channel. "I'd drop my crawdad traps off of one side and fish off the other!"

"If you fished off of a rock," said Charlie, nodding his head, in agreement, "that's got to be it. That's the only large rock I've ever seen in Bayou Blanc. I've always wondered how the heck it got way out here in the middle of nowhere. By the way, that's White Bird Island on the left, and that waterway is the way in to where the Princess lives. Her houseboat is about a mile straight down there. Ike—you'd better let me take it from here," he said, walking into the houseboat. "How about you and Cowboy get the poles out and each one of you get in the front on different sides. I'll keep the motor running at an idle, and you boys try to keep us punched off of snags and away from the bank."

"Man, I've paddled up and down this old channel hundreds of times, boys," the doctor said, with a nostalgic tone in his voice. "My Papa died when I was 12, and I had to take over as head of the family."

"Man, that's mighty young to assume a responsibility like that," Maxy said, shaking his head.

"It was for a fact," the doctor replied. "I had to quit school and make a lot of other adjustments that a kid that age shouldn't ever have to do, but I took to it like a duck to water—Papa was a good teacher. I had dozens of crawdad and fish traps all along this channel, and I always had my trusty .22 with me for ducks and wild game—I didn't have any problem keeping food on the table. I even kept up on my school work at night. I was a very busy young man!" he chuckled. "When I wasn't fishing or running my traps I was repairing my gear to keep everything in working order. My biggest problem was finding enough bailing wire to keep things tied together. In a pinch I would use willow bark or wild grass to bind things with, but bailing wire was the real answer—It stayed put! Big turtles and alligators will wreak havoc on homemade traps if they see fish in them. Needless to say, I always kept my eyes peeled for wire that needed a good home."

"Hey, Charlie we've got a big floating log coming up!" Ike yelled. "You'd better ease off a little!"

"I'll put her out of gear for now, Ike," Charlie yelled. "You tell me when we're clear."

"Man, the birds are getting thicker the farther in we go," said Maxy. "This is bird heaven!"

"This is the real beginning of bird country," said Charlie. "They stay away from areas where people are, but this is how all the back country is—needless to say, where there's a food source like this, there are lots of alligators. You want to be careful about putting your hands in the water around here—especially under trees where birds are nesting. The gators are used to snapping up any nestlings that have the misfortune of falling out."

"Okay, Charlie—we're clear," Ike yelled.

"When we get around this little bend in the channel, you'll be able to see the Princess' houseboat," Charlie said, as he pulled the gear shift down. "It's only another hundred yards down there."

"I don't really know where the old home place is," the doctor admitted with a bit of frustration in his voice—"it's just been too long. I do know it's on this channel though, and it would be on the left side," he said, with a gesture of his hand; "we have to be very close to it right now. It's probably grown over where I wouldn't recognize it anyway."

"Did you have a house, Doc, or did you live on a houseboat?" Charlie asked.

"We had a house," the doctor quickly replied. "My Papa built it with his own two hands. It sat back away from the swamp on a knoll about 50 yards. It was really a nice place to live."

"The only high spot in this whole area that I can remember is right down here about a hundred yards—in fact it's right behind where the Princess' houseboat is moored—come to think of it, I remember seeing a few old bricks and the odd board scattered around out there."

"If that's the only high spot then that's got to be where it was," the doctor replied. "This is definitely the right area. Wouldn't that be a coincidence?" he said, grinning and shaking his head.

"I'll almost guarantee you that's it," Charlie ventured. "Oddly enough that's the Princess' favorite spot—she's got a picnic table up there, and she and her critters spend a lot of time out there. She's has a ramp from the houseboat to the bank—there's a trail leading right up there."

"Well, it would certainly be nice to know there's someone else who appreciates it as much as I did," said the doctor. "The happiest days of my life were spent there."

"Well, there's Miss Hattie's place in the sun," Charlie pointed, as the houseboat began coming into view.

"My goodness!" the doctor chuckled, with a look of amazement on his face—"a piece of Southern culture right out here in the middle of nowhere."

"Yeah, Miss Hattie is a class act," Charlie proclaimed. "You'd think she's was still living in the middle of New Orleans the way she keeps this place dolled up."

"It's certainly eye catching the way she's got it fixed," said the doctor admiringly. "You can tell an awful lot about a person by seeing the place they hang their hat. White, pink and blue must be her favorite colors."

"Yeah, it must be," Charlie agreed. "This is about the third time she's painted it a variation of the same thing."

"*Hola Senores,* it is so good to see you," Miss Hattie yelled, coming around the end of her houseboat waving both arms. "I am so very pleased that you are here."

"We're going fishing, Missy," Doctor Cedric yelled, walking quickly to the front of the boat. "My friends and I were wondering if you would like to come with us."

"Oh, yes, Walter, I would very much like to come, but it will take a little time for me to get ready."

"We're in no great hurry," said the doctor—"we're just out for the day to have some fun."

"Oh that is wonderful!" Miss Hattie replied. "Tie your boat to my walkway and get out for a little while. I will hurry and get ready."

"As soon as we get close enough," Charlie said, "some of you guys jump off on the walkway and make sure we don't destroy it. This monstrosity is really heavy and it's hard to control."

"We'll take care of it," Ike said. "Bud you get the back and I'll take care of the front," he said, leaping off onto the walk.

"Aww, now that's the way it should be done," said Charlie, as the houseboat slid gently in beside the walkway with the combined assistance of Cowboy and Ike. "I don't really think we'll need to tie it fellows. The current will keep it here."

"Well, I see the snake hasn't swallowed the monkey yet," Doc Cedric observed, as Juevito leaped onto the houseboat and went bounding around the deck.

"Believe me—it's just a matter of time!" Charlie said, with a certainty in his voice. "She is so oblivious to the danger that little guy is in. I really dread the day when it happens though—she really loves that little guy."

"Oh well, life goes on," said the doctor. "Gentlemen, let's get off and look this place over."

"Please come in and sit down," said Miss Hattie. "I will hurry and get ready. Where are we going to go fishing?"

"We haven't actually decided," said Charlie. "I was telling the guys that fishing off your houseboat is about as good a place as I know of. We've already got all the bait we need."

"Oh that would be very nice," Miss Hattie agreed, sticking her head out of her bedroom. "I catch all the fish I want right here."

"Hey, I just saw three big bullfrogs suck their heads down when I went down the walkway," said Cowboy. "Maybe we can even get us a mess of frogs."

"Yes, there are many of them here!" Miss Hattie agreed walking out of her bedroom adjusting her clothing. "I can hardly sleep for their loud noises."

"Well now, I think it would be plum un-gentlemanly of us to leave a lady in such distress—don't you boys?" said the doctor with a smug grin. "Why go any further? I'd like to look this place over anyway."

"Doctor Cedric would like to see the spot up on the hill where your picnic table is," said Charlie, looking directly at Miss Hattie. "This may be the spot where he was born and raised. That could possibly be the place where his family home stood."

"Oh my goodness—Walter!—Your name is up there! I wondered who Walter was—who are Chrissie and Judy?"

"Those were my two sisters," the doctor replied, with a stunned look on his face. "How do you know this?"

"You must come with me right now," said Miss Hattie, grabbing Doc by the hand and heading down the walkway, almost in a run.

"WC—Walter Cedric plus—DC—Who is DC?" asked Miss Hattie, looking back at the doctor.

"Missy—hold on a minute—this is all happening just a little too fast," said the doctor, pulling Miss Hattie to a stop. "Where are you getting all this from? DC stands for Doris Claiborne, my late wife. How do you know about that?"

"Come, I will show you!" Miss Hattie insisted continuing to tug on the doctor's hand and heading on up the hill. "There—you see! I found it about a week ago! I was trying to drive an iron stake in the ground to make my umbrella stand up, but no matter where I drove it—it still wouldn't stand up. I spent an hour shoveling all the dirt off of it. See—Walter—Chrissie—Judy!"

"Oh my God!—the door step to our old house!" Doc gasped dropping to his knees, and running his hands gently over the surface. "I helped my Papa pour this when I was 10 years old. Like all children my sisters and I wanted to put our name and handprint in the concrete," he said with a slight break in his voice. "Walter, Chrissie, Judy—June

6th 1879. Oh Lord Missy, you don't know what this means to me," said the doctor, as large tears started forming in his eyes. "I'm the only one left of a beautiful family that once thrived on this very spot. How time does fly!"

"Oh Walter, I am so very sorry," said Miss Hattie, kneeling down and taking the doctor by the hand. "Maybe I should have left it buried."

"Oh Lord no, Missy! I owe you a great debt of gratitude. I have wondered all my adult life if I could ever find where I was brought into this world. Things don't last long in the swamp—nature takes them back. Now my mind can rest on the subject," he said struggling to get to his feet.

"There is one more thing, Walter," said Miss Hattie, taking the doctor by the hand and leading him to a large old rotted tree trunk.

"Oh my God—more shades of the past!" said the doctor, as he viewed the initials carved into the ancient tree. "My late wife and I stood here one beautiful summer evening holding hands, and I carved these initials as a sign that we were betrothed. I am the last of a fading dream that began on this spot so very long ago—life has passed over all the rest. Folks, I think I've seen what I came here for," said the doctor, looking at everyone gathered around him—"life is for the living, and as you've just witnessed—time waits for no one. We're burning fishing time, folks," he said wiping his eyes on his shirt sleeve. "Let's impale some of those fine minnows we've got and catch us a fish fry!"

"That's a fine thought for a fine afternoon, Doc," Dad agreed. "I'm going to hunt me up a good fishing pole down here in this little bamboo thicket, and get with the action."

"I'm with you," said Maxy. "I can't wait to get me one of those nice shiners on my hook."

"Swampy, your friend Wenoch is here," said Miss Hattie, pointing down the hill. "I just saw him go around to the front porch."

"Okay, I'll go down and see what he's up to. Maybe he'll stay and fish with us," said Charlie.

"Tell him we will have a fish fry later," said Miss Hattie.

"Missy, I've got a fishing setup ready to have the hook baited," said the doctor. "Let's get down there and find us a good spot before these other bums get ready."

"Oh Walter, you are so funny! I too have a pole," said Miss Hattie with an impish grin. "Let's hurry before they get back," she whispered. "I know the very best spot—I will show you; I catch big fish there all the time."

"Missy, you are truly a lady after my own heart—but I think I've told you that already—haven't I?" said the doctor with a sly grin.

"Yes you have, Walter, and I like it very much when you say nice things like that to me. I feel very good when I am with you."

"I am equally touched by your presence, my dear," the doctor said, taking Miss Hattie by the hand. "It's been a long time since a member of the opposite sex has aroused my feeling like you do, and I want you to know that every minute I'm spending with you is becoming more precious."

"Oh Walter, that makes me feel so wonderful to hear you say that," said Miss Hattie, holding the doctor's hand in both of hers. "I am so tired of being alone. Life here could be very good here if I had a proper companion."

"Well, dear lady, let's make the most of this day that we know we have together," said the doctor, stopping and taking Miss Hattie by both hands. "At this point in time I have a dear friend that is in grave trouble, and I have a solemn duty to see him through his ordeal. For now let's just enjoy each other and see which way life leads."

"I like that thought very much, Walter. We will enjoy today, and hope for many tomorrows. Now let's go catch some big fish and prepare for an evening fish fry."

"Like I said before, you're a woman—er, well I don't want to over work the same line, but you are very special, to me, Missy!"

"I like it so much when you call me that—I have never had a special name before!"

"All I can say, kid—you've been around a lot of ignorant men. You're a lady of class, and you're not afraid to attack the world—I find that extremely attractive. I'll get us a bucket of bait while you get your fishing gear. Holy cow—did you see that fish right there!" said the doctor, as a big swirl broke the surface. "He had to be two feet long!"

"Hurry and get the bait, Walter. This is where I catch the big ones. I will get my pole."

"Hey, Doc, I've got a good one on," Ike said, walking around the end of the houseboat, with his pole bent and the green linen line singing.

"Dadburn you Ike, I thought we had you aced out," said the doctor. "How did you get back down here so fast?"

"I hurried," Ike said, with an irritating grin.

"I will get the net," said Miss Hattie, running around the end of the boat.

"My God what a beauty," the doctor exclaimed, bending over to better see the struggling fish. "Man, that's a two or three pound crappie, Ike. Hurry Missy, we don't want to lose this one. That's all the fish right there one person could possibly eat," said the doctor, smiling and twisting his moustache.

"Here Walter, you do it!" Miss Hattie exclaimed, handing Doc the net.

"Get him back up here again, Ike. I saw him awhile ago but he's down too deep now."

"Yeah, he's evidently gotten around a bush or something down there. I can still feel him, but he's not moving."

"Well, just give him a few seconds or two more, and don't horse him. He might come loose."

"Hey, he's loose, Doc—get ready—here he comes!" Ike said, applying more upward pressure on the tiring fish.

"Oh man, what a beauty," said the doctor as the big black and white sunfish rolled to the surface. "Welcome to dinner," the doctor said softly, with a wide grin. "You're the guest of honor."

"Oh my goodness, that is really a big one!" Miss Hattie yelled excitedly, as Doc dumped the slab side crappie out on the deck.

"That fish will weigh three pounds, Doc. That's the biggest danged crappie I've ever caught. We need a tub or something to put him in."

"Wait a minute, Ike, and I'll cut us a forked willow limb to put him on," said the doctor—"then we can hang him back in the water."

"No sir-ree, I'm not letting that critter get anywhere near the water, Doc," Ike responded. "I'm going to eat that fish!"

"I will get you a tub, Senor Ike," Miss Hattie said, heading quickly around the houseboat.

"Holy mackerel, who caught that slab side?" Cowboy questioned, as he, Dad and Maxy came walking up with their newly cut fishing poles. "That is the biggest danged crappie I've ever seen," he said, stooping over for a closer look.

"I caught that slab side, Bud," Ike said, in a taunting voice. "Now you see the value of thinking ahead? What was that you said?—cheaters never win! What do you think now?"

"I think you better not get too close to me, right now sucker, or you're going to be sucking up branch water," Cowboy said. "I'm still going to get you—just you wait and see!"

"Poor sport," Ike taunted.

"Cheater," Cowboy instantly replied, looking at Ike with a sour smirk.

"Hey, where's Charlie," Dad asked. "We need some tackle to go on these poles."

"He must have gone with his friend, Wenoch," said Miss Hattie. "He will probably be back soon."

"Hey, soon don't cut it fellows, when there's fish like this being caught," said Maxy, looking around at the other guys. "Let's go find what we need, and get our lines in the water."

"My thoughts exactly," Cowboy replied, as they all three went hurrying toward the other houseboat.

"Hey Ike, do you have more bait over there?" the doctor asked.

"I've got a half dozen minnows in a small can, Doc, but you're welcome to use them as long as they last."

"What I'd like to do is borrow one to bait Missy's hook and get her in the water, then I'll have to go fetch my pole. I'll bring back one of those bait buckets and we'll get down to some heavy fishing."

"I've got a better idea; you stay here and get Miss Hattie fixed up and I'll go get your pole and the bait. How does that sound?"

'That's mighty gentlemanly of you, Ike. That sounds just fine. I will return the favor."

"No problem, Doc. The minnows are in that little can sitting right there on the end of the deck. I'm going to dip some water up in this tub to put my fish in and then I'll get your pole."

"Come on my lady—let's get a minnow on this thing," said the doctor heading toward the end of the deck. "I suppose we might as well fish down here where the bait is," he said, reaching into the can for a minnow. "There—that should do it," he said, dropping the impaled minnow into the water, and adjusting the small red and white bobber to about 4 feet. "Here—take the pole quick," the doctor prompted as the little float instantly sank to about three feet deep.

"Catch him, Walter," Miss Hattie yelled excitedly, backing up and refusing to take the pole.

"Oh my Lord," said the doctor, quickly bracing his feet and pulling up strongly against the fish. "Ahh—he's a good one, Missy," the doctor yelled! "Are you sure you don't want to land him?"

"Oh no, Walter you catch him!" Miss Hattie proclaimed exuberantly. "Get him in quick before he gets away!"

"Alright—Doc—you've got one!" Ike hollered.

"Here, Señor Ike, you do it," said Miss Hattie handing Ike the net. "I don't want him to get away!"

"Okay, Doc, bring him on up here. I want to get my rig back in the water."

"Hey, you boys are going to have to shove over a little," Dad said, as he and the guys came walking up—"we want in on the fun too."

"Yeah, you guys are hogging the best spot," said Cowboy. "I'll wait until you land this one Doc—then it's every man for himself—or her self," he said, winking at Miss Hattie.

"I think he's just about ready to give it up Ike," Doctor Cedric professed, putting some extra effort on the fish—"get ready!"

* * *

Well, the afternoon went by all too quickly, but it was a delightfully productive time. The washtub ended up with thirteen large crappie, a four pound large mouth bass that Maxy added, and a 10 pound flathead catfish that Dad lucked into. All in all, the day was a huge success: The cruise on the bayou, the fish fry with everyone eating his belly full, the re-connection of Doctor Cedric with his roots, and a new set of feelings between him and Miss Hattie. When it was all over the tired participants all agreed it was a time to remember. Everyone kept watch for Swamp Rat but he failed to return, so about six o'clock the guys fired up the Model A engine, and leisurely cruised back to their parking spot across from the island.

"I just wonder what could have happened to Charlie," said Maxy, as the crew went about anchoring the boat.

"Yeah that's a little strange for him not to come back; I'm a little worried about him," said the doctor. "As we all know, there are some very unsavory characters that hang around these parts."

"There is the possibility that he ran into trouble," Dad said calmly, "but I'd be more inclined to think he got held up some way by the Indian tribe."

"Yeah, that would be the more logical line of thought, Dave. He'll probably show up hale and hearty before we know it," said the doctor. "Boys, I want all of you fellows to know—today was one of the finest days of this old mans' life, and without a doubt it was the best fishing trip I've ever had."

"Now Doctor Cedric—you being raised in this swamp, I'm sure you must have had lots of fishing of this caliber before," said Ike.

"Yeah that's certainly true, Ike—I did a lot of fishing back then, but most of it was done alone, and all of it was done for base survival. Today I fished for the pure pleasure of fishing with my very best friends. I can't think of any greater pleasure that I could possibly have had than what I've just experienced."

"It was one heck of a day, Doc," Dad agreed. "I think a good night's rest now will revitalize us all. You had a great idea Old Buddy, but tomorrow we have to get back to the reason we're here. I'm really worried about my little man."

CHAPTER THIRTY-THREE—Spirit Man and the Wrath of God Is Lifted

That night the crew observed a change of tactics in the on-going Indian war against Jhondoc. All the torch-lit canoes had been abandoned for solid positions on the island, and there were large bonfires burning approximately every hundred feet apart around the entire island. Before bedtime the crew gathered on the front deck to have a last look around before hitting the hay. "I really can't imagine just what those people are up to," Doctor Cedric postulated, as they all stood observing the sea of lights.

"They certainly don't intend for old Jhondoc to get away—do they?" said Maxy.

"Yeah, that's for sure," Dad agreed, "I'm a bit like you, Doc. I can't figure why they don't just go in and get him. They've got plenty of man power—why all this rigmarole they're going through?"

"I'm starting to believe there's some kind of ritual being played out here, Dave," said the doctor.

"What do you mean, Doc?" Cowboy questioned.

"Yeah, what kind of ritual do you mean?" Ike asked, with a puzzled look on his face.

"Well, a ritual can be as simple as us getting up and having our morning mug or going to church on Sunday, but primitive people sometimes have rituals that are pretty bizarre—even matters of life and death. That was part of my paleontology studies. What I see going on over on that island leads me to believe this could be one of those cases—they can even think their very existence as a people depends on the outcome.

For example, the Aztec Indians of Mexico used to believe that the sun would cease to rise if a certain number of human hearts weren't ripped from the living bodies of captive slaves each day and offered up as sacrifice to their God. The fact that the Spaniards conquered them in the 16th century and put an end to the practice, pretty well proves it was all in their imagination—since the sun is still coming up more than four hundred years later. Now—granted—that's an extreme case, but you get the point."

"What do you think about what we're seeing here, Doc?" Dad asked. "Do you have any idea why they're doing this?

"No I don't, Dave. We may find out if we stay around here long enough, but right now I haven't got a clue."

"Well, whatever it is they're taking it danged serious," said Maxy.

"Yeah, that's what makes me think there's more to it than meets the eye," said the doctor. "Fellows, as good as this day has been, I think this old man is going to hang it up—I'm bushed."

"Yeah, I'm with you, Doc," Dad said, stretching out his arms with a noisy yawn. "Anything else can just wait until tomorrow."

* * *

The next morning early, the crew was awakened by Swamp Rat pounding on the front door. "Hey you guys in there, get up," he yelled. "I've got some stuff I want to tell you."

"Well, at least we know he's still alive," the doctor grumbled.

"Yeah, he certainly sounds alive—he's loud enough," Dad said, rolling out of bed and heading for the door. "Man, it's good to see you Charlie. We were afraid you might have run into trouble."

"Naw, I didn't have any trouble, but it was certainly a long drawn out day. I actually ended up staying at the Indian village last night. I've got so many things to tell you guys I don't even know where to start."

"Sit down here at the table," Dad said, "and you can talk while I get us some coffee going. Hey, you guys! Get up in there; we've got company."

"Top of the morning to you, Charlie," said the doctor as he ambled slowly into the kitchen, tucking his shirt into his pants. "We were a little worried about you."

"Yeah, it's a little unbelievable what I ran into at the Indian village. Those people think you guys are some kind of spirit beings!" Charlie exclaimed.

"Spirit beings!" Dad said, stopping dead in his tracks. "What could possibly have given them an idea like that?"

"Wenoch took me straight to the Chief's house and that's where I spent the whole day," said Charlie. "Man, you guys have Wacanabbi-Min-Coto in your hip pocket. He asked me a thousand different questions about you guys."

"What kind of questions?" the doctor inquired. "Why would he possibly be interested in us?"

"Well, first of all, he wanted to know if I could touch you, or if my hand would pass right through you. Boy, you guys really have him spooked! He's most interested in Dave though—he calls you Daveed," Charlie said, looking straight into Dad's eyes.

"My God, what is happening here? That's what that girl that ran away from us called me!"

"That girl that ran away from you guys is the Chief's youngest daughter, Wayrayah. She says Daveed rescued her from the pit of hell, and brought her back home. I don't have a clue what she's talking about, but those people over there think you guys are spiritual beings sent here to rescue them from the torment of the evil ones."

"Oh my Lord, Doc, what are we going to do?" Dad lamented. "This thing is getting way out of hand! How are we going to get past all this interference? I've got to find that dog and get back to my family!"

"I'll agree, it's not going exactly like we planned, Dave," the doctor said, scratching his head and twisting on his moustache. "Right now I'm a bit shy on answers."

"Well, for starters why doesn't someone tell me about this pit of hell thing?" said Charlie. "Maybe I'm the one who's fooled. You guys aren't really spirit beings are you?" he said, reaching out and grabbing Dad by the arm.

"I'm afraid not," Dad said, shaking his head with a slight grin. "We're just hard-working old boys that have run into a major problem in life."

"Well, tell me about Wayrayah; what's this thing about the pit of hell?"

"You tell him Doc," Dad said, sitting down at the table with his head in his hands—"right now I don't feel like I can deal with it."

"The Sloyd brothers of whom you are well acquainted, not only ravaged the countryside where we live and burned half the town of Sugar Grove, but they were holding Wahrayah and two local women as sex slaves. They were being held in a large tunnel complex which the scum bag brothers had built on their old farm. Dave is the one who discovered where Wayrayah was being held and went in and rescued her. The other two women were both deceased. I guess it was as close to the pit of hell for Wayrayah as it could possibly get. In her broken English she calls Dave 'Daveed,' for David."

"Hey, I can see why she would be impressed," said Charlie, shaking his head. "A man she has never seen before shows up out of nowhere and not only rescues her from a fate worse than death, but treats her good and even brings her back to her people. That is a deed worthy of a saint. Boys, these people are backward and uneducated, but they are good honest people. They are very taken with the fair treatment they have received from you, and they are well aware of what has happened to the bad guys at your hands. Whether you are *Los Santos*, as they are calling you or not, you have made some very fine friends."

"*Los Santos*," mumbled the doctor, shaking his head. "The Saints— holy moley, Dave; now I'm starting to get worried."

"Hey, Charlie, I was just wondering," said Maxy, "did you hear anything about what's going on over here on that island?"

"Just a lot of mumbo-jumbo that I couldn't understand—something about the blood of the Old Ones being separated from the Blood of Evil."

"Yeah that's just about what I figured," said the doctor. "They've got some kind of old ritual running on Jhondoc. That fellow is in real trouble. Before this thing is over he's going to wish he'd been a good boy."

"Hey, I brought you boys a present, from the Chief," said Charlie. "I told him how much you enjoyed Indian sausage and he had his Missus make you up a special batch. I'll go get it and we can fry it up for breakfast if you want to.

"Oh, man, let's do it," said Cowboy. "You boys can eat that leftover fish we brought home, and I'll take care of the sausage."

"That's what you think, Sucker," said Ike. "I'll fight you over Indian sausage."

"Boys, after we eat we need to clean the barrel on the old buffalo stick," said the doctor. "The bore on those old guns start rusting real quick after you fire them. We need to run an oiled rag through it and oil the breach too."

"Hey where is it?" Ike asked, looking over in the corner.

"I left it right there," said Cowboy, looking at the other guys. "Somebody had to move it."

"I haven't touched it since we've been here," said Maxy.

"Me neither," Dad added.

"That makes three of us," said the doctor. "As far as I know you two fellows are the only ones that have handled it,"

"The last time I touched it was when the Indian buildup started," said Cowboy. "I took it out on deck."

"You don't suppose it could have fallen overboard, do you?" Maxy asked.

"No it didn't fall overboard," Dad replied. "I'm positive I saw Cowboy set it back in the corner, and you also set the box of shells you took back next to the other box on the stand," he said, looking at Cowboy. "Gentlemen, both boxes of shells are gone too. We'd better have a look around."

"Yeah, that gun has become a very integral part of our game plan!" said Charlie.

It didn't take long for the crew to exhaust all the possible thoughts on where the old gun could be and what could possibly have happened to it. In the end there was no other possible explanation—someone had come on board at night and taken the weapon. "That's mighty hard for me to accept," Dad said, shaking his head. "How could anyone come on board and us all here and take that gun, especially in the dark?"

"It's certainly hard to believe, Dave," Doc Cedric agreed, "but the fact that it's gone, proves it did happen, and we just have to accept it."

* * *

The loss of the big gun had a dramatic impact on the Sugar Grove boys and ultimately the entire Bayou Blanc Committee for Action. After the quick elimination of two of the main bad guys and the commandeering of their vessel, everyone had high hopes of being able to take the fight to the remainder of the offenders at South Bayou, and completely break the back of the criminal element, but the loss of the buffalo stick really took the life out of their plans. The old gun had turned out to be the ultimate weapon for the job. After a couple of days of nursing their frustration finally everyone got their heads back together and began working on a plan. Since Swamp Rat knew the South Bayou area and the general layout of the islands and settlements they decided he would be the captain of a three man team that would include Ike and Cowboy, and they would take one of the larger canoes that was capable of carrying the three of them and enough supplies to last for a few days and sneak into the enemy's backyard and do some very low profile exploring. Their main objective was to find out where the other four Sloyds were holed up and maybe even find where they were keeping Old Trailer. There was about twelve miles of open water between Mission Point and South Bayou, so the plan was for Frank to tow the canoe with the launch and drop the guys off in a mangrove swamp two or three miles from the nearest settlement. The entire insertion plan would be done in total darkness and the team would work mostly on the fringes of the settlements, asking questions of people that were unlikely to be connected to the bad element. It was a very tense moment for the boys and Swamp Rat as they boarded the canoe and pushed away from the launch. "Gentlemen, it's three o'clock," said Frank. "We'll be back for you in two days at this same time. This is the central waterway leading into South Bayou so we shouldn't have any trouble finding you, but if we can't make connections, fire three shots, one from your pistol and two from your Winchester, like one—two—three, and we'll know it's you."

"We'll do our very best to be right in this general area," said Swamp Rat. "I don't want to be here a minute longer than I have to."

"That makes three of us," said Ike—"right Bud?"

"Absolutely," Cowboy agreed, with an affirmative nod.

"You boys be awfully careful," Dad cautioned as the canoe began sliding away into the darkness.

"We're going to ease back out of here as gently as we can," Frank said to the guys, beginning to idle the big launch back towards open water. "We've got to be well away from here before daylight. We don't want to alert anyone to your presence."

"Godspeed, boys," the doctor said softly as the darkness swallowed up the canoe.

"Damn, I wish I was going with them!" Maxy stated, shaking his head. "I can't hardly stand seeing them go off like this."

"Yeah, I know what you mean," Dad replied. "I don't imagine we'll be thinking about much else until they're safely back. I sure hope they can find out what we need to know. Man, I hope everything's alright at home."

"Dave, I know this is danged tough on you," said the doctor, "but those three men out there are a force to be reckoned with. If there's anybody that can do this job—they can. I'd damn sure hate to be any-body that gets in their way. What you and all of us need to do now is just relax and give them the time they need. Then, we'll know more about what we've got to do."

* * *

The scouting team paddled steadily for more than two hours through the mangrove swamp toward the larger of three small islands that make up the South Bayou settlements. As they slowly picked their way through the flooded forest using only the light of the full moon they became aware of a presence that seemed to be some distance behind them and off to their left. They would occasionally hear a branch snap or the sloshing sound of water as if someone was following them at a distance. "Boys, someone knows we're here," said Swamp Rat, looking back over his shoulder—"and that is not good."

"Yeah, we are definitely not in friendly territory." Cowboy replied, with a frown on his face. "Let's just pull over behind this big green bush and wait on him. We don't want to get shot in the back."

"You've got that right," Ike agreed, quietly jacking a shell into the firing chamber of his .30-30. "We might as well take care of it right now!"

As they sat there waiting for what they were sure would be one of the criminal element of South Bayou gliding out of the darkness, a curious thing happened—no one showed up—instead the entity continued forward but circled around them. "He's over there about a hundred yards now," said Swamp Rat, pointing to the front of their position.

"Yeah, a big crane flew out of the top of that tree over there," said Cowboy. "I could see it in the moonlight. That's where he is all right, but how in the hell did he know where we were?"

"Good question," said Ike—"it's as if he can see us and we can't see him. I don't know if you guys have noticed, but this guy isn't following normal rules."

"Yeah, that's just a little spooky to me," Cowboy whispered. "What do we do now, Charlie?"

"Let's cut back across his path a little bit more to the south and see if he follows—if he does we'll have to figure out a way to take care of him. The tip of Dragon's Head Island, where I was heading, is back in that direction a little more anyhow."

For the next hour the scouting crew tried several diversionary tactics to lose the unwanted tail they had acquired but to no avail. Everything they tried was clearly anticipated by their adversary and easily avoided. "That's the dambdest thing I've ever seen," said Ike, shaking his head with a look of frustration on his face.

"Yeah, there's nothing we can think up that he hasn't already thought of and sidestepped," said Cowboy. "If this guy wants to kill us, fellows, he damned sure can and there's no doubt about it. He's just playing cat and mouse with us now!"

"Yeah, we've got a problem here I don't know how to solve," said Swamp Rat. "I don't understand how this is possible, but, the truth is—if we want to stay alive we better get the hell out of this swamp fast. This guy is way out of our league. I can't figure out why he hasn't fired on us already."

"The only reason I can think of," said Ike, "is he just don't want to— or at least not right now! He's probably got something special planned for us and he's saving it for the finale."

"Boys, I don't think I want to stick around to see what he's got in mind," said Swamp Rat. "The quickest way out of here is to turn back to the right and paddle as hard as we can. The main channel is only about a half mile in that direction. If we lay our backs into it by daylight, we can be halfway back across the lake."

"We can't start too quick to suit me," said Ike. "Spook hunting is Brother Dave's thing! Let's get the hell out of here!"

* * *

The scouting crew had only traveled about fifty yards back towards the main waterway when suddenly an ominous but very familiar voice rang out loudly from the darkness.

"Well, well, who do we have here!" the voice called out as brilliant light from sealed beam headlights suddenly flooded the whole area.

"Well now, wouldn't you just know it—it's the boys from Sugar Grove!"

"God damn it!—it's Dud Sloyd!" said Cowboy, shaking his head in disbelief. "I'd know that rotten bum's voice anywhere!"

"What brings you farm boys off down here to this infernal swamp? Surely it's not that little old black and white mutt. No dog in the world is worth dying over," Dud chided, looking down from a large platform built in the top of a huge cypress tree. "I wouldn't be touching no weapons there if I were you fellows," he warned, shaking his head. "You see—these short barreled shotgun's are loaded with double ought buck. You wouldn't stand a chance! Me and old Luke here will kill you before you can blink your eyes—won't we Luke?" he chuckled, looking at his brother with a sadistic grin.

"You betcha we will!" said Luke, with his eyes dancing and a malevolent grin rippling across his ugly face. "Let's—let's—do it right now, Dud. I—I—I ain't kilt nobody in a long time—and I—I want to!" Luke stuttered.

"Good Lord, boys, we are in grave trouble," Cowboy whispered. "The only chance we might have is to turn this canoe over and try to swim under water out of this light. They're going to kill us, there's no doubt about it!"

"That's not much of an option, Bud," Ike whispered, shaking his head, "In five minutes they'd hunt us all down."

"Well, it's better than just sitting here and getting shot all to hell," Cowboy insisted.

"Turning that boat over won't get you out of this swamp, fellows," Dud said, anticipating what the boys were thinking. "You're mine now, and there's nothing you or anybody else can do about it! I swore that time at the wagon yard when you stole our money, I'd get even with you tough guys, but now there's even a better reason—you killed my brother Wag! He wasn't much, but he was my brother! You guys shouldn't have done that," he chuckled, shaking his head. "Rat man—you oughtened to have listened to these farms boys—they got you killed! You see—I'm going to make alligator food out of all of you—right now," he said, raising his shotgun to firing level. "Damn you Luke—get that shotgun barrel away from my ear you damned nit-wit," Dud sneered, as his younger brother stepped forward to get a better shooting position. "You could have deafened me for the rest of my life—you danged fool!"

"I—I'm sorry, Dud—I just wasn't thinking," Luke replied nervously, stepping sideways a couple of steps.

"Well, start thinking, or I'll knock your stupid brains out!—you hear?"

"Yes sir, Dud—I—I'll—I'll do better next time! I—I promise!"

"Well, see that you do! I just might feed your worthless butt to the alligators too!"

"I'm sorry Dud, I—I really am."

Just as Dud was about to lower his shotgun again a soft whistling sound broke the quiet of the swamp as it whizzed over the heads of the scouting team. Before anyone could say—"what was that"—the whole top of Dud Sloyd's head from his eyebrows up seemed to vaporize like a overripe watermelon hit by a runaway freight train.

"What the he-hell!" Luke screamed, running backwards with blood and brain matter splattered all over his face and clothes.

"I think we've just found our buffalo gun, boys," Cowboy yelled, as a small thunderclap roared through the swamp.

For an instant Dud was still standing with the whole top of his head gone and blood squirting six inches straight up into the air. Just as he went crashing headlong into the murky water below, another whisper of impending death whistled out of the night and hit Brother Luke with the sound of a baseball bat swung into a wet mattress. Instantly he flew ten feet backwards into the swamp, as if some invisible giant had smote him with a mighty backhand. "God damn, boys, let's get ourselves out of here fast!" Swamp Rat yelled, as another thunderclap roared through the bayou. "I don't know who's in charge of that damned gun, but right now I don't think I want to find out."

"My thoughts exactly," said Cowboy. "I'd just as soon learn about it second hand!"

"Yeah, maybe next week sometime over coffee," said Ike, as everyone dug their paddles deep into the yellow water of Bayou Blanc.

Within four or five hard strokes the guys were out of the blinding light and passing under the platform atop the giant cypress. "Look at that!" Swamp Rat yelled, in a muted voice; "there's the other launch tied behind this big tree. If we could commandeer that we could get out of harm's way in a hurry."

"Man, that's for sure; let's give it a try," said Ike. "We know how to operate the other one, and this one looks identical."

"Hey, if we hurry we might just pull it off," Cowboy agreed, peering around the side of the huge tree off into the darkness. "The man with the cannon has to be at least 200 yards in that direction, and that puts this big tree directly between him and us—let's do it! Pull alongside and I'll get in and check it out."

"Man, it really gives you the creeps to see what that buffalo gun does to a man's head, doesn't it?" Swamp Rat said in a low voice.

"Yeah, especially when its maybe aiming at one of us any second now," said Ike, glancing backwards. "I want to be gone from this place right now!"

"Oh man, the key is in the ignition!" said Cowboy, running to the front of the boat.

"See if she'll start, Bud," Ike whispered, holding the canoe up alongside the big launch.

"Yeah, let's hurry; that shooter could be getting into position to do a number on us by now," said Swamp Rat, looking back over his shoulder.

As Cowboy turned the key a feeling of desperation ran through the guys as a small electrical clicking noise sounded in rear of the craft. "Oh no, the battery is dead," Cowboy whined.

"Boys, we'd better get back to paddling, quick," said Charlie, peering into the darkness. "Our nemesis could be nearly on top of us by now,"

"Wait a minute Bud; let's give it one more try," Ike insisted, jumping over into the boat. "It might be just a loose connection," he said, jerking open the battery compartment—"try her now."

As Cowboy turned the key the second time the big engine sputtered for a second or two then roared to life, and the desperate situation suddenly turned hopeful. "Charlie, pile your butt in here; we're going home—Ike, get out there and untie us quick," Cowboy yelled. "Just leave that canoe right where it is, Charlie. Trying to tow that thing through this brushy swamp will slow us down, and right now we don't need slow."

"That's for danged sure," Swamp Rat agreed, crawling over into the boat.

"We're untied," said Ike, as he jumped back into the launch. "Let's get out of here!"

As Cowboy threw the big boat into reverse and began backing away from the giant tree, Ike was searching the dash for the toggle switch to the headlights. "It's got to be right in here somewhere," he said, running his head over the dash. Suddenly the whole area in front of the launch was bathed in brilliant light.

"Alright, now we can see where we're going," said Cowboy. "There's a chance we might see home again fellows."

"Man, let's put some distance between us and the Wrath of God," said Swamp Rat. "The short hairs on my neck probably won't go down for a week," he said, rubbing the back of his head. "That is a weapon I definitely don't want to get shot by."

"Yeah I can't believe we let it get away from us that damned easy," said Ike.

"What I would like to know is—how is this person firing it that accurately in the dark?" said Cowboy.

"Yeah, there are a whole lot of questions here that need to be answered," Swamp Rat agreed. "Not withstanding the fact that this person must be able to see clearly in the dark, which is highly abnormal—what I really want to know is—is he just a psychotic freak that likes to kill people, or is he only shooting the bad guys!—who's side's he on?"

"Somewhere in my heart of hearts, Charlie," said Cowboy, shaking his head, "I believe we would be just as dead as those other guys if he had wanted it that way."

"Yeah, me too, Bud," Ike replied—"the way he nailed those guys—one shot—one kill, doesn't leave much of a question about that. He could have done us in anytime he wanted right there at the beginning but he didn't—it's almost like he knows who we are!"

"Yeah, me too," Swamp Rat agreed. "Alright, Cowboy, this open area coming up leads directly into the main channel, and it's plenty deep for this boat. Let's get this thing moving; I want to leave this bad dream behind us just as quick as we can."

"Amen to that," Cowboy replied shoving the gas pedal to the floor, "Hold on boys, we're going home," he said as the big boat roared up to a plane.

* * *

Within ten minutes the launch flew out the mouth of the South Bayou channel and headed out into open water, with the scouting crew starting to feel like they might actually live to see the sunrise. "Man, I've never been so scared in my whole life," said Ike, looking backwards into the darkness. "Did this thing actually happen to us or did we just dream it? It seems like only seconds ago we were getting ready to be alligator food!"

"It was only seconds ago!" Cowboy said, shaking his head. "I've never felt so helpless in my whole life. Knowing you're about to be blown to hell by crazy people with shotguns sure brings home just how much you enjoy living!"

"That's a fact!" said Swamp Rat, "I don't think I'll ever look at a sunrise the same way again—sort of changes your whole perspective," he said. "I'm really sorry we didn't learn anything about Dave's dog though; this is really going to be a letdown for him. I guess it wasn't a complete failure though, we did get away with their powerboat which is bound to slow them down a little, and there are two members less of the South Bayou crud gang we won't have to deal with."

"The fact we're still alive and able to tell the story is the best part," said Cowboy. "We looked instant death in the eyes, fellows. This is liable to change the way we think about every day life—you know!"

"Yeah, I may be ugly as hell and all beat up, but I danged sure like hanging around the old planet," said Charlie.

"Hey, man, you're selling yourself short," Ike said, with a mischievous look on his face. "You're just beat up—this is ugly," he said, grabbing Cowboy's swivel chair and turning him around.

"Ike, you're cruisin' for a bruisin'," Cowboy said, clenching his fist at Ike. "You're just adding to the misery you're going to suffer as soon as I get around to it. If you mess around any more I'm going to stop and throw your gangly butt in the drink."

"Hey, there's the light from the Mission Point Marina over to the left, Cowboy," said Swamp Rat. "You need to make a slight course correction here."

"Hey, I just thought of something," said Cowboy. "If we try to pull this launch up alongside that houseboat, we're liable to be fired on before we can explain who we are."

"You know, that's an absolute fact," Ike agreed. "They're going to think we're the bunch from South Bayou."

"Yeah, somehow we need to let them know," said Swamp Rat. "Hey, I know; we'll do the signal we were supposed to do for pickup—then when we get their attention we'll move in closer where they can tell who we are."

"That ought to work," said Cowboy. "Man, I sure wish it was daylight. Let's get the guns up here and make sure we're ready."

"Steer clear of the island, Bud; we don't want any more problems than we already have," said Ike.

"No problem there," Cowboy replied. "That place is lit up like a Christmas tree. I'm going to approach the houseboat on the opposite side anyhow. We're just about center with the island right now, so the shape of the boat should be showing up pretty quick."

"I think we're a bit too far to the left, Bud; what do you think Charlie?"

"That's a possibility, but we're getting close," said Swamp Rat. "It'll be showing up soon. There it is—right there," he said, pointing off to the left. "I can barely make it out."

"Yeah, I see it too," Cowboy replied. "What do you guys think?—are we close enough?"

"We're actually in back of the houseboat right now;" said Ike—"let's get in a little closer and a bit more forward. We need to approach from the front. What was the signal—two rifle or two pistol?"

"One pistol—two rifle," said Swamp Rat. "We're ready to go, but let's get forward just a little more. Alright—let's kill the engine. Here Ike, you do one shot from the pistol and I'll do two from the rifle."

"Are you ready?" Ike asked.

"Let her rip," said Swamp Rat.

Pow—boom boom, the shots rang out across the water, instantly causing a flock of wild geese to take to the air somewhere nearby.

"We'll have to sit here awhile, and see if we aroused anyone," said Swamp Rat.

"I sure hope we don't alarm the Indians and cause them to send out scouts," said Cowboy. "I don't want to get shot by accident now that we're home."

"Yeah, this boat has always belonged to the bad guys too," Swamp Rat replied. "It might be a little hard to explain."

"Hey, I believe I just saw a light over there," said Ike, looking into the darkness toward the houseboat.

"Yeah, there definitely is," Cowboy agreed. "Maybe we're going to get to come home after all. Somebody just walked out on the porch with a lantern."

"It's probably Dave," Ike said. "I'll see if he can hear me. Hey Dave, it's Ike!—can you hear me?" Ike yelled at the top of his lungs. "You've got better hearing than me, Bud—see if you hear him answer."

"I can hear people talking," said Cowboy.

"Yeah, I heard it too," Swamp Rat agreed.

"Well, what are they saying?" Ike questioned.

"I can't make out what they're saying, Ike, but I would assume they're discussing what's going on," said Cowboy. "They probably can't see us out here. Yell again, and maybe they'll respond."

"Hey, Dave—Doc—Maxy, it's us, can we come on in?"

"Why are you asking?" came a faint reply.

"That's Dave," said Cowboy, "he wants to know why we're asking."

"Well, what do I say?" Ike asked.

"Tell him we're in a different boat than we left in, and we don't want them to fire on us," said Swamp Rat.

"We're in a different boat," Ike yelled—"a motorboat and we don't want you to shoot at us."

"They're mumbling again," said, Swamp Rat.

"What's the pickup signal?" Maxy yelled.

"Let's give them the signal, boys," said Swamp Rat. "You do the pistol again, Ike."

Pow—boom boom, the signal went out.

"I think he said come on in," Cowboy relayed, shaking his head, "but my ears are ringing so bad I'm not really sure."

"I'm like you," said Swamp Rat, "I think that's what he said though. Fire up the engine and let's approach real slow and we'll keep talking to them as we get closer."

"Yeah, that'll work," said Ike. "We'll just keep talking. Take her in slow, Bud."

"I can see them out on the front deck now," said Swamp Rat.

"Hey, boys, we traded our canoe in on a better boat," Ike yelled, as they slowly approached the front of the houseboat. "Isn't she a beauty?"

"Man, how did you guys pull that off?" Dad yelled as they got close enough for the guys to see.

"It's a long story fellows, which we'd really like to forget about," said Cowboy. "Man, I didn't think we would ever see this place again."

"Let's tie this thing up and you boys come in and tell us about it," said the doctor. "Man, that's one fine machine you boys have acquired."

"I am so tired I'm just about to fall down," said Cowboy.

"Me too," Ike agreed, as they started unloading. "I could sure use a few hours sleep. Come on in Charlie," said Cowboy, heading for the front door. "Let's see if we can find us a place to fall."

"Well, I can see right now we're not going to get much information out of these guys," the doctor grumbled.

"We've been through hell, Doc," Ike moaned. "What I can tell you right up front though, is we're damn lucky to be alive."

"That's a fact," Swamp Rat agreed. "We'll tell you guys all about it as soon as we rest a little."

"Dadburn it, I don't know if I can wait that long, fellows," said the doctor impatiently. "My curiosity is just about to get the best of me."

"I'm sorry, Doc, but right now I just can't do conversation. We'll make it up to you!" said Ike apologetically.

"Go to bed, Son," said the doctor, patting Ike on the shoulder "We're just glad you're home safe."

"Fellows, you need to get in there and get rested as quickly as you can," Dad said. "We have a distinguished visitor coming around 10 o'clock. Padre John is coming over to meet us all—Frank is bringing him. The rest of us will be cleaning up the house while you guys rest up."

"It feels like I could sleep a week," said Cowboy, as the gang all entered the houseboat.

CHAPTER THIRTY-FOUR—Padre John's Visit and Secrets Unveiled

Dad was very apprehensive about what was going to happen when the priest got there because he could see the task he was there to do being diverted farther and farther off course. Somehow he had to maintain his sense of direction and not get bogged down in what was happening around them. He would be just as cordial as possible but try not to get involved in anything outside of what he came there to do—at least that was his reasoning.

As everybody went about doing their respective chores—Dad, Maxy, and the doctor doing a thorough cleanup, and the intrepid explorers, resting up from their ordeal, finally the doctor broke the silence. "I just can't imagine how those boys acquired that boat," he said, shaking his head. "Did they just find it parked and stealthily sneak off in it or did they actually meet the enemy in combat and commandeer it? Darn their hides they could have told us a little more about it!"

"Look at it this way, Doc," said Maxy, "as much as those guys like to talk—it had to be a really tough ordeal, or they would have been blabbing their heads off about it immediately."

"Yeah, that's what makes me so antsy—I just know there's a really good story behind it, and here we are about to have company, and I probably still won't get to hear about it even when they wake up—what a predicament!"

"Well, I just hope we can get through this visit with the Padre and not find ourselves diverted somewhere off into left field," Dad said. "We're down here for one reason—to get my boy's dog back, and get back home. With everything that's going on around us that fact is threatening to get lost! As much as I'd like to be a Good Samaritan, I just can't afford to take my eye off the ball here. We must remain on task, fellows!"

"That's a fact," Doctor Cedric agreed, "and we need to get it done quickly. Our little buddy's life is hanging in the balance."

As the morning wore on and the cleanup was finalized, Dad said, "Fellows, I think we should be getting the boys up—it's 9:30 right now," he said, pushing his railroad watch back into his watch pocket.

"Yeah, we need to give them a few minutes to get straightened up," said Maxy. "I'll go in and roust them out."

"Doc, I think we need to get us a new pot of coffee brewing," Dad advised, heading toward the cook stove.

"That's a fine idea, Dave; we're probably going to need all the help we can get. When the priest gets here, I'd suggest we do a whole lot of listening and head nodding—the less talking we do the better," said the doctor. "Maybe we can read between the lines and get an idea of what's going on around here so we can stay out of the way and get our job done."

"Fellows, that's exactly what I was going to suggest," Swamp Rat agreed, as he walked into the room. "The Padre is a walking index file on everything and everybody in this area, and the scouting crew has some questions we desperately need answers to."

"Man, that's for sure!" said Cowboy. "I'm still not sure if all that really happened or we just dreamed it."

"The trouble with Padre John—he'll clam up tighter than Dick's hatband if you ask him direct questions—he tries to protect everybody, and he's afraid he's going to say something he shouldn't. He's getting up in age and he doesn't trust his memory."

"Well, now since the subject has come up," said the doctor, "why don't you boys tell us a little bit of what you ran into over there? It's been wearing on my mind something awful."

"Well, for starters, Doc, we found your buffalo gun," said Ike. "Whoever has it shoots it in the dark just as good as if it was daylight."

"Now fellows, that answer needs a whole lot of explaining!" said the doctor, looking at Maxy and Dad.

"Yeah, I'd say that's a near impossibility. Well, if you found it," Dad questioned—"where is it? It's like the doctor says, you fellows need to give us some answers here."

"We found it, but somebody else was using it, Dave," said Cowboy.

"Gol-durn you guys, quit with the double talk!" said the doctor irritably—"tell us something we can understand. Charlie, tell us what's going on here!"

"What's going on, Doc, is whoever took your gun was at South Bayou last night. He blew two people to kingdom come, right out in front of us—it so happened it was two of the Sloyd brothers, but he scared us so bad we're still shaking. Seeing what that gun does to a man's head does a real number inside your mind. We've got to find out who this guy is and whose side he's on."

"If he shot the bad boys it stands to reason, he's got to be on our side—doesn't it?" Maxy suggested.

"Yeah—well—I'd sure like to think so!" Swamp Rat replied hesitantly, "but I want to make damned sure before I do much paddling around out in the dark again."

"Whoever he is, he's a cat of a different color," said Ike. "He is definitely not a normal person, and he scares the holy hell right out of me. Just thinking about being anywhere near him and that damned gun, makes that stiff stuff in my back turn to jelly!"

"Well, if there's anybody in the Padre's parish that would be capable of such a feat, there's a 99 percent chance he knows about it, but there's also a 99 percent chance he won't tell us if we ask him straight out. We'll have to ask unrelated questions then figure it out for ourselves."

"Hey, guys, here comes the launch," said Maxy looking out the window.

"Dad blame it, fellows, you're killing me here!" the doctor groaned, shaking his head. "I still don't know anymore than when you first got here—dang your hides anyhow!"

"Doc, just give us a little more time and we'll explain it all," said Swamp Rat.

"Now you've got to promise me—as soon as this visit is over you'll tell us everything about your trip!" said the doctor, "and I do mean everything!"

"Okay, Doc, you've got our promise," said Cowboy. "We'd be doing it right now except for this visit."

"Fellows, I've been around the Padre a long time, and I know how he thinks," said Swamp Rat, "so if you'll let me do most of the talking I'll try to maneuver him into giving us the information we need. If he discovers we're picking his brain—the game is over!"

"Alright, you've got the floor," Dad said. "Let's go on out and help dock the boat."

"Hey, where did our boat go?" Ike exclaimed, looking around at everyone.

"We took the liberty of dragging it around to the other side of the houseboat while you guys were asleep," Maxy volunteered. "We needed the parking space."

"That's a good thing," said Swamp Rat. "I'd just as soon Frank and the Padre don't know anything about it at least until our conversation is over. We need answers, and having to do a lot of explaining will slow up our process."

"Good thinking," Ike agreed, "that way we can get right down to business."

* * *

"Bring her right alongside and point the bow forward, Frank," said, Swamp Rat, with a semicircle gesture of his arm. "That way we can tie her down solid."

"How was that?" Frank asked, looking at Swamp Rat with a grin as the big boat slid smoothly up against the houseboat. "Man, I never expected to see you guys here," Frank said, looking around at the crew.

"We'll tell you all about it after our visit," said Swamp Rat—"keep it on the QT for now—Okay?" he said, in a quiet tone. "We've got a major problem! Padre John, how are you, my old friend?"

"I'm well, Charlie, and I am very pleased to be greeted by such a distinguished reception party. I have waited very impatiently for this moment—several times I have almost made it only to be delayed again. Thank God I am finally here!"

"Padre, let me give you a hand up," Dad said, stepping forward to grasp the priest's hand.

"I am so honored to finally meet you gentlemen," said the padre. "You have brought hope to a despairing people."

"Padre, let me introduce you to the boys from Sugar Grove," said Frank, stepping up onto the deck. "Boys, line up right here," he said, turning the padre to face the crew. This is, Maxy, Doc, Cowboy, Ike and Dave," he said, pointing each one out separately.

"Gentlemen, I am extremely pleased to finally make your acquaintances. Your presence here has changed everything in the lives of these people. There is now hope where there was no hope. Whatever you think of yourselves, there are those of us who feel that your journey here was guided by a higher power, and we are so very grateful for your presence."

"Padre, let's go on inside where we can be more comfortable," Dad said. "We just made a new pot of coffee if you're interested."

"I would be very interested," said the Padre, following Dad toward the door. "It's one of the vices I very much enjoy."

The Priest was a man of about seventy years old and it was apparent that his age was catching up with him. He was somewhat stooped and walked with the aid of a homemade cane whittled from a stout black walnut sprout. It was very apparent that he had seen better days, but the zeal with which he still attacked life and the fire in his sparkling brown eyes, left no doubt that he was very much in control.

"Padre, you can sit right here at the head of the table," said Frank, as they all gathered in the dining room.

"There you go, Padre," Dad said, sliding a full coffee mug in front of him.

"Thank you so much, for your kindness. I can't tell you folks what a great pleasure it is to be here. Your arrival and the bold action that you immediately displayed raised us from our pit of anguish. Over the years, we had settled into a state of helpless despair that went clear to the marrow of our bones—but your appearance has changed all of that. We are now of one mind and one spirit, and we intend to have peace and dignity in our lives or we will all die trying," he said, pounding his cane on the floor with his brown eyes flashing. "As you know the arch enemy of the whole of Bayou Blanc is now the prisoner of the Indian tribe, and I will assure you he has ceased his earthly malice."

"Padre, why is it the Indian tribe has gotten so involved in this affair with Jhondoc?" Swamp Rat asked. "If they want him why don't they just go in and take him; they certainly have plenty of manpower."

"Yes, that's a fact; they certainly do," said the priest hesitantly.

"Then what's the hold-up?" Swamp Rat, asked looking directly into the eyes of the priest.

"That's sort of a long involved story, Charlie," he said, showing a bit of stress in his face.

"I don't think there's anyone here that's in much of a hurry," said Swamp Rat, looking around at the others, "and we would really like to know what's going on over there."

"That knowledge is a very touchy subject, and I really hate to talk about it at all," said the priest, shaking his head—"but—since you fellows are involved here I suppose it's only right to give you an answer to your question. I must swear you to complete secrecy on the subject, though!"

"You have our solemn word; it will go no farther than this room," said Swamp Rat. "Go on Padre."

"Well, you see—Jhondoc is, in actuality, Chief Wacanabbi-Min-Coto's grandson. His father—if one can call him that, was the animal and arch criminal—Bojoc Breen. He has been dead for some years now."

"Yeah, we know about Bojoc," said the doctor. "We were instrumental in his demise."

"Oh praises be!" the Padre responded instantly, pounding his cane on the floor with his dark eyes alive with excitement. So you are the ones! You were already helping us in our struggle, and you didn't even know we existed. The Lord was using you even then my friends!" he declared, striking his cane against the floor again. "I desperately want to hear the full story at your earliest convenience."

"We would be glad to oblige you sir," the doctor replied, "but please continue; we want to hear the rest of your story."

"Well, Bojoc's death gave us a small space of breathing room, but it was too soon filled by this seed of evil that he left behind. You can well understand why the chief is so determined not to allow him to escape."

"Explain to us how the chief and Bojoc's blood got mixed up," said Swamp Rat. "I've been around the Indian tribe a lot and I've never heard anything about that."

"As you can imagine it's a very sensitive subject, Charlie, needless to say, the Chief is devastated by it, so out of respect for him it is never spoken of."

"What actually happened?" Charlie asked—"how did it all come about?"

"The chief's oldest daughter, Wahrina, her husband, and their 2 year old son were out canoeing, and Bojoc and a bunch of his thugs encountered them in the back country—true to form they shot Wahrina's husband to death and carried her and the little boy off to South Bayou—it doesn't take much imagination to know what happened after that. The Chief's daughter had a son by the most evil man on the planet, and he grew up to be a malefactor of the same type as his father, plus he had an inborn hatred for Indians. Just a few days ago he and his thugs raped and killed the wife of a dear friend and left him with three little children to raise alone."

"That's Wenoch, my good buddy I was telling you guys about," said Swamp Rat—"but Padre, that still doesn't answer our question why don't they just go in and get him? Why are they just sitting on top of him like that?"

"That's another sad story," said the priest. "As hard as I've tried to teach them the ways of Christianity, they still cling to a lot of the old ways. The shaman has assured the chief that his magic can separate the blood of the Old Ones—the blood lineage of the chief—from the blood of the evil ones. You and I know that's an impossibility, but the chief still believes in him."

"So what they're doing over there is some part of the process of separating the blood," said the doctor, searching the priest's face for answers.

"Yes, that sadly is the truth. The shaman says they must first weaken the blood of evil to the point of death, and only then can the blood be separated."

"So what you're saying," the doctor deduced, "is they're going to starve him almost to death, and then the ritual of separating the blood will take place."

"That would seem to be the process," Padre John said, nodding his head in agreement. "They hold a lot of stock in the purity of the earth. The shaman has told the chief that when the blood of evil has been sufficiently weakened it will be spilled out upon the pure earth and the blood of evil will die instantly—but the blood of the Old Ones—the millions of people from the past in the chief's lineage, will be preserved."

"Holy cow, that almost sounds reasonable," said Ike, shaking his head with a perplexed look on his face.

"Doc, you were dead right!" Cowboy exclaimed, looking directly at the doctor—"that is a life and death situation!"

"It almost had to be," the doctor acknowledged—"it definitely had all the earmarks. Well, whether the blood separating process has any merit or not there is a definite plus factor to what they're doing."

"What's that, Doc?" Maxy asked, with a confused look. "What kind of plus factor?"

"The bum won't be killing any more women and children," said the doctor with a slight chuckle."

"That's the way I look at it too," Padre John said, sitting up straight in his chair and pounding his cane on the floor. "The earth will finally be rid of Bojoc Breen!"

"Okay, Padre, slide your mug out here, and I'll give you a warm-up," Dad said, bringing the pot to the table.

"Padre John, I think I understand what's happening on the island, and how the chief got into this terrible mess he's in," said Swamp Rat, "but what happened to Wahrina?"

"Yeah, and what ever happened to her little boy?" Doctor Cedric questioned.

"Gentlemen, you are forcing me into an area which I am not prepared to talk about!" said the Padre. "As the keeper of the flock, I have a duty to keep family secrets in complete confidentiality. This thing that you ask is an extreme case, and I have been sworn to secrecy on it for well over 20 years."

"Padre John, we understand your need to protect your flock," said the doctor, "and like we told you before, this knowledge will go no farther than this room. You have expressed confidence in us as being sent here to help you, and we will be leaving this area soon, so the secret you are protecting will remain protected. We would very much like to hear the rest of the story."

"Yes—yes, of course—I am ashamed of my behavior gentlemen, please forgive me. In my old age I am becoming unsure of myself, so I am trying to be as careful as I can. I have never revealed this to anyone before, and even now I am very anxious about doing it."

"You're a fine man, Padre John, and we applaud your kindness," Dad said. "The people in this area are very lucky to have you. We will guard your secret with our lives."

"Thank you so much, my friends, for your understanding. It will probably do me good to finally be able to tell someone of this horror story I have carried in my heart for so long. Chief Wacanabbi-Min-Coto is a dear, dear friend of mine, but tragedy seems to have found a permanent home among his people. The indignities they have suffered at the hands of Bojoc Breen and the South Bayou bunch have been unbelievable and is still ongoing. I will try to relate the story as accurately as I can. There are many members of my parish who live at South Bayou and for about two years after Wahrina was abducted I was able to get word of her occasionally, but after that time she completely disappeared and has never been heard from since."

"What about the little boy?" Swamp Rat asked—"what happened to him?"

"That my friends, is the extreme secret I have been protecting," said the Padre. "At this time he is 27 years of age, and he has never spoken a word. He was found floating in the swamp in an empty canoe with a severe head injury about the same time his mother stopped being seen. He was four years old at the time. Since he has never talked, no one knows whether a good Samaritan set him adrift to save his life or if he did it on his own."

"That is such a tragedy," Doctor Cedric, commented, sympathetically. "Trauma of that magnitude can easily cause a child to grow up abnormal. He probably saw his mother brutalized and went into a state of severe shock."

"Whether it was the physical and mental abuse of himself and his mother or the head wound or both, it took a terrible toll on him," the padre answered.

"What's his name, Padre?" Swamp Rat asked.

"His name is Wacanabbi-Min-Coto the third. His parents named him in honor of the chief. The chief's natural son had died many years before of pneumonia. A sadder state of affairs I have never witnessed," said the priest, shaking his head. "The child that was named to honor him has grown up to be a very introverted individual. He lives with his grandparents—the Chief and his wife."

"Padre John—why is it I've never heard anything about this before?" said Swamp Rat. "I've been in the chief's house dozens of times and I have never heard anything about Wacanabbi-Min-Coto the third—in fact I didn't know such a person even existed!"

"It's like I told you, Charlie, he's a very reclusive person. If I told you what the local people call him, you would recognize him immediately."

"Well, tell me Padre; what's he called?"

"He is known as—The Ghost of the Night, Charlie."

"Oh my God—Mewatha-Min-Chato! He who walks in shadows is the Chief's grandson!"

"Now you know the whole truth," said Padre John. "The chief has underground living quarters for him beneath his house."

"That's a bit strange!" said the doctor, looking at the priest inquisitively. "One would think the more exposure a person like that got the better off he would be. Why is the chief hiding him?"

"It's actually to protect him, Doctor. Due to his tragic beginning, he suffers from severe vision problems. His eyes can stand very little light. Being in constant darkness is how his life is lived—what made things even worse, as he began to grow up he discovered he wasn't like everyone else, and he began to rebuff any interaction with the tribe and became more and more introverted—needless to say, it's a sad thing. The Chief calls him Buddy, and he is very fond of him."

"That's amazing," said Swamp Rat. "I could tell that Wenoch didn't want to talk about the subject, but I had no idea why. Does Buddy function at all in the real world, or is he a complete recluse?"

"Oh—on the contrary!" the padre replied, "he is very intelligent, and he is eager to do anything he thinks will please his grandparents. All the chores that can be done at night are always left for Buddy. He does a lot of hunting and fishing too—he is a crack shot with that rifle of his."

Suddenly Swamp Rat, Cowboy, and Ike's eyes meet with a slight rise of their eyebrows. "You mean he can even shoot a gun at night!" said Cowboy.

"Oh yes, he probably has close to perfect vision on moonlit nights. His eyes are really strange looking—they're almost white with a light tinge of blue."

"That is strange," the doctor replied. "I've never heard of a case quite like that."

"I think it's really great that he's eager to please his grandpa," said Swamp Rat, with a smile. "Wacanabbi-Min-Coto is a fine gentleman. Does Buddy know anything about the trouble the chief is having?"

"Oh yes—he is well aware of everything. His grandmother is a bit concerned about him right now; he's been gone on a hunting venture for two or three days now. He has never stayed away so long before."

"How does he handle the daylight when he stays away from home like this?" Swamp Rat asked.

"He finds a secure place to park his canoe—usually way back in a heavy patch of tulles, and he sleeps all day. He carries a heavy black hood that he wears over his face."

"That is truly an amazing story, Padre," Doctor Cedric replied, shaking his head. "I see what you mean about an on-going affair—Bojoc left a real legacy of despair behind him. Does Buddy have any contact with anyone except his grandparents?"

"Not as far as I know. They spend a lot of time down in his quarters with him, but that seems to be the only thing he will accept. His world is right there or at night out in the swamp. I really don't know what's going to happen to him when his grandparents are gone. It's a sad thing."

CHAPTER THIRTY-FIVE—Double-Cross and the Crew Gets Tough

After the Padre's visit and after a thorough explanation of everything of interest about the scouting trip to the doctor and the rest of the crew, the guys all settled in to discussing just what kind of position they had suddenly found themselves in. It was obvious to the scouting crew who the mystery gunman had been and why he was taking such vengeance on the South Bayou group. He was, without a doubt, unleashing years of pent up frustration, on the Evil Ones—as the Indian tribe called them. Even though the scouting crew felt that Buddy was actually on their side they still felt very insecure when they thought about going anywhere near him and the buffalo gun.

"Well this sort of leaves us in the lurch, boys," Dad said. "I don't know which way to go from here. If we could just find out where the dog is being held we might be able to go in and get him—now that there's only two of those bastards left!"

"Yeah, as much as I hate to," said Ike, "we may have to go back and just hope that Buddy don't decide to lay one on us—damn that gun anyway! If we knew for sure he wasn't going to whack us, the diversion he's causing might benefit our cause."

"You know—I'm suddenly starting to wonder," said Swamp Rat, with a far away look on his face.

"What's that Charlie?" Cowboy questioned. "What are you thinking?"

"I was thinking maybe it's us who have been duped. We were so intent on learning who the South Bayou night stalker was we might have settled for only half the story."

"Charlie, tell us what you're talking about," said the doctor.

"What if Wacanabbi-Min-Coto has actually given Buddy permission to stalk and eliminate as many of the South Bayou hard cores as he can—and what if Padre John is actually in on it, and has given his blessing to the event."

"Yeah—what if!" said the doctor, with a skeptical look on his face. "Speaking of blessing, a few days ago he was all fired up to bless the buffalo gun—even called it, The Wrath of God, and was prepared to sanctify its use—what happened? He never even mentioned it!"

"That's because he knew it wasn't here," said Maxy, looking around at the group. "He had already sanctified its use for another purpose."

"I'll be damned," said Ike—"there's no other answer—is there?"

"Gentlemen, it appears our dog hunt has been hijacked," said the doctor, twisting his moustache up in a knot.

"Yeah, the bums—they took our weapon for their own use," said Cowboy. "That wasn't real neighborly of them if you ask me!"

"I wouldn't hold that against them too much," said the doctor. "Maybe that old weapon out of the past was the medicine the chief needed to fire his people up and give them hope again—no doubt the padre has used his position to inject a goodly amount of divine assistance into the program also."

"Well, they've got themselves the perfect killing machine," said Ike. "A man with night vision and years of pent up hatred. If I thought he was after me I would leave the area post haste."

"Something like this was exactly what I was afraid of," Dad said, shaking his head. "Now we're probably looking at an impossible chore."

"Don't give up yet, Dave," Doctor Cedric, grumbled, "We still may pull it out."

"I can see at least four people that had to be involved in this," said Swamp Rat.

"I see three," said Cowboy—"the chief, the priest and Buddy—who's the fourth?

"Wenoch," said Swamp Rat, "he had to tell the chief where the gun was, or it was him that took it—at any rate he's involved."

"You know—even though he was here for only a few minutes when we were having our little celebration," said Maxy. "I did notice him eyeballing that gun."

"Fellows, I would be thrilled to death to see every one of these modern day assassins with their boot heels turned up," Dad said, "but I don't have time to take part in making that happen. Old Trailer is somewhere over there among that bunch of riffraff, and I'll be damned if I'm going to leave here without trying to find him," he said, with his jaw clinched and stress showing in his face.

"Then it's time to get down and dirty," Cowboy said, looking directly into Dad's eyes—"we'll go in and get him just like we planned to do in the first place!"

"Yeah, we'll go in the day time," said Ike, "that way we won't have to worry about the buffalo gun—any son of a bitch that fires on us—we'll blow him right out from between his galluses. Charlie, where should we begin?"

"Dragon Lodge would be the right place to start. That's where the meanest of the lot hang out, and anything they consider of value would be kept somewhere close by. What we need to do first though is get with Frank. He's got four more guys plus Marco that want to join our group."

"Boys, let's start getting everything together that we're going to need," Dad said. "Tomorrow we're going to find that dog or know the reason why."

"How about I take the launch into the marina and fill her up with fuel and get with Frank on the subject, while you fellows get everything ready here," said Swamp Rat.

"Let's get after it," Dad replied. "We're going to do what we came to do."

"Yeah, this is what we expected in the first place," said Cowboy. "Let's get it over with and get back home."

"I'll be back in a couple of hours," said Swamp Rat, "and we'll start loading all our gear."

"I think I'll hitch a ride to the store with you and see if I can get in touch with my missus, Charlie," said Maxy. "There is a telephone there isn't there?"

"Yeah, it's in the back of the store," said Swamp Rat.

"Is there anything you guys think we should get while I'm there?"

"We're going to need something we can eat on the move," Dad said, reaching for his wallet—"maybe a block of cheese and a box of crackers.

"Hey, how about a stick of that dry salami too?" said Ike. "I really like that stuff."

"Have you guys got plenty of shells for your weapons?" Swamp Rat asked—"we're probably going to need a bunch!"

"I think we're alright in that department," Dad replied, "We took care of that before we left home. Gentlemen, let's get with the program. Let's start by getting all our fire power out here and checking everything over."

"We'll see you in a couple of hours," said Swamp Rat, as he and Maxy headed for the launch.

As the crew went about the duty of getting everything ready, Dad suddenly fell quiet as he began to contemplate the reality of what was about to happen and what would be the consequences if they failed—suddenly Doctor Cedric spotted his downtrodden demeanor and broke into his thoughts. "Dave, I know you're really troubled about how this thing is going, but I'd like to remind you—the night is always darkest just before the dawn. By this time tomorrow afternoon we might have your dog and be headed for home—so don't let this thing dig into you too hard."

"Yeah, I know you're right, Doc, but when you suddenly find yourself in a position where everything your life consists of is riding on one turn of the cards it's a bit hard to get your mind off it!"

"I realize what you're saying, Dave, but throughout my lifetime I've always found—the stress we put ourselves through beforehand is usually worse than the actual event, so try to stymie it as much as you can. When tomorrow gets here we'll give it the best shot we know how."

"Well, there's one thing good about it," Dad replied, "one way or the other it'll be over with. I've got to get back home whatever the outcome."

"It's a sad thing children get so attached to critters like this," said the doctor, shaking his head. "There are scads of cute little puppies everywhere you look, but not one of them can replace the one that's been lost—childhood can be a rough time!"

"Doc, I can't imagine what's going to happen if we can't find that dog. Dell and I lost one little boy already, and she almost didn't make it through that. I'm really afraid if I lose one of them I'll lose them both!" he said, with a blank stare on his face.

"You need to distance yourself from that kind of thinking, Dave," said the doctor, looking Dad straight in the eyes. "We will get your boy's dog back and your family will become stable again. It's very important that you believe that! Tomorrow is the day of reckoning, and we have right on our side—God help anybody that tries to stand in our way—now you buck up here, good buddy—things are going to be alright!"

* * *

As the afternoon dragged on, as hard as Dad tried to keep his mind off the subject of—what if—his mind had to constantly be dragged back to reality by Doc and the boys. Finally Maxy and Swamp Rat got back from the store and for a short time things seemed to be shaping up, but one could tell there was something amiss by the depressed attitude of Maxy and Swamp Rat—It was clear that something had changed. Finally when Dad was in the bedroom, they motioned for Doc to follow them out on deck.

"Boys, it's obvious something's wrong," the doctor said, when they got outside—"what is it?"

"Doc, we've got to go home," said Maxy. "The situation at Dave's house is out of control. The boy is still bad and Dell is starting to go down

A FUR COAT FOR MAMA

hill. June went by to visit them yesterday and she said Dell looked terrible; she's losing weight and has big dark rings under her eyes. The girls are crying behind her back wanting daddy to come home. We wanted to consult with you before we tell Dave. This is going to hit him really hard."

"Man, this is a tough one!" said the doctor, looking at the floor and shaking his head. "I just finished giving him a major pep talk to try and stabilize his mind—how am I going to tell him this?"

"I guess the only thing to do is just come right out with it," said Maxy. "I guess I should be the one to do it."

"Well, let's get the deed over with," said the doctor. "There's no use putting it off. Sometimes life can be a son of a bitch, boys—and this is definitely one of those times—just to think that little black and white dog could solve this whole problem—damn the luck anyway!"

* * *

Within the next 15 minutes the depression on the houseboat went from bad to worse, and just when everyone figured it was as bad as it could possibly get another problem popped up—an entourage of fifteen Indian canoes were seen heading directly for the houseboat.

"I wonder what the hell they want," said Cowboy, as everyone gathered on the front deck. "As far as I'm concerned they've already done enough!"

"I'll second that motion," said Ike. "I'd just as soon they'd leave us alone!"

"That's Wacanabbi-Min-Coto in the front canoe!" Swamp Rat exclaimed, running over beside Cowboy—"and that's the medicine man seated behind him!"

"Oh Lord," Dad said, "what else can happen? Boys, you'll have to handle this; I can't deal with it right now! I'm going to go in and keep packing."

"You go ahead, Dave, we'll take care of it," Doctor Cedric replied.

"This has got to be something special!" Swamp Rat exclaimed, looking around at all the guys. "The chief is wearing his full ceremonial feathers. See that single eagle feather stuck through the top of his braid—that indicates he's bringing a gift."

"Maybe he's going to give us our gun back," said Cowboy, with a disgruntled look on his face. "If he hadn't interfered, things might have turned out right."

"What's done is done, boys," the doctor grumbled. "Let's try to be as congenial as we can."

"*Hola,*" the Chief cried out, standing with his arms outspread. "I must speak with Daveed."

"Damn it!" the doctor exclaimed quietly. "What are we going to do, boys? Dave can't handle this!"

"It's alright, Doc," Dad said, walking back out on the deck. "I've never turned a friend away in my life and I guess I shouldn't start now. My name is Dave Walker, sir," Dad replied, walking toward the chief's canoe; "what can I do for you?"

"Daveed—I am Wacanabbi-Min-Coto—chief of this tribe, and I have come to thank you properly for the great kindness you have shown to me and my family."

"May I give you a hand up, Chief?" Dad asked, as the canoe pulled alongside the houseboat.

"You are a man of great honor, Daveed," said the chief extending his hand. "The Great Spirit has blessed us by your presence. My only daughter was in the pit of hell and you brought her back to me. My life is in your hands," he said, kneeling down in front of Dad with his head bowed.

"No my friend—I'm just a man the same as you," Dad replied, helping the chief back to his feet. "We are brothers of the flesh trying to exist against the evil of this world. The evil ones that took your daughter have also taken my son from me, and I have no way to get him back. My heart is broken and my family is destroyed," Dad openly began to weep, wiping bitter tears with the back of his hand. "I am forced to return home in defeat!"

"I have brought a gift for you Daveed—my daughter Wayrayah has told me of your son and how the evil ones have caused him to fall into a great sleep. My grandson Me-Watha-Min-Chato is the greatest hunter of all my tribe. I sent him personally to try to find your son's dog in hope that I could return your son to you as you have returned my daughter to me. Suddenly the chief began a slow dance around Dad letting out a loud series of Indian chants, and flashing his ornately feathered costume. *"Eh Yeh Yeh—Hey Yeh Yeh—Et Ney Ha Ka."* As the chief finished circling around Dad suddenly at the far end of the deck Dad heard a familiar whining sound that ripped at the very core of his being—as he turned—his mind was stunned by the sight that greeted his eyes—there on the end of the deck stood Wayrayah in all her Indian princess finery holding Old Trailer on a light cotton rope.

"Oh My God!" Dad exclaimed, falling to his knees in front of the chief. "Now my life belongs to you, my friend."

"As you have said—we are brothers of the flesh, Daveed," the chief said, helping Dad to his feet. "Though our lives are very different, we share a common bond—the love of a father for his children. You and your braves have given life back to my people, Daveed. The Great Spirit has smiled upon us this day. I desperately hope my gift returns your son to you in health and happiness."

"What can I say good friend," Dad said, grabbing the chief in a strong embrace. "There are no words that can tell you how I feel right now. I owe you my very life!" Suddenly from the other end of the deck came a blur of black and white as Wayrayah slipped the rope through Old Trailer's collar. "Oh my God, little buddy, you are a sight for sore eyes!" Dad said, grabbing him up full in his arms. "I know a little boy that will sure be glad to see you—if I can get there in time!" he said, pitching Trailer back down onto the deck.

"The evil ones who took your son's friend are no longer among the living," said the chief, "as are many others of their kind. I now return to you the gun of small thunder which the Great Spirit made available to us. Come!"—the chief exclaimed, motioning to Wayrayah, who was now holding the ancient weapon. "My daughter wishes to thank you also, Daveed," said the chief, taking the heavy gun and the two boxes of shells from her.

"*Daveed me Salvador*," she whispered, softly as she dropped to her knees in front of Dad. "I live because of you, Daveed—you will be in my heart as long as there is life in my body."

"Wayrayah, you don't need to do that," Dad said, taking her by the hand and helping her up. "I am so very pleased to see that you made it back to your family—I was worried sick wondering what was going to happen to you."

"I am sorry that I acted so badly, Daveed. I was very scared and confused; thank you again for my life. I leave you now to my father," she said, with a curtsy and a few steps backward.

"This weapon of the past has given hope again to my people," said the chief. "I return it to you with our undying gratitude."

"I'll take it Dave," said Cowboy, stepping forward to get the old gun.

"You are a great hero among my people, Daveed. We will remember you always," he said, with a nod of his head and a couple of steps backwards. "We go now!" he yelled out, motioning everyone back to the canoes.

As soon as the Indians were all back in their boats, Dad grabbed Old Trailer and began rough-house playing like he always did at home and Trailer went bolting around the boat dodging and dashing around everybody in a frenzy of pure delight.

"This sort of changes things, doesn't it, Dave?" said the doctor, approaching Dad with a wide grin.

"You can say that again, good buddy. Now I might have a chance of salvaging my life. Boys, let's get these anchors up," Dad yelled. "We're going home!"

"Hey, here comes the other launch," said, Maxy, looking back to the left of the houseboat.

"Frank and the recruits were probably going to spend the night on the houseboat so we could get an early start in the morning," said Swamp Rat, "but I guess we've had a change of plans."

"Yeah, we'll be heading home as soon as we can get things ready," Dad said. "I've been gone way too long."

* * *

As the launch neared the houseboat it was easy to see that it wasn't carrying an invasion force because there were only three people on board and they were all easily recognizable—Frank, Padre John and Miss Hattie.

"Gentlemen," Frank yelled—"I've brought some folks who want to say goodbye to you!"

"Thank goodness," said the doctor, smiling at Miss Hattie, as the launch pulled alongside. "I thought I was going to have to leave without seeing you. Come over here, my dear, and I'll help you up."

"Oh, Walter, it is so wonderful to see you again!" said Miss Hattie, stepping around the padre and taking the doctor's hand. "My heart was broken thinking I might never see you again."

"That's not going to happen, Lady," the doctor stated, looking into Miss Hattie's eyes. "I know a good thing when I see one," he said, with a wink and a smile.

"My dear friends, we meet again," Padre John, exclaimed. "The Lord has been good to us. I see the chief has already been here," he said, observing Old Trailer running around on deck. "I must apologize for keeping you in the dark on the recovery efforts but we didn't know just how it would all turn out."

"All's well that ends well, Padre," Dad replied, nodding his head at the priest. "You and the chief have done me and my family a great service. I will forever be in your debt. Frank, I can't thank you enough for the use of this marvelous houseboat. The gang and I are certainly going to miss it. You fellows come on in and chat awhile—boys, leave those anchors down for a little longer."

As everyone began to gather around the table, Frank said, "Dave, I know you boys brought a court order with you to be signed for due process on the Sloyd boys and I was thinking that Padre John here would be the perfect person to attest to their demise."

"That would certainly fill our needs," Dad replied. "I'll get it out of my bag."

"The Padre and I have a favor to ask of you fellows," said Frank. "We were wandering if you would, by chance, feel like donating the buffalo gun to the Citizens for Action Committee—it has suddenly become the icon of our struggle."

"You'll have to talk to Doc about that," Dad said, heading into the bedroom.

"I think Grandpa Cedric would be very pleased to have his old gun used for such a fine purpose," the doctor replied, nodding his head. "All it's been doing for the last 50 years is gathering dust in my closet."

"If you should ever want it back we will return it to you," said Padre John.

"Better yet," said the doctor, "when you're through with it, present it to Wacanabbi-Min-Coto as a gift from the Sugar Grove Boys. Between that gun and his grandson he seems to have found the cure for what ails Bayou Blanc—a no nonsense approach to crime control."

"Then that's the way we'll do it," said Frank. "Thanks to that gun and The Ghost of the Night the crime level is certain to be on the decline. The grapevine has it that the bad boys that are left over there, are all scrambling to find a hole to hide in, so keeping peace now shouldn't be a problem for the Citizens Committee—especially now that we've got both launches and several more new recruits."

"Between the Citizens Committee and the Indians, we can form an active watch group that will spot trouble before it gets out of hand," said Padre John.

"That sounds really good to me," the doctor replied. "This was once my home, and there's a good chance it will be again—and I'm very fond of peace and quiet. Missy, how about a stroll out on deck—if I'm not mistaken there's a full moon about to rise."

"Oh, yes Walter, I would like that very much!" Miss Hattie agreed, taking Doctor Cedric by the hand.

CHAPTER THIRTY-SIX—Renewed Hope and the Crew Heads Home

Due to the late visit from Frank, the priest and Miss Hattie, the crew spent one more night aboard the houseboat, but early the next morning around five o'clock they were already loaded and headed for home, with Old trailer asleep on a blanket in the floorboard. "Boys, how many days have we been down here?" Doctor Cedric asked, as Maxy turned off the Mission Point Road onto the main highway.

"It can't be more than eight or ten days," Maxy calculated.

"It seems more like a year," Dad commented. "I sure hope my little man is still hanging in there."

"Well, I think we've got the cure for what ails him, now," Doctor Cedric, replied, "but there is a limit to how long a child can hang on."

All that day and through the next night Maxy pushed the Model A just as hard as he possible could and the next morning around eight o'clock they came rolling up in front of the Walker house. "Oh, my goodness, Mama, it's Daddy!" Nellie yelled, holding the front door open.

"Thank God!" Mama exclaimed, as she and Dorothy ran out onto the porch.

No sooner had the back door of the car opened before Old Trailer had shoved his way through under everyone's legs and was outside checking to see if any other dog had invaded his territory. "Oh, Trailer it is so good to see you!" Nellie said, dropping to her knees and grabbing on to him.

"Hoytie! Hoytie! Old Trailer's home," Dorothy screamed at the top of her lungs, hurrying back toward the front door.

"Oh, thank God you're home, Husband," Mama said, grabbing onto Daddy, as he stepped out of the car. "I don't know how much longer we could have lasted!"

"My Lord, woman, you're just skin and bones!" Dad said, holding Mama in a close embrace. "How's our boy doing?"

"He's still hanging on," Mama whimpered softly, wiping tears with the back of her hand—"oh thank God—I've missed you so much."

"Well, you've got help now, Good Lady!" said the doctor, grabbing Mama by the other arm. "I'm putting you straight to bed. The rest of us will take over from here on. Gentlemen, for the next few days life around this house is going to be centered on bringing this family back to health, and everyone of you is going to be on call," he said, as they all entered the front door. "I want this house warmed up until it's comfortable in your shirt sleeves, and I want enough water heating to thoroughly bathe both of my patients. Dave, I need you to kill three or four chickens to make soup, and the rest of you can catch up on whatever needs to be done. Girls, I want you to strip your Mama's bed and put clean sheets and covers on it then we'll do the same with Hoyt's."

* * *

Within the next week, due to the doctor's expert handling of the situation, life started taking on a degree of normalcy in the Walker household. As he slowly diminished the amount of sleeping drug I was being given, the dreams and dark shadows of my mind began to fade, and I started to realize the situation I had been in. The last night of my dream-filled ordeal I awoke very early in the morning to feel Doctor Cedric's cold stethoscope sliding up between my shoulder blades. "Oooh, that's cold," I said, curling up in a little ball.

"Hey, that's what I like to hear—a little bit of complaining," the doctor chuckled, sliding the scope around to my chest. "Do you think you can stay awake for us awhile today?"

"I think so," I replied. "Man, am I hungry!"

"That's a very good sign," he replied. "Hey, there's a friend of yours here that really wants to see you." As the doctor stepped back Old Trailer reared up on the side of the bed and began whining and licking my face—suddenly all the dreams and shadows I had been used to, began to fade into the background, and I realized this wasn't just a vivid dream—this was Old Trailer—my soul mate in the flesh, and I was his master.

"Oh my goodness!" I exclaimed, "I've got to get up!"

"Now, hold on there, Little Mister Walker," the doctor cautioned, "you're in no shape to get up and go chasing around. How about I rustle you up some breakfast, then we'll see how you feel after that."

"Can Trailer get in bed with me?" I pleaded; "I haven't seen him in a long time!"

"Why not?" the doctor grumbled, lifting Trailer up onto the bed—"he had a good bath yesterday too."

Within minutes after Doctor Cedric left the room, and Old Trailer and I had our get reacquainted romp and settled down, Nellie and Dorothy came creeping into my room with their kerosene lamp in hand. "Oh, Little Brother, when are you ever going to wake up?" Dorothy lamented, setting the lamp on my night stand—"we miss you so much!"

"Hey Dot, look at that!" Nellie exclaimed, pointing to Old Trailer's head sticking out from under the covers.

"I'm awake!" I yelled, throwing the covers back with a squeal and a giggle. "Here, get in bed with us; I'll shove Trailer over some more and you can both get in beside us," I said. "I want you to tell me everything I've missed since I've been asleep!"

"Oh Hoytie, you are awake!" Nellie said, grabbing me in a tight hug.

"Well, the biggest thing that happened while you were asleep—you scared us all out of our minds, you little brat!" said Dorothy, reaching over and scuffling up my hair.

"Yeah, we were afraid you might even die, Hoytie!" Nellie said, hugging me even tighter.

"Well, you should have known better than that," I replied smugly.

"Now, how were we supposed to know better?" Dorothy challenged, raising up onto her elbow.

"Because we haven't finished Mama's coat yet—that's why!" I said with a big grin.

"Oh, you ornery little turkey!" Dorothy whispered, reaching over and putting her arm around me. "It is so good to have you back, Little Brother; please don't ever do that again—Hey, I'm going to go tell Mama you're awake!" Dorothy said, jumping out of bed and running to the door. Very quietly Dorothy sneaked into Mama and Daddy's bedroom in the dark and whispered next to Mama's ear. "Mama, Hoytie is awake! Do you want to come in and see him?"

"Oh my goodness, baby, is he alright?" Mama asked swinging her feet out of bed.

"He's just fine, Mama—he's laughing and talking and everything."

"Oh thank God," Mama said, with her hands up to her face. "Maybe this horror story is finally going to be over!"

"Come on Mama," Dorothy said, taking her by the hand. "Nellie and Old Trailer are already in bed with him. I hope you don't mind about Trailer."

"Right now honey, I could care less, just as long as my little man is alright. Let's just let Daddy sleep for now," she whispered.

Within seconds Mama and Dorothy were quietly approaching the bed as Nellie and I continued to laugh and giggle. We were discussing how good it was that we were going to be able to catch more mink and finish Mama's coat. Suddenly Nellie stopped, and whispered, "shhh"—with her finger up to her lips.

"Hey, Hoytie! Mama's here," Dorothy said, "you guys scoot over so we can get in. Hey, what were you talking about?" Dorothy questioned. "I saw you whispering!"

"It's a secret," I replied, "and we're not going to tell, are we Nell?" I said in an impish tone.

"Oh my precious little man! Are you really okay?" Mama said, leaning across Nellie to run her fingers through my hair.

"He's fine Mama—just as rotten as ever!" Dorothy exclaimed, with mock spite in her voice. "Hey, scoot over so we can get in!"

* * *

From that moment on our family started to gain back its momentum, and within two more days Doctor Cedric felt things were going well enough that he could safely leave us on our own. He left mother a big bottle of blood building tonic and told her and Dad that he would be back in a week to check everybody out. The following week Sheriff Dan showed up on the front porch and he and Dad spent more than two hours discussing the action surrounding the Sloyd gang and their demise, and Dad presented him with the court order signed by Padre John. The 500 dollar reward was split up evenly between the crew—all five got a crisp new one hundred dollar bill. All in all, it just about paid for the trip to Bayou Blanc. The good thing about the whole affair was—Old Trailer was home again where he belonged and the Sloyd brothers would never be coming back. The county took their old home place for back taxes and closed the file on the Sloyd gang. The old house was burned to the ground and all the caverns were dynamited and filled in. Everyone in the whole area breathed a welcome sigh of relief.

* * *

In a couple of days when all the sleepy feeling was gone from my mind, Old Trailer and I were just like we were never apart. The only thing different was Mama was so overly protective of us kids it was almost unreal. I guess she had a right to feel that way after all the trauma she had been through. Dad, on the other hand, was just the opposite; he was more playful and energetic than we had ever seen him. It was like he realized how close he had come to losing his family and he was trying to make up for lost time.

The school year started the first of September and the girls and I couldn't believe how much coat talk Mr. Roberts was immediately doing. It was obvious—to our extreme delight, that he and his wife had been doing some very intense planning. They had even visited the coat factory at Fort Smith and learned exactly how a fur coat was put together. That was pure joy to us because we had already done a couple of forays down on the creek just to make sure Old Trailer was still in mink mode—man was he ever! The second time we did it though we decided we had made a big mistake because we had to drag him almost all the way back home. He didn't understand why we wouldn't let him dig the mink out.

"We're not going to do this any more until trapping season," Dorothy stated flatly, as we finally reached the top of the hill leading up to the house.

"Well, we found out what we wanted to know!" Nellie exclaimed, with a broad smile. "There's still mink down there, and Trailer still wants to get them!"

"That's for sure," I grunted, tugging him along on a short rope. "We'll be lucky if he doesn't decide to go without us now!"

"You know—that's the truth!" Dorothy replied, stopping and looking back at Nellie and me. "It was really dumb of us to do it again!"

"Yeah, but it's so much fun!" Nellie insisted, with a little squeal of delight, "and we've been waiting so long to do it. Hoytie, it feels so good to have you and Trailer back home with us healthy and happy again."

"Yeah, Little Brother, we were really scared!" Dorothy said, looking back at me with that big sister smile. "As ornery as you are, Nell and I found out that life without you isn't nearly as much fun."

"So, now do you believe what I said about Trailer being a one in a million dog?"

"There's no doubt about that! It was stupid of me to treat you and Trailer that way. I didn't know just how special both of you really are!"

"Our whole family is special," I replied proudly, "and we're going to prove it by finishing Mama's fur coat and presenting it to her on Christmas morning."

"Oh yes—and we'll get Daddy something really nice too, and we'll buy gifts for each other." Nellie said, with excitement in her voice. "Why didn't we think of doing this a long time ago? This is the most fun I've ever had!"

"We only learned how to do it last year, silly!" Dorothy replied, looking back at Nell.

"Just think—we're probably the only kids in the whole world who can do this," I said proudly.

"Well, it stands to reason—since Trailer is a one in a million dog, there's at least a million other people who can't do it," Dorothy deduced.

"Yeah, and they don't have a cousin like Steve to teach them what to hunt and how to take care of the skins either," I reminded. "I still say we're the only kids in the whole world who can make money hunting mink."

"Well, I don't know about that, Hoytie," Nellie said, as we came up into the back yard, "but I certainly know one thing, I can't wait until we can dig them out and put them on stretcher boards."

"Yeah, me too, Sissy," I replied exuberantly. "We're going to catch a pile of them this year!"

"Speaking of stretcher boards," said Dorothy, "we need to start making more new ones while we still have plenty of time."

"Yeah, I'd say we're going to need at least twice as many as we had last year," I answered, "and right now we don't even have any boards to make them out of."

"We've still got plenty of time," Dorothy added. "We'll collect a piece here and a piece there until we get enough."

CHAPTER THIRTY-SEVEN—Bad News for S.G.B. Enterprise and the Walker Family Takes Another Hit

As the Walker kids were quietly getting ready for the opening of Mink season—December the first, there were other factors at work that were destined to change our lives dramatically. It all started one early morning in the middle of November when Uncle Ike revealed that he had received an induction notice from the army and was ordered to report to Camp Chaffee within the next week. In the two weeks that followed it seemed that everything our family had been counting on began to disappear. Cowboy decided that since his buddy was going into the service he might as well go too and get his military duty behind him, but the straw that broke the camel's back came just two days before opening day of mink season when a young mule that Daddy was trying to break to the wagon kicked him in the hip and he became bedridden overnight. From that moment on the whole family's plans began to change. The first week of the mink season after school, the girls and I dug out four mink—three sows and one boar, and meticulously removed the skins and put them on stretcher boards; there was only one small problem. Without the smell of mink from Dad and the guys trapping—no matter how much we washed, Mother could easily tell we were catching mink—there was just no way to hide it.

"What are we going to do, Hoytie?" Nellie asked, as we got together in my bedroom to talk it over. "Mama can smell us—I know she can!"

"Yeah, and she can definitely smell Old Trailer," I replied. "I don't know how we're going to catch mink and keep it secret. The smell is just too strong. What do you think, Dorothy?"

"Well, maybe we can catch enough to finish the coat and give some to Mama and Daddy too," Dorothy replied.

"Yeah, that way we'll have a reason to smell like mink," Nellie said excitedly.

"Hey, we might just be able to do it," I answered. "We'll hunt really hard, and get just as many as we can!"

After another week in which we kids caught three more mink and presented two of them to Mama and Daddy—all stretched and ready for curing—we got a very big surprise! Sunday morning as we were getting ready to go hunting again, Daddy called us into the bedroom and had us sit down.

"Kids, your Mother and I have something to talk to you about. It appears this injury is going to cause us to lose this trapping season unless you and Old Trailer can do something to help. As you know this is our winter time survival money, and losing it is going to put us in a real bind. What you've already done is probably worth about 50 dollars in cash money, and that's going to go a long ways in helping us stay afloat. Now what your mother and I have been considering is—well, do you think if we took you out of school for the rest of the season to let you make the most of it—do you think you would be able to handle it?"

"Oh, yes Daddy, I know we can," Nellie exclaimed, bouncing up out of her chair, leaving Dorothy and I sitting with our mouths open.

"Hoyt, what do you think about it?" Dad asked, looking directly at me.

"I know we can catch a lot of mink, Daddy; there's no doubt about that," I said, nodding my head affirmatively.

"Dorothy, what are your thoughts?" Mother interjected. "Would this interfere too much with you kids and your schooling?"

"It would be hard, Mama, but we could do our school work at night—yeah, we can do it." she said, looking over at Nellie and me with a determined look on her face—"can't we?"

"Yeah, we can do it!" Nellie and I both yelled in unison.

"Alright then," Daddy said, looking at each of us individually, "as of right now you are the official breadwinners of this family. Tomorrow morning your mother will go with you to school and let Mister Roberts know what's going on, and then each morning I'll help you lay out a new place to hunt. This is now a Walker family enterprise," he added, with a smile and a wink. "With the Sloyds gone, you can hunt my old spots down on Sugar Creek."

"Daddy, can we take the .22?" I asked. "We could kill squirrels and rabbits to bring home."

"Yes you can, Son, but be really careful with it. We've got enough problems without one of you getting shot. As you already know there's lots of wild game on Sugar Creek, and right now we could sure use it."

As we left the house to go hunting and began to talk about what had just happened, we quickly became aware of just what a daunting task we were facing. For me it was the fulfillment of my fondest dream, to be able to quit school and go hunting, but it also meant we would be working really hard right through Christmas with no chance of finishing Mama's coat.

"What are we going to do?" Nellie asked, with uncertainty in her voice. "It's less than two weeks till Christmas! There's absolutely no chance of even catching enough mink to finish Mama's coat, much less getting it made. "

"We'll talk to Mister Roberts about it tomorrow," Dorothy replied, "but it looks to me like it's going to take a lot more time than we've got."

"Come on girls, let's get going," I said, as Trailer came running by us. "Get 'em, boy I yelled as we headed towards the creek on a run.

The next morning we were having our breakfast getting ready for school when Dad came limping into the kitchen with the use of a heavy cane. "You kids are biting off a big chew here," he said shaking his head; "I hope you realize that! There are a lot of grown ups who wouldn't tackle what you've taken on."

"We can do it, Daddy," I replied enthusiastically.

"Yeah, and we're going to have fun doing it too," Nellie stated. "Hunting mink with Old Trailer is the most fun I've ever had!"

"Well, I'm going to tell you right now it'll get tougher as it goes. It's a short intense season, and to make anything you've really got to hustle. It's certainly not a job I like putting you kids on, but it seems like the only choice we've got."

"We can do it Daddy," Dorothy insisted. "The hard part will be keeping up with our school work, but we'll get it done."

"Well, I'll help you every way I can—catching them is only one part of the game," Daddy said. "I can't help you there, but I can do skinning and taking care of the pelts. Between all of us we'll give it our best shot."

"Okay kids, let's get on over to the school, and see Mister Roberts," Mama said.

"Yeah, let's hurry, and we can still get in a good day of hunting," I urged.

* * *

"Mister Roberts, our mama has come to talk to you," I announced loudly as I entered the school ahead of Mama and the girls.

"Oh she has, has she," Mister Roberts said, with a little chuckle. "Well, why don't you pull up some chairs close to the stove there, Hoyt, and I'll be right down."

"Come in ladies," Mister Roberts hollered from up on the stage. "I'll be right with you. Hoyt, how about chunking the stove up a little and throw in a couple more sticks of wood."

"Mister Roberts, I need to talk to you about the kids," Mama said, as she and the girls entered the room.

"They're all doing really well, Mrs. Walker," Mister Roberts replied, jumping down off the stage, and approaching the group.

BAD NEWS FOR S.G.B. ENTERPRISE 373

"Well, that's good because we've had a real problem develop that requires us to take them out of school for a while."

"I was afraid of that," Mister Roberts replied. "Dave's injury is preventing him from trapping, isn't it?"

"Yes it is, and we don't have any idea when he'll get to where he can work again," Mama replied.

"That's truly unfortunate," Mister Roberts replied, "especially at such a critical time. Well, it looks like you little mink catchers are going to be very busy," he said, looking at the girls and me.

"Yeah, we're going to have to work right through Christmas too," Dorothy said, looking directly at Mr. Roberts with a sour look on her face. "That's the worst part."

"Well, sometimes life requires us to change our plans," Mister Roberts conceded, looking specifically at me and the girls, "and it would appear this is one of those times. Mrs. Walker, since you folks don't own an automobile I would be pleased to make mine available whenever you need it, and it would also please me to take the kids to the fur market and watch over them while they do their business."

"That's very generous sir," Mama replied, with a relieved look on her face. "That fur market isn't a place I like sending my kids, but under the circumstances there doesn't seem to be any choice."

"Well, with my supervision, I'm sure we can get their furs sold without any difficulty."

"Their daddy will certainly be pleased with your offer, Mister Roberts. We were talking just last night about how we were going to handle that situation."

"Well, you can consider it handled. You and Dave have raised some outstanding children—they're a pleasure for me to be around."

"Mr. Roberts, we're going to be keeping up with our school work at night," said Dorothy. "Can we come once a week and get our lessons?"

"You certainly can; I will lay them out complete with instructions, and you can bring your completed work as you pick up your next lessons."

"We really hate doing this, Mr. Roberts. Dave and I thoroughly understand how much education means to a child, and we will get them back in school just as soon as possible."

"I know you will; tell Dave hello for me, and I hope he gets back on his feet real soon."

"I'll certainly tell him. Well, I need to be getting on back," Mama said. "Kids, as soon as you finish things up here—you come straight home—do you hear?"

"We will Mama," Nellie replied.

"It won't be more than 30 minutes or so, Mrs. Walker."

"Thank you again, Mr. Roberts—we appreciate your help very much."

As Mama walked out the door, Mr. Roberts said quietly, "Well Walker kids, it looks like our coat project is going to be delayed. There's not even time to finish it by Christmas even if we had all the skins ready. I guess we really didn't think it out too thoroughly—did we?"

"Yeah, dadburn it, we really wanted to have it ready for Christmas too," I exclaimed.

"I have a suggestion," said Mr. Roberts. "Why don't we sell the pelts from last year and then when we do get to start on your mama's coat all the skins will be new."

"Yeah, that's probably the best way to do it," Dorothy agreed, looking at Nellie and me.

"Maybe we should just take the money and buy Mama a real nice regular coat," said Nellie.

"No, I want her to have a fur coat like those other fancy ladies," I insisted emphatically.

"Okay, Hoytie," Nellie said, shaking her head, "but Mama really needs a coat. The one she has now is really getting old and ragged."

"How many new pelts would you have ready to go by next Saturday?" Mr. Roberts asked, looking intently at me and the girls.

"We've got seven pelts right now," I answered. "Those will definitely be ready and we could possibly have two or three more by then that could go. It takes about five or six days to dry them out."

"I think it would be the best idea to get the money from those frozen ones as soon as we can. I'm positive they'll still be good, but I don't think we should press our luck any longer than we have to, and we could sell your new catch at the same time—how about we plan on going next Saturday?"

"That sounds alright with me," I said, looking at the girls.

"Okay then, that's our plan," said Mr. Roberts, as the girls nodded their heads in agreement. "Hoyt, how early does the market open?"

"It opens at seven o'clock."

"Well, we don't need to be there that early! How about I pick you up at your house around 8:00 and that will put us at the fur market about 8:30. I'll lay the frozen hides out the night before and we'll sell the whole batch."

"That sounds really good," I replied. "That way we won't have to go again for another month."

"Mr. Roberts, do you think we could buy some things while we're there?" Dorothy asked. "This is the only chance we'll have to buy Christmas gifts."

"You certainly can; in fact, I would make sure to get the exact size of your mother's coat just in case you see something you can't resist."

"I wear the same size coat as Mama does," Dorothy said, "so if it fits me it'll fit her."

"Okay, then—now let's get your lessons put together and you can go on home," Mr. Roberts concluded.

CHAPTER THIRTY-EIGHT—Walker Kids
at the Fur Market

It was a dream come true for me to have Daddy interacting with us each morning giving us our day's instructions and setting up the hunt. Suddenly he was talking to us just like he had talked to Cowboy, Ike and Maxy. In essence we were the Sugar Grove Boys—well almost!—but we felt like it anyway. After each meeting we would go away fired up to the point we could hardly contain ourselves and ready to hit the day running—our daddy—the best mink trapper in Arkansas was tutoring us and helping take care of the mink we caught—we felt like we had life in our hip pocket. The following week we caught four mink—two big males and two females. Daddy estimated our catch was worth between 75 and 85 dollars. He and Mother were elated over our hunting success, and Old Trailer was being treated like royalty.

Saturday morning we were up early getting ready to go to market, and anticipating the arrival of Mr. Roberts when Nellie said, "Hoytie, do we have all the mink skins we're going to take?"

"Yeah, we've got five that are ready to sell," I replied. "They're out on the front porch wrapped up in a clean toe sack. You know something— with the furs from last year—if I haven't counted wrong, we should have close to 500 dollars in cash money when we sell them today—that is—if the prices haven't changed.

"Oh my gosh!" Nellie said, with astonishment in her voice, "If you're right we're half way to being able to buy Mama a factory made mink coat."

"Yeah, that's out of the question though—the family needs the money!" Dorothy replied, a bit despondently.

"Hey, here comes Mr. Roberts," I said, heading out the door to the front porch.

"Good morning, Hoyt, are you kids ready to go?" Mr. Roberts hollered, stepping out of his car.

"We're ready," I yelled back as the girls quickly came outside.

"Hi Mr. Roberts," Nellie said, as he headed onto the porch.

"Good morning, ladies; I need to speak with your parents before we go."

"Come right in Sir," Mother said, swinging the door open. "Dave is in the kitchen."

"Top of the morning to you, Dave, how is the hip doing today?" Mr. Roberts asked, reaching out to shake Dad's hand.

"Excuse me if I don't get up," Dad replied, reaching for Mr. Robert's hand. "She's sore and stiff, but I guess I'm lucky it's not any worse than it is. That mangy critter really laid one on me."

"Getting a young mule properly broken can be a real chore," Mr. Roberts acknowledged, "but Lord knows, what we'd do without them?"

"Yeah, my old mule team is as gentle and trustworthy as an old hound dog, but they were just as knot headed as this one when I first got them. The missus and I really appreciate what you're doing, Mr. Roberts. We will make it right with you as soon as we get some cash coming into the house—in fact, you be sure to fill up your gas tank as soon as the kids get paid."

"Dave, there's no payment needed here; this is just as exciting for me as it is for the kids, and I'm looking forward to it with great anticipation. This is a part of life I've never encountered before and your kids have inspired me greatly—they are highly motivated and I like that. Helping young people to better themselves has always been my goal in life, and in this case I feel very lucky they count me as their friend as well as their teacher. I will watch over them as if they were my own. By the way—I thought I'd better let you folks know, this outing is likely to take most of the day, so don't look for us until you see us coming."

"Yeah, I want to take them to Maynard's for chili, for sure," I replied, excitedly.

"Oh, yes, I can't wait," Nellie shrieked, putting her arm around my shoulders. "We're going to have so much fun!"

"Well, you kids enjoy yourselves," Mama interjected, "but just you remember—you pay attention, and mind everything Mr. Roberts says."

"We will, Mama," Dorothy replied.

"Kids, let's get on the road! We've got an adventure ahead of us, and I'm anxious to get started."

With my prior knowledge of the back entrance of the fur market through the wagon yard I guided Mr. Roberts to the usual parking spot right behind Maynard's Diner.

"So, this rail car is where the best chili in the world comes from, is that right, Hoyt?" said Mr. Roberts, looking at me with a big grin.

"You said it!" I exclaimed. "Come on—let's go say hello to Maynard. He's a good friend of mine and Daddy's."

"Well, I'm going to lock this bundle of pelts in the trunk then," Mr. Roberts said. "After we say hello to your buddy we'll come back and get them."

"Hey, Maynard!" I yelled in the door, as the rest of the group started coming up the ramp. "I brought you some business!"

"Alright, it's the bean flip man," Maynard said, walking around the counter. "Hoyt, it's good to see you again. Hey, this isn't your usual crew," he said, as the girls and Mr. Roberts came in.

"Yeah, Cowboy and Ike joined the army, and Daddy got kicked by a mule," I said, "but I've got me a new crew now, and we're all going to be having chili for lunch."

"Hey that's great, little buddy. I'm just starting to get her on right now," said Maynard."

"Maynard, this is Mr. Roberts, our school teacher, and these are my two sisters Dorothy and Nellie."

"Well, I can say one thing this crew is a whole lot better looking than your last one," Maynard said, smiling at Nellie and Dorothy. "I'm very proud to meet all of you."

"Right now we've got to get on over to the fur market," I said, "but we'll be back to have chili and soda pop a little later."

"That's good," Maynard replied, nodding his head in agreement. "I'll get the chili on and be sure there are plenty of crackers when you get here."

"Let's get our furs, and go get in line," I hurried. "We don't want to be behind everybody."

"Yeah, we've got a lot of things to do today," Dorothy agreed—"let's get to it!"

* * *

The smells of the fur market, as we entered the back door, brought back the same old excitement of my first visit, but there was another feeling that was brand new. Even without Daddy and the crew—I wasn't afraid anymore—in fact, I was the man in charge and I liked it.

"That's Mel's station in the middle," I pointed out.

"Boy, he is big," said Nellie, with her eyes locked on Mel.

"He's really a great guy," I said, as we made our way through the crowd. "We got here just in time," I stated as we walked up in front— "we're up next! Mel, how ya doing?" I yelled out confidently, as the last customer turned to leave.

"Hey, it's young Mr. Walker from Sugar Grove, and I'll bet those are all mink hides you're carrying."

"They sure are," I replied proudly, rolling the bundle off onto the counter.

"Hey, where's your pa and all the gang? I've been expecting you boys for a week now," Mel said, easing the bundle of furs out of the bag.

"Everything has changed since last year, Mel," I explained, shaking my head. "Ike and Cowboy joined the army, and Daddy had a run-in with an ornery mule and got his leg all bunged up right before trapping season—but don't worry, the girls and I are going to get you lots of good mink. We caught every one of these all by ourselves."

"You're kidding," Mel said, shaking his head, with a questioning look on his face. "These are excellent furs, Hoyt. You can bring me just as many of these as you want to."

"Mel, this is Mr. Roberts, our teacher, and these are my sisters Dorothy and Nellie. Mr. Roberts is helping us out while Daddy's crippled up."

"I'm very proud to make all your acquaintances," said Mel, extending his hand first to Mr. Roberts and then to each of the girls. "Girls, you might want to go check out my new boutique over in the corner of the building there," Mel suggested, pointing to a well lighted store front inside the big warehouse.

"What's a boutique?" Nellie whispered to Dorothy.

"I don't know," Dorothy whispered back, with a puzzled look on her face.

"A boutique is a small store that sells expensive ladies wear," Mr. Roberts said quietly to the girls.

"We won't have any money until we sell the furs," Dorothy said, looking sheepishly up at Mel.

"Well, if all these pelts are as good as the ones I've seen so far, you're going to have a pile of money here pretty quick."

"Hey, I can take care of this if you want to go look!" I said to the girls.

"Mr. Roberts, will you come with us?" Nellie asked. "We're not supposed to go anywhere without you."

"I certainly will—let's go check it out."

"Tell me young Mr. Walker," Mel said, as Mr. Roberts and the girls walked away, "how did you kids come up with this many quality mink skins in this short a time? These are all excellent furs and you've got a bundle of them!"

"We had a secret project last year that Mr. and Mrs. Roberts were going to help us with," I said, "but we didn't catch enough mink so Mr. Roberts stored the cured furs in his freezer for us."

"So basically what you're saying here is—part of these furs are from last year."

"Yes, sir," I said hesitantly, looking down at the floor. "I hope they're still alright."

"I can't see any difference in them, Hoyt; they're all prime furs. By the way—what was this secret project you were planning?"

"We were going to make our mama a fur coat and Mrs. Roberts was going to sew it for us, but we didn't catch enough mink."

"Man alive, Son!—I can't believe you got as many as you did—and they've been perfectly taken care of! This is a monumental feat you kids have performed. Having that kind of knowledge of trapping for people your age is phenomenal."

"Oh, we're not catching them with traps!" I replied.

"Now, wait a minute here—what other way is there but catching them in traps? You've got me a bit confused here."

"Old Trailer helps us get them," I replied proudly.

"Old Trailer—helps you get them!" Mel repeated, with a questioning look on his face. "I still don't understand; tell me how Old Trailer helps you!"

"He trees them in the creek bank and we dig them out with a shovel," I replied. "He snaps every one of them right through the head.

"Old Trailer is your dog then—is that right?"

"Yeah—and he's the best mink dog in the whole world," I replied. "He's a wind hunter—Daddy said he's one in a million."

"Well, I certainly can't argue with that. I've never heard of such a thing! You know something, Hoyt—that critter of yours is probably worth a small fortune. There's people who would kill to own a dog like that."

"Yeah, I know!" I exclaimed. "The Sloyd Brothers stole him and ran off down to the Louisiana to try to hide in the swamps, but Daddy and the crew went down there and killed them all and got Trailer back."

"Holy hell!" Mel said, scratching the back of his head. "I can see one thing right now, I've got to go visit your pa and get the skinny on that story.

Well, Young Mr. Walker—by my calculations you and your sisters have 480 dollars coming, but because you are such a budding asset to my business I'm going to make it an even 500. Does that sound alright to you?"

"Man, Mel that sounds wonderful!" I exclaimed. "That's a lot of money!"

"It certainly is, partner. At this rate you and your sisters are going to make a pile by the end of the season."

"We were thinking we might make enough to just buy Mama a fur coat, but Daddy got hurt, and now the family needs the money real bad—darn-it!"

"Hey, Little Buddy, didn't you say that 12 of those mink were from your secret project? Does that mean you haven't told your folks about them yet?"

"No—they don't know yet. We were just going to give them the money then tell them."

"Hey, since I don't have any customers right now, why don't we go on over to the boutique—maybe we can work something out to get your Mama a coat after all."

"Oh man, Mel that would really be good. Do you have fur coats over there?"

"I certainly do—I have a fairly good selection of Magnus and Son's fall line. We just might find something your Mama would like."

"I don't think we have enough money to buy one, Mel," I replied, shaking my head. "We looked at them in the catalogue and they cost a lot!"

"Yeah, they do, Hoyt, but when you've got cash, you can drive a hard bargain. The way I figure it those 12 secret pelts are worth at least 300 dollars, and you can buy a really nice coat for that—especially whole-sale," he said, with a wink.

When Mel and I walked into the store I could see that it was a lot bigger than it appeared, and there were fancy girl clothes everywhere.

"I think they're in the back over there," Mel said pointing across the store.

"Yeah, I can see the top of Mr. Robert's head back there," I replied.

As we walked around the corner and started towards the back of the store there were fur coats of every descriptions hanging on both sides of us—short ones, long ones, mid length ones—suddenly Mel and I walked up right behind a young lady that was being fitted and I became aware of just how gorgeous a fur coat really was. The clerk had the lady up on a fitting stand about 12 inches off the floor and was measuring the length of the coat—pulling and adjusting it.

"Hoyt, what do you think about that one? That's a very nice coat right there," Mel said. Instantly the young lady being fitted turned around where I could see her face—I couldn't believe my eyes—It was Dorothy!

"Isn't it beautiful, Little Brother," she whispered, hugging the fur up around her face. "Wouldn't Mama look great in one of these?"

"Oh my gosh, Sis—I can't believe that's you!" I exclaimed, with my eyes bugged out. "That's the prettiest thing I've ever seen!"

"I know—I fell in love with it the minute I saw it—Nell did too. She and Mr. Roberts are over on the other aisle searching for a full length one in this size.

"This is a mid length Silver Fox, Hoyt, and it retails for 400 dollars," Mel said. "The full length ones are 500, but since you are such enterprising young folks and the offspring of my good friend Dave Walker, I'm going to make you a much better deal on it than that," Mel said.

"We finally found one!" Nellie exclaimed, as she and Mr. Roberts appeared around the end of the aisle. "This was the only full length one left in the right size."

"Man, Sissy, I thought this one was pretty—that is even more awesome!" I said, as Nellie presented the coat to the female clerk.

"Would you like to try this one on, Dorothy?" she asked politely.

"Oh yes Ma'am, I certainly would," Dorothy replied—"it is so elegant!"

"Mama would look so good in that!" I exclaimed, shaking my head.

"I can tell you one thing," Mel replied, "she'd be the talk of her quilting club if she showed up in that."

"Hoytie, we looked at the mink coats first and we didn't like them near as much," Nellie said. "What do you think? Isn't this coat gorgeous?"

"It certainly is, Sissy. I don't need to look at any other coats; this is the coat I think Mama should have," I agreed, as I let my eyes drift over the beautiful fur; "I just wish we could get it for her—Dadburn it!"

"Now Hoyt—like I told you, if you kids want this coat, I could make you a very special offer on it. I'd let you have it for exactly half the retail price—just what I've got in it—the mid length for 200—the full length for 250. That's a whole lot of coat for that price!"

"Oh my gosh, Hoytie, do you think we might actually buy it?" Nellie questioned, with a wide eyed squeal of excitement.

"Girls, we just sold 500 dollars worth of mink, and we will be making more money next week. I think we should get this coat for Mama, right now while we have the chance, but I think she would like the long one best. What do you think, Dot?"

"Oh, yes, Hoytie," Dorothy replied, clutching the voluptuous fur around her. "This would definitely be the one, but do we dare spend that much money? Ohh—I want to so bad," she whined softly, wringing her hands, and looking at Nellie and me with uncertainty—"but, I just don't know!"

"Dorothy, you're a worry wart!" I exclaimed. "We could buy this coat and even spend 50 dollars more on Christmas presents and still give Mom and Dad 200 dollars. That's even more than they're expecting."

"Oh yes, let's do it then!" Dorothy exclaimed, with her face all aglow—"yeah, let's do it!"

"You've made a fine purchase, kids. I'll guarantee you there are loads of people who would love to get their hands on this coat at that price."

"Oh my goodness, I can't believe it," Nellie said, with her hands up to her face—"we're actually getting Mama a fur coat for Christmas!"

"Not just a fur coat, Sissy!" I exclaimed—"an awesome fur coat."

"With me being in this business, my wife has a coat of about every kind Magnus and Sons makes, and she wears her Silver Fox three times as much as she does any of the others. Your Mama is a very lucky lady— now I've got to get back to work. When you get ready, come on back to the station and I'll pay you the difference you have coming. Evelyn, you might want to wrap this as a Christmas gift for these young folks," Mel said. "They've worked mighty hard to get it—it's for their Mama."

"I certainly will, Mr. Flood. I'll do an extra special job on it too."

"Thanks Mel," I replied as he started walking away.

"Oh, yes, thank you so much, Mr. Flood. You're very kind!" Dorothy said, hugging the coat with a smile of satisfaction.

"Well, I must say—as your mathematics instructor I am very proud of the way you handled your finances there," Mr. Roberts spoke up. "That was very well done."

It took Evelyn about 15 minutes of wrapping and ribbon curling to get Mama's coat ready to go, and then she produced a beautiful Christmas card which we all signed and she slid it gently under the strings on the package.

"There, that should do it," she said. "Your mother is going to be one surprised lady when she opens this box. I would really like to be there and see her face. Kids, I would like to take this time to wish you and all your family a peaceful and happy Christmas," she said with a smile, "and may the Good Lord bless and keep all of you in the new year."

"Thank you so much, Evelyn," Nellie replied, extending her hand. "This means so much to us. Merry Christmas to you also and a happy new year."

* * *

After we left the boutique, we collected our money from Mel, and headed back to the car where we locked Mama's coat in the trunk and walked through a narrow alley way to the front of main street and spent the next two hours buying Christmas presents. After we completed our shopping we walked back through the alley to the wagon yard and

A FUR COAT FOR MAMA

deposited our presents in the trunk with Mama's coat and headed straight to Maynard's for our much anticipated lunch. The girls and Mr. Roberts had never experienced the culinary delight of which Daddy and I were so fond—a large bowl of steaming hot chili with lots of crackers and a bottle of soda pop—either Orange Crush in a heavy brown glass bottle or the unbelievably delicious little 6 ounce Grapette. When we were ready to go Maynard filled a quart fruit jar full of chili—capped it tightly, wrapped it in a clean towel and put it in a paper bag to take home. "There," he said, handing the chili across the counter, "if there's anything that will get old Dave back on his feet it's a big bowl of good chili—tell him I said hello."

CHAPTER THIRTY-NINE—Christmas Morning at the Walker House

That Christmas that had started out so bleak turned out to the best Christmas we had ever had. Old Trailer's skill as a mink dog just kept getting better, and Dad and Mom began to relax in the fact that we could actually handle the family's financial situation, and get our school work done too. We cut the family a nice blue spruce Christmas tree and decorated it with strings of popcorn and silvery icicle decoration we had bought in town and put all our presents under it.

Christmas morning was unbelievably special. We got Daddy and Mama seated next to the fireplace where it was nice and warm, and gave them each a present to open. Mama's present was a nice dress that the girls thought would look really good with her new coat, and Daddy's was a new Old Timer pocket knife. The one he'd been carrying for years was just about worn out. It was easy to see they were touched by their gifts, but they really came unglued at their next present. Daddy's present—which he opened first with us all watching, was two new pairs of overalls and two new flannel shirts. Daddy as a person never showed much emotion, and we were very surprised to see a single tear escape down the side of his face before he turned his head. Mama, on the other hand, was an outwardly sensitive individual and we basically knew what was going to happen when she opened that box; what we didn't know was that Daddy was just as bad as Mama when he lost control. The longer he sat there the more emotional he got, and when Mama opened her coat—they both fell apart, and we all had us a crying session right there by the fireplace holding onto each other. We finally settled down enough to help Mama get her new coat on and the crying started all over again—they were dumbstruck with the magnitude of the gift. In the next week Mama wore her new coat to Sunday church services and her monthly quilting club and just like Mel had predicted—her coat was the center of attention, and the Walker Kids were so proud!

Doctor Cedric came by and checked out Dad's hip and brought everyone a Christmas gift, as usual, and got his hug from us kids. Then he announced that he would be returning to Bayou Blanc in the spring, and that he had a strong suspicion he and Miss Hattie would be getting married. Ike and Cowboy came home on furlough and we found out all about service life, and how much they hated it. They were both farm boys and homebodies and military life didn't suit them at all.

Maxy didn't get to do any trapping until after the first of the year. He was able to continue running his sawmill due to the lack of heavy snows—he had 8 or 10 workers who depended on the job. It turned out just about right, though, because Dad's hip improved steadily. He and Maxy got in the last month of mink trapping together.

THE END